Disaffections of Time

Disaffections of Time

W. Thomas McQueeney

Copyright © 2018 by W. Thomas McQueeney.

Library of Congress Control Number:		2018903138
ISBN:	Hardcover	978-1-9845-1464-6
	Softcover	978-1-9845-1465-3
	eBook	978-1-9845-1466-0

All rights reserved. No part of this book may be reproduced or transmitted in any form or by any means, electronic or mechanical, including photocopying, recording, or by any information storage and retrieval system, without permission in writing from the copyright owner.

Scripture quotations marked KJV are from the Holy Bible, King James Version (Authorized Version). First published in 1611. Quoted from the KJV Classic Reference Bible, Copyright © 1983 by The Zondervan Corporation.

Scripture texts in this work are taken from the New American Bible, revised edition© 2010, 1991, 1986, 1970 Confraternity of Christian Doctrine, Washington, D.C. and are used by permission of the copyright owner. All Rights Reserved. No part of the New American Bible may be reproduced in any form without permission in writing from the copyright owner.

This is a work of fiction. Names, characters, places and incidents either are the product of the author's imagination or are used fictitiously, and any resemblance to any actual persons, living or dead, events, or locales is entirely coincidental.

Any people depicted in stock imagery provided by Getty Images are models, and such images are being used for illustrative purposes only.
Certain stock imagery © Getty Images.

Print information available on the last page.

Rev. date: 04/28/2018

To order additional copies of this book, contact:
Xlibris
1-888-795-4274
www.Xlibris.com
Orders@Xlibris.com
772561

CONTENTS

Acknowledgements vii
Prologue xi
1. Into the Blue 1
2. The Boracle of Wi-Fi 7
3. Walter Bailloch 23
4. Theta Barnwell 33
5. Prof. Thomas Leon 47
6. The Nexus of the Sixties 53
7. Billy Grayson 66
8. Jackie and Frieda 70
9. Sunshine 84
10. Maria Delgado 88
11. Sunday Swim 92
12. Theoretical Algorithms 112
13. Simmons Barnwell, Esquire 117
14. Come Away with Me 121
15. Joey Preticos 130
16. Seatbelts 136
17. Hal Butters 149
18. Heartfelt Letters 154
19. Penalty Kick 164
20. Pablo Gutierrez 175
21. Recovery Discovery 185
22. The Other News 190
23. Providence 204
24. Requiem 209
25. Chance 214
26. Little Ashton Grayson 219
27. Beauty Within 225

28. Dr. Ramsey	233
29. A Dark Reappearance	238
30. The Fixers	241
31. Who Is Charlie Landon?	245
32. Police Escort	252
33. Remington Reality	257
34. Viola Butters	271
35. Established Residency	277
36. Keepsakes	283
37. Mithridates	289
38. Flights	294
39. Dream Site	298
40. St. Croix	302
41. Rest Stop	311
42. The Frumpy Bellman	315
43. The Wish	335
44. A Record Deal	339
45. The Bracelet	347
46. Itineraries	357
47. And Do You?	361
48. Little Conch	370
49. Eternity Never Waits	385
50. The Urn	391
51. Retrospective Commitments	398
52. Pocket Watch	405

| Epilogue | 413 |
| About the Author | 415 |

ACKNOWLEDGEMENTS

The "novel experience" of writing a novel could not be possible without the valuable input, mentorship, and encouragement of others. I am forever grateful to Fred Whittle, the editor of my second book, *Sunsets Over Charleston*. Fred is a stand-up American who has served our country as a U.S. Marine and served our community earnestly. He is a true friend.

My appreciation also goes to Mary B. Tutterow, a fine graduate of the University of Georgia who became the prime mover for Healing Farms Ministries—a magnificent organization that benefits the developmentally disabled.

Without the timely input preened from an incredibly talented best selling American novelist, the book would not be possible. Profound and sincere thanks are certainly in order for Dorothea Benton Frank's kindnesses extended. Dottie's 19th novel, *By Invitation Only*, is due out in the spring of 2018. She's amazing!

The support and diligence of the professionals at XLibris Publishing could not be overstated. My appreciation to Rica Caro, Angelie Sage, Lani Martin, Lyn Mayers, and Nina Arden is matched by my honor to be associated with their team. They earned my complete confidence. Together, we will "team up" again.

What you may hold weighs more than what a scale may indicate. It has been a lifelong ambition. My final appreciation is to you, the reader. Without your consignment of time and interest, there is no reception of the effort tendered. You are my judge, assessor, and final critic. Bless you.

PROLOGUE

The universe is a beginning unknown and an ending undetermined. All unexplained phenomena tax science to prove its nonexistence. The list grows with time—UFOs, near-death experiences, ghosts, psychics, space aliens, and time travelers. Believing in an unconventional existence presents an edgy social proposition.

There have been other aberrations that have escaped reason—apparitions, atmospheric oddities, colossal engineering feats in antiquity, and historical figures of mystique. All beg additional clues to rationalize their lingering enigma.

In varying degrees, sculptured literary characters have emerged with other-worldly powers attributed to separate them from the masses. They change energy, mimic animals, transform, regenerate, read minds, levitate, and disappear. The ages have given them names that paint them forever in our minds. They read as Merlin, Hag, Medea, Aladdin, Cassandra, Gandalf, or any number of witches, wizards, sorcerers, magicians, shamans, or prophets. We want to believe they exist because they know the potions that surrender answers to other unknowns. The practice of the mystique reaches back to names that have been recorded through millennia as other factual creatures of intrigue such as Nostradamus, Rasputin, and Sybil of Cumae.

No less a wizard saunters among us. He is a man extolling powers that required seven decades to materialize fully. His perceptive nuances are balanced by his unique ability to solve, resolve, and conjoin. Witnesses have reported this savant within their recorded experiences reverently. The benevolent savant lives because he said he would become complete. But we will, yet again, lose his address.

A romantic tale began with the record of a medieval poem written by Blind Robert Barrow in the year 1279, seventeen years after a travesty he witnessed. Lightning blinded him. His words survived.

The poem's challenging translation from Gaelic to Latin to Modern English loses little over time but the resonance of medieval sounds. It describes a midnight attack upon Castle Sween that ended the dominion of Dubhghall mac Sween, Lord of Knapdale and Kintyre. But the poem is not as much about the bloody takeover as it is about the talisman stones that guided the prophecy of two lovers. The fall of Castle Sween occurred in the early morning hours before the lovers were to celebrate their exchange of nuptials at noon.

The Fall of Sween

The earl sent tidings from Innis Court
A handsome celebration nigh
The hand of the chaste Maire
The bride with alizarin hair
And Dubhghall, Lord Knapdale
Contented with his domain

A slovenly bearded ignoble crew
Blackened attire and lances
Braved the crusty sea
Only hours from nightfall
As the wedding party drank Meade
And the nectar of the vine

Flashing shields and grapples
Weapons of death
They climbed the darkness
At once they converged
The unattended walls
The gate ajar in the howling wind

Maire in the tower
Dubhghall in the keep
And the wizard Cailean
All fast asleep
Startled by horror
Awakened in blood and fright

The castle embattled
Victims were strewn about
Cailean the Wizard
Awakened Dubhghall in time
To take him to the tower stairs
Where the door was barricaded

Maire was shielded away
Protected by her lover
Cailean followed up swiftly
Their death's thought assured
By Bailloch's swords
Sent to extinguish the bloodline

The door was shattered
The tower was breached
The lovers held the talisman
Violet stones ethereal
Forty men approached them
Swords drawn in zeal

The wizard directed the lovers
By Gaelic words uttered to the heavens
She clasped the lavender amulet
He the matching stone ethereal
Their salvation was ordained
They could not be harmed

They waited without defense
And by the wizard's command
The three leaped from the parapet
Into a thunderbolt
They disappeared in the flash
Hidden by the turbulent sea

Souls surrendered to a tyrant
Passed to evil, cold and silent
But alas, Bailloch had failed
The stones were united
And the bloodline remained
To render his demise

Time would be their comfort
Scattered each to a path
A bride awaiting her lord
A lord awaiting her beauty
A wizard purposed to unite
Their timeless passion of pursuit

In an eerie consequence seven centuries later a shadowy person emerges as Walter Bailloch in search of two stones. A classically statuesque lady with dark reddish hair appears to the delight of a chivalrous young man enamored. An old man relates to each circumstance as if he had expected every potential variation. He is considered a savant. His age belies his abilities. He flourishes in the evaluation of external elements, the conclusions drawn from sensory input, and the education of inspired youth. He senses that his life's quest must be fulfilled above all other wishes.

The modern-day found the four vestiges of Sween's conquest emplaced for a confrontation, collision, and conclusion. The wizard had ordained the timing.

The savant's re-emergence into a classroom setting was at the request of a friend. He treasured friendships above all else.

"Contingencies have tendencies to become dependencies," the guest lecturer declared.

The elder explored the point before nineteen college students in awe of the man's clear grasp of all knowledge. Nearing his seventy-seventh birthday, the guest lecturer never referred to notes or used props. He spoke in compelling tones reserved for uncommon sages.

"Contingencies," he continued, "they rule us. Our lives are a balance beam of unanticipated events. One either falls tragically or lands propitiously at the culmination of an artful dance."

His herringbone suit was dated and wrinkled. It draped his gaunt frame. Yet his collared shirt and bow tie were crisp and stylish. He wore cufflinks, and a belt loop was adorned with a gold chain that led to his unseen pocket watch. His light-blue eyes were warm and glared over his thin-rimmed glasses that held position halfway down the bridge of his Welsh nose.

"The width and breadth of our meaning lie within the nebulous ideals of vitality, love, success, eternity, and God. They are—each and all—random conceptual contingencies.

"Our vitality is the course of purposeful living, cordoned by time. We know not the tribulations of this temporal resource. It is ordained.

"We seek true love, though we may never become truly lovable."

The class laughed at the insight.

"Success is an island triumph beyond a sea of obstruction. Riches should never define its reach. Each of us has a differing personal sense of its fulfillment.

"And what is eternity other than the antidote for oblivion? Do we really want eternity? Will we be alone in eternity? Is there any phase beyond its lure?

"They all bow to the ideal of a belief in a benevolent master—a righteous God. That is the largest contingency of all. If he or she exists, then everything else matters. If not, what matters?"

The savant gained their full attention. The class could have been listed in the college offerings as Knowledge Expansion 402, but it garnered a more officious title for second-semester seniors—Theoretical Algorithms.

"You get to decide which contingent concepts will guide your world. Your life, thanks to the modern ideal of liberty, is largely under your control.

"At the other end of the calendar, my contingencies became dependencies. I believed in living as a duty to others, love as a perfect design, success as a composite progression, eternity as a preferred alternative, and God as a subjective reality. He'd better be there—or my train will plunge into a chasm of despair."

They giggled at the visualization of the old man's long life finding no terminal station. He had been speaking for forty minutes.

Oddly, the old man walked to the door and reached for his umbrella. He turned and gave a slight bow before walking out. The unusual departure was accommodated by the quiet. It was as planned. It was how he always left.

The man knew the ages, the eras, and the epochs. He knew joy, warmth, and anguish. He knew relationships and responses and reveled in reminiscence, sentimentality, and nostalgia. He became both enamored and repulsed by the disaffections of time.

CHAPTER ONE

Into the Blue

(Sixty-Six Years Prior)

ONCE THE LANTERN dimmed, the dawn began. Vacations, motels, and summer camps were products of the world's latest confidence in peace and prosperity after World War II. The Crystal Lakes Summer Camp for Boys was established in Pennsylvania's Poconos near the Delaware Water Gap in 1947. It grew out of Philadelphia and New York cocktail parties into fashion for wealthy couples to source away their children. Their parenting responsibilities were dispensed to bossy college kids in matching T-shirts. The counselors were paid well to become high society's babysitters.

The swimming platform was moored to the middle of the lake where summer's boys ran and jumped like tumbling frogs. The late July sun shimmied across the surface. The cotton-ball clouds were huddled at each horizon as the trees at the shoreline slumbered in the stillness.

The crew-cut lifeguard Eric D'Angelo sat perched in his eight-foot chair facing the old screened-in canteen at the shoreline. The bronze meal bell hung silently. He was nearly finished reading Marvel Comic's latest Captain America. The fantasy world was suggestive of extraordinary powers every male teen of the 1940s wished to possess. His towel hung at the back of the chair, and his whistle was wrapped around the flat wooden arm. The climactic final pages of the comic book were too captivating to ignore. It was the worst timing for Eric to look up to acknowledge a sudden silence from the playful swimmers. It was the moment that the panic began.

Belligerent boys laughed loudly as they dunked the youngest camper away from the platform. The taunting seemed natural enough that Eric never needed to glance up from the comic pages. Gasping for air, the nine-year-old swimmer became exhausted. A pugnacious kid named Wally Bailloch waited above the surface to dunk the freckled lad wherever he might pop up next. The young camper was too traumatized by the bullying activity to cry out, preserving his breath for the next scornful dunking.

The last submersion quelled the activity. He did not reappear to the surface. The seven boys who had taken turns dunking him looked around for signs of their prey. There was no sighting—no floating body. Wally Bailloch raised his hands in a boxer's victory when the swimmer did not reappear.

Eric looked down from his chair after the short onset of the eerie quiet. The band of conspirators turned to him. One suddenly yelled out, "He's still down there!"

"Who?" The lifeguard boldly inquired as he stood up. Even Captain America couldn't be summoned. The comic book was dropped.

"That freckly kid from Boston, Sidney somebody!" another kid yelled. "He went down but didn't come back up. Help!"

Sidney Toile was the only child of double-Harvard graduate parents Arlene and Norman Toile. Arlene was from a well-to-do Hartford family. Ted was an adjunct professor at Boston University. He grew up in Weston, Massachusetts, where median home prices were among the highest in America. The Toile family social calendar made child raising a part-time provision with diminishing priority. Young Sid was an awkward boy—pasty-skinned, boney, and nerdy. He was sickly and sheltered with minimum parental interaction. He was an accident brought on by revelry that included Armand de Brignac Brut Rose followed by Dom Pérignon. Sid's home life created a cold loneliness that the warmth of interaction at a summer camp could repair. The socialite Toiles of Boston proper had no idea that their only child was in an advanced state of severe duress.

The panic had turned into the frantic.

Eric looked all around from the high perch of the lifeguard chair. Seeing no sign of the freckled kid, he dove in.

The other boys began looking to the other side of the platform and to the shoreline. One dove under the platform to no avail. Two of the boys cried in despair. The orange-haired, freckled nine-year-old son of high-placed Boston gentry had completely vanished.

Constant surface dives by the entire search group did nothing but to cloud the water and exhaust the rescuers.

Eric had dispatched one of the young swimmers by canoe to the cabins to seek emergency help after he had gone underneath the platform twice. Other counselors came running. A patrol of canoes and kayaks from the shore was utilized. Calls went out. "Sidney! Sidney!" It was as if the young boy could hear from under the lake.

The terrified camp director, Hugh Callison, called the local sheriff, Roy Mercer. The sheriff was a Louisiana transplant and liked to fish the lake with Hugh. The camp director usually found a contraband six-pack of beer for their mutual diversion. But this was not a time to exchange pleasantries.

"Roy, we have a real emergency up at the lake. A young swimmer has apparently drowned," Hugh reported. His loud voice implied that the emergency should be shared and that the sheriff should come quickly enough to mitigate the suspected disaster.

"Dammit, Hugh," Roy said. "Who was in charge? Dammit," Roy repeated. "Scour da area an' don't let anyone touch da body, if found, till I get there. This iz gonna be a huge mess, Hugh. An inquiry. Prob'ly a lawsuit. I'll b'dere in twenny minutes. Dammit. Dammit. Dammit."

Hugh was a single thirtyish summer-timer—an employee who would return to a full-time career in the fall. He worked as a public high school math teacher in Pittsburgh. He began his short inquiry after slamming the phone in his office—the only phone on the property. Hugh hurriedly rowed to the platform.

"Eric, how in the hell did this happen, son?" he asked. The veins were bulging from his neck. Anger and judgment were beginning to chart their separate courses.

"He was swimming out over there and disappeared." Eric pointed. "The fellas were playing like they always do. When it got quiet over to my left, one of them yelled that he was still down there. I dove in immediately. Sidney was a good swimmer, so I can't imagine what happened. Maybe he got a cramp."

It was as if all of the searchers realized that Sidney was already dead. It was a gruesome prospect that had several of the campers whimpering at the shore.

"This is going to be a nightmare," Hugh replied. He turned away disgusted. He rowed back to the shore and took the camp bullhorn up to his mouth.

"All counselors, you are responsible for your team. Sidney Toile from Team H is missing and presumed to be in the lake. Emergency help is on the way. Meanwhile, your entire teams are to be accounted for. Take roll. Once the roll is completed, all counselors are to employ the canoes and try to find Sidney. Chef Jim will assume command of the teams at the canteen."

Chef Jim, the canteen cook, came outside while donning his white apron. It was the same apron he had donned aboard the aircraft carrier *Ranger* two years earlier, one of the few deployed in the North Sea during the war. He began to scope in the shoreline with his navy-issue binoculars. The Sard 7x50 set was pulled from its worn leather case. They had spotted German U-boats at two miles but could not locate movement across the reflective lake water. The nine-year-old victim had not resurfaced in over fifteen minutes.

Chef Jim ordered all campers into the canteen to sit at the wooden picnic tables. He knew of no protocol for a drowning. He had them form a line for ice cream.

The sheriff arrived with the entrée of a siren and red lights flashing. He had already called the coroner. He was pulling a flat-bottom, motorized boat and trailer and began backing it down the landing. Hugh assisted by unhooking the tow straps as the stern reached the waterline. He slid the aluminum boat down farther. The sheriff pulled the car up and trotted to the boat. Hugh jumped in with him. The small engine cranked at the second pull, and the two men began to troll the lake in anticipation of disgust.

"Ya got 'iz parents' numba?" Roy asked.

"It's in the office. This is our last day. All of the parents will start showing up by ten tomorrow," Hugh countered. "I'd bet they're on the road now, coming from Boston."

"Almighty damn!" Roy exclaimed. "Dey on da way. Dey got no way a knowin'. We'll have volunteers out here tomorrow mornin' draggin' da lake if we don't find that boy's body 'fore nightfall. No way a gettin' 'round it."

"Yeah, I know," Hugh replied. "That may close this camp for good."

"Any foul play suspected?" Roy followed. "Ya betta tell me now while we're out here. Kids horsin' around, maybe? A fight? Some a dem rich kids are nuttin' but hoodlums. You and I know it, Hugh. Wouldn't want dat to come out, wudja?"

"The lifeguard, Eric, said he thinks the kid got a cramp," Hugh offered.

"A cramp? Really? Dat won't hold up," the sheriff replied while changing positions to look in another direction for the body. "We're gonna hafta do an inquiry. Get dat lifeguard and put him in yo' office when we get back."

"OK." Hugh nodded.

"And we'll getta list of da witnesses and a separate statement from each. Ya find out a lot when ya start writing da facts down," Roy explained. "Somebody's gonna tell us da real story, and I'd betcha a fifth o' Johnnie Walker it ain't cramps."

As the daylight dimmed, lanterns were lit and dispersed to the counselors. They walked the shoreline while looking for a body—and hoping for a miracle.

Hugh and Roy saw something move about a hundred yards off the bow. Roy noted it was just a mullet jumping. He then turned to state the obvious to Hugh.

"By now, that boy oughta be floatin' up. We better find him b'fo' his folks git 'ere in da mo'nin'," Roy said. "First, they're told their boy's dead, and if the body's found later, it'd be like dat boy died twice."

"Dammit ta hell. Let's git that boy's body out b'fo' nightfall."

CHAPTER TWO

The Boracle of Wi-Fi

(Modern Day)

THE BEGINNING OF December is spurious. It is no season at all. It is the waft of autumn leaving. It is the deciduous trees defrocked and the winds changing to the northeast. And this rainy morning was not perceptibly varied from the others, except for the muted distant thunder. The keyboard chorus in the corner of the bookstore café was a virtuoso. The clickies had come to check their e-mail and post the weekend's adventure on Facebook.

A curious and weathered man was slowly sipping a café grande while checking his Apple iPad XG for the latest news on his *USA Today* app. The stories connect to a series of unrelated inquiry subjects that he jotted down on his brown napkin.

The Bib and Bibliothéque does a steady business as cyber information fused with the aroma of the many South American blends. Short order breakfasts and lunch sandwiches are available. Fresh-baked cookies draw the parents in with young children.

However, the man sat alone. He had no schedule; only time. He was impassioned unto himself. In what seemed to be a person out-of-place in the setting, he wore cufflinks and a button-down white shirt. His dark tan herringbone suit was dated and wrinkled. He had a muted ruddiness in his worn face. The redness came from his seventy-six years and the blood pressure medication he had taken daily. He got up to throw away his cup.

A female book shopper appeared and asked for directions. She thought the old man might have been a greeter like one might find at a Wal-Mart.

"Would you know where I can find cookbooks?" she asked.

"Sid, Sid Toile at your service, ma'am. Cookbooks are on aisle nine, left side. But if you look at the table by the register, there are some overstocked or dated ones marked down," he instructed.

She easily followed his directions to find her purchase. She checked out and left believing the old man to be an employee of the B & B.

He sat back in booth 14 and began to study and update his electronic charts. He clicked a tab to open his stock portfolio. He has tailored impressive graphs so that his azure-tinted eyes could distinguish the ups or downs more readily. This day, however, was a bit down. It's Apple, AT&T, and Pfizer. All fluttered upon a recovery. He remains stock-wealthy, and even while his stocks grimace, his portfolio smiles.

He had found the café soon after he moved to Mount Pleasant three years prior. He had moved to the area from France. Incidentally, France was the first place that he moved from without the forewarning he had experienced in other locales. He had lived in worldly places absent of fear until the medieval dream returned. It was the repetitive nightmare of being pursued. The evil was always near. He would reluctantly steer his life clear of the anxious specter. A man named Bailloch reappeared too often.

He had lived on Coronado Island near San Diego. Before that, he lived in Thun, Switzerland, and Cabo San Lucas, Mexico. There was a longer stay of six years in Quebec and a four-month hiatus in Santiago,

Chile. There had been more addresses and cafés along the way. He stayed until the nighttime called him away.

"Excuse me, sir, are you the Boracle?" a rotund young man asked.

"Sid Toile, at your service. How can I help you?" he replied nonchalantly.

"Oh, it's not me, Mr. Toile. It's my mother. Can I bring her to see you?" he redirected. "I'm fine, but my mother. You see, she thinks I'm doing drugs. But I'm not. She's paranoid, and I can't seem to get through to her."

"Yes, son, your mother is right to be vigilant. Addiction is a serious matter," the old man began. "But I can see that you are not a drug abuser. Though you may have a little trouble with alcohol, I surmise. Peer pressure. Beer probably. But I don't see this as a habit either."

He drew upon his highly acute senses to decide that the rouge-cheeked youth was straightforward and honest. He chose to assist.

"Let your mother know that you met an old man who wants to leave some of his fortune to charity. Tell her to look for me at this booth any day this week after eleven o'clock but before twelve thirty. OK?" Sid suggested.

The boy was relieved. "Yes, sir. Please tell her that her intuition is off. I will never do drugs," the boy conceded. "And tell her that I have good friends too."

Sid could see that the boy was on a mission to stop his overreaching parent from falsely accusing him. He would resolve the issue as he had always done. He assessed. He solved.

Sid commands timely answers to riddles, but no person has approached him to pose the next riddle, conundrum, or puzzle. He assumes all inquiries will eventually find him. They have always found him in his past.

The old man has Googled information to verify the exact numerical formula that proves the world is spherical, not round. Yet the workmen who paved the driveway at his condominium complex last week could not make the correction needed for the curvature of the earth in a forty-foot strip of asphalt. The new driveway collects the day's rainwater.

He has Googled other questions that have intrigued him for six decades, like what language is spoken in Estonia, where to find a Bactrian camel, and what ingredients are in guacamole. He has a thirst for knowledge and a secret hope that someone will ask him something other than directions to the restroom. His brilliant mind of inquiry can never be quenched. The innovation of the Internet has accelerated his obsession with knowing all things of all time. He remembers everything he reads.

He is the Boracle of Wi-Fi. He received his name from the sarcastic multi-pierced cappuccino clerk. The name developed naturally because she once asked him why people wait to see him at booth 14, his regular seat of choice.

"I suppose it is much like why the early Greeks traveled to the temple of Apollo at Delphi—the center of the known world more than three thousand years ago. They needed questions answered from the Oracle," the old man answered. "I try to steer friends who visit me to helpful answers just like the Oracle at Delphi once did."

Callista Jantzen, the sneering clerk, is unimpressed by the old man that others seek. She quit college in her freshman year but never returned to her family in Chevy Chase, Maryland. Her parents disapproved of her lifestyle choices. Her next poor choice was to re-engage the gentleman of her most recent ire.

"But, surely, they are driven out of their minds when you tell them anything. Nobody can understand old folks like you. You are more like a bore-acle, the bore-acle of our Wi-Fi." She protested as she made a clever play on the word to describe the man she loathed each day.

"Yes, I suppose I could be a bore-acle, miss." He surprised her in the agreement. "The answers I deduce are often plain and without frills. Perhaps if I gave each person a balloon or a candy cane, the answers would become more interesting."

Callista did not respond. She just walked away.

Others who sought him for advice admired this gentle man's tolerant disposition. The name stuck. And he returned the favor to the clerk, naming her Callous, as a nickname for Callista. Though few patrons called Callista Callous, nearly all accepted that Sid was the Boracle, a name he enjoyed. It was a moniker of honor.

Some days, the B & B was like a magical train station. The locomotives would come in from distant and mysterious hinterlands. The platform of their short visitation was booth 14. The trains all left to better places.

Though the sassy counter clerk took some minor glee in insulting him because the old man routinely refused to leave her a tip, she enjoyed that he was kind to everyone. Callista proudly coiffures streaked magenta and cerulean in her stringy base of orange hair. She prefers a rebellious attitude and a counterculture appearance.

The old man seems glad that she does not work for him. No tip had ever been left, not even copper cents from his change.

Callista sees the Boracle every day. She grabs a cup for his café grande before he reaches the counter. She tries to avoid his sneer of inspection. She always asks for the tip—without success. He gives the same trite answer.

"I prefer to tip all at once . . . At the end of service. My service will be complete after my last café grande here," the Boracle reminds her. "I've got the running total in my head. So hang in there, Callous. You'll get what you deserve."

She bristles at hearing the repeated explanation. She tells the next customer her reasoning and adds her insight about her disapproving parents. The unsuspecting customer just nods. They have their own problems to resolve.

"It's the same every day. Same size and flavor, same booth, and same tip—nothing!" Callista shot back, "Then you sit freely for hours to bore the regular tipping customers and wear out our Wi-Fi."

There is a constant clash of the two from nearly every aspect—age, culture, ideology, and personality. But the day proceeds at booth 14. It is where the Boracle dwells.

Sid Toile became a widower before he turned age forty-six. He lost Ida to cancer thirty years prior. He never remarried. He adorns himself in the gentleman's style his deceased wife preferred and last saw—a bow tie, suspenders, a vest, and a rotation of wrinkled old herringbone suits. He clipped a gold pocket watch through his belt loop and rested the gold chronometer into a worn-out watch pocket. Pants with watch pockets have vanished from society.

The watch face had stopped at 10:27. It was the time of the morning that Ida breathed her last breath. Sid was at her side. He only opens the watch to be reminded of the love of his life. The small circular insert opposite the watch facing was a 1970s Olin Mills studio portrait of Ida Crutchfield Toile before she turned thirty. He would have Ida with him every day for the rest of his life. They never had children. Yet Sid was far from being alone in the world. He was gifted and gregarious. His daily life thrived on a self-imposed lifelong mission. He must help others.

He came to Charleston because he knew of her history. Charleston was once the city of defeat—where invective slander precluded its resurgence to its storied past of old-world grandeur. Its low profile brought in the inspiration of wind, the majesty of sunrises, and the natural bliss of what once was . . . in centuries past. Its compact peninsula held more mysteries immersed in the long-suffering of tested souls than any place in America.

Sid lived across the river. Driving across the modern Ravenel Bridge provided him with a magnificent vista to witness the meteoric rise of America's finest rediscovery—Charleston.

The septuagenarian was spry for his age. At 150 pounds over a frame that stretched to five feet ten inches, he had avoided much of the aging process. He walked fast. He ate little, and he stood upright without knees that buckled or a back that slumped. He avoided doctors and hospitals much like the Bushmen of Botswana avoided lions. He believed the medical establishment to be for emergencies—but not for the maintenance of health.

He would substantiate his medical viewpoint by repeating his mantra, "More infections come from hospitals than from any other source."

Sid had the countenance of a younger man. His well-groomed alabaster beard hid some of the imperfections and discolorations from his seven and a half decades. His matching hair was barbered short on the sides and was thinning on the top. His blue eyes were friendly and focused. His most distinguishing mark was a light-tan birthmark on his right temple partially covered by his beard. The birthmark looked much like the Nike swoosh affixed at a darker tint than the rest of his face.

The Boracle had a voice that was mindful of a church usher whispering loudly. He was ever kind in his certainty. And just like the church usher would direct, one would take the seat appointed merely because this pleasant man asked one to sit.

Sid not only knew the facts but also knew the numbers and reasons that composed them.

He once lived in exotic and lonely places, but the road was a poor substitute to fill the chasm that led, inevitably, to the void. He arrived in Charleston from Nice on the Côte d'Azur. He loved Nice. But a sense of duty, rather than fear, moved him. Nice is where youthful lovers strolled along the Avenue des Anglais in contemplation of finding true happiness.

Sid enjoyed his morning coffee at Le Koudou Brasserie, a block from the Hotel Negresco. It was propitious that Sid noticed a father-owner of Le Koudou mentoring his daughter. The daughter had been away all night and came in to work late.

"Vous devez diriger votre vie avant que votre vie ne vous dirige" (You need to direct your life before your life directs you). The advice was succinct and life-changing. The expressive père was talking to the world beyond through his truculent daughter. The coquette turned away from the chastisement. Sid was within earshot. The point was made to the wrong listener.

Sid internalized the advice. He needed to honor Ida by completing the task he had known since his childhood. He could respect the past by having an impact on the future.

From his loneliness, his senses began to converge and expand. The phenomenon made him acutely aware that he could broaden his service to humanity. He encountered, engaged, and encouraged. His mind retained all. The father's scolding to the daughter was his impetus moment for Sid's arrival in Charleston.

His condominium home was within walking distance of the Bib and Bibliothéque. Fiddlers Cove Condominiums had two sun-faded lavender four-story buildings and sixteen end units. Sid's was on the fourth floor. His top-floor balcony captured the coastal breezes and the long view of the salt marsh between Mount Pleasant and Sullivans Island.

The balcony also welcomed the sunrise to the American continent. Sid sat there often contemplating the mysteries of life. His habit of calculating lightning strikes across the marsh view produced uncanny predictability. The afternoon electrical storms often found the grounded television tower two blocks away. He sensed the rise in electrical charges from the falling cold air into the swelter.

A trusted employee cleaned Sid's two-bedroom unit daily. Maria Delgado was a mother of two "anchor babies." She was an illegal immigrant from the Dominican Republic. She arrived every weekday morning from a long bus route by 9:00 a.m. and left before noon. Sid paid her for fifteen hours per week. She received nearly the same wage that her husband made for forty hours of operating a mobile hot mix tar machine for a local roofing contractor.

The adornments to his condo were simple. He had a few old furnishings from his marriage, one old twenty-three-inch box television in the den, a few of Ida's handmade pottery pieces, and a large painting over the mantel. The canvas revealed his brown-haired bride in a flowing white-laced Raphaela gown. It was Ida's wedding portrait. Her eyes looked down into the room as if she were greeting him each morning. And she did.

Sid was a man of routines. He was usually home at the condominium by twelve thirty for lunch. He liked meatless salads with pecan chips.

His second bedroom was converted to an office library. There, he immersed himself into world knowledge and associative contemplation. He amused himself with information not found in books—but available within the most significant nuance imaginable—the World Wide Web. He stocked facts like a doomsday planner stocks a large bunker.

He had few rules. The primary precept is that he is never to be thanked. He preferred not to be appreciated because he felt that his life's calling was a duty—not a favor. His attitude of assistance to others became a passion.

The Web followed him from foreign countries and into coffee shops. It was his most alluring companion. He supposed that in some future society, the Web would emanate without the convenience of Wi-Fi. It will simply transmit directly to any inquiring mind anywhere. Nonetheless, he enjoyed the reception he received at the Bib and Bibliothéque.

Every Monday at the Bib and Bibliothéque is a new day full of the old habits, management procedures, and stilted customs. They usually preclude a destined regression into what was the routine yesterday and the day before. Each day systematically degenerated to become mundane.

This Monday would be different.

The distant thunder was foreboding. The wet wind had commanded the mood of this ominous morning. Sid drove his 2003 Volkswagen Beetle to the B & B. His black wood-handled umbrella leaned dry in his selected booth. He sensed higher atmospheric energy arising.

The old man had left his cell phone plugged into the corner socket—a reason he initially chose that particular booth. The outdated iPhone rang with the innocuous melody "Morning Has Broken," a church tune reprised by Cat Stevens in the 1970s. Sid found out that the singer was no longer Cat Stevens. Google informed him that Stevens now calls himself Yusuf Islam. Sid answered the phone before the melodious tune reached the line's ending.

"Sid at your service," he answered.

It was his CPA, Will Henry. In the never-ending world of tax catch-up, his latest return dictated another $239,000 to the Feds. Wonderful. This was the extension of the extension tax return. It could have been worse.

"I'll come by after two o'clock," he stated to the accountant, "but don't expect a stock tip." Sid studied stocks like baseball managers study pitcher-batter matchups.

"Will, my friend, let's transfer the funds from the money market account. You did a great job. I expected mid-six figures," Sid cited. "And you always seem to find depreciation that is moving faster than the breakdown of my physical infrastructure at age seventy-six."

A quarter of a million dollars was sometimes made or lost in an hour from the frumpy man's Fortune 500 portfolio. Sid owned timber and development acreage, certificates of deposit, bonds, collectible artwork, rental property, and precious metals.

What he didn't have that he longed to have again was his most meaningful and most cherished wealth—his wife, Ida. She was his reason for happiness. Her memory was in his watch pocket. He checked it often. Ida was his constant reminder not to fear death. He would see her again. He believed, all the sooner.

The intensity of the morning's stormy weather rumbled closer. The violent sounds foretold a calamity in the distance that was moving to the southeast. The sky blinked within a sudden surging downpour.

Lightning hit nearby. The loud flash illuminated the rainy parking area in a sudden burst. The boom of thunder was a split second behind. It was a storm that tumbled quickly within striking proximity of the trendy emporium. Callista winced as the last bolt lit the atmosphere.

"Damn, Sid, that was close!" she yelled across the room. "It's the heavens opening. Your chariot awaits. Can you meet it in the parking lot?"

"Never mind, lassie. It's not the spirits but the convergence of air masses. You're safe on that rubber mat. It's best to stay there lest you get fried," Sid replied. "You'd be missing your final tip."

Suddenly, the coffee shop lights popped off like a champagne bottle opening and then flickered back on momentarily. The seemingly directed bolt struck again as the old man was calling his housekeeper. The phone inexplicably burst from the old man's hand, shattering the glass facing. The lights in the coffee shop had one more flicker before they shut fully off. The cappuccino machine arrested its obnoxious grind in mid-cycle. All background noises ceased.

Within seconds, an emergency light beeped and came on—thrusting a powerful beam onto the serving counter. The Boracle's phone was partially shattered, the facing glass cracked and the casing destroyed. Sid placed the exploded device down with one hand. The other hand applied pressure to his ear with the coffee napkin, where blood had suddenly trickled. The startled Callista and a housewife waiting in line rushed to his side. The housewife pulled off her scarf as if it might be used as a tourniquet. The sudden bleeding oozed from his right ear. Pressure from a brown napkin was applied to stop the flow. The man sat up composed in a newfound dignity, assessing that there was no damage done to his other electronic miracle—the Apple iPad XG.

"I'm fine," Sid proclaimed as he was being attended. "I have not ruptured my cochlea. There is only a minor abrasion to the Eustachian tube. No medical attention is necessary."

Callous and the scarf lady were relieved but also amazed. The Boracle then asked to have his café grande refreshed.

"But the electricity is off," the sassy clerk replied.

He paid her no attention; instead, he asked the scarf-wielding housewife to sit a minute. She instinctively obliged. He then turned his attention back to the clerk.

"The electricity is back on now," the old man stated in calm frankness. The lights came on as his sentence ended.

The scarf lady was fortyish, fair-skinned, and dressed nicely. Her face was framed with ringlets of dark hair. She was apparently an upper-middle-class socialite, though she seemed wholly unpretentious. Sid surmised that she was a patron of the arts and a regular volunteer within charitable organizations. She exhibited a soothing Southern accent softly lilted.

"You sure know a lot about ears. Are you a doctor?" the lady asked.

"Ma'am, I'm no doctor. I'm simply Sid," he responded with the napkin against his ear. "Your name?"

"Evelyn. Evelyn Rhett. I'm here to meet my friend Louise. But I'm very early," Evelyn noted.

"Your friend Louise is likely headed back home to avoid this awful storm," Sid replied.

Evelyn's phone rang. She waved her hand up to Sid to excuse the short intrusion. As she waved, Sid noticed a deep bruise on the underside of her arm between her elbow and her wrist. He suspected that it wasn't from a fall but rather from a defensive posture.

"No, I understand," Evelyn said back into the phone. "It's still coming down hard over this way too."

She paused. Then she answered the caller. "OK. Thursday at nine o'clock. See you then."

She placed her phone into her handbag, looked up, and said, "You must be a clairvoyant. That was my friend canceling because of the rain. Are you telepathic—a psychic—or something?"

Evelyn smiled at the question, signaling that she knew her friend's call to be a circumstance and not a prophecy. But Sid answered her more seriously.

"Heavens, no. I'm a synesticist," he said with conviction. "I get that psychic tag all the time. Clairvoyant? Telepathic? Not me. I am not any of those words. Just a plain old synesticist."

Sid knew she would engage him by his subtle response.

"I have no idea what that is," Evelyn remarked as if she was supposed to know the descriptive word the old man gave to himself.

"Synesticist. Nobody really knows what that is, Mrs. Rhett. But it describes what I do perfectly! I take in all information from the five senses so that a sixth sense compels me to truth. It is not like a synthesis you'd know in photosynthesis, biosynthesis, or nucleosynthesis. There are synthesists and synesticists. I'm the second one."

The lady nodded as if knowing that either profession ever existed.

"So what does a synesticist do?" she asked.

"It's simple. He tells the truth. But being reserved and wishing not to cause anyone discomfort, I try to tell the generalities of the truth as a way of coddling the exigencies of life," Sid offered.

"Do you feel a truth getting ready to exit now?" she inquired.

"Exigencies are not exits, my dear. They are the troubled priorities that one sometimes must face, like death, divorce, loneliness, or—in my immediate case—taxes," he noted.

"Your exigency is the troubled priority of relationships. It is seen in your body language, the color of your scarf, and the way in which your hair is tousled. It's a faint smell of Estee Lauder. It's the book in your lap and the grasp you have on your pocketbook. It's hesitancy in your voice, the inflection you have on random words, and a slight pout you probably do not even know that you are displaying. Your relationship issue is probably with your daughter. She is sixteen or maybe fifteen.

She cannot understand you. She thinks you do not love her. She told you that she would never grow up and be like you, but she will," he rambled. "I hope I have not said too much."

The old man knew even more than he was admitting.

The lady was startled at the insight and looked around suspiciously to see if anyone heard the explanation. She then looked down at her book. She paused. Her soft voice mellowed into a sniffle. Sid knew she was hiding other sorrows. She got teary-eyed and looked back up. She was stunned by the accuracy of the revelation and the emotion she had driven inward for months.

"Are you licensed?" she inquired as if to make an appointment. Her wet eyes were yet focused to a response.

"There is no such thing as a license for a synesticist, ma'am. There is no formal education or Ph.D. You either are . . . Or you are not. I am the only synesticist I know." He said the words solemnly, knowing he had struck a deeply set emotion with the now introspective lady.

There was a pause as she gathered herself. She adjusted in the seat and placed her pocketbook to her side.

Sid's new coffee arrived. The clerk brought it over instead of characteristically calling his name out into the void of airspace claimed within the realm of Wi-Fi. The landmark science of wireless transmission of the Internet brings the minions to this café.

"Is he boring you?" the clerk asked sarcastically.

"Boring? Quite to the contrary, miss," the lady responded. "I find him quietly charming."

The clerk noted the sadness of the moment and, not wanting to engage, returned to the counter. The old man was discomforted by the lady's weeping onset but unapologetic. It was as if he knew she should cry a moment to face the truth. It was simply what synesticists knew within their timing of revelation.

She cleared her voice and looked away at the counter while she composed herself to ask the next question.

"Do you have office hours?" she followed.

"Yes." He nodded the response to the realization that he frequents the same booth in the same café nearly every day. "I'm here every day from nine o'clock to eleven thirty or so. My time is free, like the Wi-Fi and the snide remarks I get from that orange-haired clerk."

"Does she not know your insight?" Evelyn asked, staring back at the clerk over at the counter.

"Oh, that she does. But she is not receptive. The messaging that goes out and travels the cyberspace that we know as our world cannot be completed until it enters another world. It has to be received. Her receptors are almost fully blocked."

Sid paused to posture the next truth.

"Your daughter's receptors are more open than you know. Go to her. Tell her that you understand what she is feeling. Listen to her message. Respond after a deep breath and a nod of your approval. Look at her as someone you love, respect, and trust. You'll see some results within the week."

It was as if a doctor ordered a prescription.

"Don't expect the full transition without beginning upon the path of patience. It's the most comforting word in the lexicon. Patience," he added.

Evelyn nodded as she looked past the old man's glasses into his Santa blue eyes.

"If I come in and see you, can I assume that I can sit here and that you will know me?" Evelyn queried.

"I will know you. When you sit here, it will be an opportunity for you to know yourself better. You cannot dupe the senses," the old man intimated. "You can only betray them for a moment. But then reality resumes its course."

Sid hoped that she would return. He knew there was a more profound and darker reality.

"Do you have a card?" she asked in a way to ascertain a name or a reference. She did not fear him or see him as a circus-type act. She innately knew him to be what he said he was—a synesticist. How could he be anything else?

"I have something better than a card that you do not have to carry," he replied. "My formal name is a palindrome. If you remember my first name, you'll know my last."

"A palindrome? Is that like Ava or Bob?" she asked. "A name that is spelled backward and forward as the same?"

"Most people seem to think a palindrome is a large building to shelter elephants or giraffes," he noted. "But it's a mostly intentional anomaly of names or phrases that make for a cute comment."

"I'll guess your middle name is Otto," she proposed, now in a lighter mood. "That would seem to fit you. Is it Otto?"

"Eliot S. Toile, at your service," he stated. "It's actually Eliot Sidney Toile, and I go by Sid. The palindrome only works with my initial. It has been a lifelong triviality perpetuated by my Harvard-degreed parents. They could have been even more belligerent by naming me Sweat N. Toile."

"Mr. Toile, your ear seems to have stopped bleeding." Evelyn noticed, looking to his countenance for any other sign of injury.

She then started to gather her things. She would remember this frumpy man for being aligned by the lightning, an inexplicably smashed phone, and a palindromic name.

"Just call me Sid. That would be fine. And thank you. I am fully auditory again. My vision is failing, I suppose. It should last long enough to see you again," he winked.

The old man looked up and started to rise as a gesture of courtesy.

"Keep your seat, Sid. I do have a feeling I'll see you again," she replied.

She was guessing. He was citing fact. He knew when, but she did not.

"Your daughter's name, Mrs. Rhett?" Sid asked as she was ready to depart.

"Anna," she stated. "It's a palindrome too."

With that, the lady departed from the booth. She looked enlightened and calm. She confidently walked out of the B & B to take advantage of the storm's passing. She had not even ordered her latte.

The old man sipped his warmed coffee, patted his ear once again with the brown napkin, and continued on his laptop. He had a new concern about Evelyn that he had not revealed. Stating it would have prevented her from sitting with him. He would get to know her better before addressing it so that it could be solved.

He opened his iPad cover and tapped to refresh the screen.

He Googled the ancient Ethiopian claim that this eastern African country has housed the Ark of the Covenant for centuries. After reading myriad articles that cited or refuted the evidence, he Googled again to find where Charles Lindbergh was buried.

Maui, the page revealed he thought to himself, *"That makes no sense at all."*

His café grande was still warm. The storm had passed. Callista was lurking. The Boracle of Wi-Fi was happily centered in his booth.

CHAPTER THREE

Walter Bailloch

SID WAS SETTLED in his booth at the Bib and Bibliothéque Emporium in Mount Pleasant, the fastest-growing city in South Carolina. He looks at his pocket watch to glance at the love of his life, Ida, who died many years before. He was expecting someone important.

His friend Thomas presently joined him with his morning latté. He asked questions and then listened intently in amazement of answers he had not anticipated. The friendly septuagenarian was considered a savant. He was da Vinci, Tesla, Einstein, and Aristotle. No living person knew as much. The old man stopped suddenly to ask Thomas a question.

"Do you know a fellow named Walter Bailloch?" he asked.

"Nope. Never heard of 'im," answered Thomas.

"You will one day," the old man warned. "If one Googles the name, there is nothing. That makes sense, but then again, it doesn't. Walter Bailloch surely exists."

"What does he look like?" Thomas asked.

"I don't know," Thomas realized. "I haven't seen him since I was nine. What I remember are eyes that are nearly black and deep set. That's all I can recall. But if he were ever to resurface, I'd know."

The elusive Bailloch had been able to move in and out of the most secure checkpoints without incident. By lore, he aged in reverse canine years—a year in every seven. It was Bailloch that dunked the young Sid repeatedly in the Pocono camp lake sixty-six years earlier. Sid assumed that this horrid adversary could move about undetected in disguises.

Bailloch had not arrived anywhere in his past with anything but deleterious intentions. His pursuit of Sid Toile had become compulsive. Yet it was something Sid invited because he felt that he could anticipate Bailloch's methods. He knew when Bailloch was getting closer. The savant determined that his synchronicity with time would checkmate the cursed malevolence of Bailloch.

Sid followed. "He is the evilest man and not to be trifled. He'll come many miles across continents just to cause and witness an enemy's demise. Witnessing his applied evil enhances the triumph of his self-image. I knew of him long ago."

Thomas acknowledged the warning just before the savant returned to the informational trail of awe requested.

The Bib and Bibliothéque incorporates a unique local enterprise. The locally owned establishment combined four elements—an exotic coffee shop with a hot short order menu, a bookstore, a reading emporium, and a Saturday children's entertainment venue.

Prof. Thomas Leon needed innovative material for his college senior lecture series that would begin in January. An elective course titled Theoretical Algorithms could not disappoint. Thomas had come to his elderly friend for ideas. The typical format of a syllabus for college students was about to become injected with steroids.

They spoke in pleasantries prior to the aging man's rare insight to his friend. A revelation was imminent. But, first, the old man brought up the name of a vengeful murderer. In time, Bailloch would find him.

The senior citizen took a sip of his café grande and continued on a stream-of-consciousness diatribe. More than a dozen exciting nuances were listed to benefit the professor's syllabus. Thomas was taking copious notes.

The old man emphasized the next thought.

"There is so much out there to cover that you should never run out of topics. Thomas, you've read that there are scientists in Switzerland working on time travel and predictive analytics. The first part is an undiscovered truth. The second subject is enthralling. These scientists believe they can anticipate world events—everything from cultural revolutions to continental droughts. I have no reason to doubt that they are correct. Skype one of them in to guest lecture and make a donation to their foundation."

Thomas shook his head indicating that the departmental budget would not allow extravagance. He had two yellow pad pages of ideas—all of the topics sure to engage creative conversation. The old man recited an endless fountain of ideas.

"How do you keep up? Were you born craving information?" Thomas asked.

The pause in their conversation was profound and mildly uncomfortable. There was a backstory to the old man's insatiable quest for knowledge that he had never divulged—not even his best friend, the professor.

"Thomas, I've never told anyone why I have come to this thirst," he explained. "It's because I really don't know. I don't think I was born with any particular skills whatsoever. In fact, I do not remember hardly anything in my life before my tenth birthday," he started.

"Something happened before I turned ten. My parents only had me . . . No siblings. I wondered if I had been adopted for years, but I was not. Anyway, they were absorbed into a level of Boston culture that nearly made me a footnote. I was likely an accident of passion that they never repeated. Many of their friends were unaware that they even had a child. They sent me away to boarding schools and to summer camps. I felt like a rental property."

Thomas adjusted his haunches and listened, realizing that this rare insight was intensely personal.

"When I was almost ten, they sent me to a summer camp in the Poconos. Their age limit was ten, but my parents must've paid them extra to take me. There, I was swimming to a platform out in the lake when some of the other kids started horsing around. They dunked me several times, and I panicked. I lost my rhythm in the aggressive play and began to drown."

The elderly savant reflected on the event by pausing to look up at the bright LED lighting in the bookstore coffee shop. It was as if he knew that another force saved him—an omnipotent God that redirected his life.

Thomas detected a most unfamiliar glare in the old man's eyes.

He continued. "I remember the water rushing into my lungs and a horrible realization that I was going to die then and there. Turtles and bottom-feeding lake creatures would eat my carcass. I was mortified by the prospect but too tired to fight anymore. My lungs had no more air. I was staring up at the surface but unable to get there. I truly believe that I died there.

"Then I entered a timeless trance of peacefulness. I saw and was directed by a vivid blue beam that kept coming toward me. It seemed to me as if it were divine. Celestial. Spiritual. Godly. I began to pray the only prayer I had learned fully from the catechism, the Hail Mary. I kept my eyes on the light. I believe I witnessed an intercession I can never explain to anyone without them declaring me as whacked. I lost consciousness. I have no recollection of what happened under the water in the stillness of that lake."

Sid continued to stare off into another dimension, his eyes upon the intense lighting above the booth.

"It was the most peaceful feeling imaginable. I had stopped fighting the weight of the water. Instead, the water took me like a baby in the arms of a new mother. I was completely contented. My fear was gone. I was no longer in a state of panic but more in a state of euphoria. That blue beam was indescribable in its richness from shades of cyan to sapphire. It was wide and intense. It moved and changed with the reflections of the surface. I stared in awe. I believe that this is where I was given something extraordinary by what I am convinced was an intercession of angels. Don't judge this as a near-death experience because it was certainly not. It was, in fact, a new life experience. I believe I was reborn under that water. I was also redirected. I was taken placidly into the life I still live without the fear of anything, including death. The other phenomena took a few years to manifest. You have just cited it. I must gather information and fit it to other information, like a wiring harness with millions of color-coded connections. I did not understand why until about thirty years ago after Ida left me alone to face the world. My thirst for knowledge is only exceeded by my sense that I must make a difference. I have to be quietly and dutifully consequential. That impulse trumps all others."

"Did they pump your stomach back then?" Thomas asked.

He wanted to know how a drowned youth extricated himself from a death situation.

"No. There was no outside earthly force that brought me back. You would assume I had a physical delivery back to the living, back to humankind. Thomas, I learned later that no one person had saved me, though they dove frantically to locate me. I simply reappeared at the bank of the lake more than a thousand yards from where they last saw me struggling. It was an unfathomable and bizarre result."

"My god. How?" Thomas asked.

"I've never figured out how and why. I just know that it became fact. The blue light delivered me, I suppose. The angels. Mother Mary. God. All of the above. I had blacked out after the peaceful intermission I described. I coughed out nine and a half years of the life before that drowning and began anew. I was exhausted and sick with the harsh release of water expelling from my lungs. I was alone and afraid. I was on the edge of the waterline, too tired to move further up the bank. I lay sprawled there for a time, maybe an hour. Once, I heard sirens in the distance, as if it was the signal to start my new life. But I could not get up. After a bit, I began to cry and gathered myself. I walked up to the road near the gate and all the way back to the shore nearest to the canteen where I heard the other kids in there—some crying, some praying. A counselor on the platform saw me first. Then the others saw me there. I was fully drained and wearied by the experience. My swim trunks were dry. I suppose I was in shock. I sat down as they rushed to gather around me. In a moment, Mr. Callison, the director, scolded me as if I swam underwater for a thousand yards. But I remained calm as he yelled at me. He presumed that I had intentionally deceived the bullies who caused my drowning."

"He didn't hug you first?" Thomas asked.

"He may have," Sid countered. "I don't remember that. A police officer was filling out paperwork on a table. He chucked it, I suppose. The bullies who tried to drown me were more in shock than I was. I suspect they had confessed their offenses to the officer and were thinking about reform school.

"I slept in the car for most of the trip back home the next day. The night after the incident, I was with my parents in Boston. I repeated to them what happened for the third time, but they didn't seem to buy it. That head guy didn't even tell them about the drowning episode. After hearing it again that night, my mom just said, 'Oh, you poor dear,' and told me to go upstairs and take my bath.

"But something dramatic did happen. I emerged with a newfound zeal and high purpose. I honestly believed that I could never die. And I believed that I was delivered by God to complete a mission. I'm seventy-six now, nearly sixty-six years past the mishap in the Poconos.

"I am unaware of any singular focus to my life's mission. Like I know that I'm not supposed to run for president or invent something indispensable. There has never been a major purpose revealed to me. I just know that I thrive on information. I am voracious in that regard. And I must become helpful to all that I consider as potential recipients of my God-given abilities to resolve. That is—to me—my personal sense of positive human consequence. My rationale tells me that I can and will die. But I have never feared it."

Thomas took a sip of his latté, hoping that Sid would continue with the personal insight that had captured his attention.

"What returns to me, my friend is that intense beam of blue light—every so often in my sleep. It's still guiding me. To what? I don't really know."

The old man paused to check his nonworking pocket watch. It was an obsessive habit with the reward of seeing the miniature photograph of his deceased wife opposing the watch face.

He looked back across the booth to Thomas, who was absorbed into the story and wanted to delve more into the interim sixty-six years. There is no doubt that Thomas believed every word of the impossible tale that the old man described.

"Was your life markedly different after the drowning?" Thomas asked.

"When I went back to school and began the fourth grade, I had already read and memorized all of my textbooks. My grandmother had given me a *Rand McNally World Atlas* for my birthday. I memorized every country, every capital, every river, and every mountain range. She owned a one-hundred-year-old leather-bound set of *The Federalist Papers* in her library. I devoured them. John Jay, James Madison, and Alexander Hamilton wrote them. I found that I could read something once and commit whatever it was, no matter the complexity, to memory. At the age of ten, I became what people often describe as a savant. But it was not like Rain Man or others you may have read about or seen in documentaries. I have no disability. Sometimes savants are characterized as those with exceptional abilities and limited social interaction. I never experienced the latter, thank God.

"My parents thought that their gene pool had delivered my expanded mental capacities. My grades were exceptional, and I rarely did homework. Instead, I visited the Boston Free Library every afternoon to seek other information on every topic from architecture to zoology."

Thomas was silent. He simply nodded, hoping that his friend would continue the backdrop details to his genius and motivation. He suspected that the only other person who may have known the drowning story was the old man's deceased wife.

The soliloquy of the savant continued.

"I cannot relate the significance of a recurring dream. I often dream in another century. There, I am a wizard. I move about without the restrictions of distance, pain, fatigue, time, or gravity. As I travel from place to place, I seem to find another dilemma greater than the one I had just resolved. These are endless encounters. They present themselves. I do not seek them. I just listen intently with a powerful sensitivity to clues that do not always come from the words spoken. It's the logic of wizardry, I suppose."

Sid gave more insight. "I have taken clues from newspaper accounts of high crimes and deduced the method, means, and often the criminal. I mail it to the proper authorities anonymously. I have done the same to solve scientific conundrums. But I am not a scientist. So I'll send what I connect to a deserving scientist. I simply reach for pieces of puzzles that are before me and link those that match."

"Don't dismiss me as nuts, Thomas. I've never revealed this to any other living person. I just absorb it all and see where and when the information takes me—whether that destination is current, rational, or ancient and mystical."

"I'm not one to judge, Sid," Thomas replied. "I have a brother who teaches gross anatomy at the medical university. His residual job is cadaver disposal. I have a sister that works for the CIA and invents new people by authentic documents. And they both think I'm the odd one."

"So we can get a dead body anytime we want with passports on demand!" Sid deduced.

Thomas laughed.

"I never ask because I'm afraid they might tell me something I really don't want to know," Thomas noted. "I hope I never need a cadaver or a fake passport."

Sid rerouted the insight of his childhood and its residual impact back to his most trusted friend.

"Over my lifetime," the old man intimated, "I have been able to commit innumerable trivialities to memory. I realized the purpose years ago. I have found that an inordinate percentage of those seemingly inconsequential matters eventually connect. Knowledge, they tell us, is power. But they never finish the thought. Infinite knowledge becomes the unlimited power to resolve. Knowledge simply being power is an age-old formula for corruption. It is infinite knowledge that elevates. Connecting the pieces does that."

Thomas was still astonished at the story of how Sid's intellect coalesced and his basis for his exceptional abilities. He never knew about the drowning story or the dreams that took him into other times. And though he knew that his friend was a bona fide savant, the mysterious source, extraordinary breadth, and profound depth of his knowledge were never meticulously explained until this conversation. Thomas felt personally privileged to know the seven-decade story Sid had never told another.

Thomas asked another question related to Sid's observable habits.

"I notice that you always show up at natural disasters too. Hurricanes, earthquakes, floods . . . why do these things attract your attention?"

"Simple, Thomas. When these things happen, people become despondent and need the most basic things like food and fresh water. I rent a U-Haul and take my sleeping bag. I want to be there early so that those in need see that we are all part of one family—humanity. It's an incredible opportunity to make a lasting impression on children," Sid explained. "They need to see that I am not government or the Red Cross or the Peace Corps. I'm an old man in a U-Haul with cases of water and boxes full of emergency rations that came because of an inner duty to be part of their recovery experience. The lesson? We need to depend upon each other implicitly. When it comes down to it, we are neighbors helping neighbors with no ulterior motive beyond. Young people will remember that."

"Make no mistake, Thomas. There is a constant of evil. It is in the disruptive intentions of those with dissociative ideals," he explained. "We see them more and more. They are suicide bombers, murderous dictators, and counterculture instigators. Their minds work differently. They plan, punish, and poison. Among the worst of these is Walter Bailloch. His passion is to seek and destroy all that is good wherever it exists. He was born without a conscience. He has no joy."

Indeed, Bailloch became a character of the worst order. The list of his impunity reads like an underworld dossier never to be exceeded in its composite malfeasance. Bailloch's grim experience altered too many lives. He bombed a church in Bulgaria; initiated a crowded cinema fire in London, a jumbo airliner explosion over Portugal, a village poisoning in Algeria, and a suburban train wreck near Tokyo. He had engineered all of the misery.

"He must not capture the stones." Sid declared.

"The stones? What stones? Thomas followed.

"The Castle stones. There are two—the Ethereals—rare lavender diamonds from another age. They were secured before Castle McSween had been overrun. They exist still. But they are separated by time. If they are reunited they become an undeniable force, one that even Bailloch cannot penetrate. But separate, Bailloch can smell them. He must never hold them, Thomas. Never. No matter what. Sid decreed.

Thomas was confused. He had never heard Sid speak of Bailloch or the stones. He took the point as information and did not explore it beyond—seeing that Sid was upset by the prospect.

Sid knew of Walter Bailloch. But they had never met. He was direct and cautiously composed in his words to Thomas. It was because of those for whom he cared. There were many people of circumstance under his protection across six continents. Every one of these was charged with but a single request from the sage. They were to assist him to locate the lavender diamonds. Evry small clue mattered. His quest to find the long-missing Ethereal Stones entailed an even more substantial responsibility—to unite them with their rightful heirs. His nemesis Bailoch had a darkened mission to seek the stones and destroy the curse of a bloodline. Sid hoped to draw in the malicious and sinister counterpart. But Bailloch was a complicated man to trap. Bailloch's most feared adversary on earth was a frumpy old man who had no fear of him. Bailloch was compelled to locate the stones so that he could then destroy the protective sage. He could then dispense with the only bloodline that could destroy him.

Sid was hesitant to explain the other-worldly dilemma to Thomas, knowing it would make him sound mentally imbalanced. The septuagenarian had never been as forthcoming with anyone about his reasons, his concerns, or his abilities. He sensed that he could speak to Thomas in candor because he knew that Thomas was trustworthy and shared his interest in the pursuit of absolute knowledge.

Besides, Thomas was part of his plan to die.

CHAPTER FOUR

Theta Barnwell

THE READING EMPORIUM was nearly full of young children on Saturday mornings. Excited youth crowded the bookstore mini-theater to be mesmerized by puppetry, mimes, dramatic readings, magic, and finger painting. A dramatic reading of *Snow White* was enchanting the Barnwell twins when their mother, Theta, saw a most familiar man across the bookstore. It was Billy Grayson. Her heart immediately leaped with joy. It had been a very long time since she had last seen Billy.

Billy was the singer-songwriter and guitarist with the new wave band The Pals. Billy's insular lifestyle and loathing of the stardom track that had ruined the lives of so many other band members gave Theta the sense that he could be approached. The band had taken a touring hiatus months earlier. Billy had registered a few solo ballads with his scratchy Kristofferson-like voice. He had a growing fan base.

His solo performances also bolstered the popularity of the band. The singer-songwriter had moved back to Mount Pleasant and recorded a few new tracks that brought him some widespread notoriety for his mellifluous lyrics.

An agent might have further enhanced the financial impact of his solo career, but Billy refused to hire one. His quest was not for money or popularity. It was for re-exploring his troubled soul.

Billy found song subjects within the most arcane and ordinary occurrences. To him, the lyrics were a journey to the unknown placed upon the sheet music of nature. The beat could mimic a swaying tree in a summer breeze, a midnight lapping of waves upon the crags, or a baby's heartbeat.

He and Theta had dated briefly when they were in high school. A mutual admiration developed before they parted for college. It was the natural order of life to Billy but a cataclysmic event to Theta. She knew that Billy was the boy that captured her soul, her heart, and her imagination.

Theta Seabrook Barnwell was born with both a silver spoon and a golden rule. The only child of Dr. Simmons Barnwell and Martha Seabrook Barnwell, Theta favored her mother's agile and lissome physique but had her father's Irish complexion and demeanor. Her dark red hair hinted of ancient Hibernia. It was long and flowing—more waved than curled. The sparkle in her emerald eyes accentuated her lightly freckled face. Theta had emerged into early adulthood donning the rarest exquisiteness of physical attributes. Her gawkiness as a child developed into an intonation of grandeur. Her maturation subtly depleted her physical awkwardness. It also summoned her innate sense of approachable candor and deep-seated humility. She was convinced that she was simple, unpopular, and unattractive.

Theta treated classmates and friends on the same level as strangers, the unfortunate, and the downtrodden. She loved all of God's children much the same. Her Sunday school upbringing helped her develop a selfless sense of compassion and understanding. Her odd preteen physique sometimes insulated her from the popular circles. She internalized much social disappointment during her formative years.

Only her father saw the hurt. He became her pillar and her strength by his wise insight into living without prejudice.

Her father was a lawyer with nearly anonymous philanthropic tendencies. Her mother was a status-conscious socialite. By the age of twelve, Theta was enamored by her father's disdain for status and his admirable empathy for the needy. He was a man of great conviction and uncommon temerity. He stood for what he believed. Theta emulated his sensitivity and demeanor.

"When a disappointment arises, there is a deeper opportunity, my dear. It is a time to put happiness over a happening," he would say.

Conversely, her mother, Martha, harbored personal advancement agendas. Her meeting calendar was marked with garden clubs, gossipy luncheons, bridge clubs, and historical lineage associations. She once worked as a bank teller, but only for the two years until she met and married the young Roper Hospital intern Simmons Barnwell. The marriage gave her permanent leave of a schedule. She became exactly what she studied to become at Wellesley—a wealthy socialite housewife.

"She was the aggressiveness I lacked when we married," Simmons told Theta. "And there were other shortcomings that I had that she complemented by her strengths. She does her own thing. I try to get out of the way!"

Theta, their only child, was often presented with decisions between grandeur and humility. More and more, she viewed her mother's status-seeking forays into societal circles with disdain. She chose to model her life after that of her father. Something happened when she was a sophomore away at college that should have altered her course. It only emboldened her all the more. She became pregnant. Her twins were born out of wedlock.

At age twenty-eight, Theta was not only a single mother but also a career-entrenched travel agency professional. She prided herself on her cultural knowledge and her insider avenues of saving customers unnecessary fees. She was also a church volunteer and a soup kitchen helper.

She kept to herself and never married. The twins were the whisper of pundits and insensitive chatterers who guessed at the circumstance of her mystery suitor for years. Theta would never divulge the name of the children's father. She did so to protect him, not her. She had a predisposition to render any pretense of an esteemed self-image to the judgment of others. She was quite comfortable just being a good mother.

There was a time that her silence required her father's constancy of advice.

Once, eight years earlier, at a discount store, while trying on two marked-down maternity outfits in the dressing room, she heard two of her school friends in the thin-walled room next to her.

"Well, I think she is nothing but a two-faced whore," Ellen Scofield said. "All of the remain-a-virgin talk was just her way of saying she was better than us. She's no better. She's a tramp if you ask me."

Her neighbor Gail Barker, whom she rode to high school with for several years, was equally cruel.

"She never fooled me. She always had that sanctimonious air and better-than-thou aura. She never stopped talking about 'my daddy this and my daddy that.' To see her now makes me feel vindicated. She was not what she pretended to be after all."

Theta cried silent tears as she waited for her two erstwhile friends to leave the dressing area. She left the maternity clothes in the stall and went directly home.

Home is where Theta gained her strength of character. It was where she listened to the encouragement of her father.

Theta was well read, highly educated, and dedicated to the proper upbringing of her twin girls. She was innately happy. Her loves included reading, soft music, chivalric manners, Victorian traditions, and a dedication to the moralistic North Star of living a good life. She didn't lie, made no excuses, and was not envious of others. She was a person of letters. She handwrote thank-you notes from the heart, along with all personal correspondence, and current entries to her personal diary. The entries were not daily but sporadic. She even sent beautifully scripted notes to customers to advertise a vacation special. She would forgo much of the digital world to make someone know that they are special. To Theta, handwritten notes served that purpose.

The green-eyed Theta seemed to float along the floor as she walked. Being reedy-thin and light, her gait was long and yet soft like an egret landing upon a lake. Though her hearing was exceptional, she had a habit of angling her head to the left when she didn't understand or was surprised by something. Some thought that she did so as if she was straining to hear. It was an evolutionary quirk. Her father, Simmons Barnwell, also exhibited this idiosyncrasy.

She was not an ideologue, a feminist, a socialite, a born-again, or an attention-getting do-gooder. She was just Theta—dedicated mother and responsible citizen. Having her twin girls out of wedlock was entirely outside of the orderly life she had planned. But she had adjusted well. Her father helped her for the first few years until he had become ill. By then, the twins were in kindergarten, and Theta had begun a career in travel. Simmons died when grandchildren Mia and Leah were only four years of age. He left Theta a down payment for a home within his estate, knowing that she would not likely tolerate staying with her pretentious mother.

The Bib and Bibliothéque attracted excited children to their unique events. It was a free path to entertainment via the arts. Theta routinely took the now seven-year-old twins to the special area for the Saturday morning emporium performances.

Theta led the girls to their seats in Lilliputian chairs formed in concentric circles facing the reader. She never lost sight of her long-ago confidant Billy Grayson. She tactfully meandered back to find Billy looking over the European History section.

"Billy, what are you doing back in the B & B? I thought you were permanently attached to Atlanta. Are you lost?" Theta began.

A short embrace initiated by Theta was enhanced by a stare and quick perusal of each other's slim physique and dazzling green pupils. They shared the verdant eye color now and in their burgeoning youth at Cooper River High School.

Billy looked puzzled. He sheepishly admitted that he had been away too long, and though he was sure they were friends, he could not recall her name.

"I'm Billy. But I did not catch your name," he confessed.

"Theta Barnwell...and you are forgiven. I didn't expect you to remember me. I know all about you from the rumors, press interviews, and even the medical journals. I just want to let you know that I'm someone from your forgotten past that has the very best opinion of you." Theta smiled in reply.

Her heart beat rapidly, and her upper chest reddened. It was evident that she was delighted to see Billy again. He was someone she once trusted.

Her insights about the press stories she noted to him were a factual observation accumulated over the last few years. She knew he had an incredible journey of difficulty. She knew that he was cruising in life's fast lane because of his latent talent, mega-income, and public notoriety. She suspected that he was part of the alcoholism and drug crowd that musicians sometimes coddle, but was careful not to judge. Innately, she wanted him to be happy—considering all that he had experienced. Much of Billy's downside had turned into an incredible upside.

They dated briefly in the springtime of their senior year in high school. Theta was Billy's date to the senior prom. Theta had not dated often prior to Billy because of her shyness and awkward physical adjustments to young adulthood.

They seemed to be an ideal match as a dating couple. Both had career aspirations. Both were excellent students. Their commonalities stacked like pyramid stones to a high and exquisite crowning apex. Their capstone was the sincerity and pleasantness of their conversations. Subjects were often academic and accentuated by another cohesion—their smiles. They brought to each other the unpretentious zest of high school optimism. Theta once indicated to her father that Billy was the man she would one day marry because they enjoyed a caring and unique attribute—a never-ending conversation.

As a dating couple from years before, they had only one lingering matter of contention. Theta was indeed chaste. She quietly reemphasized her desire to remain as a virgin until her wedding night each time their romance began to exceed a comfortable level of warmth. She insisted that Billy respect her promise to herself. Billy was grudgingly compliant.

The matter of her virginity seemed to become a new discussion at the conclusion of each date, Billy believing that he would eventually erode the defenses. Theta's willpower was stronger than Billy's willingness to accept the caveat. Billy knew that his rampant testosterone would not win Theta. They departed after graduation as close friends who depended upon each other for the next stage of their lives as insightful friends. Billy believed they would eventually meet again. Theta was devastated that they parted.

He went off to Georgia Tech to study engineering. Theta pursued her love of journalism at Scott College in Decatur, Georgia. But she changed majors early to the college's highly regarded hospitality management program. Scott College was Theta's secondary attraction to the Atlanta area.

She had often spoken to Billy by phone over the prior year but wanted to be closer. Her conviction of remaining a virgin remained foremost, but she felt a strong desire to be near Billy. She accepted that they would not date and that he would likely be dating others. She was content that they could speak more often and even meet for lunch on occasion. Billy enjoyed seeing more of Theta as well. When pressed, she reassured him that her virginal status had not and would not change. Theta knew that she was happiest in her life when he was near. Their conversations drove their relationship forward.

Seeing Billy so many years later in the emporium recalled her once-bubbling sentiments. She still loved Billy. The surprise of seeing him rekindled her warm feelings for the man she told her dad was the love of her life.

"Seriously, what brings you to the bookstore, Billy? I come here sometimes with my twins but haven't seen you here before," she asked.

She stated her reasons in a way to remind herself that she had moved on from the mysterious past that everyone scrutinized years before. The Billy Grayson she once knew was not the same person standing in front of her. It was taking her a hard moment to realize his trying circumstances. Much had changed. She suspected that he was unaware of the state of affairs that made her quite uneasy at their chance meeting.

"Theta. What a pretty name. Theta, I've been away for too long. Did you know another Theta here by any chance?" Billy asked.

Theta answered and inquired back to Billy, "No. Why do you ask?"

"My friend Jackie Mann told me about a girl named Theta that I evidently knew in Atlanta. He said that we were platonic friends but that she moved away. Then there was another Theta my mother told me about who raised money to help pay my medical bills. I owe her a lot. Are you either of those Thetas?"

"I'm both," Theta proudly admitted. "And you owe me nothing. I did it out of concern. And, yes, we were platonic friends. I have missed that."

Reality had returned to capture and cage the concept of circumstance. The entertainment press and medical journals detailed Billy's horrendous accident and slow recovery from death's grasp. He became a medical journal miracle. The unfortunate remnant of the ordeal was his memory loss. To Theta, Billy was the love of her life and the boyfriend that got away in high school. To Billy, Theta was a complete stranger. She knew that she would need to detail how he may have known her. She was happy to explain why she helped from afar so many years ago.

"We were great friends in high school and even dated, Billy," Theta explained. "We remained the best of friends. So when you had the accident at Tech, I tried to step in and help. By the beginning of February, we found out from your roommate Jackie that your insurance ran out. We just tried to help your family cope with the avalanche of bills. With so many others, we raised some money to assist. But you were still kinda out of it so you would not have known us or anything about that effort. You would have done it for others, so it was a given that we were there for you."

"My god, Theta. That was you," Billy restated. "You are so nice. Mom told me about you, but I had no memory of anything before September 4 . . . Eight long years ago. I'm so glad that we get to finally meet—or in your case, we meet again."

Billy paused to take in the view of someone he found quite stunning who knew him before his accident.

"Why would we have quit dating? Did you get married to someone else? Was I a jerk? Tell me. I've had the chance to start over. Please forgive me if I have done anything to upset you," Billy apologetically offered.

He hoped that the response coming back would not be embarrassing.

"Billy, it wasn't you. It was I. We both wanted to start college without strings. I was the one who was difficult, and I regret it to this day," Theta explained.

Their smiles belied the underlying abruptness of their former relationship. Billy and Theta were among the most popular senior couples at Cooper River High. Theta was a cross-country runner and played volleyball on a state championship team. Billy was the team captain and played midfielder on the soccer team. They were considered among the most likely of the senior couples to marry. But that had all changed.

When Georgia Tech offered an athletic scholarship, it cemented Billy's immediate future. The chance to become an architect enticed him more than the soccer program. The contortions of time left him in another dimension outside the graph of his chosen academic major. He became a musician.

"Thankfully, we remained friends. I saw you the week before the accident," Theta retold.

She hoped Billy would reconnect even a morsel of the time they had together. But the reference did nothing to reattach a memory for Billy.

"Billy," she continued as baby tears welled in her green eyes, "you had nothing at all to do with our parting circumstances. You were the consummate and perfect gentleman always. When you were struggling to live, my heart was breaking. You were far from being a jerk. I prayed that you would live. And now you have reappeared. I am fully pleased."

Billy was concerned about the sudden emotional reply.

"Theta, I'm sorry. Is there anything I can do?" He focused upon her fallen eyelids as if he had caused her tears.

Theta's face quivered temporarily within her reestablished memory of the long-ago disconnect. She had not reconciled the circumstance. She despaired. She became angry. She scoffed at the unfairness of life.

Billy's parents never knew of the pain she held deep inside. She remained independently strong throughout. And after a while, she adjusted to the new life that was still before her. She never reencountered Billy until this chance meeting in the Bib and Bibliothéque.

"No, Billy, I'm sorry. I get caught up in the past sometimes. What did you say brought you back to the B & B?" Theta asked, pulling herself back together.

"I'm here to meet an old friend named Sid for coffee, but he has someone with him," Billy replied. "Sid is like a father to me. I met him by chance about two years ago, and we remained in touch. I saw him the last time I was in town, and he really helped me come to grips with a few things. He's fascinating."

"Are you talking about Sid Toile, the Boracle?" Theta asked.

"You know him, Theta?" Billy asked.

"It seems everyone knows Sid. He's helped most everyone over the last few years. I should see him myself," Theta replied with a newfound smile. "I met him once just in passing, but we have never formally spoken at his 'booth office.' Amazing man, I'm told!"

"He once opened the B & B door for the twins, and I have never forgotten what he told me. He said he had just met three new 'friends-to-be.' I was instantly taken by his kindness. Then he told me that he collected friends as a hobby," Theta continued. "He assumed that I had too few friends. I don't know how he could have known that. It was eerie. He said that he was a 'frillionaire,' a man rich in friendships. I liked the word and thought to myself that I know no person who spends their lifetime collecting close friends. What a wonderful pursuit!"

Theta then inquired, "Are you just seeing him to say hello or to get advice?"

Theta was intrigued by Billy's sudden appearance at the bookstore and wanted to continue the conversation. She loved revisiting the boy she admired so much in high school.

"Well," Billy hesitated sheepishly, "I have a music career issue that I wanted Sid—the Boracle—to help me to direct. He is great at simplifying matters and lending advice."

"I hope it's not lyrics, Billy," Theta interjected. "Your lyrics have captured the hearts of all the young fans, especially the girls."

Her memories drifted back before she added, "I especially liked the lines in your 'Soul Mate' song that explored 'memories in the mists of mushroom fields.'"

Theta's comment was a poignant reference to a memory she shared with Billy years before. Somehow she had hoped that Billy would remember seeing mushrooms sprout in a wetted field.

"You have a devious way of reaching a chord of romance," Theta blushed. For a moment, she was hoping he would remember a time she cherished.

"Theta, memory is something I've tried to recapture, but it only frustrates me more each time someone asks, 'Remember when . . . ?' There is no magic elixir. Fact is, I don't remember when or then or whatever. What happens happens for a reason, I suppose. I have to look at life as now and beyond. People who knew me tell me that I was good to them. That's comforting. But given my injury, maybe they're telling me just what they'd like me to hear. Perhaps there was a fantastic period in my life that I can never reconnect," Billy intimated. "Someone like you, for instance, would surely be a great remembrance."

Theta didn't know what to say. She cocked her head to the left.

"Billy, I knew you before, so I understand. You have come from a tragedy to the top of the music charts," Theta assured him. "Everyone is happy for you. And you have handled so much more than most."

Inside, Theta felt the pang of memory. She had such high regard for the celebrity, but could not let her feelings overcome her cynicism for all else. She dared not trust anyone. There was just too much at stake. She would be wise to withdraw with cordiality. She knew that Billy would leave to some other place exotic and enjoy an enchanted life. She was proud that she helped him and elated that he had flourished beyond her efforts to find a new life and a public following

The twins came running back to find Theta as the reading of *Snow White* ended with applause. She introduced them.

"Billy, these are my girls, Mia and Leah. Say hello to Mr. Grayson, girls," Theta directed. "He went to high school with your mom."

DISAFFECTIONS OF TIME

"It is my pleasure, young ladies. What grade are you in?" Billy asked.

They almost simultaneously said, "Second grade, sir," when Theta spoke up over their reserved young voices to tell Billy, "They're at Pinckney School here in Mount Pleasant. It's a wonderful place for them with small classrooms and great teachers."

Theta bent over to adjust Leah's hair ribbon and tuck in her blouse.

"Do they have any siblings, Theta?" Billy pursued.

"No, Billy, these two are a handful." Theta offered incongruous small talk as the girls darted back into the children's playroom. "I can't imagine doing more than I do now just to be a good mother. They both take piano lessons and gymnastics in addition to their schoolwork. There's homework, sleepovers, birthday parties, and shopping."

"Understood. I have a little one myself. He's three, and he stays with me. He's at my mom's today. Name's Ashton. He's in half-day kindergarten at Westminster here since I moved back," Billy divulged. "Great kid, but I never thought I'd be a single parent."

"Why are you a . . ." Theta started. She had intentionally not divulged to Billy that she was also a single parent.

"Oh, my fiancée, Emily, you probably wouldn't know," Billy interrupted. "She had some habits that came back. Some of the paparazzi had it right. They didn't know about Ashton."

"So sorry, Billy. What happened to her?" Theta continued with a quizzical look.

"I loved her with all my heart, Theta. She couldn't change. Sad. After Ashton was born, she went right back to the demons that had stolen her life—and had taken away our marriage plans as well. I tried to help her four times to get into centers at about $40,000 a shot. She O.D.'d a year ago. Since then, the band got off the road. I came here so that my mom could get to know Ashton, and Mom has really helped me out. She loves that little guy."

Billy paused to reflect.

"Ashton never really knew Emily, his mother. Sad. She had a good heart. She seemed to know that her adventure was to be a short one. Her sudden passing affected me more than anything."

Billy paused to reflect. Theta saw that he was hurt.

"I felt like—as much as I loved her—I was completely helpless. I was at first angered, then victimized. Later, I felt so incredibly lonely. It was the sense that I was needed by another human being that pulled me out of my self-pity and depression."

Theta was stunned by the personal insight. She knew much of the hurt that she had internalized before moving on to find comfort in her quest to become a new person impervious to sorrow. She could empathize with the tragedy of Billy Grayson.

"But I'm a new person now. I have Sid to thank for guiding me," Billy allowed, knowing that he had made the person he couldn't remember from his past most uncomfortable.

"I hope I have not burdened you. Please do not feel sorry for me, Theta. I am convinced that my life—through it all—has been charmed," Billy smiled.

Billy glanced across the bookstore to the corner coffee booth. The Boracle was free.

"Theta, I would love to catch up sometime," Billy summed up as he saw the opening at the booth. "Maybe you can tell me who my high school friends were and whom I dated. I'd like to thank a lot of people, but I wouldn't know who they are unless I had someone like you to guide me."

Billy produced a card with the simplest information—his name, his cell number, and his e-mail address. There was no occupation, no logo, and no tagline.

"Theta, you are obviously a special person to have helped me from afar. There was no 'thank you' and absolutely no communication from me. I feel I owe you much. I can tell that there is beauty all the way to your soul. Please do not throw the card away. I need friends now more than ever," Billy offered.

"Well, I hope we can catch up sometime. I'd love to meet Ashton," Theta replied.

Theta knew that she would never call the number on the card. She did not want to re-engineer the past into the simplicity of the present. She knew that chapter had been ripped away from the manuscript. It was much like the extraction of a wisdom tooth—necessary but painful. The Billy Grayson she knew so fondly from before did not even know the new Billy Grayson, an iconic celebrity who overcame all medical odds.

Somehow, Billy was puzzled that he had not known what had become of Theta, though he had heard her name from Jackie Mann, his parents, and from two of his therapists.

Their small talk filled the time before the opening at booth 14 gave Billy a sense of suitable opportunity. He would need to dart to the booth. Another good-bye might mean ten more years of silence between the reconnected high school classmates. Meeting again would merely be a reintroduction to Billy now that he saw Theta, at age twenty-eight, for the first time.

"I understand, Billy. Go and see the Boracle man. I'll catch you later," Theta said. "You can catch me anytime."

Theta had sensed his fidgety impatience to see Sid. She leaned over and kissed Billy on his cheek as she departed to retrieve the twins. The kiss left Billy with a countenance of both surprise and apprehension.

Theta's eyes watered anew as she walked away to retrieve the twins.

He hesitated before turning to join Sid a dozen steps away at the booth. He knew that he had touched her memory most emotionally. He was concerned.

Theta had just encountered the man she had not planned to ever meet again. She winced to describe their mutual past and their devotion to each other.

The pleasantries belied the reality. They were lovers scattered by the cruelty of circumstance—another disaffection of time. Billy's accident changed both lives immeasurably.

Billy Grayson's name was initially on the birth certificate of the twins Mia and Leah before Simmons Barnwell assisted her to have their names legally changed. She did so to protect Billy. Billy had no idea that he had fathered twins and that they were playing in the Emporium area next to him. He did not remember that he loved Theta honestly and implicitly. The details of that long-ago romance lingered to Theta as if it was a third person in their chance meeting at the bookstore. She would cry for days thinking about meeting him again. But she would move past it.

CHAPTER FIVE

Prof. Thomas Leon

BY MIDWEEK, THE cloudless skies had begun to deliver the uninhibited winter shadows. Days were shorter. People feel the pull of night in December, it seems. The early morning darkness incites employee yawns that pass from book display stockers to the clerks at the registers. They awake to harbor an even deeper addiction to the java.

"A tip would be nice," Callista announced as she delivered the Boracle's morning café grande.

"You'll get your tip, Callous. I have an adding machine in my head. Despite yourself, the tip will come, and you will be pleased," Sid countered.

"Well, would you break it up into smaller parts and give it to me when served? If you die, your adding machine goes with you," Callista shot back with sarcasm.

She hated that Sid called her Callous but had to accept the return-moniker in fairness because she had named him "the Boracle."

Sid objected to her conclusion that he would expire owing her.

"I can never die. There is a synchronicity to my world that you do not have in yours. Because of that fact, I will still have a calculator well beyond the time that you come of age and accept a path toward proper manners."

The background music was instrumental and played an acoustic version of Paul Simon's "Kodachrome." The adjoining bookstore employees were putting up stock and changing the sale signs. Coffee customers were coming in to get their caffeine fix.

By his routine, Sid the Boracle was usually waiting when the next expected visitor arrived. It was his best friend, Thomas.

The kindhearted professor from the Engineering Department at the Citadel stopped by to see him. Dr. Thomas Leon only taught one course since his semi-retirement. Theoretical algorithms was so futuristic and mind-bending that it was remanded to general academia as an elective. Yet it became trendy. Engineers took the course, as well as other academic disciplines. It was highly recommended by the School of Business. Professor Leon was well ahead of his time. He was brilliant and had an exceptional penchant for relating to students. They liked him. His course also charted nearly a half-grade higher, on average, than other departmental course offerings. He explained this anomaly to the academic dean. The course bred better grades because the nature of it demanded more participation than other courses. In his mind, a willing student who would be challenged by the immensity of this course deserved extra credit.

Though Thomas's friend Sid did not take engineering courses in college, he had a keen mind for it, re-edified by his constant absorption of new information available by Wi-Fi at the Bib and Bibliothéque. Thomas had the first twenty minutes booked with the Boracle nearly every Monday. Even so, their meeting was usually more social than advisory. A turn of a phrase, an odd faculty function, or an absurd newspaper story usually provided the levity.

"Can you believe that this guy shows up at the Halloween costume party wearing an end table and a lampshade?" Sid pointed out. "Nobody could guess his motive for the outfit. He finally divulged that he came as a 'one night stand.' I got it!"

Thomas smiled. "The kids are right clever these days."

Sid continued from his perusal of the morning Internet news. "A lady near Sacramento called the police to report a robbery in action. A neighbor's teenager was chopping sections from her backyard marijuana crop."

Thomas responded, "It's California. I suppose that happens more than we know."

Though Sid was in high demand, given his penchant for not charging, the good professor always slipped a prepaid coffee card to Sid, indicating that it was a gift to him from a struggling student. He told Sid that he couldn't drink all the coffee that the years of gift cards would allow. He did not want to waste them or insult the student donors.

Sid knew that the ethical professor would never accept a gift from a student. Thomas bought the gift cards at twenty dollars each online simply to give them to Sid. He felt that Sid would not accept them otherwise.

He should have guessed that Sid would measure his friend's pupil dilation, skin tone, mannerisms, and breathing pace as he accepted the gift cards. Thomas glanced away when telling him he received a gift from a student instead of telling a white lie. Fooling the world's only synesticist is hard. Sid only accepted them because it made Thomas feel better about himself. Otherwise, Thomas knew the First Rule of Toile. A slight nod was acceptable, but Sid considered a 'thank you' with disdain. He was not to be thanked.

The professor was in good physical condition for his near-retirement years. He was a highly decorated Army Airborne Ranger. He distinguished himself in the Desert Storm conflict of 1991. His brown-and-gray hair was short for a professor but long for a military veteran. Like the Boracle, he was inquisitive. His brown eyes were friendly but focused. His tall frame had filled out more in recent years, but he still jogged at Hampton Park instead of enjoying lunch with his fellow academics. He was among the most respected professors at the small military college that heralded principled leadership.

"What's up at school, Thomas?" Sid asked as Thomas adjusted his posture across the booth.

"I'm still working on my syllabus for the spring semester, Sid." The professor began. "These kids are so bright these days that I have to present the mystery of science two steps beyond their thinking.

"Theoretical algorithms is a growing field. The provost is behind me. I only teach this one class, and the new material comes faster than I can catalog it. I wrote down everything you gave me last week. Kids are lining up to take the course, but I need to expand my mind into other tangents to keep the course of high interest. Opening minds to new concepts is what drives me to continue teaching, but I have to be more creative personally."

Sid knew that the visit wasn't just about added material.

Sid replied, "Thomas, you are teaching something that no professor at any college, Ivy League or otherwise, has ever attempted. So let's talk about it. My iPad can locate everything the world has developed, along with most of what could be later developed.

"Society grew from fire to the wheel to Gutenberg in a flash. Now we have the creativity of Steve Jobs, Bill Gates, and Stephen Hawking. The nuances and concepts are nearly a daily story. I read recently that in six months' time, the world will have more new inventions than have happened from the first Egyptian pyramid at Saqqara to the flight of the Wright Brothers. Not sure that could be true, but it attracts scientific readership."

Thomas raised his brow. "I've heard about that along with the steady diet of doomsday philosophers. Sometimes what we discover is that society, especially the western world, is in great danger. The signs seem to be indisputable, Sid. If you're like me, I'd rather know about something bad in advance than have to react to it in an emergency."

Sid nodded agreement. Yet Sid seemed to calmly compute the predictable variations of weather, culture, economics, and warring regimes anyway.

"What about DNA?" Sid introduced.

"We are mapping it at light speed. We may become able to locate genes of distress and then eradicate them forever. Will the cure for most cancers come from simply replacing a small piece of the nucleic sequence? Darwin shows us that we evolve. Can we explore a way to devolve? We must have millions of dormant genes from our evolution. Can we locate these and, for instance, redevelop a man with gills to swim underwater?

"Advanced societies have diminishing birth rates. Is that good or bad?" Sid continued, "And who governs the planets?"

"Forty years ago, a professor at Princeton charged his class with a project—space colonies. Read *The High Frontier* by Gerard K. O'Neill. These students effectively solved most of the permanent space existence issues. Who will build it? Who will own it? Will there be condominiums and hotels in orbit?"

"We're just scratching the surface, Thomas. From the premise that all knowledge connects, I began drawing conceptual results from the obscure. I suppose that one day, there will be another like me and the world will hold two synesticists," Sid stated. "But until then, I still dream blue dreams, absorb luga-bytes of connective information, and still harbor this ridiculous sentiment that I will never die."

The professor smiled. "What's a luga-byte, Sid?"

"It's a cache of seemingly useless trivia that is held to the end of time. It's more like a giant jigsaw puzzle that can only be pieced together by providence or forces of the unknown. The smaller locking pieces complete smaller purposes. In theory, all trivia in a luga-byte will eventually connect. So a luga-byte is both science's largest unresolved puzzle and a cache of all that is known. Oh, and, Thomas, a luga-byte is a word I made up because there is no word for it otherwise."

Thomas Leon sat in awe, realizing that Sid could lift young minds. He was the perfect visiting synesticist. And Thomas would love to explain that the world had only one.

"Once we resolve the puzzles, we can produce more PHCs. PHCs are why life matters to the living," Sid added.

"Huh? Do you mean PCBs? The contaminants from large electrical transformers that poison the ground?" Thomas asked.

"No. PHCs are more important to our civilization," Sid replied.

He further explained. "This acronym is key to everything we expect from our culture. A PHC is a positive human consequence. Yours is quite evident. You expand horizons for inquisitive students. You are at a heightened stage of fulfillment to your consequence. So many have no PHC defined. They are the lost souls. Can you imagine if we could guide every person to his or her full PHC? Can you imagine the innovation the world could attain?"

Professor Leon half-heartedly raised his hand as a student would do in his cutting-edge classroom. Sid stopped to see what he wanted with a wry smile at the gesture.

"I've never heard of that acronym, Sid. Is it your invention?" he asked.

Sid nodded, expecting that Thomas should have conceded that not everything he would hear on this day was in a textbook or gained from a Wi-Fi signal. Sid assembled his conclusions from extensive data and assigned a new vernacular where needed.

"I think I found a solution for my course in theoretical algorithms, Sid. Can you come as my first guest lecturer on January 16?" Thomas asked.

Sid knew that Thomas had come to that conclusion as soon as the professor sat and handed him the gift card.

"I think I said too much," Sid acknowledged with a smile before hesitating with a reply. "Just let me know what time to be there."

Thomas could learn more about life's perspectives by sitting for twenty minutes with Sid than a full sabbatical semester at the finest university. He would quantify the sentiment since he received his Ph.D. from Oxford University in Cambridge, England. His thesis was written on chemical modeling—something he found that Sid knew more about than anyone in Oxford.

Sid would never refuse a request from his best friend. Besides, Thomas knew the Second Rule of Toile. Duties are not favors.

CHAPTER SIX

The Nexus of the Sixties

(As It Happened, 1967)

IDA CRUTCHFIELD MARRIED Sid when the civilized world had succumbed to an unrelenting swirl that banded out into a category five hurricane. It was more than a generational clash of definitive eras. The winds were vehement. The seas were violent. It was a counterculture that would heave forward by its sheer mass. The previous historical convergences of this magnitude produced the Renaissance and the Industrial Revolution.

Ida selected her handkerchief pocketed Ivy Leaguer in the clearness of a moment when nothing else around her seemed clear at all. Music chronicled the nexus of time. The mellifluous counterculture of the 1960s ceded the chaos in chords. Every element of every strife related back to the sounds. Buffalo Springfield sang "For What It's Worth."

The Animals hit song was "War (Good God, What Is It Good For?)." James Brown reminded his packed audiences to "Say It Loud: I'm Black, and I'm Proud." "Fortunate Son" came from Credence Clearwater Revival as a protest. The surge of the women's movement had many titles including "Different Drum," a song from Linda Ronstadt. "All I'm saying is I'm not ready for any person, place or thing to try and pull the reins in on me."

The sexual revolution was in its infancy. Within a handful of years, books introduced the idea of recreational sex well past the Victorian mores of a hundred years earlier. *The Joy of Sex* by Alex Comfort and *Sex and the Single Girl* by Helen Gurley Brown opened minds and changed attitudes. The birth control pill was a suitable companion to the love generation.

The multifaceted culture was daunting yet vibrant. Newspaper reporters wrote about the busy intersection that managed the American civil rights protests, the unpopular Vietnam War, free love, flower children, music festivals, rampant drug use, along with hair and clothing styles that went amok. But these aberrations did not faze Sid. He was pursuing the love of his life.

Ida Crutchfield was a Tennessee farm girl—one of seven children. She was a twin. Ida was loving, wholesome, and bright. She was patient and proud of her more traditional femininity. She enjoyed conversation, having friends, and a few of the old domestic standards like cooking and cross-stitch. She even made some of her own dresses. Her high school classes included courses in home economics, stenography, and typing. She loved state fairs and pig pickings. She attended her local Baptist church every Sunday and every Wednesday evening. She wore her best outfits for the occasion. Otherwise, she wore overalls and dungarees like her siblings. Blue jeans became the natural fashion genesis of a farmer's dungarees.

Her twin brother, Arlo Crutchfield, was her antithesis. He was cruel, temperamental, and vengeful. His cocooned farm family only promoted his deleterious behavior. He was compulsive in his pursuits. He had killed farm animals for sport, even poisoning a calf. He had mixed fertilizers to create small crude explosions, once destroying a silo.

He was expelled from his third academic institution midway through his ninth-grade year. His father saw no reason to challenge him with further education. He was comfortable in agricultural employment as long as he had time to secretly destroy things—or animals—outside of his chores. Arlo had a strange affinity for his twin sister. Ida instinctively and foolishly protected Arlo during their youth. It was an instinct that twins seemingly inherited. During the 1950s and 1960s, there was little counseling available in rural areas for the symptomatic tendencies Arlo exhibited. Arlo's misogynistic aggressive and destructive behavior was never corrected. People feared Arlo Crutchfield with good reason. With sweetness and optimism in her heart, Ida stood by her twin.

Their father, Maynard, operated the second-largest farm equipment dealership in the United States. He inherited it from his father. The John Deere tractor dealership was located in Sparta, Tennessee, and was established by Grandfather Jake Crutchfield in 1922.

Arlo accepted his lower responsibility role as a farmhand who was to stay away from the dealership. Older siblings would work in both businesses. All shared the financial benefits of the dealership profits. Arlo was to remain out of the public eye. The older Crutchfields referred to him as "the family hemorrhoid." Arlo did not like Sid from the first time they met on Christmas Day 1967. He had a strange sense of overprotection for Ida. It was an obsession.

Ida met Sid in Knoxville when she attended the University of Tennessee. Sid had begun a career at the Y-12 plant of Union Carbide. Twenty miles west of Knoxville, Oak Ridge was the genesis town of the Manhattan Project. What the federal government owned across sixty thousand acres was either retained or leased to leading U.S. companies of science and technology. Union Carbide became a substantial partner in the atomic age.

Sid and Ida's chance meeting was from an automobile accident on Kingston Pike after a Tennessee Volunteers football game. Sid attended with a ticket given to him by his supervisor at Union Carbide. Ida was a student who was leaving after the game to attend a sorority party at the Deane Hill Country Club. The accident backed up traffic for several miles. Ida hit Sid's 1963 International Scout in the rear with her

'65 Datsun. No one was hurt, and minimal damage was exacted upon the sturdy International. But Ida's Datsun could not be restarted. The radiator was destroyed, and the fluids drenched the pavement beneath the sporty four-cylinder.

Sid hurried from his rugged four-wheel vehicle to check on the driver who had hit him. Traffic was immediately snarled.

"Miss, are you OK?" Sid began with a genuine concern for the hard impact.

"Just shaken. I hit you hard. I'm so sorry. I was just adjusting my rearview mirror to check my lipstick and didn't anticipate the light changing," Ida explained. "I'm such an idiot. Should we flag down the police?"

"We could be here for an hour before they can get through this gridlock. I'll pull up so that the traffic can get by," Sid told her. "I'll come back to get your car off the road."

Ida emerged from the Datsun, holding her pocketbook. She was a cute coed with a bouffant style fashioned of her dark brown hair with russet tints haloed by the street lamp. Barely over five feet tall, she wore an orange Tennessee sweater. Her knee-length skirt was nearly the color of her hair.

"Miss, you should stay on the sidewalk. Many of these fans have been drinking, and this accident will only make them angry," Sid insisted.

Tennessee had just tied Georgia 13–13 in Neyland Stadium, a result that no fan enjoyed. The early season game was to be a barometer measuring each team's viability for the coming season. Both teams were seeking the NCAA national football championship.

After moving his car into a bank parking lot fifty feet up the highway, Sid returned to attend to Ida's car. He pulled a white handkerchief from his rear pocket to wipe his brow. He then entered Ida's car and placed the stick shift gear into neutral. He got out with the door open and began to guide the small car to the service station up at the next intersection. Three young Tennessee students that were behind the accident saw the effort and decided to assist in pushing Ida's car. Two got out to push. The third student followed them with hazard lights engaged. Ida walked on the sidewalk in apprehension, visibly upset by the situation for which she felt entirely responsible. Once the car was secure near the service station bathrooms, Sid thanked the students and decided to see if Ida needed further help.

Sid recommended that she call someone to have the car towed.

He immediately went back to retrieve his Scout. Ida wasn't sure he would return. In a moment, Sid pulled in with the Scout and jumped out to make sure she had arranged a way home. His keen sense of helping others was evident. Besides, he did not want the upset young lady to be stranded in the night. She had not attempted to call anyone, being confused by the frenzy of her first automobile accident.

There was no phone booth near. Sid pointed to the service station building as a likely place to have a working telephone.

"Miss, you can likely use their phone inside to call a tow truck. Do you have a friend to bring you home?" Sid inquired, ever the gentleman.

"My brother, Arlo, will come to get me, but he lives two hours away near Sparta," Ida replied without realizing that she assumed the role of the distressed maiden. "I have some girlfriends here too. I'll call one of them."

Kingston Pike was no place for a tow truck, a police car, or an ambulance after a Tennessee football game. It was an ocean of orange-clad students and fans heading for a sea of partying. Home football games happened six times a year. They were the primary reason that Knoxville swelled by nearly fourteen thousand hotel room occupants in the fall. Volunteer football weekends controlled the farmer's harvest, the wedding calendars, and the stress for services in traffic, restaurants, and even hospitals.

Sid waited in his Scout while Ida made arrangements to be driven home.

Ida returned. She looked perplexed.

"I can't reach Arlo. My roommate is at the party. I tried to reach my dad, but nobody seems to be home on a Saturday night," Ida stated. "I spoke to the owner here, and he said I could leave it until tomorrow, but I have to get it moved before 9:00 a.m. I'm just a few miles from where my roommate is. Would it trouble you too much after what I've caused to drop me there?"

"Only if I can call you another name than miss," Sid replied. "I'm Sid Toile."

"Ida. Ida Crutchfield." She offered her hand, palm facing down.

Sid took her hand deliberately and held it as he replied. His formality was a habit encouraged by his parents.

"Ida, I'd suggest that you take anything valuable from your car. And I would further suggest that you release yourself from worry. Neither my vehicle nor I am damaged."

"I'll grab my books and my spare change from the ashtray," she responded.

Meanwhile, Sid went around to open the passenger door to the Scout. Ida moved briskly to the seat and swiveled to place her legs inside. Sid closed the door carefully so that the loudness of the tin-clad interior would not offend Ida.

Sid was smitten. It was by Ida's sweetness in her demeanor and her confidence in her choices. She was petite, but her smile was gargantuan. It warmed the mood.

Sid figured that he had just three miles to the Deane Hill Country Club in slow traffic to develop a relationship. He told Ida of his palindromic name, his Harvard parents, and his love of trivia. The exchange being pleasant, Ida spontaneously invited Sid to join her at the event. It was a leap of faith, she thought. But she sensed that Sid was a good man. She had no idea that he was much, much more.

"This is just a celebration party, not a date-like invitation. The ladies in my dorm are hosting it. It was the Beat Bulldogs Bash. But I suppose a tie will have to do," Ida started.

"If you're asking me to come in, I accept. If you're explaining why I shouldn't come in, then I also accept that as well," Sid replied. "But I would like to secure a mailing address or your dorm number at least to take you to dinner formally."

"That's not necessary," Ida shyly replied. "I wanted to see if you would like to come in—that is if you have no other immediate plans?"

"I had planned to cruise Kingston Pike looking for other damsels in distress, but I can pass on that for the privilege of attending the beat bash," Sid stated. "I hope I am dressed appropriately."

"You're overdressed, believe me," Ida said. She immediately liked the formal sense of the man who delivered her to the country club dance.

They enjoyed the party—a dance with a disc jockey spinning records. Sid studied her small button nose and her lips shaped like Cupid's bow as she spoke. He was mesmerized by her southern-paced voice of pragmatism. Her eyes were a Pacific blue, unusual for girls with dark brown hair. She had a habit of looking right into Sid's eyes when she talked as if their eyes were friends from another life.

A vehicle accident had caused them to become friends. In just a year and a half, Ida dropped out of the University of Tennessee to marry the brilliant gentleman Eliot S. Toile. Their wedding in Sparta was the event of the spring season.

Sid's marriage to Ida brought them great joy and adventure. Sid, as a young engineer, earned an income that could accommodate their passion for travel. Ida could visit her family in Sparta frequently, as they were less than two hours away. They spent their nurturing years in the clutch of each other's dreams— except a haunting sadness. Ida had four miscarriages. Tests were done in clinics. They could not have natural children. They had resigned themselves to the reality. They had each other. Their love was profound.

Sid's career had blossomed because of his sincere demeanor and his ability to retain scientific and marketing information. He had become the general manager of the Y-12 plant. He placed valued items into the lockbox of their Oliver Springs home. He saved twenty-four $200 U.S. savings bonds each year. He had Union Carbide stock and also hoarded silver by saving pre-1964 "Mercury" dimes.

Ida came from a wealthy family but declined any assistance from her father in her marriage to Sid. Sid was self-sufficient, responsible, and a wise investor. They had no financial needs. Ida knew that Sid was self-made and would object to any assistance at all from anyone, including her father, Maynard.

Their love was evident daily. He brought her coffee to wake her; she fixed cream of wheat or oatmeal on the cold Tennessee mornings. They enjoyed driving vacations to Florida's gulf coast. She was an artful gardener, liked to cook, and painted acrylic scenery. He enjoyed crossword puzzles, Scrabble, and reading biographies. They both enjoyed peaceful weekend drives to the foothills of the Appalachians. They would often drive through idyllic Townsend to picnic at Cades Cove. They exchanged unusual gifts for birthdays and on each Christmas morning. At their twentieth Christmas together, Ida presented Sid with a gold pocket watch and chain. It had to be wound each morning manually. The inside of the cover opening contained a small round formal photo of Ida.

"I want you to see me as you see time," she said as Sid opened the gold watch in complete surprise.

Their lives together were charmed and idyllic. Happiness could not evade their grasp. They even bought a funeral plot together just off Kingston Pike near where they first met.

But the life of the charmed has the highest probability of sadness and remorse. In their twenty-fourth year, everything changed. Ida had become ill. Her foreboding diagnosis was told to Ida and Sid simultaneously at Fort Sanders Hospital. Ida had pancreatic cancer.

It was deemed untreatable. They had little time left together.

Shocked by the report, Sid swore to Ida that he would strive day and night to find a cure. He read every article in every available medical library about the disease. The conclusions were all the same. Pancreatic cancer killed 99 percent of its victims within a year of its detection. The extreme measures Sid took to save her life included an arduous trip to Mexico to try experimental research drugs never approved by the U.S. Food and Drug Administration.

The close-knit Crutchfield family of middle Tennessee scorned all of Sid's efforts. But Sid would never give up on saving her life.

"Let her die with dignity," Maynard Crutchfield advised Sid, distraught by the circumstance. "She is too fragile to transport."

Maynard had seen many of his relatives pass over the years. At the age of seventy-one, he never thought he'd be burying his daughter.

Sid doggedly refused to give in to the inevitable. Ida believed in him and trusted that he would find the best possible solution to save her life. His diligence took Ida away from the Crutchfield family. The emergency strategy subjected her to other experimental trials her family would disdain. He wanted to discover anything other than an expedient avenue to death. To Sid, life was a puzzle to be solved. Conversely, death was a resignation that should not be an option considered.

The Crutchfield family became incensed, especially Arlo. In their view, Sid hoarded Ida's dying time from them. Sid was trying to connect the most unlikely of miracles. Increasingly, he became distraught by the result.

Ida breathed her last on an early May morning.

The funeral service at Cedar Springs Baptist Church was attended by some of Sid's associates from Union Carbide, their close neighbors, and some of Ida's friends from her high school in Sparta. The Crutchfield family arrived together and sat as a group in the very back of the church. Sid felt their vitriol.

Sid, timid as a speaker, eulogized the love of his life bravely.

"Today is Saturday. We met on a Saturday, married on a Saturday, and found out about her cancer on a Saturday. Ida and I found each other in a world blinded by pursuits of little consequence. We paid little attention to that world, instead focusing on our world together.

"We were different, but different for us was our normal. On occasions such as this, I suppose I could tell you about the things Ida liked. It was the gurgle of mountain brooks and the songs of wrens, the sweet aroma of lilac and lavender in her garden. She inhaled the cold freshness of the first snowfall. She marveled at the beauty of driving through Townsend as the sunshine sprayed through the forest. She was taken by the simple joy of tasting wild honeysuckle."

Sid's eulogy was truncated by his visible emotions. He struggled to finish.

"I would have probably never married had I not met Ida. She was my soul, my breath, my purpose, and my joy. I wished that I could take her pain away. But most of all, I wished that I could hold her hand like I did the first time we met."

He hesitated momentarily to wipe a tear away. "People die. People live on. I cannot fathom that I will not see my beautiful Ida again. Neither can I fathom that I would have had the honor of her love for a quarter of a century. Her life has compelled my life. I have to find a direction that is beyond the grasp of her delicate hand. I will never see another sunrise without beholding her morning warmth or hear the rainfall without drenching my entire being in the love of her."

Sid lost the ability to say anything else in his intense emotional state. He stood for a moment looking out with tears flowing. The minister joined him once the pause became elongated. He then went to sit. He pulled out his gold watch and stared at it. Sid had not wound his watch since the morning that Ida passed away.

Sid's despair was deeply imposed, causing him the loss of his career as well. After fourteen months of grieving, he answered an advertisement in the *Wall Street Journal* to intern at a brokerage house in Hartford, Connecticut. It was not the change of scenery that he sought but the change of purpose.

Sid would never marry again. He retreated from social life. Instead, he dedicated his life to enhancing tools of success so that he could fulfill his boyhood convictions of assisting others. He rationalized that Ida would want him to pursue the dreams he shared with her. His strength of character and tenacious sense of purpose would compel the remaining years he forecasted were left from his calculations. He never feared his own passing, yet his boyhood whisper of evading death remained.

"Immortality has had a 100 percent rate of mortal endings," Sid would say. "And life is the pursuit of consequence for the benefit of innumerable inconsequential others."

He did not become a cynic, though he had much reason. Instead, he became a principled idealist. Sid would read about every facet in pursuing the optimum result in every lost cause.

Sid's love of Ida convinced him that death was an enviable transition that could reunite them. He did not fear his own demise and felt there was much more to be accomplished along the way.

Sid began studying history, culture, and religion. He wanted to learn more about the idea of reincarnation. The sense that it could be possible was thematic among world religions and historic civilizations. The ancient Greeks, the Egyptians, and the Chinese had scripts that described it in detail. The Buddhists and the Hindus harbor its inevitability. There are those born with odd birthmarks that relate the epidermal oddity to a previous life. Sid's right temple displayed a prominent birthmark. Sid wanted to know more.

With humility, he mourned, and he wept over the coming years. No new day was breached without the ever-present sense of loneliness and despair. He missed his princess.

The only constant beyond Sid's seclusion over the grieving period was the untimely and inappropriate contact from Arlo. He persisted in his verbal attacks directed at Sid. Sid knew of his demented pursuits as a teenager through Ida's childhood stories.

Three stories chronicled incidents of Arlo beating another school classmate with the use of brass knuckles. There was a stabbing that most attributed to Arlo. But his father seemed to protect him each time. The only incident that placed Arlo in the county jail was gruesome. He had managed to hang a neighbor's Shetland pony on a playground swing set. The evidence was overwhelming, and Arlo spent nine months in a reformatory facility near Pikeville. It failed to reform him.

Arlo hounded Sid by phone and sent several short notes of contorted spelling and vocabulary. They warned Sid that Arlo was a disturbed and angry man.

One came just two weeks after Ida's funeral.

"I will make yer life as bad as a trapped doe. You won't know what hit you. I will hide yer ugly carcass where the buzzards can have lunch."

Another was handwritten on a blood-stained page. "Yer life ain't worth two cents. Yer life will get cashed in when you don't expect."

Sid never responded. To the degree that Sid was saddened Arlo encountered an ever-building rage. Sid presumed that Arlo was suffering from mental depression or a bipolar disorder. He thought Arlo's senseless wrath would subside over time.

Arlo was not likely to vanish into the past. He swore vengeance upon Sid Toile. He could never accept that the disease doomed Ida. Arlo blamed Sid for the choice of treatment that took his twin sister away. His disagreement with Sid's course of trying to save Ida heated to a raging fire after the funeral. Arlo became a vehement antagonist. His disdain for Sid grew obsessive.

"You can't hide from me. I'll hunt you down like a stray fox. Yer dead, Toile."

Arlo grew up close to his twin, Ida. Her moving away to marry Sid was never accepted. He thought Sid to be too "cityfied" and not willing to get his hands dirty in the Tennessee soil that fed and clothed the old south. Arlo believed in hard work and a hard life. His view of the white-collar elite who escaped manual labor and earned incomes by investments while sitting at a desk came with a most salacious contempt. He hated the intellectuals and detested those with creative aspirations.

Sid married Ida out of love and in defiance of her twin brother. He noted that Arlo was entirely different but assumed that he would always remain in the rear view of Ida's path. Ida pursued a life outside of Sparta and the inherent joy of advancing her life's experience in the magnificent world before her. Sid provided companionship, security, and the full commitment of love.

Arlo was devious and straightforward. He would never contemplate leaving the family farm. He received a more-than-comfortable income from his father's lucrative tractor and equipment business. His associations were with farmers who knew dawn by the roosters and the evenings by the mask of dusk. Clocks were superfluous. They planted by almanacs and harvested in earnest to maximize the tonnage to the marketplace. The industry is a most honorable and selfless commitment and yet a chosen curse upon individuality.

Arlo was as thin as Asian noodles and tanned like an overworked cabana boy. He had oily black hair and steely dark eyes. He seemed to consume more Winston cigarettes than eggs and bacon. He wore overalls often, proud of what they represented. He had pursuits outside of farming, but they were also quests presented by the land. He liked freshwater bass fishing, trapping, and hunting Tennessee white-tailed deer. He learned how to hunt with a crossbow as a teenager. He liked to live by seeing other creatures die. Like a red fox, he was an expert in the wild. His favorite nine-inch fishing knife was a gift from Ida for their joint birthday at age eighteen. It was an indiscreet gift that only a farming family could fully appreciate. It was given to the worst possible recipient.

Arlo, Sid considered, was years overdue for institutional incarceration.

Arlo never married. Set in his ways, he had all the family support he needed at home. He said he was protective of his family's hard-earned wealth and presumed that most women wanted to date him "to win the lottery." His attitude toward women, bankers, insurance salesmen, other races, other religions, and especially preachers was of snickering disdain. Yet he promoted his views as if everyone shared them and that he could not be challenged because he was always right. Sid had long dismissed him as incorrigible and incapable of redemption.

Sid was most careful in his conversations with Ida about family. His parents were societal pillars of both the WASP class of Boston gentry and Harvard-bred academics. They were not initially accepting of Ida and her Tennessee Volunteer sorority. They assumed that she was crudely unsophisticated. For this reason, Sid rarely returned to Boston. He surmised that, as absentee parents, they did not know much more about him than they did about Ida. He was an inconvenient child.

During their marriage, Arlo was rarely an intrusion because of the two-hour commute to Sparta. Sid lamented that Arlo would find his life's purpose by encroachments for many years and miles beyond Sparta after Ida's passing. Sid was too distraught to deal with Arlo's ill-tempered protestations. He needed to leave their Oak Ridge home and build a new tomorrow.

The move to Connecticut was unannounced to anyone in the Crutchfield family. One could easily get lost in Hartford.

CHAPTER SEVEN

Billy Grayson

BILLY WAS CONFUSED. He had just walked away from a strange person who knew him well. He was equally intrigued. He had seen pictures of dozens of people with whom he had been photographed before the accident. He had scanned them many times to try and connect to a past that had evaporated. His mother found Theta Barnwell in two separate albums. Both were from high school. There were only two photographs of Billy and Theta together more than ten years earlier. Billy wondered what she knew about his past before the accident that drew tears to her eyes spontaneously. There were plenty of photos with a handful of unrecognizable girls whom he had dated from his college years, but none of the college-era photographs showed Theta. He sequestered her lovely face to the era of his late high school years.

He assumed that Theta was happily married but still hoped that he would see her again out of curiosity. Maybe she could explain her sadness to him.

The Boracle was adjusting his reading glasses in booth 14. He was studying his personal financial graphs on his iPad just after a visitor left. He had two visitors in succession and was getting ready to check on a blue-chip stock, anticipating a sell-off. He was fully immersed into the exciting financial market that he understood better than a convention of Wall Street tycoons. But there was a gentle interruption.

"Sid, I know you're getting ready to leave, but I will just take a moment," Billy started. "You got time?"

"Step right into my office," Sid offered with the wave of his right hand. "I believe I might be of assistance."

Billy sat immediately on the edge of the booth seat with his back turned to the wall. His body language and posture of escape indicated that he was looking for a short answer.

The Boracle was already seated. Sid's iPad screen went dormant. He looked into Billy's eyes after a pause of adjusting his posture. He read the moment correctly.

"You are considering a life change, Billy," the Boracle saved him the preface remarks. "Your son is your priority. You have to rebuild a career that cannot be done here. But the road is no place for a young preschooler. Does that about size it up?"

Billy nodded sheepishly. He realized that he would not need a long explanation.

"You're amazin', Sid," Billy replied with a knowing grin. "You have the essentials. If I take him, it will be a sacrifice for him to be on the road. He'll have to be with me everywhere. If I don't take him and leave him with my mother, I'll miss him terribly. He'll miss me too. I don't know when I'll get back. My recording contract is through a studio in Detroit. But Sony has other sessions scheduled with other musicians that will take me to LA. The contract calls for dubbing sessions in Nashville as well."

"I get it," Sid interrupted. "You have an open-ended career commitment and the trappings of parenthood on a collision course. Hide the magnet."

"The magnet? I don't follow," Billy answered with a questioning tone. "What magnet?"

"It's a saying my wife liked, Billy," Sid replied.

"It's part of a magician's trick. You can move anything around that's metal and have an audience believe you have special powers if you can effectively hide the magnet."

"I see. But how does that saying solve my dilemma?" Billy asked.

"The magnet is your emotional well-being," Sid countered, knowing Billy would ask.

"Unfortunately, this is what really controls everything, and it is hidden below our rationalizations and so-called common sense. You will not succeed in any endeavor without that special magnet. Your Detroit trip will be a disaster when you force opposing magnetic fields together. They repel for a reason. The magnet will work best here when you are centered, and your force field is aligned."

"Your wife must've been a genius," Billy offered.

"She was brilliant. She never finished college. She took a Mensa IQ test just after we married at my insistence—186! That puts her above the category of most Pulitzer Prize recipients and MIT professors," Sid answered factually. "And that was not her best quality."

"Well, Sid," Billy shot back, avoiding another trip down the nostalgic trail Sid often cited, "I guess you think I should find a third solution for Ashton. That means I should stay and work the solution from a different vantage point."

"You have to internalize the best solution so that it becomes yours, not mine. I simply readdress the facts devoid of outside agents like finance, emotion, and history," Sid pointed out as if revisiting a mission statement of his life.

"However, working from the correct emotion-charged solution always makes you more creative and better settled within your own psyche. You'll be emboldened in your decision by recruiting a new partner in your decisions—the 'Big E' . . . enthusiasm!"

Sid continued, "Billy, I do not subscribe to the vagaries of clairvoyance. But I can read many signs and deduce elements that others might not notice. There is a more significant force at work here. Your career is not the music, my son. Music is a career you are living now. But you'll not be wholly immersed into music later, given time's impact. Other responsibilities will find you.

"The universe moves in patterns that do not deviate without reason. You are part of that universe and will cycle into the proper orbit so that all the meteors of your life burn harmlessly into the atmosphere. Life requires synchronicity. Believe that. Never forget that" Sid summarized.

Billy had a new resolve. He would pursue a balance that kept the meteors from crashing. He rose to leave by extending his hand to Sid. They shook, and Billy nodded reverently.

He knew not to thank the man who brought stability back into his life. Sid sensed that he would find more ways to assist Billy in the coming months.

"Hide the magnet, son. It works."

The Boracle had spoken.

CHAPTER EIGHT

Jackie and Frieda

(As It Happened, Eight Years Earlier)

TROPICAL DEPRESSION JULIA remained stagnant in the Gulf of Mexico, only 120 nautical miles due south of Pensacola. The wide rain bands were predicted to drench the southeast for the next seventy-two hours should it follow a predicted path of north-northwest.

Theta consented to a conditional invitation to accompany Billy to his roommate's family's cabin for a relaxing weekend. He would pick her up in Decatur. She would accompany her friend Billy—but only within the condition of strict "Victorian rules." The tropical depression would dictate the events of the weekend.

Though they dated for nearly three months before their high school graduation, they both felt that the excitement of going away. Yet they both arrived as freshmen fraught with the regret of parting.

Theta accepted a partial grant-in-aid to the University of North Carolina before the longing to see Billy changed her locale and her academic major. Scott College's reputation as a top women's institution extended well past the Atlanta area. She thought she wanted to pursue a fulfilling relationship with Billy.

Billy felt otherwise. Their cordial relationship had been pleasant but did not become romantic. He deeply respected her. But Billy wanted more and felt that Theta was not likely to become more than an endearing friend. It was in this understanding that Billy asked Theta to the weekend excursion. Theta would not know that she was the prospective third date he had invited.

The rain was steady. Billy ran up to her dormitory entryway to retrieve her two small bags. Theta was holding her small pocketbook and a folded orange Myrtle Beach towel. The constant precipitation made their weekend adventure awkward. She was waiting in the lobby, wearing dark blue shorts and a tan-and-blue print top. She smiled when she saw him run to the cover over the entryway.

"Right on time, Billy," Theta noted.

She hugged him. "Now what are you going to do to keep us dry?"

"Obviously, I'm the dummy who has no umbrella. I'll put these two bags in the back and open the passenger door. Just wait thirty seconds. You'll have to run for it!" Billy replied.

He dashed to the car with her small tote bags.

Theta smiled. She was glad that she wasn't wearing dressy shoes or had spent time on her hair. Billy went first, and Theta followed in a dash thirty seconds later. She hopped into the old SUV and wiped the rain from her eyes. Billy handed her a golf towel from the backseat, but she lifted the Myrtle Beach towel from her lap to show him that she was more prepared than him.

Her hair was pulled back into a scrunch. Her print shirt was more wet than dry. She draped the towel across her chest to absorb the moisture from her blouse.

"OK, we're dry. Now what?" Theta asked.

"On to Guntersville. You're the navigator. Here's the map Jackie drew," Billy assigned. "Surely, there is sunshine in Guntersville!"

The Victorian rules were what he most remembered from their high school relationship. Theta was awkwardly pretty, bright and interesting, conversational, fun—but not intimate. She reminded Billy on the phone of her idealistic virginity. She was now twenty, more appealing than ever, and still off limits.

Strong-willed, she made this stipulation clear to Billy back during their dating period, never retreating from the self-imposed rule.

Billy's hormones had to break out of the corral, like a stampede of Wyoming's wild stallions. Like those horses, Billy had grazed in other pastures over the past fifteen months.

They accepted fate as the catalyst to end their high school relationship. Though they stayed in touch and met a few times for lunch, the romance simply fluttered to a halt. Theta's angel's wings cooled Billy's devilish pursuits. Billy wanted to venture out and date others before beginning college without the restrictions imposed on their past. Theta instinctively surmised that it was because Billy knew the stop signals she placed upon their mutual physical attraction. He wanted more than she would provide, and she demanded control.

Not much had changed in the interim. Theta and Billy were more friends of convenience than a dating pair. She studied hospitality management and played cello in the Scott College student orchestra. She became an exercise and fitness advocate—scheduling her runs and swims within her busy schedule.

Meanwhile, Billy became more athletically toned as a result of the Yellow Jacket training room facilities. His soccer career was enhanced by his midfielder speed. His skills developed nicely to compete in the tough Atlantic Coast Conference.

Neither Billy nor Theta envisioned the next chapter of their relationship. It hinged on chance.

Billy's Georgia Tech roommate, Jackie Mann, had invited him and a date to his father's lake cabin near Guntersville, Alabama. Rodney Mann was a soybean farmer in North Alabama. His son, Jackie, gave Billy a handwritten map of how to get to the cabin from the nearest highway. Billy called two potential weekend dates, Amanda Weathersby and Gracie Catton. Both had other plans. Amanda was Billy's latest interest, but she had committed to a wedding shower in Brunswick given for her older sister.

Billy had a tepid affair with Gracie Catton for several weeks after Christmas. But Gracie's family was on the way to Vienna with her in tow. Their affair had cooled when Billy realized that her pampered life was never going to backpedal and settle for a pauper. She was at Tech studying to be an architect as well. Her eyes were affixed to anyone who came from a wealthy family. Billy was just an experience for her. He had no financial pedigree. Once Billy realized this, he saved Gracie the pain of departure. Besides, she had already targeted a doctor's son.

He respected Theta and consented to the rules, knowing that the weekend would be endearing. Theta was just the kind of girl Billy wished to fall in love with—but even he knew that he was too young for a marriage commitment.

Billy rationalized that he could revisit the lovely Theta later in his life if the timing of all humanity consented. Even as striking as she had developed over her freshman year, she was a faraway dream. He invited her because she was much more—a confidant, a comfort, and an amazing companion. Besides, they had a most important quality in common. They were conversationally compatible. They spoke to each other on the level of adults well beyond the age of twenty—with deep-seated mutual respect.

It was not unusual for Theta to ask a profoundly interesting question in a most eloquent sentence structure and be answered by Billy as if he were reading from Lord Byron or W. B. Yeats. They had a love of language to nurture in their loquacious and reflective conversations.

Billy noted that Theta's physical maturity also included her graduation from the unwieldy resemblance to a baby giraffe. She was fully grown. Theta was ethereal. Her voice, her mannerisms, her facial expressions, and her long flowing reddish hair—they all seemed to have reached the conclusion of her clumsy youth. That youthful awkwardness served his timing well, Billy thought, because no other suitor had noticed the stunning transition. She had evolved into a splendid goddess, even more beautiful in her soul than in her physical aura.

Billy had matured as well. From the time he saw her hop into the Toyota next to him, he realized she could easily become the focus of his fate. She was delightful. Given the sacrifice of the delineated boundaries, it was exciting to have Theta there again next to him.

"We need to swing west on I-20 and then pick up State Road 21," Theta advised. She turned Billy's front defroster on to clear his view.

"It's raining a river. Help me look for I-20 west, Theta. I don't want to end up in Florida," Billy asked.

Theta watched the passing highway signs.

Theta had also blossomed in her confidence of adulthood. She was naturally bright and earnestly caring. She was completely different than anyone else Billy had dated at Georgia Tech. She was statuesque and conservatively dressed. Yet she was demure, spontaneously playful, and looked lovingly into the slate-green eyes of the Billy she held in girlish esteem for the last fifteen months.

Theta was elated that Billy had called and had no idea that she was a "fallback" choice. Billy had run out of options and did not want to report the failure to his roommate, Jackie. He decided that he would spend the weekend as a gentleman in conversation with a girl that he had frequently confided—before, during, and after their dating sequence in high school. Besides, she was a good-time guarantee. She was pretty, pleasant, and lively. He acquiesced that there would be no invasion of physical space between the two. Billy prepared himself for his perception of a fishing cabin's old musty sofa.

The relentless rainfall continued to blanket northern Alabama and eastern Tennessee. It made the trip to the cabin longer and slightly dangerous. The windshield wipers wisped away the droplets at a steady pulse. They had driven for three hours, only stopping once for gas and a restroom break.

"You sure we're on the right road?" Billy asked when a turn placed him behind a large Massey Ferguson tractor being moved across a soybean farm.

Theta took Jackie's map and turned it upside down, mocking Billy.

"Is it possible that the Gulf of Mexico is north of Birmingham?" she asked, feigning confusion. "Your friend's map has some scribbling I can't read. I think it says, 'No matter what, trust your navigator.'"

Billy smiled. "You mean this is a highway?"

"That's what it says on here. Besides, I saw a sign that said Highway 21 a half mile back. Never doubt your navigator again," Theta said. "And never pass a large farm tractor in the rain. He'll tell you when it's clear."

As if on cue, the tractor driver waved Billy around him. He was on the right road with the right navigator keeping him humored.

Jackie's father's cabin was across the creek from a game preserve. No other buildings were within two miles of the old rustic 1970s structure. The "Mann Hole" cabin had the only electrical service of the co-op from the pavement to the rut-laden dirt road all the way back down to the creek. The seclusion and the waterfalls made a weekend at the cabin peaceful, quiet, and carefree.

There were four map-marked turns on red clay roads along the way. Theta warned of the upcoming road turns to Billy well in advance. The route was arduous with washed-out potholes and the constant driving rain. Billy's Toyota 4Runner moved slowly, as he did not want to get stuck and require towing. He tried to dodge every soaked pit. The conversation strayed because of the driving hazards. It was further interrupted by Theta's map directions. The wipers were barely effective. At each pounce of the front shock absorbers, Billy apologized.

"Oops, didn't see that one. Tighten the seatbelt, Theta," Billy reminded her.

"If I get it any tighter, I'll be separating the bottom of me from the top," she replied. "Seatbelts. Why was there ever a time without them?"

They finally arrived in the still-steady drizzle. They were relieved that they had found the fishing cabin. Jackie's Jeep Wagoneer had been there since the day before. He and girlfriend Frieda were tidying up the guest room when Billy and Theta skirted the puddles to the front porch.

Jackie opened the door.

"Just in time!" he exclaimed. "The sun is rising in Fiji and should be here by Sunday." Frieda grabbed Jackie's right arm as a signal to be introduced to Theta.

Jackie caught the signal. "This is Frieda. And you must be the Theta that Billy has talked about for a solid year. I'm Jackie."

"Pleased to meet you." She coyly curtseyed to Jackie and shook Frieda's hand. Her genuine smile immediately made her welcome.

"Frieda, I can help you with the spaghetti Billy mentioned," Theta interjected. "I picked up some French bread at the BI-LO when we came through Guntersville. I like to cook, so I am at your disposal."

Frieda answered by looking at Billy. "Keep this one, Billy. None of the others ever offered to help."

Billy displayed a contrived indignity.

"Frieda! You act like I've brought a harem before you for approval. Don't give Theta the wrong idea. She could end up liking me! It's possible."

In reality, Billy had dated less than a handful of coeds from Georgia Tech during his freshman year, including Amanda and Gracie. Theta knew of a couple of them because Billy told her some snippets at their occasional lunch meetings. Theta assumed that he was only serious with one—a petite brunette named Georgiana. She was studying to become an architect, like Gracie. Billy had shown Theta a photo of Georgiana and him together at Lake Lanier. Georgiana was sexy and smart and came from a fine family near Valdosta. But she was what Billy called an OCD freak. Her obsessiveness was not deigned as a medical condition by any psychologist but was nonetheless certified by Billy. Georgiana and Billy decided to discontinue the relationship because Billy could not adhere to the precise scheduling she had demanded of him.

The secluded cabin was a short walk from Creek House Falls where the Tennessee River rushed to a series of nature's gravitational marvels, including a hydroelectric dam near Guntersville. Its small tributaries included branched brooks and a swirl of short waterfalls that pleased the farmers and fishermen alike. The stream from the river's lower falls could be easily heard from the rustic clapboard cabin. It was only a short distance down a walk path to the creek bank. Water slid down a series of large granite rocks—vestiges from a Pleistocene Era glacier 1.8 million years ago. The rocks extended up eighteen feet where the water continued to detour over smooth bevels. The highest fall ledged out at ten feet was nearest to the cabin.

Jackie and his girlfriend, Frieda Brouthers, drove to the cabin often on getaway weekends. Frieda was in nursing school. She was outspoken, lively, and talkative. She loved to cook and was a hobby cyclist. She read romance novels and had an affinity for older country music and some of Jackie's heavy metal CDs. Jackie loved that Frieda was always doing something to titillate his imagination—whether an adventure, a new hobby, or an intimate encounter. Frieda liked wearing boots, jeans, and tops that gave a reveal of her healthy endowment. Her dark brown hair was curly and full. Her olive skin hinted that she loved the sun.

Jackie's dad built the cabin for fishing weekends and to just get away from the soybean farm. Jackie said that he won the spit of land near the falls in a poker game when he was truck farming in the 1970s. The seclusion of the falls and the stars that hung low in the sky—lacking the ambient light of a city—were magnetic impulses. Frieda and Jackie loved coming to Creek House Falls.

Frieda convinced Jackie that her favorite times were yet to be had and that her favorite place to have them would be at the cabin by the falls. Her strong hints of a permanent relationship did not go unnoticed by Jackie.

Billy ran the last of the groceries and the cooler in by the front door. He was dripping wet from the rain's sudden intensity. As he toweled off his face and hair, he suggested that they open one of the six bottles of the pinot grigio that Theta also bought at the Guntersville BI-LO Grocery. They had been warned that Marshall County might be "dry." No alcoholic beverages are sold in many counties of North Alabama, a vestige of their strong Baptist religion conversions a century before.

"Frieda, I hope you like the whites. I didn't buy any reds," Theta informed.

"Honey, my favorite wine is the wet kind when I'm looking for a good time. That stuff there will be perfect. But we only have these plastic twelve-ounce cups," Frieda countered. "Wine in a Dixie cup—perfect!"

"Better than a coffee mug, I suppose." Theta winked. "This has the makings of a great weekend."

The two couples interacted seamlessly. Frieda was humorous and forthcoming. Jackie was obviously smitten with her. Frieda's country southern drawl was fascinating. She and Jackie displayed an obvious sense of intimacy. They held hands, exchanged spontaneous kisses, and led each other to double entendres—sexual interpretations of innocent responses.

"If I admitted that I craved your sexy body, would you hold it against me?" Jackie offered.

He was relentless in his pursuit of both the giddy laughter from Frieda and the intended inducement he desired. Jackie got it and was demure in her replies. Theta understood the innuendo as well and smiled. She hoped to change subjects.

"I'm part Welsh and part French. Have you had any part of either in you?" Jackie asked Frieda. Frieda winked. It inspired Jackie to continue.

"Frieda, dear, come sit on my lap, and we'll talk about anything that pops up." Jackie added, "Oh, that's a wrinkle-free blouse. Let's scrunch it up on the floor next to the bed and see how it does. You know what would look great on you? Me!"

They laughed in their secret enticements. But Billy knew that the comments were too edgy for Theta. He suggested that they come to the table for dinner.

The two couples ate dinner and slowly sipped from two chilled bottles of pinot grigio while listening to the rain pour in pulses upon the tin roof. They told each other stories for nearly three more hours. After the giggles of old stories from their respective high school proms, the four of them agreed to retire early and get up at the crack of dawn to see the sun come up. They parted with the salutations of long-termed friendships.

Though their bedroom door was closed, Frieda and Jackie began their audible lovemaking within fifteen minutes. Frieda was uninhibited. They both would laugh about it in the morning. They assumed that Billy and Theta were intimate as well.

Theta knew that Billy would live up to his sworn promise. They took turns in the bathroom, Theta coming out first in her full robe and jammies. She hopped into the comfort of an old double bed with a loud creaky box spring. She threw one of her pillows to the floor next to Billy's sleeping bag. The room had no sofa.

Billy turned out the light before going into the bathroom. He came out in the darkened room in his boxer shorts and headed to the old sleeping bag that had been in the hall closet. The uncomfortable sofa that he would have preferred was in the den. The sleeping bag, he thought, was better than a thinly blanketed floor. Billy lay awake on his side in the sleeping bag; Theta staring at the ceiling covered by a frilly spread on an old mattress. It squeaked as she moved. From the other room, a crescendo climax meant that they could now turn to sleep. Theta flipped to her side as the squeak interrupted the new silence. Their backs were to each other—each glad that the ardent and rhythmic sounds from the room across the den had subsided. They each pretended to be asleep until the endorphins captured them.

The steady Alabama drizzle persisted throughout the night. It helped to ease both of them into their dreams.

The next morning disappointed the four of them as the rain fell even harder. Rain is the conductor of many a destiny. The two couples found joy in card games, baseball and golf broadcasts, music from old 78 LP records that belonged to Jackie's mother, and a few board games from the hall closet shelf. It appeared that the rain had won the weekend.

Jackie and Frieda planned to leave to drive back just after lunchtime on Sunday. Frieda could not miss her Monday vital metrics class.

The four of them got out of the cabin just once. It was Theta's idea as they had reached midafternoon incarcerated by the weather.

"The rain is wet, the river is wet, the waterfall is wet—so why are we not wet?" she challenged. "I'm going to get wet."

They went as they were—in shorts and T-shirts. They didn't bother to carry towels.

They spent part of Saturday afternoon dancing in the rain and swinging from the short tree rope into the natural pool created by the waterfall. The cabin fever made them into fun-seeking children for an hour and a half. They became soaked and playful, dunking each other into the waterfall area where the water was past waist deep. Theta and Billy explored the area from the top of the granite rocks, seeing the water collect into a small pool before exiting at the ten-foot falls. Other water washed across the rocks as gravity danced in the beauty of nature. From the stream, the area was thickly wooded in all directions. They saw Douglas firs, pines, white oaks, and maples interspersed in the thick green forest. Only otters would have enjoyed this respite better than the two wet couples.

Neither Billy nor Theta knew that a local Guntersville tree festival each November lauded the area's natural stand of the verdant surrounding forests. A Guntersville forest is a resource they celebrate much as other communities celebrate a wine harvest or a watermelon crop.

"Billy, thank you for not looking. I think the rain has made my shirt and bra almost invisible," Theta said.

Billy tried not to look, but after the private notice given, he had to summon even more discipline. She should not have said anything.

The sudden rage of the rain gave them the impetus to return to the cabin. Yet Theta's suggestion turned into an unforgettable adventure. Once they returned, Billy dripped from the porch swing while Theta changed into something dry to wear.

The dusk crawled to the falls as they prepared for dinner and pinot. More card games were in store. Wet clothes were wrung out and hung to dry in the two bathrooms. Being dry was a reason for a toast.

"To Theta, the 'creata of good times.'" Billy raised his red cup.

"To Theta!" Frieda added. "I told you she was all wet."

The four of them got out their favorite partner game—Trivial Pursuit. Theta was Billy's best asset in the challenge. She knew way too much trivia.

"This cute little South American animal has three stomachs and hums," Frieda challenged. "I added the cute part."

Theta answered in her most academic chide.

"Well, it would seem to me that if you're in South America, you're likely to speak either Spanish or Portuguese. Either way, when you put two *L*s together, it makes the sound of a *Y*. So, Frieda, dear, I wonder if I hummed the answer if I could get extra points? My final answer is the two-*L*'d yama."

Billy looked at Jackie with a smile.

He explained, "She's like that. She could have just as easily given the simple answer, but she wanted to teach and inform at the same time. If we married and had children, they would be calling those cute little guys 'yommas.'"

"You snobs have won again," Jackie intoned.

He pointed to Frieda in jest as he added, "Nice boobs. No help."

They all chuckled. Theta and Billy won three straight games and were nearly unbeatable. Frieda was ready to retire for the evening instead of starting a fourth game that would produce the same result.

"I'm getting a bit chilled, sweetheart. I need to be warmed." Frieda fluttered her eyelids at Jackie.

"You don't want little me to have chilly bumps and catch cold, d'ya? I'm goin' to get under your momma's comforter. Wait five minutes and come see if there's a prize under there for you."

Frieda said her good nights and headed to their room. She turned on the nightstand lamp and closed the bedroom door behind her. Jackie brought the Dixie cups to the sink and helped straighten the room. He placed the cork into the opened bottle of pinot grigio and put it into the refrigerator. Theta rebagged the uneaten pretzels and put up the board game. Few words were said as they all straightened the room until Jackie broke the silence with his own quip.

He took a theatrical bow before entering the bedroom.

"Good night, my servants. Good night. I'll be seeing a little less of you two and a lot more of the queen's bosom."

Since there was no partner-accepted alternative, Billy continued to retire to the sleeping bag by the bedroom door. The bathroom sequence of "lady's first" began. The light went off when Billy left the bathroom. He assumed that Theta was starting to sleep since the box springs had no squeak. He tiptoed to his Coleman XL insulated sleeping bag, navy blue quilted with a Scottish clan-patterned interior.

After Frieda's newest warmth hit its audible peak from the room across the den, the mating couple seemed to fall off to sleep. Theta was not so lucky. She was wide awake. The lovemaking made her nervous about Billy's promise and embarrassed, as she had never heard a couple making love until the last two nights.

"Billy," she whispered, "are you awake?"

"Yes. Who could sleep after that opera across the way?" Billy answered with low-toned sarcasm, wishing that the performance could be copied in his room.

"Billy, this is awkward for me. I hope you understand," Theta started. "I told Frieda I was a virgin, but I don't think she believed me. She just smiled as if I was saying, 'I wish I were still a virgin.'"

"Theta, all you need to know is that I concede that fact and respect your wishes. Frieda is sweet and comes from a fine home. Her not being a virgin is not a condemnation. She loves Jackie, and Jackie truly loves her. They do not hide their affection. In a sense, it's great. But for us this weekend, it's like 'in your face.' I get that," Billy stated. "Frieda . . . I'd bet she does not have a female friend that is a virgin. So she may be a little curious, if not confused. Don't take it personally."

"Billy, I'm also worried about you. You shouldn't have brought me here. I'm a drag. You could have brought Georgiana or someone who did not have my hang-ups about premarital sex," Theta continued in a lower whisper as if she assumed that Billy would have enjoyed an otherwise sexually active weekend. "I'm sorry I put you through this."

Billy hesitated a moment to gather his thoughts. He knew that Theta would remain a virgin until she betrothed herself to a marriage partner and the ceremony was performed. There was no use in fighting a battle that could not be won. Besides, he truly admired Theta's conviction and her clear sense of morality. He regarded Theta as a close friend, a confidant, and someone to be admired for her convictions. She was a brilliant student and a fun companion. In Billy's mind, he profoundly hoped that he would find someone much like Theta when he was ready to marry and to begin a family.

"Theta, for a perfect person with all of your abilities and your iron willpower, you sure beat yourself up. There is not one thing wrong with you whatsoever," he strained to whisper.

He continued.

"You are perfect in every way. I could not have had a better time than to have you here. You have known me for a long time. You know that I am not a virgin and that I've been with other women. Yet you befriend me with great trust. I hope you leave here this weekend knowing what an honor it is for me to be with you despite my shortcomings. In the end, all you need to know is that I deeply respect you, and I always will."

Billy couldn't see Theta as her eyes watered. He had alleviated her misgivings, solidified her trust, and, most importantly, touched her heart.

She whispered in the voice of a quivering angel, "You make me happy, Billy. Your friendship is essential. Thank you for understanding. Good night."

The formality of Billy and Theta's relationship was not breached over their forty-eight hours together in a private bedroom. Their mutual friendship had blossomed into conversational intimacy devoid of physical interaction. They were most comfortable with each other, with deep-rooted respect at the forefront of their unquestioned friendship.

Billy fell off to sleep, wishing that Theta would surprise him under a comforter one day.

CHAPTER NINE

Sunshine

(As It Happened, Eight Years Earlier)

THE WINDS BEGAN to relent. The tropical depression was showing signs of breaking up.

Billy made cheesy scrambled eggs and bacon with toast and strawberry preserves. Theta made the coffee and put out the cups, milk, and sugar. Jackie smelled the breakfast and woke Frieda to join him while the breakfast was warm.

Frieda came in first and grabbed two cups to pour black coffee. She smelled the bacon and told Billy, "We'll be decent shortly."

She took the two black coffees into the room to give one to Jackie.

After breakfast, Jackie began to give Billy last-minute instructions about locking the cabin. Billy and Theta were staying over for the extra day. Jackie then went to shower and shave after Frieda had finished in their private bathroom.

The retreating lovers, Jackie and Frieda, were packed and ready to wrestle the muddy back roads before their return to Atlanta by midmorning. They were heading to the Mann family farm over near Tuscumbia first. Their departure would leave Theta and Billy to the assumed honor of respectful coexistence for the next twenty-four hours. Nothing romantic was suggested or expected by either.

Frieda rushed around to tidy up the larger bedroom. She came out with bed sheets, towels, and pillowcases. Before she could place them into the washer, Theta came to her.

"Frieda, don't be silly," she started. "I'll wash these and place them back on the bed before I leave tomorrow. With this steady rain, I'll be looking for something to do."

Frieda heard the last part of the sentence as if it were a commitment to remain chaste.

"Theta, I am so glad that I met you. I wanted to talk to you a moment anyway while the boys are getting the car packed," Frieda began.

"I want to apologize for my insensitivity. I know that you are trying to balance a situation, and I have been of no help. I am not whom you think. I love Jackie, and he loves me. I know we get carried away, but that's what we do. He is so much fun, and he is part of my life. I know that we've made you uncomfortable."

"Please say no more. I understand. You do not have the problem here. I came under a set of rules, and Billy has accommodated the rules. I hope that I have not spoiled your weekend," Theta offered.

"To the contrary. I got to know you, and I already knew that Billy needed to step up his game. Just friends or not, you need to grab that boy before he drifts toward a miserable person and ruins his life. He's Jackie's best friend at Tech," Frieda added.

Theta blushed.

"Maybe one day. But I'm not ready for a commitment to anyone," Theta said. "But when that day comes, I do hope I find someone like Billy. He has the sincere personality, gentlemanly qualities, and the moral bearing that impresses me deeply. And he is really funny when he gets on a roll. But don't tell him that. I like that he has no large and uncontrollable ego."

Frieda followed, "Theta, why don't you just kiss him once? He's under your control. We can see that. If the kiss is magic, the life you build together will assume magical qualities. You don't have to go further than the sincerity and truthfulness of a kiss."

Theta blushed again while looking down.

"Thank you, Frieda. I hope I'll see you again soon," she replied sheepishly.

They hugged.

Billy continued helping Jackie pack his Jeep in the slow drizzle. Stepping down from the slippery porch, Jackie leaned over with his back turned to Frieda and whispered to Billy, "Good luck, buddy. She's an ice cube, but she's probably worth the melt time."

Theta smiled curiously, though she did not hear Jackie's "ice cube" whisper to Billy. She wondered what Jackie said but did not pry. Boy talk—she imagined.

Packed, they got into the boxy Jeep. From his car window, Jackie bellowed the last instructions through the drizzling raindrops.

"Billy, when this rain stops, can you take out the trash to the bin by the gate?" Jackie asked. "Dad gets a little pissed if I don't leave the cabin as I found it. And flip the breaker off to the hot water heater."

"Sure, Jackie. Be careful dodging the potholes and ruts. Wear your seatbelts!" Billy yelled. The Jeep Wagoneer started pulling away. Theta approached Billy on the porch as if they were the actual hosts waving good-bye.

"Seat belts! It's all about safety and not letting go." Theta winked as she suggested another level of safety. Theta squeezed Billy's arm a bit tighter. "Seat belts!"

She chided Billy.

"I'll make sure you leave everything in perfect order. And we'll wear our seatbelts too. Right, Billy?"

The Jeep headed to the gate.

There was a purposeful underlying meaning in Theta's remark, Billy surmised. He had no plans to break his promise to Theta. It was a tantalizing prospect, but there was definitely another stop sign recorded, he deduced. Besides, he deeply respected her wishes and found her so pleasant that he would fight the devil to keep her special and trusting friendship intact.

Once Jackie and Frieda left the front gate area, Theta was completely comfortable with the chivalric Billy to stay until Monday morning. Jackie left instructions for them to leave the cabin key under the porch planter.

"Well, Billy, we have it all to ourselves," Theta noted.

"But with freedom comes responsibility," she added in a cautious pause. "I'll straighten the place a bit and finish in the kitchen. You're the 'cruise director' for the day. Maybe we can go for a walk in the forest if the rain stops."

"I'd like that," he consented. "With luck, we can explore the property beyond the falls."

Billy gazed to the horizon looking for a sign in the sky.

'The clouds may be breaking up. Keep your fingers crossed. At the very least, we can go back to swing from the rope in the drizzle."

"I'm in," Theta responded. "But let's keep it strictly cordial, OK?"

She added, "You can sleep in the other bedroom tonight. No more floor! I'm so sorry to cause such an imposition, Billy. I really am, but I know that you understand. You have been every bit the gentleman I expected."

Before Billy could respond, Theta began to plan the day.

"I'll wash the bedsheets and towels if you don't mind getting our two towels for me," Theta asked.

"Your back will appreciate a break tonight," she added. "And we'll have the whole afternoon to do as you like, Mr. Director."

"Really?" Billy smiled boyishly.

Theta sensed the insinuation.

"Yes, really. But as two good friends who respect each other well enough not to cross the line," she further qualified.

Billy smiled, feeling that the ice would not melt anytime soon.

He replied, "And I'll clean the playpen and stack the toys in the corner."

CHAPTER TEN

Maria Delgado

MARIA DELGADO MARRIED Pablo Lopez Gutierrez out of necessity. Her work visa was not likely to be approved. From differing cultures sewn by the commonality of the Spanish language, they fell in love after their nuptials.

She had escaped from the Dominican Republic where she had been charged with *gran robo*, or grand theft. She had stolen her stepfather's 1991 Ford Fiesta with 209,000 miles and no spare tire. She had also taken five hundred pesos from his wallet. She left the farming village of Moca and headed for the port town of Puerto Plata, where her oldest brother, Hector, arranged passage on a commercial ship to Miami. She was a known stowaway. Hector then returned the Ford Fiesta to a conspicuous location away from the port to be readily found the next day. They had successfully decoyed the stepfather away from the trail.

Maria arrived at age sixteen with a knapsack of essentials and a mindset to find her way in a land of opportunity. She hoped that the torment of sexual abuse would distance itself in the large wake of the container vessel. She cried as she left her brother and her homeland.

Arriving at the Port of Miami, she was given a stevedore's identification card through Hector's arrangement. With this ID, she was able to visit the city outside of the high fencing as if she were on leave from the ship's duties. The custom's officials approved her day visa.

Maria knew that her stepfather had relatives in Miami. She obtained directions from other Spanish-speaking residents to find a money exchange and the Amtrak station on northwest Thirty-Seventh Street. She selected the Silver Meteor to Charleston for the eighty-five-dollar fare. She arrived with twenty-six dollars left from the stolen and converted pesos. Her knapsack had a stale loaf of Miami bread and an empty water bottle from the Amtrak station. Her lone guide to obtain her full independence was a Spanish-to-English lesson book she brought from her tenth-grade classroom. She wore her faith—a silver crucifix on a thin leather strap that once tied a farmer's boot. Her mother had given her the silver crucifix at Navidad the year prior.

She walked from her Amtrak arrival to the place other Latinos directed so that she might find work. She needed a job, knowing she was within twenty-six dollars of destitution. She stood at the foot of the bridge connecting the Charleston peninsula to Mount Pleasant with a cardboard sign that simply read, "Domestic."

Sid Toile was returning from the main Charleston library on Calhoun Street when he spotted Maria's sign. Sid had lived in Mount Pleasant for less than a year.

He pulled over before passing her. He instinctively knew that she would not speak English and inquired, "Puedes cocinar?"

Though Sid had not taken a course in the Spanish language over his sixteen years of formal education, he had memorized the language in his dotage. He had also memorized Serbo-Croatian, Russian, Mandarin, French, Swedish, and Italian. He could recognize all other major languages by his keen sense of tones and inflections. Speaking to Maria seemed both natural and adventurous to the old man.

"Si. Ama di casa," Maria replied, hoping that the innocuous gray-bearded man would give her a chance. She announced herself as a housekeeper.

Sid invited her to come to his home as a trial of work. There, he would assess her ability and continue to employ her should she prove to be proficient. She accepted the terms without divulging that she was underage, homeless, and suspect of strangers. Sid knew all of these secrets without asking.

Other than cooking out of cultural necessity, she had none of the skill sets that Sid would require. He had laundry, dusting, sweeping, vacuuming, mopping, maintenance, and plant nutrition in mind—in addition to cooking.

Sid arranged her first night in an American hotel, a Holiday Inn Express that provided breakfast. For three weeks, the young Maria stayed there until Sid found her a small one-bedroom furnished apartment just off of Coleman Boulevard. Sid picked her up at eight o'clock each morning and delivered her back by twelve thirty. He encouraged her to find an afternoon employer. She found a job as a dishwasher at a Shem Creek seafood restaurant. Sid provided a social security number that she used to assure the owner that she was legal. Since she worked hard and drew a minimal wage without complaint, they did not pursue other proof. She worked there from two o'clock to ten o'clock on three weekdays and from twelve o'clock to eight o'clock on Saturdays and Sundays. With Sid's primary job, Maria was working sixty-three hours every week and saving her money to afford her future American life. She was an illegal immigrant who shopped for discount groceries in the evenings and never dined outside of her apartment. She feared extradition back to the Dominican Republic and a return to her sexual deviate stepfather.

Over the next three and a half years, Maria Delgado learned English, found a suitable home, got married, delivered two children, and became an expert domestic. She owed her life to Sid. Her marriage to Pablo Lopez Gutierrez was for the convenience of both. Pablo, from

Puerto Angel, Mexico, near the border with Guatemala, was also an illegal immigrant. They met on a city bus. They dated and married in a whirlwind, each knowing that a deportation could emerge. Their fears formed a mutual reason. Their love for each other developed after their marriage. Their toddler boys became what politicians call "anchor babies."

CHAPTER ELEVEN

Sunday Swim

(As It Happened, Eight Years Earlier)

THETA CLEANED THE breakfast dishes while Billy showered and shaved. Billy noticed from the window a spark of sunlight drifting across the wet shrubbery. As he came out of the bedroom, he announced to Theta that he was going to the falls while the sun was slightly visible. He hoped that she would follow.

"I'd like you to join me. It should be nice to feel the sun after all that rain," Billy invited. "Come lie out. We waited all weekend for the sun, so let's enjoy it."

Theta looked to the window. She was not sure she should follow and wanted to think about it, not putting herself into an awkward situation.

"Maybe," she offered. "Let's see if it clears."

As the warming sun poked through the midday cloud cover, Billy took the short foot trail to the creek bank. Theta stayed to finish cleaning the kitchen and to take her morning shower. The sun changed her mood. She wanted to not only join Billy at the waterfall but also show off her new bright green bathing suit. With a cooling August breeze wafting across the meadow from the kitchen window, Theta envisioned a very pleasant and relaxing afternoon.

Theta put on her new two-piece that she had been hoping to wear since Friday. The emerald green contrast to her delicate skin settled her concerns about beachwear. She had an aversion to intense sunshine along with too much exposure of her lithe figure to others. She was innately conservative and private. But she felt quite comfortable that Billy would compliment the color and style of her new suit.

She sauntered down the short path barefooted to see Billy standing under the falls. She placed her large yellow-and-orange Myrtle Beach towel across a slanted grassy area away from the spray of the rushing water. It was not as muddy there. Billy swam in circles near the falls for exercise and then floated to within yards of Theta.

"I know the boundaries, Theta. But it is no fair wearing that bathing suit. You are simply dazzling in that. I can tell that you spend too many hours in the gym," Billy observed. It was the first time he had ever seen that much of her revealed.

Theta blushed.

"Get back, Billy. You're blocking my sunlight!" she kidded him. "You like it? I'm glad. I bought this at Ginger's on Peachtree just for this weekend. Fair-skinned redheads have a hard time finding bathing suits. But I am happy that you noticed."

Billy responded, "You found the right one. But if I were you, I'd lather up with lotion. I don't mind applying a coat to your back."

There was an awkward pause.

"Billy, you know the rules. I want to be with you, but not in that way. Let's keep our spacing and still have loads of fun, OK?" Theta replied as if she was scolding a schoolchild.

She at once felt remorseful in chastising him in her assumption of sexual aggression. Billy was just being Billy.

Billy had turned to wade back to the noisy ten-foot falls. He had not meant to draw the comment. He was simply courteous. The raging water sounds and the return of the various songbirds made the setting seem idyllic.

Billy returned to the deepest part of the natural pool created by the rushing volume of water. It came tumbling down faster than usual, a result of the weekend's steady rain.

Theta removed her sunglasses and straightened up her beach towel to enjoy the partial sun by the small sugar maple that swayed in the assuring breeze. The tree rope hung still from a white oak on the other side of the stream. It was installed to the reach of the deeper waterfall pool.

The sun danced across shadows of wide leaves upon the repose of Theta's exquisite body. She had the benefit of a slope to the creek and the security of the maple tree shade to protect her tender skin.

Indeed, her bright emerald bathing suit accentuated her well-proportioned figure and her matching eyes. Her dark cedar hair flowed across her milk-skinned shoulders. Irish lineage had given her splotches of muted freckles and a skin tone that always looked young and tender. Tanning lines were not present since she was woefully underexposed to the outdoors. A slight pinkish glow on her upper chest and her arms suggested that she enjoyed the sun as a jogger or walker only.

She pulled down her Oakley's as the sunbeams intensified. Theta turned to her side watching Billy glide gracefully in the water over the top of her sunglasses.

She had changed the mood of the moment and felt she could not take back the way she had snapped at him. She realized that she had been too stern and suspicious. Billy was being kind and not overtly forward. She immediately felt that her deep feelings for him were now jeopardized by her staunchly defensive words. She did not want to be vulnerable, but she certainly did not want to be a bitch. She hoped that the wonderful man she had just insulted might be her true love, though he could not be her lover. She was resolute in her self-commitment. Billy was sincere, respectful, and true to his word. She began feeling awful about the last few remarks.

From the water, Theta looked like a statue of a goddess in semi-recline. And Billy was now certain that she was made of marble or granite. He would not apply sun lotion or even mention the intense August sun again.

On reflection, Billy was similarly uncomfortable about their last exchange. He thought he might have been misunderstood and may need to apologize but was not sure he had said anything inappropriate. He decided to accept the circumstance by avoiding the subject entirely and cooling off in the waterfall.

Billy turned back toward her. The waterfall was only two dozen slow steps from the creek bank. He waved to her awkwardly.

He half-heartedly placed his hands up to the sides of his mouth to call to her over the sound of the pouring water.

"Come on in, Theta."

She sat up to respond. Though she had been lying comfortably in the quiet of nature and the newly audible chatter of the sparrows, larks, and warblers, she acquiesced by standing up to hear him. Not hearing him clearly because of the waterfall noise, she waded in closer to him.

She was not an avid sunbather for obvious reasons. Her exquisite skin tone was meant for shaded areas and moonlit nights.

Theta was still thinking about her last comment to Billy. It was uncalled for and may have been too confrontational. Wading to him was her way of saying, "I'm sorry."

As she got closer, Billy pointed to the falls.

"I wanted to show you the prism in the falls from the sunlight. It's a permanent rainbow, but you have to see it from the angle at the underside," he motioned. "The sun is high in the sky, so you have to stoop to look up into it."

The sunlight prism was dancing across the falling water. The welcomed sun filtered through the pines into the glaze of the creek like a mirror reflection. The spray had created Billy's discovery—a mini rainbow. Billy was not sure Theta would venture to get her hair wet.

She waded even closer to Billy, though reservedly. She immediately drenched her dark reddish hair into the rush of the falls, the rivulets of fresh water streaming to the side of her face. She went to the underside where Billy pointed, looking through the fall from under the crest of the upper granite rock that spawned the wide current of gravity and the pool beyond. Billy was elated that she came to him. The awkwardness of the suntan lotion comment was forgotten.

"We have our very own rainbow," Theta remarked as she squeezed the water from her hair while leaning aside. "What other magical mysteries will we find today while we're not wearing seatbelts?"

Billy smiled. He thought of her playing in the water the day before in their shorts and T-shirts. Billy had adhered to his gentlemanly vow in the rain. He avoided glancing at Theta's rain-soaked T-shirt that exposed much of her full bosom. Theta warned Billy that he would see too much as she turned her torso away from his view to avoid that temptation.

Billy enjoyed the frolic in the falling rain a day earlier as he tossed her over and over again into the waterfall. She laughed like a young teenager.

Billy wondered, "Will she play again now that they were alone?"

The T-Shirt situation had given way to a less-revealing bathing suit. She was no less voluptuous. He would find out presently.

Theta's spontaneity was not a character flaw but a wisp of adventure that she frequently presented. She liked being unpredictable.

"Can you still lift me like yesterday, or are you too weak?" She enticed him.

Billy stepped forward and lifted her up by her waist and dipped her back to the underside of the falling water. She laughed in the new joy of their playful solitude. The episode of the lotion confrontation had been washed away in the moment. A new bond was formed. She had acquiesced to enjoy their watery playground.

"Somehow, I knew you couldn't be trusted," Theta said as she smiled. The contrast of her satin pearl teeth against her thin lips was delectable.

"Ah, but I can be trusted . . . trusted to have a good time even when it looks like it could turn out to be a boring and lazy time."

Billy was still cautious about Theta's commitment to playfully interact, even in the backdrop of the falls. He would go as far as she would allow in the tossing frenzy, always ready to back away.

Theta smiled demurely. It was as if she had a devious side that needed exploring. He had no idea of her newfound spontaneity and the pure joy of being with Billy in the moment. The ice was melting away.

"Boring and lazy, you say?" Theta implored. "I am a lot of things, but boring and lazy will never describe me. You should know that by now!"

She splashed him with two open hands of water.

Before he could be offended by the affront on his polite chivalry, she jumped back to him and wrapped her arms around his athletic neck, swaying her lower body to his side playfully as if to be lifted and thrown into the waterfall again. She was temporarily embraced as if he was not going to toss her. She laughed loudly in the enjoyment, knowing that Billy was getting ready to throw her even higher. She clutched tightly but was giddily prepared to let go.

Droplets were gathering in rivulets from the ice, it seemed.

"Nobody has ever gotten sunburned underwater," Billy chided her. And there she went, higher yet. She splashed and came back up, cocking her head to the side to squeeze her dark rusty hair again. He knew she was coming back for more.

Billy was immediately taken by her playfulness and her touch. She was angelically beautiful. She was indeed someone he could love forever.

Theta stooped to shoulder level in the water to rearrange her hair yet again and check to make sure her bathing suit top did not slip down. She retied the bow at the back of her neck tighter. She emerged a few feet away while twisting her locks away from her shoulder. She jumped into his arms again to be thrown back into the high roaring waterfall. She was fully cradled across his curled arms, her tight grip around his neck. She looked up to his neatly groomed chin of whiskers, her sheepish eyes asking him to please make her joyfulness complete.

Billy instinctively folded his sinewy arms under her legs and her upper back to pull her closer. She was cradled, awaiting the height she would be thrown. He threw her nearly straight up but caught her back into his arms before she reached the water and then threw her clumsily into the falls.

Theta laughed as a young child running on a playground.

She came back to Billy laughing while squeezing her wet hair. She reached for his neck and clutched it in a new death grip. She used it as a fulcrum to jump to him again, throwing her legs up in unison for Billy to cradle. She held him tight enough that she felt that she would never want to be separated again, even in their playfulness.

Billy moved closer to the falls as she anticipated a submersion from his strong toss to the water. With a stilted pause to look at her happy and enticingly wet face with her glowing green eyes, Billy paused. She looked up demurely. Their eyes locked. He kissed her.

Theta remembered that an hour before, Frieda had suggested that she just kiss him to know that feeling.

The kiss released Billy's imprisoned yearning for her. The desire had been bound for much too long. But he had knowingly crossed the line. He expected a reprisal, perhaps even a slap. But Theta did not pull away. The kiss was everything.

The long, fervent kiss was not diverted. It momentarily took Theta by surprise. As their lips parted, Theta turned her head away hesitatingly, though still in the clutch of Billy's muscular arms. She paused and turned back to him. Without words, her brow raised to assess him quizzically. She was cradled still. The smile was gone. Water dripped down from her eyes. Her tears mingled with the moment. She loved that first kiss. She was searching her soul for what to do next. Billy's dreamy eyes had captured her. She looked down and then up again.

The spray from the waterfall began to make her blink. Billy turned her to protect her face from the spray while wondering if he should let go or pull her back to his lips.

Theta's spontaneity won out. She placed her free right hand to the side of his face and initiated the next kiss. It was as if she had been waiting a lifetime for that moment. The second kiss was longer yet.

It was in the same moment of the second kiss that Theta's life assumed a storybook cadence. Her pulse increased. Her sweet breath invaded Billy's heightened senses. Billy was deeply aroused but knew that the stop sign could materialize any moment. In a sense, that overhanging codicil of the relationship rules had made the second kiss all the more enchanting. It was she who kissed him.

There was something forbidden in the seclusion of the falls. What was prohibited and banned as illicit had become central to the moment.

Theta's mind found a comforting rationalization. Undoubtedly, this rapture she felt throughout her sensuous and wet body was love—pure and vibrant. She was weakened by the first kiss and submitted her soul to the second.

Saying nothing but glancing deeply—green eyes locked upon green eyes—they kissed a third time, longer and more passionately yet. Billy dropped his right arm, releasing Theta's lower body to stand closer to him, but continued to clutch her in his left arm around her supple back. She offered no resistance.

Theta moved even closer. Her height made it easy to stand nearly face-to-face. She wanted him to hold her. She had never been held by anyone before. Instinctively, Billy drew her closer in a securing embrace.

Billy's thoughts were to honor the moment. It was special and one he would never forget. Though highly aroused, his mind was not directed to an outcome of his natural desire. It was focused upon the angel clutched in his arms, lips to lips. As they were entwined, Theta rubbed her hands into his shoulder blades softly. They were still showered by the waterfall spray.

Billy stroked her lower back tenderly. He had become hesitant like a spin-the-bottle participant. He wondered how far she wanted him to go. He decided to become bold, knowing that out of respect for her, he could stop if she desired.

He lovingly kissed her again. They were waist high in the waterfall pool. He slowly unhooked her bathing suit top. It draped freely on her chest from the tie around her neck. He kissed her again and simultaneously untied the bow and removed it, revealing her full, firm bosom. Theta hesitated, but no protest was given. No man had seen her breasts. She simply cocked her head quizzically to stare into his loving eyes. Billy's eyes remained locked upon her puzzled face. He looked to her for a hint of what could follow. He was still not sure what might happen next. He remained entranced upon her melting eyes without a glance to her voluptuous and newly exposed chest. She had surrendered herself completely by the fourth long and fervent kiss. She looked at his eyes as he looked at her expression. He expected the sudden halt at any moment.

"Theta, I can stop. My heart is filled with you, but I can wait," Billy whispered.

But she was suddenly expecting more. The permafrost was warmed by the diligence of the sun and Billy's full and caring attention. All of the ice had melted into the kisses that silenced the protests and enthused the participants equally.

The cooling water had raced through them. The curvature of Theta's lissome figure was as beautiful as the classical work of Renaissance artists. She wilted to his strengthened embrace. They kissed again, joined as if they were one. Theta was at once clear in her life's direction, free from her inhibitions. She had fully surrendered her stilted convictions for this one perfect moment with this ideal and chivalric suitor. His commitment to stop appealed to her sense of full trust. Alone in a forest, she wanted him to move her life and her long-reserved desires further yet.

Billy kissed her again and again. Smaller kisses were targeted to her neck, her ears, and her soft clavicle. She swooned with each. He placed his right hand on her bare back and slowly moved her closer. He could sense her quickened heartbeat as he pecked smaller kisses to her bosom.

"Billy, I'm not sure what I'm doing, but I am sure that I do not want you to stop. Hold me close and please be gentle," she implored.

Billy could not detect whether her sparkling green eyes were wet with joy or from the natural spray of the waterfall. He assumed the former.

"Don't worry, Theta. We will go at your pace and take it slow," Billy whispered back. "We're alone. We're in love. And there is no hurry. You are in complete control."

Theta was reassured but was not entirely sure of what was to come and how far she would allow the passion to rise. She could stop at any time. They kissed again and again without the sense of a pressured conclusion or rhapsodic crescendo.

They were immersed waist deep into the water and fully unto each other. Theta wrapped her long bare arms around his neck while standing flat-footed and cooled in the fresh pool from the falls. Her heart trumpeted the moments, ecstatic in the sensual pace of emboldened bliss.

Cautiously but deliberately, Billy slipped his hands down inside her bikini bottoms to her bare buttocks under the waterline. Theta pulled his neck closer still. She was suddenly tepid in the excitement. Billy slowly brought the top elasticity of the emerald bottoms to Theta's knees underwater. She helped him in his clumsy effort to take them off by pulling her left knee up and then the right. She giggled as he set them adrift. She then chased them for a few steps to direct them to the shore. As her lower body was partially exposed, she coyly retreated back to Billy, her folded arms covering her breasts as if she suddenly did not want him to see her fully *au naturel*.

Billy laughed. They embraced anew. He took off his trunks. He threw them in the direction of the shore near her empty beach towel. They were both now fully nude and in the mood for whatever the stillness of time and place delivered.

"I never would have expected this minute or this moment!" Billy exclaimed to Theta with his eyes fixed on hers. I had no idea that you could be so exciting yet so reserved."

"Billy, I am certain that I am not making a mistake. I am in love with you. If you feel for me as I do for you, all is right in the heavens and on earth," she declared, still poetic in her expressions.

Billy clasped her hand and led her back to the sun prism under the waterfall. They sensuously initiated their first fully naked embrace in the drench of the sun's dance upon muted light, sprayed by the coolness of the falls. The larks continued to bicker as a light breeze shook the longleaf pines. The water and the wind yielded to the moment. With Billy's hand behind the bend in her knee, he softly lifted Theta up. Theta wrapped her long nervously flinching legs around Billy's waist.

She stopped to peruse his face and eyes again, her body inviting the bliss she had only imagined but had never known.

Theta gave a slightly grimaced glance to Billy's eyes as they began lovemaking below the waterline. Her eyes were furrowed as if she expected a tetanus shot. But the penetration was slow and not abrupt.

It acclimated her hesitance and ceded her acceptance of him. Billy stared deeply into her eyes, now fixed upon his. Billy knew that Theta had, within this emotional instant, given up something incredibly special to him. She had saved and protected her virginity as if it were the vast vein of golden treasure the Aztecs sought throughout Middle America over eight centuries.

Accepting the responsibility of her vanquished dream engendered yet another level of Billy's care and commitment. The physical engagement was fully about her. She maneuvered willingly but uncomfortably. He was committed to her being contented and relaxed and in full control of the experience. Billy's impulses were remanded to the highest level of his subconscious. Making love to Theta for her first time would be something he knew she would never forget. His focus was to make it an experience with the highest possible benefit to her.

Their lovemaking sounds were muted by creation's elements—the rushing water, the thrusting breeze upon the forest, and the menagerie of forest animals in their sun awakening.

They fervently copulated as a rapturous crescendo—as if the sky, the fluttering leaves, the birds, and the water were orchestrated in every clasp, release, and swoon. The waft of wind swirled anew. Their connection below the waterline was enhanced by its stimulating flow.

To Theta, this would become the most perfect submission imaginable. She would not dissuade his natural instincts, though the recently forbidden activity was still so new and so foreign. There was discomfort, but it was a noble ache muted by the soothing current.

She kissed him deeply and vigorously, unaware of the extent of time that would be considered normal for this thrilling union. The warblers whistled amid the delight. Rustling sways of the leaves accompanied nature's bursting indulgence. All was right in time, pulse, and pace. They were alone unto their naked desires. They had merged their hearts. Theta never knew that the experience could be so perfect, so sensual, and so fulfilling. It is doubtful that any female could have experienced a more loving and dramatic indoctrination throughout the history of mankind, she surmised. She felt loved, honored, and unique.

The ecstasy was like the first embrace of Adam and the first surrender of Eve. They said nothing. They kissed, they clutched, and they writhed in the joy and the freedom of being isolated and in their own private Eden. Billy's care and attention to Theta in this new and tantalizing experience were particularly chivalrous.

The waves of the seven seas surged. The migrations of great herds intensified. Sunbursts swallowed the darkness. Theta received him with tears of overwhelming joy.

Theta emerged from this primal experience contented from her participation despite the expected discomfort. She had no psychological remorse. She worried that Billy might feel responsible beyond its profound meaning to her life's experience.

They embraced anew, cuddling in each other's afterglow. The waterfalls still commanded the sound of the moments in its continuous delivery of the swollen river above.

"Billy, you're worried about . . ." Theta started as a new and tighter embrace was secured.

"No, Theta. Don't say it. I know. I feel as special for you as you feel for me, if not more. I feel like I have waited to make love to you my entire life. No words could describe the warmth and passion I've had for you. And you must know that I have maintained all respect as well."

Theta immediately began to cry.

Billy did not fully understand. "Theta, you OK? Did I hurt you? Are you bleeding?"

"No, Billy, it was a hurt of tremendous joy. It was not that." She paused to collect herself and her passionate thoughts. Her sense of a fairy-tale ending was fully attained, though the wedding night promise was now gone forever.

"I knew that I loved you so much, and yet I pushed you away for so long. I hope you can understand that" Theta said as she wiped away the happiness of her tears.

They were both comfortable in the fully nude embrace as they drifted with the current further from the pool and falls. Billy assumed they were heading slowly to the shoreline to retrieve their bathing apparel.

Theta reflected. "I realized that I wanted to be loved more than I wanted to be, well, to be a virgin for a special night. What I wanted all along was to love you. And it took me a year and a half to understand myself. It's me, not you."

"Theta, I will always remember this moment and will always love you," Billy remarked. "Our life ahead can be amazing."

They embraced and kissed again and again by the shoreline, ankle deep in the stream. They were enraptured by each other's total joy. Theta smiled and then pulled away as Billy still expected her to retrieve her swimsuit by the streamside. She walked away from him and completely out of the water where Billy could not divert his eyes from the entirety of her beauty.

He followed her out to the steep grassy bank.

They had retrieved each other's bathing suits. He assumed that they would dress and return to the cottage. Theta turned to look at Billy. In a simultaneous notion, they realized that though they had made passionate love, they had not seen each other fully naked out of the water. They both smiled wryly as they perused each other's full daylight attributes unabashedly.

"Billy, do you like what you see?" Theta asked innocently. "No man has ever seen this body. I'm imperfect, but I hope I'm perfect for you."

The moment was the Genesis story in reverse. They realized they were naked and found it to be of great comfort to each other. They stood by the shore momentarily in the perusal of each other's flawlessness, with no imperfections noted.

"Theta, if I began to tell you how gorgeous you are, you will blush and feel embarrassed by the talk. Just know that there is no creature on earth more tantalizingly beautiful."

Theta blushed and slightly turned her head.

The athletic Billy was firm and fit, shadowed by a thickened layer of masculine chest hair, dark brown in the wetness. Unlike Theta, he was suntanned from the outdoor soccer practices and the love of the beach. His two-day chin growth was not an oversight but purposeful. He had shaved his neck and upper cheeks earlier to leave a hint of a well-groomed beard in the making. He rarely shaved on weekends.

Theta was eminently feminine, fully proportioned at the hips despite her lengthy five feet nine inches. Her thin lips were perfect adornments to her narrow face. Her soft skin only interrupted by the randomness of umber-colored freckles. Her figure was the dream of any man and every man.

Billy and Theta were immediately intrigued by their mutual exchange of perusal. It was an uninhibited permission extended. There was no protest to the propitious circumstance of memorizing the mystique of the opposite sex in living, breathing reality. They were both enamored. Theta's shyness was washed away in the waterfall.

Instead of dressing back into her wet two-piece, Theta threw it to her towel near her sunglasses. Billy saw the hint and smiled. He threw his on the towel too. They had both mutually accepted their bodies as meant for the eyes of the other without reservation. The sense that there was no hurry to dress was a surprise to Billy, it being Theta's initiative.

Theta was still in the swoon of her most meaningful physical moment she had ever shared. She moved to spread the oversized towel sideways for Billy to join her. She sat on the towel to a knee bend next to the wet bathing suits, her feet under her buttocks as a landing party may have seen the native Pocahontas. She adjusted to move her legs to the left, leaning on her right arm as Billy sat up next to her.

Theta again cocked her head to the left as she squeezed the water from her darkened hair.

"Theta, I—" Billy started.

She interrupted. "Billy, don't say anything. You know that I wanted it as much as you did. You have stirred my passion. I had no idea that you were both so sensitive and so honorable. I will not let you feel guilty about something so perfect. It was something that moved me and that I was drawn to share with the only person I could ever love."

The clouds were drifting away. More sunlight was focused upon them as intermittent rays of warmth skirted across them. The cloud shadows flickered. The ambient temperature was perfect.

She leaned over to kiss Billy again. Though the kiss was a confident gesture of appreciation to his caring and honorable treatment of her first total sexual experience, she also felt that he could have her again and again. They both lay back on the towel looking to the sky.

As the foliage swayed softly into the treetops of their view, their conversation drifted to their mutual appreciation of each other's attributes. Theta especially liked hearing what Billy expressed.

He gazed up and down. "Your body is exquisite and exceptional. It has surely been classically anointed by the gods."

He continued to apprise her poetically. He raved about her dark and thick red hair and the differing patterns he found in the freckles on her upper chest. He told her that she had perfectly shaped and incredibly sexy breasts.

The intimate talk, at first, made Theta blush. But it also made her feel most cherished and wanted. She became the dreamy complement of his manly frame.

Billy turned to be supported by his elbow and repeatedly kissed her soft rounded shoulder. Except for her hair, Theta was nearly dried by the breeze.

"Billy, I hope I can always be exactly what you want in a woman. You are everything I ever dreamed," Theta admitted.

Saying nothing, Billy reached to hold her again. He initiated yet another sensitive kiss. He moved his left hand to her wetted hair as they simultaneously reclined in another full embrace. Billy pulled her right knee out and up as he slowly initiated the delicate return to their newfound bliss. Theta breathed deeply as he maneuvered with a most gentle and soothing desire. She was enraptured by his gentleness and control of his actions to please her fully.

This second tryst of love on the wide towel found them more uninhibited and more passionately engaged. They would not be interrupted by nature, guilt, or protest. They were both self-assured that time would stand still for them, that the thrill and beauty of the outdoors was their domain, and that this session of pleasure would last even longer than the first. Sparrows sneered. Doves cooed in the distance. She was inflamed with the surrender of passion, her wind-dried skin shimmering from the slight perspiration of the energetic activity. His hair-covered chest dripped with both sweat and the wetness of the creek they had exited. Soft and blissful moans of delight emanated from their union until the uncontrollable zeal of its tawdry conclusion.

It was a reaffirming session of pure and selfless love that had them now panting with passion and mutual insatiability. They wanted each other profoundly.

At the conclusion, Billy rolled over to prop up and look into her green eyes again.

"Theta, are you OK?" He was nearly out of breath.

"Yes, Billy. Don't worry. I'll be fine. I am so happy that I can fully please you. I had no idea that it could be so good," Theta assessed.

They lay in the peaceful aftermath. Enthralled by the physical euphoria, Theta sat up to catch more of the breeze as Billy lay back down and rested. Theta again waded to the stream. Her sensual tingling was still evident as she stooped into the water. She bathed as a maiden of antiquity. She returned to the shore after watching Billy begin to doze off on the grassy bank.

As she lounged by the rushing fresh water, still immodestly nude, she perused the Adonis body of Billy Grayson. She wanted to memorize it. Billy dozed in the harmony of knowing the thrill of his life's new direction. She knelt down quietly before lying next to him. She studied him in his slumber—his countenance blended in the peace of a pastoral calm. She then curled in the crux of Billy's arm. She peered up to witness the clouds drifting farther apart. The sounds of the forest were as soothing as the brook rush of the water moving next to them. Billy and Theta slept in the concordance of nature.

The sun warmed them. Billy awakened, suddenly worried about Theta's fair skin in the August sunlight. He whispered to her.

"Lotion?"

She smiled and kissed him. They were kissing intermittently when Billy proposed the next detail of this unforgettable encounter. He suggested that they remain completely naked until they returned to the cabin.

"Our clothes and the towel are wet. There is no use in putting them back on to walk a short distance to take them off and then put on something dry," Billy reasoned. "Besides, Theta, if you don't mind me saying, I much prefer you naked in the sun."

Theta smiled at his conclusion. Theta was elated by the erotic realization that Billy genuinely liked seeing her naked. She loved being naked with him. She was humbly critical of her tall and gawky body and its pale hue. But it was way too late to start being modest, she concluded.

"There is nobody within miles of this place, Billy," Theta countered. "Why not extend the time a bit? I have always wondered what the Garden of Eden would feel like. Let's enjoy it as long as we can. The first of us to cover up loses! Dare?"

It was a challenge Billy would relish presently. It was a dare that could not possibly develop a loser since they remained excited by each other's physiques.

Billy was surprised that she was willing; thinking that his initial suggestion was very forward and boyishly hedonistic. But he had just made love to her twice within the past forty minutes. She was even more incredible in her lilted voice and spirited conversation, he realized. She was the epitome of feminine perfection and yet surprisingly mischievous.

"Theta, you never fail to amaze me. We've gone from me sleeping on the floor for two nights to making passionate love under a waterfall and again here. You've stolen my heart away. I am perfectly content enjoying our private Eden here and now. We can decide on when we become prudes again later!" Billy smiled. "I'm running out of dry clothes in my gym bag anyway."

Theta lifted herself upon her elbow. Her hair was still heavy with the creek water.

"Well, we can change our minds at any time. But once we dress, this chapter of our experience and memory will be gone forever. I'd like to see it last as long as possible," Theta suggested. "I want to be here for you as much as you may want to be here for me. You've seen me naked—so what?"

With that, she thought that her nakedness was now his secret alone and forever, as it inevitably was.

She lay back down as Billy rested his head in his opened left hand while leaning toward her. He yawned and decided to close his eyes again. Within a few minutes, he drifted back to a contented nap. Seeing this, Theta smiled. She leaned over to rest her head on Billy's chest. She, too, began to catnap in the security of Billy's affection and the peacefulness of the exquisite pastoral setting. They slept for a half hour.

As Billy awakened, he moved his arm to support Theta's back as she curled into him. The steady breeze had dried her skin and his hands.

Feeling him rustle awake, she leaned to kiss him. Their mouths locked before their arms embraced fully. He reached down and gently rubbed her lower back, made warm by the sun. It was already pink. She placed her hand softly upon his chest. Theta discerned that she was in the grasp of genuine and total love. It was a condition so rare, pure, and extraordinary that it had to be embraced for the brief time it may exist.

Crickets harmonized as the rushing stream gurgled past. The breeze freshened as the two of them embraced. She knew that her love was absolute and her curiosity was fully nourished. She craved all of Billy Grayson—his throbbing heart, his captivating eyes, and his physical fullness. The symphony of birds continued. Frogs croaked in the shadows. Squirrels chattered in octaves. Even the blue jays seemed enamored.

They were secluded and not likely to be disturbed. Their conversation turned to their mutual joys and the humor in things they had shared in high school.

They lay motionless before rising and lazily retreating to the shallows of the stream, hand in hand. They embraced as they dipped to sit in the cooling wash of the current. Theta waded away momentarily to enjoy the natural shower of the waterfall. She swayed her twisted and mangled strands into the refreshing flow. Billy viewed Theta in the waterfall as if recalling the Greek tale of Diana and Actaeon. Her beauty entranced him as she bathed. In the legend, Actaeon turned into a deer. Billy escaped the myths and gained the mindset that he would remain as Theta's only lover.

Billy couldn't stop staring at the perfect female form in the ideal setting after the most sensual lovemaking he could ever imagine. He waded to her, thrilled to hold her yet again. They embraced anew, kissing at every opportunity in the splash of the falls.

"I'm not putting a stitch back on until you do," Theta intimated as she expressed the exuberant joy of their carnal interludes. "I'm staying in Eden. Please do not offer me an apple!"

After the wash of the waterfall and the fine spray wetted them back into the giddy realization of their erotic interchange over the past few hours, Theta splashed Billy playfully. Billy's retribution followed. They dunked each other with childlike joy. They were both soaked again. After squeegeeing her thick hair with her cocked head, she turned to go and retrieve her sunglasses, bathing suit, and towel from the bank. Billy simply followed behind her. He caressed her as she turned back to him for another long kiss. Lithe and well proportioned, Billy realized he would never know a vision as lovely as Theta or a time so deliciously exquisite. She turned spontaneously and pressed him to her lips as if it were the most important kiss of her life.

Billy had noticed her pinkish skin tone as she walked into the rushing stream. The color developed as much by the sun and her natural blush—as by the engorgement of her passions.

"You sure you don't want me to rub sun lotion on you?" he asked.

They both laughed at the suggestion, as it was the refusal of lotion that began the chain of aroused events.

They slowly moved to stand at the bank where their eyes locked, green to green. They were each fully confident in their mating selection.

"We have to come to this waterfall in the morning," Theta announced. "Deal?"

"Deal. And you have to bring the towels for drying. But that will be all that we bring," Billy stated. "Deal?"

Theta looked up with her gorgeous emerald eyes as if answering a challenge. She at first hesitated, knowing that she had never slept in the nude. Her spontaneity would override her sense of privacy.

"Done deal," she responded.

She wiped the water spray from her face with the damp towel. She dabbed his face, as he stood before her entranced in the admiration of her beauty.

They gathered their towel-encased bathing suits and retreated to the cabin for leftover pasta and a waiting half bottle of pinot grigio. Theta reached to gather her sunglasses, as Billy took her towel and suit to place with his wet bathing trunks.

"We won't need these bathing suits anymore!" he said.

"No, Billy, and we won't need anything else but you and me and the stars tonight. Please do not wake me up from this dream, this Eden?" she asked as she thought about the romance that had stolen her heart forever. "Seriously, let's not eat the apple. Let's hold on to these moments."

CHAPTER TWELVE

Theoretical Algorithms

THE SPRING SEMESTER arrived, and after the indoctrination class, Professor Leon brought in the Boracle to lecture for forty minutes in his popular Citadel class on theoretical algorithms. The syllabus had announced the visiting septuagenarian as the world's only synesticist and an intriguing savant. The Boracle, a man of quiet humility, did not mind the introduction because it seemed to benefit the standing of his friend Thomas.

"Thank you for the graceful and promising introduction, professor," Sid began. "And I hope to take your minds along the trail of enlightenment by asking you to close them a moment before you open them."

He further explained, "Close everything you anticipate and then open yourself to what you are able to imagine."

"I'm soon to be seventy-seven years old. Today in the USA, men are expected to live 76.4 years. So in life expectancy terms, I am dead," Sid observed.

The class broke out in laughter.

"I am 0.6 over my limit," Sid began. "Giving you forty minutes of my borrowed time must be worth more to me than it is for your time. If you're juniors in college, let's assume that you are about 20.5 years old. If the expectancy charts are right for males, that will place you fellas at 73.17 percent of your life in front of you. It goes fast. Females are the beneficiaries of longevity. You live to be 81.4. That means that you have 74.82 percent of your life yet to live.

"So let's get to some life algorithms before I croak!"

The class gave the septuagenarian their full attention. He was speaking without the benefit of notes.

"Before anything is ever invented, a need or a want emerges. Questions always precede answers," Sid postulated. "There must be something to warm me when I'm cold. Fire! I wonder if mankind can ever fly like birds? Airplanes! As a society, therefore, we should always begin with questions we should be asking ourselves. In other words, we would not likely recognize an answer unless we have a relevant question that precedes it.

"Frequencies seem to be the invisible threads of the universe. What Guglielmo Marconi and Alex Bell did to enhance communication seems to have no end. We have satellite radio, Bluetooth wireless, microwave technology, and even radio telemetry telescopes for space exploration. We accept that someone somewhere knows how these things work. Question. Could we take the frequency technology down to a permanent contact lens that has endless frequencies and even download what we currently recognize as cloud-stored files? If so, could we record all that we know in our experience for the next generation to view and comprehend? Will this technology, in effect, allow us, as brain depositors to the cloud, to live forever?"

The class was in awe of the Boracle. He continued.

"Suppose we are trying to solve past conundrums. Suppose a professor like Dr. Leon reaches a breakthrough societal enhancement that's even bigger than Jiffy Pop, but his semi predictable longevity gets in the way. With the demise of the inventor, the idea may die forever. It's happened.

"Can we assume that John Keats, who died at twenty-six, would have surpassed all poets? Or that Alexander the Great, who died at thirty-three, would have conquered China? Or Vincent Van Gogh, at thirty-seven—or Raphael at thirty-three—would have further elevated the art world? They had more potential left ahead of them than what was produced for the world before their premature deaths."

It was evident to the class that the savant had no notes. He spouted off the information from his incredible powers of recall alone.

"Could a frequency theorist connect that eye lens with, for instance, sunglasses, to multiply the information a thousandfold? Will there be a new and larger information storage unit invented next week? I'll call that uninvented cache the mega-yadabyte, or myb. The myb will equate to all known human information to date. But let's suppose that in your next sixty years of life, your myb contains a multiple of what mine and Professor Leon's myb would hold today. We are the past. You are the future of mankind. So let's call the future myb an myb to the second power or myb2. We're on to something. We just invented the future by its quantity. I will be there because I will never die. My body will cease to function. My dentist will cancel my future visits, but I will live on and on."

The class was amused again.

"Change is all around us. Carbon fiber is replacing steel because it's lighter and stronger. It's much more expensive to produce, but with innovation comes saturation. That price will come down. Nearly three-quarters of all carbon fiber production comes from the U.S. and Japan. Think automobiles. But the other applications are mind-boggling. Zirutek produces carbon fiber in four countries. But prices are falling. I sold my Zirutek stock last July. Instead, I invest in the finished end of the product because of the price drop of the material. Follow the innovation to its best use.

"Robots serve us more and more in manufacturing. Why not send robots to space? Then the only errors made are inhuman errors. That's a nuance. Let the robots build the habitats. We'll move there when they're finished. It might be more out of necessity than curiosity.

The class laughed again.

"Have you ever thought about the other world we know but cannot decipher? Dreams. We all have them. Is there a dream technology that might unlock potentials we never imagined? Do dreams have gravity? Can you die in a dream and still dream? Do loved ones reappear after they have left us at the expiration of their longevity in dreams? Can you get younger in a dream?

"When someone wishes us peace and harmony, how much of either can we stand? One report stated that over the last 3,500 years, there have been only 270 years of world peace. In the twentieth century alone, nearly 110 million people have died because of conflict. Like lightning in a dying forest, is this nature's way of dealing with the stress of humanity? Lightning is thought to be the catalyst that burns the dead trees to make way for the new forest growth.

"Harmony anyone? We could argue that Cuba has harmony. A communist regime dictates harmony. China has harmony as well, but no Chinese citizen legally has a first cousin. Think about that. Is that the harmony we seek?

"Raise your hand if you've heard of a 3D image printer," Sid continued.

A dozen of the eighteen students raised their hands.

"What could this mean? An instant auto part? Maybe. A mail order for your home that prints at your home seconds after the order is placed? Yes. A new kidney? A new heart? A new brain, even? What about a border collie already housebroken?

"Will someone create an outside influence that takes people off of blood pressure medication? There is both a need and a want. It will be invented in your lifetime. I suspect it will come from music, not pharmaceuticals.

"Will supercomputers either certify or nullify the significant questions of life? Will an IBM like the one they named as Watson conclude that there was a God, but He died? Or will a MacBook resolve that the best economic avenue for Venezuela is to seek a merger with Ecuador? Can man-made monstrosities reverse global warming or disperse a hurricane? Will laser technology save the world from predicted-path meteors? Can we develop a serum that can entice humans to hibernate? Will we begin to mine valued materials from the moon or from Mars?

"The universe swirls in mayhem, yet it seems synchronized. There is life somewhere else. Believe it. It may exist as we do on hundreds if not thousands of planets. And there may be old beliefs that resurface in the new technologies. Reincarnation could be a possible consequence of interactive worlds.

"I haven't had any déjà vu lately, but it seems as though that has happened before."

Some chuckled.

"Opening the mind to endless possibilities, we have much to anticipate and much to avoid as well. Would you have any questions? Questions always precede answers," Sid reiterated.

Several smiled at the return to the initial theme.

The class began on the proper footing that Thomas desired. Curious students asked the brilliant savant a barrage of questions. Sid answered with numerical facts that were apparently not in notes he had before him. IBM's Watson had nothing on Sid Toile.

At the conclusion, Sid shook hands with his best friend Thomas and quietly left. It seemed to be an odd termination before the class had run its full fifty minutes. It was silent.

The class had been warned not to show their appreciation. Sid was as uncomfortable with applause as with any other form of gratitude. Minds were opened. Sid fertilized a class for new growth.

CHAPTER THIRTEEN

Simmons Barnwell, Esquire

IT WAS A very long day at the offices of Dr. Sonny Prioleau. His old friend Simmons Barnwell had come for his annual physical two weeks earlier. He called Simmons back to report and comment on some troubling results.

"Simmons, let's take a moment to go over some data that came from your blood tests and your EKG. Both are mildly concerning for a fella only sixty-one. You're in good physical condition, but it doesn't mean that you are necessarily in good health," the doctor began.

"Sonny, we're old friends," Simmons interrupted. "You know you don't have to mask your findings. Tell me what the concerns are and the avenues that are needed to countermand them. We old-time lawyers never try to fool the old-time judges. We just put it out there."

"Well, that makes my approach easier but doesn't change the data, Simmons," Sonny replied. "You have two major issues we have to look at immediately with follow-up. Sorry to break it to you. They are both in the direction of being life-threatening. Your EKG says you have trouble in your right ventricle wall where blood pumps into your pulmonary artery. That may be minor, or it may mean significant heart repair. There is a protocol for this issue that must be followed."

"Yep. Knew that. Tests and more tests until each testing doctor pays off the Mercedes, right?" Simmons interjected.

"That's right. I'll already get my cut from your Blue Cross, but others are waiting, you SOB! Now, do you want to listen or just be obstinate?" Sonny followed.

"I'll need to send you to get a calcium test—it measures the amount of blockage you may have by a standard relative to arterial sclerosis disease. If that test proves positive, which it likely will, then we're off to a cardiologist for a nuclear stress test. He gets his Mercedes payment before his test sends you on to get a heart catheterization. The 'heart cath' then directs the next lucky doctor to either put in a stint or do a bypass. You still wid me, Simmons?"

"OK, OK. Let's get scheduled before I croak in your office, Sonny," Simmons surrendered. "Is that all you got?"

"No. That's the easy one. We can fix hearts. The next one is hard," Sonny stated. "You wanted me to just put it out there."

"Dammit, what's worse than waiting for your heart to stop?" Simmons asked.

"Blood tests are not always conclusive. A complete blood test—a CBC—can indicate harsh variations in blood counts. You have that situation. In laymen terms, the blood counts could tell us that you have cancer. It's too early to tell, but your blood is out of whack," Sonny said. "Let's hope this is just an aberration."

"Type, doc?" Simmons asked.

"Too early to know. We have to take a closer look. This protocol may take longer and involve more doctors. You won't like it. There are measurements, biopsies, and radical treatments that I'm sure you've heard about," Sonny related. "But there are nuances too. If it's cancer and it's early, there are cutting-edge treatment centers most everywhere—Houston, New York, Cleveland, and LA come to mind."

"Give me a name of the cancer you would suspect, Sonny," Simmons pressed. "I want to know what they'll write on the death certificate before I die from the stress of waiting to get a professional opinion from you."

"Leukemia is the most likely cause of your blood abnormalities, Simmons. Leukemia. But don't fret that now," Sonny detailed with concern. "It has to be tested by the experts. I'm setting you up with an oncologist this afternoon. You should get in immediately."

Sonny continued, "Your heart calcium screening will be at two o'clock on Monday at the University Hospital Clinic in Mount Pleasant. Cancel your appointments. Be there."

"Sonny, I can't say it's been good to see you. But I am glad that whatever may come, you will guide me as a friend. Hellfire, I might become the very first person in history to have my cause of death to read 'cancer and heart attack.' I'd make all the medical journals. If we do this just right, they could both kill me at the same exact moment."

Though amused by Simmons's untimely humor, Sonny was too distraught at the prospect of losing a lifelong friend to smile at the suggestion.

"Simmons, you have always had and will always have my prioritized care. You can call me at midnight or on weekends. You know that. If there is something you do not understand going through these tests, call me. I may not have every answer, but I can sure find them when you need them," Sonny stipulated. "What are you going to tell Martha?"

"Not a damn thing, Sonny. And I don't want anything coming from you either. Our secret," Simmons explained. "She'll be worse living with by a multiple if she gets wind of this. Let's hold out until this god-awful news is vital. I may tell Theta because she can handle it and she'll be there for me when I need a lift."

Simmons got up to shake hands with his old friend.

"And don't send me a bill for staying in your office five minutes too long," Simmons concluded.

The words that Simmons feared came in twos. He may have a life-threatening heart impairment and leukemia simultaneously. Being ever mindful of others, he immediately decided to find out about leukemia before he decided on his heart remedy. If he was to die slowly of cancer, why prolong the event by disrupting his wife's and daughter's lives with recovery from heart surgery?

Wouldn't a sudden and fatal heart attack be a much more desired result anyway? He thought.

CHAPTER FOURTEEN

Come Away with Me

(As It Happened, Eight Years Earlier)

BILLY LIT THE fireplace—though the heat was not needed in their blood-hot encounter. It was not necessary to reignite a tender mood, but the fire made the evening setting perfect. The flames flickered, and the logs hissed from the moisture. They lay side by side on the worn leather sofa, a bedsheet easing the friction from the cowhide surface stitching to their warmed and bare skin.

Billy plugged his black iPod playlist through a jack into a cheap surround-sound system that went to the nonworking console television. The speakers played perfectly when turned down to a background setting. Billy's melodic mixture set the evening's ambiance to a subtler mode than the heavy metal that Jackie had played the night before. Van Morrison, James Taylor, and Allison Krause regaled the cooing couple with old love ballads. There were old standards their parents knew—from Cat Stevens, John Denver, and Carly Simon. The mood was slow and quite romantic. Billy's iPod was plugged in and charging so that the soft music would not stop for hours.

Staring into the flames with the chill of wine emboldened them for the evening's rediscovery of their conversational compatibility. After speaking about their commonalities over the music and the fire's spitting surges, the conversation turned to childhood adventures. Theta detailed cuts and stitches from her mishaps. Billy had a broken foot from a sports injury and detailed a scary bout of cat-scratch fever. The infection swelled his left arm for several days.

They spoke of their family vacations and grade school teachers. Billy made an observation that was appropriately timed.

"Talking with you when we were in high school, in the times between, and now is, well, something I would not have predicted. But I realize this is crazy special. It is a never-ending conversation of such interest that it heightens my mood and intelligence at the same time!" Billy detailed. "And there is more to you than a lovely face. I knew that all along."

"Ditto, Billy. I knew that about you before you knew that about me!" Theta replied as a boast of calculated insight. "We fit each other intellectually. We have a common interest level. We are suited in our temperament as well. We're both easygoing and mellow. Would you agree?"

"I'd just add that we fit each other. Take that to any particular ideal of our romance," Billy announced as he smiled.

They discovered new passing enticements, new chides, and new taunts to seduce each other into the dreamy and blissful dusk. She aroused him, and he titillated her. They held each other in the welling of passion—seeing, feeling, and caressing each other with coy conversation—followed by quiet and then short peaceful reflection.

In an elongated pause, they embraced and stopped to stare into each other's eyes. They were entranced. Ironically, the background music was playing Alison Krauss's "When You Say Nothing at All." The musical lyrics came forth softly in their quiet pause. They didn't speak until the song was nearly over.

"Theta, if I never made love to you again, I would be heartbroken but so very happy that we have reached a complete contentedness together," Billy reflected. "Let's always remember this fire."

They gazed at each other contentedly.

"I would be a fool to not crave you every waking minute," Billy added.

The musical chorus continued as they listened.

The smile on your face lets me know that you need me.
There's a truth in your eyes saying you'll never leave me.
The touch of your hand says you'll catch me wherever I fall.
You say it best when you say nothing at all.

Theta spoke up as the stanza drifted. She reflected upon her loss of virginity.

"Billy, I didn't know what to expect. It hurt, but I suppose it was natural. But, Billy, the tingle is also natural. I feel so close and connected to you. It's maybe a woman's emotion or intuition. Do you feel anything special like I do?" Theta offered. Her eyelids fluttered sweetly.

"Theta, I never thought I could fall so deeply in love with someone so fast. But I admit that I have always felt like we would end up together. It was because we could relate to each other in that never-ending conversation," Billy explained. "To always be elevated by words spoken and feelings shared—that, to me, is what makes a relationship permanent."

Theta was gladdened. She found a heightened confidence of commitment in Billy's insight. They exchanged loving glances even more prosaic than their verbal interaction.

She readjusted her torso to a twist so that she could initiate a heartfelt kiss as her reassuring response to Billy's last words. They touched her. Another pause of conversation ensued as they caressed. The embrace coincided with the song's final refrain from the mantel's speakers.

The touch of your hand says you'll catch me if wherever I fall.
You say it best when you say nothing at all.

Theta whispered after they both absorbed the words.

"My personal discovery of true and innocent passion will never leave me. I will yearn for you always. And it sends me flying to know that you want me as much as I want you," Theta interjected. "Let's hold each other. And you are permitted to discover me all over again as you wish. But let's wait a bit more on the lovemaking if we can."

The seat belt warnings from their ride to the cabin on Friday were no longer needed. Their entire world was unfastened.

Billy immediately brought Theta's angelic face to his. He kissed her and held her next to him in recline. She adjusted from the awkward twist of her shoulders and moved closer, placing her dark hair on his muscular chest. She was unabashed by it all as if she had accepted that their natural state was to be nude and entangled.

Billy reached around to the small of her back and began rubbing the area softly with the knuckles on the back of his right hand.

"Theta, I'll adjust the fire, and we'll leave the music on. But let's go to bed," Billy suggested.

Theta took her half glass of pinot and the bedsheet with her. She coyly wrapped the sheet around her shoulders and pulled it to a clasp at her neck. The pull of the endorphins made her sleepy like she experienced as a little girl at the reading of a fairy tale.

This adult fairy tale was as much an enchantment as any she had memorized, but it was charmingly real.

Billy poked the simmering logs back to the rear of the fireplace and replaced the safety screen folded back to the wall. He turned the music down a notch and opened the two windows wider to expose the cabin to more of the natural airflow. He felt the persistent breeze stream from the den into the bedroom. It was as if the cooling gusts had guided him to a destiny he would cherish forever.

As Billy came through the bedroom doorway, the freshening air ruffled the bedsheet from across Theta's legs. It showed her lying demurely on her stomach with her head up, waiting for Billy. He joined her, forgetting that Theta's bed had the creakiest box springs in the county. His bodyweight brought the springs to a new pitch. They both laughed at the creakiness.

"I was afraid to move last night for fear that I might wake not only you but Jackie and Frieda across the den too," Theta stated. "This box spring is a nuisance—or like something from a bad fright movie."

"Maybe we can get it to play a song tonight," Billy hinted. "Or at least it can humor us if we get too frisky!"

Theta winked demurely.

She sipped the last of her wine, placing the glass on the nightstand. She and Billy began talking anew about dreams they wished and the providence of circumstance that had them in a state of euphoric happiness. As Kelly Clarkson's "A Moment like This" played from the den mantel, Billy fell off to sleep. Theta looked at the man she loved, kissed him on the cheek, and followed off to join his dreams.

Some people wait a lifetime for a moment like this.
Everything changes, but beauty remains.
Something so tender I can't explain.

Just after midnight, another shower came through, the rain landing softly on the turned tin roof. Theta got up to check the den windows for water, but the overhangs prevented its intrusion. The music from the iPod was still playing softly from the mantel. Theta turned it down slightly.

She tiptoed back to bed and cuddled to Billy's torso, smelling the freshness of the rain. She tried to limit the creak in the springs and not wake Billy. But Billy had stirred and turned back toward her, half awake.

Theta opened her eyes to see him looking at her. She began to stroke the furry hair of Billy's abdomen.

"Billy, do you want to go back to sleep?" she asked coyly.

"And miss this moment with you?" Billy whispered back. "I'm dreaming that I am with the most beautiful creature on earth and that she lies next to me. I am stirred by the lure of rain as it marches in spurts across the roof. Rain is such a great mood setter. I'm dreaming that these moments will never end."

"Billy, would you do me a favor?" Theta asked innocently.

"Anything, Theta. I can't think of a reason I'd ever turn you down," he replied willingly while turning up on his shoulder. The bed creaked loudly.

"I'm awake, and my mood is such that I'm selfish. I want you to be awake with me. I love this rain too. It's so relaxing. I never realized how sexy rain could be at midnight. I want to feel you close beside me. I want the softness of the breezes on my back and hear the nighttime speak to me, to hear the roof play tunes and the gutters gurgle the water away. I want to listen to the loons and owls so that this moment will always be. And I want to make love to you again!"

Billy was enamored by the lilting angelic voice of a willing and wanting partner. His eyes glared in the consumption of a new passion. They kissed vehemently as Theta moved her stomach to his.

She raised her head to look into his eyes.

"I want you to teach me to be a great lover so that I will always exceed your expectations," she intimated in a low tone.

"But you are already the greatest lover ever, Theta," he answered.

Billy was surprised to hear Theta wants to learn to be even sexier than she had unintentionally been by being soft, caring, patient, and natural.

"There is nothing we can teach each other, Theta," Billy continued to speak tenderly in whispers. "You are classically gorgeous, receptive, willing, selfless, and sensuous. You are brilliantly conversational, and best of all, you are spontaneous. It is you that teaches me. Our love could not be deeper. Our lovemaking couldn't be any better. We are ideal lovers."

Theta was turned on. The catalyst of rapturous rain, the mystique of night, and the whispered words conspired to develop their consensual longing.

The box springs creaked anew.

They started slowly by moving the pillows up to the head of the bed. Theta took Billy's hand slowly to her fully anticipating right breast. She placed her hand on top of his. He kissed her neck before moving his exploring lips to her bosom. The bed creaked with each affectionate move. Theta moved her hands like a masseuse in circles of sensual patterns to his upper chest. Billy rolled toward her. Their slow explorations were both delightful and encouraged.

The flickering embers from the den fireplace cast shadows upon the opposite wall. The iPod music began playing an old Cat Stevens's song, "Into White." Billy turned his focus to other parts of Theta's desirable figure. The bed creaked with synchronicity. The moistened breeze from the screened window cooled them both. They could hear the trees rustle to and fro as the pulsed winds brought in the flourishing sprinkles of the midnight shower.

Theta spoke in low tones, expressing great comfort in the care Billy exerted in his caressing attention. He was fully prepared by her suggestive hands to forgo his desires in favor of her full and genuine pleasure. No words were said for several minutes in the building crescendo of passion that led to their next ecstatic engagement. It was as if the creaky box spring lost its voice over the moments.

Theta was fully ignited within her petition of surrender. Billy was momentarily surprised as she rolled over to lie on top of him. She was sexually emboldened, and he enjoyed the nuance. They were delicately engaged. The physical interaction was not rushed.

"Billy," Theta swooned, "please go slowly. I want this to last forever. And know that I want you always."

A most unusual thought crept into Billy's mind. It was at a time when they were fully interlocked. He had to ask.

"Theta, what about protection? I know this is a bad time to ask..." Billy glanced at her delighted facial expression. Her forehead was intense with anticipation of the joy Billy enthusiastically accommodated. They were compelled by their mutually selfless attention.

"Billy, you have nothing to worry about now. I am just a few days past my new cycle. Two weeks in would be different," Theta reported as she moved lovingly in syncopation of nature's accord.

"Do you want me to stop now?" She challenged him in jest. She was wriggling in a new and previously unknown passion as the initiator of the conjugation. The activity thrilled Billy. He realized that Theta had an unexplored bedroom spontaneity. The future permeations could be delightful.

"No diseases, of course," she added as she giggled.

She was slightly embarrassed by each new sensation of joy she was experiencing for the first time. Billy knew that this was yet another new level of rapture for Theta. He was gentle—yet energetic. He focused solely on her satisfaction. She began to cry with joy in her release of passion and appreciation of Billy's controlled lovemaking. Their breathing heightened. Their hearts were ablaze.

The iPod played a Norah Jones ballad softly in the background, "Come Away with Me." The words were a natural syncopation of the moment.

And I want to wake up with the rain
Falling on a tin roof
While I'm safe there in your arms
So all I ask is for you
To come away with me in the night
Come away with me.

Billy kissed her neck and then her opened mouth. They stayed in the clutch of full and complete love for moments beyond. Eric Clapton's song "Change the World" filled the background of their afterglow. In a moment, Theta disengaged from her top position and rolled over next to him. They both lay face up listening to the soothing Clapton lyrics and feeling the fresh rain air waft across them.

For several long minutes, they exhaled together, catching their breath and slowing their heartbeats. Theta took Billy's hand in hers to her bare right breast again to feel the intense thumping of her heart. The breeze felt soothing to both. The rain continued its tin march. No words were spoken as they slowed to their concordant realizations. They loved each other without hesitance, without borders, and without reservation. The long Clapton tune played through. The lovers remained contented in their post-coital silence.

A Rita Coolidge song drifted from the den speakers.

All I wanted was a sweet distraction for an hour or two
Had no intention to do the things we've done
Funny how it always goes with love, when you don't look, you find
But then we're two of a kind, we move as one.

Billy broke the silence with humor.

"Yeah, I have no diseases either." It was a response from Theta's last words nearly ten minutes earlier.

Theta laughed at the timing.

They had explored nuances, desires, and fantasies consensually. The creaky springs were in the rhythm of their overactive contortions, but they did not hear them.

Billy then added, "You know, Theta, this was the first time we made love in a bed—our first indoor experience."

She giggled again. "And I suspect we'll find a better mattress and box spring in our future."

"I never heard it," Billy cajoled.

They had made love three times since the noon hour. They both felt that three lovemaking sessions in a day would be a temporary record. Their relationship was well beyond lust. They genuinely cared for each other in what both believed was rapturous love overflowing like the statue-laden promiscuity heralded through the ages in the fountains of Rome.

What followed was a resolute goodnight kiss that sealed a relationship poetically. They both lay together nude under a single sheet. The unrelenting breeze was their whisper of forever love.

They fell off to a dreamy, secure, and contented sleep.

CHAPTER FIFTEEN

Joey Preticos

"AT&T HAS MOVED up three-eighths. Sell, man, sell," Joey Preticos suggested.

The Boracle looked up to see a balding forty-something-year-old man with a scruffy shadow of a beard. His voice was a rasp contorted within another grating sound.

Joey Preticos was of Greek lineage but was a seventh-generation Charlestonian. His grandfather Demetri was one of the last of the corner grocers who pervaded the Holy City peninsula in the 1880s. The Preticos Grocery at the corner of Rutledge and Vanderhorst carried milk, bread, cereal, and candy. But their most profitable retail sales came from beer. Burger Beer was cheap and cold. His back driveway was paved with Burger Beer bottle caps and crushed rock.

It can be said that Charleston's earliest country clubs were the Greek corner grocers who kept the beer cold near the rear ceiling fan out of the view of the Charleston youth. The workers from the State Ports

Authority and the naval shipyard repair facilities would gather after five o'clock each weekday. The blue-collar crowd assembled. Demetri Preticos sold nearly eight cases a day, one beer at a time.

Grandson Joey Preticos had a small home on the newer side of the Old Village in Mount Pleasant. On his business card, it said that he sold commercial real estate. But Joey Preticos only made three commercial sales in ten years. One was his mother's flower shop. He boosted his income from being a bookmaker of mostly illegal bets.

"Joey, why would you want me to sell anything that had a healthy dividend?" Sid countered. "That's the problem with financial markets. People guess at highs and lows to move something because they become personally fidgety. The only time I ever lost significant money by holding stock was the W. T. Grant stock I bought in the 1970s for two dollars a share. I figured that stock couldn't go any lower. Well, zero is lower than two."

They both laughed at the sarcasm.

Joey Preticos was a good-natured guy without the benefit of direction. He was gruff, interruptive, urbane, and loud. He liked the Boracle and was apt to stop by to see what all the fuss was about as people waited to see him at booth 14.

"Sid, you wanna make real money quick, take the Dolphins at home and nine and a half against the Chargers on Monday night. It's a lock," Joe offered.

Sid smiled. Joey knew that Sid would never gamble.

"No thanks, Joey. I have a lock on other investments. They may take a few decades longer than yours, but I enjoy the stagnant joy of a slower success," Sid replied.

Joey Preticos wore an open button-down shirt, high-tide blue jeans, penny loafers, and white socks. His white socks made him unique enough to fit the role of a recognizable bookie. It was his "marking insignia" to advertise his chosen vocation to new bettors. They saw the white socks as the signal of his professional commitment much like a journeyman plumber would have a crescent wrench on his business card.

He was forty pounds past his last diet. His right hand was adorned with a large signet ring. He wore a magnetic copper bracelet and two gold-plated chain necklaces. One was a twenty-inch choker, the other a thinner twenty-seven-inch chain with a silver cross. He was not religious. He immersed himself in the trinkets of luck. Luck was his north star. His hair was dark and long on the sides—combed back and shiny. A Chicago Cubs ball cap sometimes covered the baldness. His tan was permanent and hinted that he may have owned a yacht on the Caribbean. He couldn't afford a used oar of a beached rowboat.

Joey took too many pills. He had baby aspirin, Tylenol, Tums, and Ambien PM. His blood pressure readings for someone so young were borderline dangerous. He drank a few beers daily. He had to have a large regular coffee every morning. He kept a small spiral notepad in his top shirt pocket. He was on his way to pick up bets for the weekend from regular clients. His payouts were made every Wednesday.

"Joey, I know that what you do can be lucrative. But I've not met many with the patience to just earn the profits in the middle. The instinct that all gamblers have is that they are more knowledgeable than the people who set the odds. Then there's a countermeasure in gambling that has been historical. The players, managers, game officials, and even the owners are 'on the take.' The know-it-all gamblers don't figure on that. In the end, everyone loses. It's the temporary exhilaration of winning that compels otherwise smart people to give it all away, knowing the final result will be the same for them as it is for everyone in that industry . . . They—"

"Sid, I get it," Joey interrupted. "It's what I do. Can't change. Been doing it for nearly twenty years. Your point is made."

"Sorry, Joey, I get carried away. What's troubling you?" Sid waited to hear what he likely already knew.

"Sid, when I sold the family flower shop by the hospitals, I took the money and put it in an account to support my mother's last few years at home. Being an only child, I was there nearly every day. I didn't work in real estate. I only brokered bets. It was the easiest schedule for me. It meant so much to her that I was there. But it was painful to see the effects of the Parkinson disease and that awful daily routine she had to face. I couldn't bear it. So when she passed last October, I lost a sense of family and even a sense of doing something legitimate. I made good money. You're right, I tried to leverage the fees into the games, and I lost," Joey admitted.

Joey wiped the sweat from his forehead with a handkerchief. He was visibly nervous about the admonition, not just to Sid but also to himself.

"Joey, what do you make in a typical week from the fees—without gambling?" Sid asked the question to ease the conversation and settle Joey's demeanor.

Joey thought for a moment before answering.

"The sports schedule determines the income, Sid. For instance, I make a ton in the fall from college and pro football going on—at the same time as the baseball playoffs. I get a big wave of bets during the NCAA basketball tournament. Volume keeps me busy but pays a lot," Joey explained.

"How much on average, then?" Sid pursued the number.

"Some of the young guys make about $400 a week. I have a wider clientele because I'm single and can get to all the joints on my route. I've had good weeks where I've vig'd out at $950. But then there are weeks we only make about $200. Typically, I make about $600 a week."

"By vig'd, do you mean vigorish?" Sid asked.

"Yeah, the vig is what we say, but we never use the vigorish term. They'll know you're a rook," Joey explained.

"So you make maybe thirty grand a year with the risk of arrest and muggings? You probably carry a weapon? Why would you feel this can vault you to prosperity unless you placed bets as well?" Sid asked questions in multiples.

"Sid, I get it. That's why I'm here," Joey continued. "I've lost all the money from my mother's inheritance. I have no sources to cover losses, and I'm in debt worse than I've ever been. I'll pick up maybe $800 next week from the vig. But I'll have to hit a long odd with that money to pay last week. I've got the Dolphins on a lock at home. I have to take it and hope like hell."

"Joey, I like you. But if you think I can predict games, well, I can't," Sid began. "I can predict outcomes from the bigger picture.

Let's suppose you win enough to put off the amount owed until you can pay it with four straight long-odds winners over the next month. That would get you even. But you would agree that this type of run in gambling is highly unlikely."

"So what do I do, Sid?" Joey asked.

"Quit," he shot back.

"And pay these thugs how?" Joey said with a touch of sarcasm.

"I'm guessing that you're into this at a manageable level. Wean from the bookmaking and go legit. List properties. You'll sell something in the next six months to take care of a $10,000 bet. Do you owe more than that?" Sid followed.

"Sid, you don't understand this business. You don't walk away. You limp away if you're lucky. And that's from a broken kneecap," Joey confided.

Sid countered, "Nobody is going to react in that manner for what you owe. It's workable. If the debt is to one person or two, just have them call me. I'll vouch for you. Then they will set up a repayment plan. You'll see."

Joey looked at Sid in a skewered glance, somewhat in the realization that he did not get across the ramifications of not paying debts in the gambling underworld. He realized that he was spilling his guts to someone who was too naïve and innocent to understand the seriousness of his position. He thanked the Boracle and got up from the booth to retreat from the conversation that had no viable direction that he'd follow. He knew that Sid's solution was both wrong and right.

"Sid, I'll consider your advice, but right now, I've gotta place an important bet. Wish me luck," Joey said as he turned away.

He left embarrassed that he had spilled his soul to the miracle man and not found comfort in the resolution offered. The only positive is that Sid did hit a nerve. Joey wanted his childhood friends to believe that he was a commercial realtor because it made him feel accomplished. He sincerely wished he could become someone more respected and legitimate.

Sid looked up and said to himself, "Poor Joey. There is no good end to a bad endeavor." He knew that Joey would not accept the solution offered.

By the week's end, Joey's fortunes had predictably turned. Sid was right. He had $9,500 bet on the Dolphins trying to raise money to pay his last locked bet loss from the week before. He did not have that $9,500 either. His unfunded bet was "booked" by a suspicious contact, Tony Muzon. Known as Tony the Blade, Joey had not considered the full consequences of obtaining funding through a crime family in Philadelphia. The weekly interest rate was 20 percent. It was the beginning of a most horrendous cycle for Joey Preticos. The Dolphins lost at home in Miami on national television that Monday night, 31–10.

Joey Preticos had no buffer, no stash of emergency funds, and no equity interest in any other ventures with which to barter. He knew the consequence that was just days away. Gamblers eat their own kind.

CHAPTER SIXTEEN

Seatbelts

(As It Happened, Eight Years Earlier)

AS BILLY AND Theta awoke the next morning, a mist appeared that rolled from the river to the cabin, made eerily beautified by the beams of the rising sun. They lay uncovered vertically across the bed on their stomachs. The sheet was draping the side of the bed to the floor. The constancy of the pulsating breeze sifted through the cabin, from the front screen door across to the windows on the creek side. Billy reached to reassure Theta that he was still there and still real. He placed his large right hand across the middle of her randomly freckled back.

He yawned aloud. Theta followed with her own quiet yawn.

"Theta, I should have put lotion on you. You are slightly past pink. Does it hurt?" Billy asked. He had not noticed her skin tone in the muted light the night before.

She turned to look at him and smiled.

"Hold that thought," she said. "I've gotta get up and brush my teeth."

She closed the door to use the bathroom, brush her teeth, primp her tousled hair, and spray a hint of her perfume. She looked at herself in the mirror to see a glow that had heretofore not existed. She was not ashamed or remorseful. She did not feel that she had broken with tradition or committed sin. It was the opposite. She felt completed and enamored with a new life with Billy that had been fully enhanced less than twenty-four hours before. It was not as if Theta had lost anything. Rather, she had found something.

She coupled the few introspective moments in the bathroom with slight adjustments to her appearance. The overnight activities had left her in a more disheveled natural state than what she hoped to present to Billy when she returned to their creaky mattress.

Theta dampened her milky skin with a hand towel. She retrieved a small dispenser of Jergens lotion from her toiletries. She brushed her hair again—back behind her ears to gain a semblance of personal neatness. She dabbed more of her Gypsy Kiss perfume to her pinked neck and chest.

Billy had gone to the other bathroom. He performed what was hygienically needed for the morning's acceptability by dabbing a minimum of aftershave on his bold and bristly chin. He was back on the bed before she returned.

Theta reentered their noisy love nest and sat next to him on the bed. They kissed good morning, each with the freshened breath of their chosen toothpaste. It was the kiss of a first morning as if they were honeymooners. They both faced the window. Their nakedness continued the natural course of mutual arousal. Their gaze was upon the small open meadow and the pathway to the riverbank.

"Now you can put lotion on me," Theta announced. She handed him the dispenser bottle and reclined to her stomach with her arms stretched upward over her head.

Billy rubbed the lotion in his hands to warm it and applied it to her shoulders, arms, back, buttocks, and back of her legs, where her skin was pink.

"Thanks, Billy. You forgot the front," Theta reminded as she turned over. "Take your time."

It was a most alluring prospect.

Theta lay out flat on the creaky bed, her head upon the pillow looking to Billy's focused eyes. They were afire with stimulation. Billy applied the warmed lotion sensually until all the pinkness was soothed.

"I can't hardly wait to get you pink again," Billy chided. "But then again, it was a lotion that caused our first misunderstanding. Let's stay away from those crazy things from now on. Honesty always works best."

Theta was feeling new sensations and wanted to kiss Billy. She reached up to him. They caressed.

Frogs serenaded the morning with mixed-pitch croaks only yards away. Squirrels were playing in stunted spurts across the old rusty turned-tin roof. The misty streams of morning's light twirled in the freshened damp foliage. The birds were louder than before as newborn chicks waited their morning feeding. Small mushrooms had popped out of every shadow across the open field and down the meandering foot trail. It was pastorally perfect.

Theta swiveled to twist her torso to Billy's side, pulling his neck down again to her. They kissed and paused to lie still silently. It was their shared instinct to ponder the succulent sensitivities of the moment. Their intimacy had simmered and boiled in both endless afterglow and tireless desire.

"You ready for day two, Billy?" Theta demurely asked. "I feel like I'm in a Brontë novel or a character from Tolstoy."

"Try Elizabeth Barrett Browning. 'Let me count the ways,' my dear!" Billy answered. "I'm still dreaming. I cannot believe this is happening," he continued. "I'm with someone so deliciously gorgeous yet so conversationally suited that I can't figure what I like best—but your body is moving into first place right now. And this fresh view of morning allows us to take in the splendor of nature, the time, and each other. I do believe I am dreaming."

Billy kissed her on her sun-splotched shoulder blades. "That's a place I missed last night," he submitted. "I want to kiss every part of you every day."

He took one more squirt of the lotion to apply to Theta's neck. He applied the lotion slowly and then placed the Jergens dispenser on the nightstand next to the empty wine goblet. Theta was expecting their next encore as Billy delicately spread the excess of the warm lotion across her breasts. She looked deeply into his loving eyes as the thrilling touch sensation enticed them both.

They lay exhilarated within their mutual tantalization. They had enjoyed a deep and blissful night of sleep. The creaky springs still reminded both of their very active lovemaking at midnight. Theta giggled at the reminder as she turned to allow Billy a better reach to her upper back and neck area. She was aware that the creaking springs could get intense again momentarily. She craved him.

The window view accentuated the morning sun burning off the shards of mist that crossed the meadow. The color and size of the fresh mushrooms became more prominent with the changing sunlight. They had volunteered from the germination of the earth in their own titillation. They grew in varied shapes and shades of gray, brown, and orange.

Theta decided to be provocative.

"I'd bet that stream water has cooled down overnight," she stated softly. "I suppose you have cooled down too," she taunted as she slightly turned away from Billy.

Billy's challenge of spontaneity was proposed. He would perform the unexpected—a cornerstone theme of their growing relationship.

"I was thinking the same. I'm hot right now. Really too hot for you! Going to the waterfall would be like taking a cold shower," he teased.

"Let's go and enjoy what nature provides, Eve." Billy referenced her fascination with the biblical Genesis. "Paradise is still sleeping."

Theta smiled at the assertion. She thought he was kidding about going outside to shower.

She replied, "Surely, the mother of all humanity had much more allure than a skinny freckled redhead. Redheads always prefer the safe indoor option of convenient comforts and creaky beds."

She began sitting up with her back to Billy. She then pushed Billy's roving hand away in jest as if she had been mistaken for a poodle needing a sudsy bath. She stared at him provocatively and then reclined demurely and to expose her full and stunning chest to him again. She assumed that he would get the sexy hint.

"If I were not naked, I'd just be another boring passerby," Theta offered humbly.

Billy changed the playful subject.

"Theta, you are most critical of yourself. Please don't denigrate the woman I love," Billy demanded. "Besides, your beauty is beyond. High-paid models will never have what you possess—a soul of beauty. As ravenous as you are, this will pass, but your soul of beauty is a constant. Your nakedness is just an extra inducement!"

Theta smiled at his insight as she blushed.

Billy then doubled down on his idea of a natural shower. "Let's retrace where it all began. Just relax. I'll carry you."

"No, Billy, it's going to be cold," she coyly protested. "Wait for the sun to warm the water. Let's stay here. I'll let you explore me in the daylight."

As she curled away from him to remain lazily in the bed, she continued pleading that they should stay inside. Her rebuttal was like an ambulance-chasing lawyer trying to convince a judge that the client's impaired income approached a Fortune 500 level. Billy was not impressed by her reticence to get wet.

"We don't need no stinkin' sun," Billy quipped much like a scripted movie line. He stood up from the creaky bed and started to lift her.

"No, Billy. You wouldn't!" she exclaimed.

Billy could not resist. He grinned deviously with a frisky plan of a new arousal. He then lifted her fully nude, quivering and anticipating body into his outstretched athletic arms.

"It's time for our morning shower, Eve," he announced.

With that, he cradled and carried her from the cabin and down the path all the way to the waiting waterfall. He counted out loud to build up the anticipation of the cold-water immersion. There were twenty-three broad steps from the side porch to the stream. He stopped the count at the water's edge, wading in with her arms wrapped tightly around his neck. She laughed loudly as he managed her folded body in his athletic stride. He rumbled in a heavy breath toward the sound of the falls.

"Put me down! Put me down! It's going to be cold!" she protested.

Their spontaneity meant no towels and no shoes would be available when they finished. Billy had no concern whatsoever—only childlike frolic and the exchange of fond caresses.

He waded in all the way to the falls and tossed her sideways into the heavy rushing shower. She was at once shocked by the temperature change.

Theta feigned being hurt, folding her slender arms in to cover her breasts as if to counteract the sudden chill. She turned away. Then she turned back with a broad and scheming smile. She chuckled at the prospect of more teasing play. She immediately leaped to him to be thrown again. They jumped and splashed and hugged and then waded away from each other. Their cold shower did nothing to quell their passion for each other.

She splattered water at him coyly as he turned to advance. He clutched her waist and kissed nearly every wet inch of her chilled curves. She anxiously caressed his craning neck, melting into the moment. Their green eyes locked before their bodies followed. Their mating sounds could scarcely be heard past the roar of the waterfall. They moved slowly to the grassy mud bank, continuing to find contorted positions untried—the silliness of mud now a part of a whirlwind romantic dance.

They kissed unceasingly and stirred rhythmically within the morning's yawn. Newfound love was presently total, exhilarating, and uninhibited. Their bodies enthusiastically intertwined in artful collusion. They were entranced into each other's full commitment of sensual and giving love. After twenty heavenly minutes of rapture, they reached the mutual conclusion of nature's happy reward.

The accompaniment of the wind played across the treetops in continuous waves over the past twenty-four hours. It was ever present and exhilarating.

They collapsed in frenzied joy, napping another half hour, her cheek upon his chest. Their heartbeats exceeded their deep breathing. Their perusing eyes gazed upon the high trees where the breeze continued to play other natural rhythms. They were completely absorbed into the place and the moment when love again invaded their souls. The muddy experience did not have to be spoken as one that was above or equal to others that they would ever enjoy. Each association was its own unique memory. Their hunger was nourished; their fantasies flourished.

There was more mud covering Theta's body than her pink-skin exposure. Billy's back was black from their earliest love position. Theta's hair was muddy. Billy wiped the creek bank from her neck and jaw. They laughed at the result of their uncaring roll upon the elements. Hog farmers had piglets cleaner than either of them.

They realized that they had not bothered to bring the towels they suggested from the day before. They were indeed alone in nature without any man-made enhancements. The biblical Adam would have been proud.

In a moment, they waded hand in hand back to the waterfall, rinsing each other lovingly. They each took their time in the fresh spray of falling water. They caressed. Theta and Billy had become as one. They waded to the shore and walked back to the cabin where they dried off with the towels they had left behind.

Theta placed the last two bagels in the toaster while Billy retrieved the cream cheese from the refrigerator. He poured two glasses of orange juice and set them upon the small kitchen counter.

"We need the vitamin C," he stated. "And I might need to get a Sam's Wholesale crate full of vitamin E."

Theta knew the biological reason for the reference. She turned to Billy after checking the toaster.

"Billy, I wouldn't change one thing about you or your vitamin mix," she assessed. "You don't need anything but me in front of you. And you're all I will ever need."

Billy smiled. He knew the statement to be honest and true.

They sat at the stools by the counter to slowly consume the simple breakfast. They continued to exchange stares, pleasantries, and short kisses. Their attention then turned to straightening the cabin and packing to leave.

Theta had already placed the linens and towels in the washer while the bagels toasted.

The wine bottles from Jackie and Frieda's bedroom and the den were collected. Billy gathered all other trash items to one large hefty bag. He tied it at the top.

They stopped to sit for a moment on the cracked leather sofa. Theta's hair was still damp from the waterfall. She did not want to get any of the cloth fabric wet that adorned the den chairs. They kissed and embraced without words.

"Theta, I have a practice match at six at Dodd stadium. I'll need to leave in time to get back. Coach Norman is a stickler for punctuality," Billy stated. "But I really never want to leave this place. I wish I could stay with you forever."

Theta showed a wry smile for an instant. She slightly nodded her wetted head while responding.

"You'd get tired of me. I'd want you all the time. That would be too stifling for a man of your background. You'd escape, and I'd be an emotional wreck. I will want you forever. But I know that our forever includes being responsible. I have my harp practice at six and need to pick up my new books for my English 201 class sometime before it starts tomorrow."

She then paused before saying words in the moment that she would never regret.

"Billy, my life changed. I am different than the girl you knew a day ago. And I'm not talking about surrendering my virginity. I have breathed you into my life. I hope this is not a passing memory but a forever state of devotion."

Theta again had baby tears as the words drifted.

Theta often cried when something touched her. Billy saw her cry from their joyous interludes so often that he accepted that her heart was pure and overfilled with love. The tears became another component that propelled Billy's love for this unique and flawless creature of warmth.

Her prosaic verbalizations were most appreciated. They enjoyed well-chosen and meaningful expressions. It would be another mutual attribute.

Billy answered her succinctly. "Theta, I will never know a more intense and profound love. Our bodies are a minor part of it. You have me forever if I am worthy."

He spoke directly to her with her green eyes melting in the moment. Theta's happiness tears continued to wet her cheeks.

She quivered anew and then simply stated, "I love you, Billy Grayson."

They embraced and held each other tightly while sitting nude on the den sofa. The embrace was long and loving, only to be interrupted by the reality of time.

"Let's get this show back on the road," Theta suggested.

They packed their duffel bags, laughing at their neatly folded and unused clothing. They straightened the room and repositioned the creaky bed together. They bagged the leftover food, partially filled the cooler with ice, and checked the lights. They were ready to go but in no immediate hurry if Billy did not get lost on the way back to Highway 21 toward Gadsden. They needed to wait for the sheets, towels, and pillowcases to finish tumbling in the dryer. Then Billy would turn off the fifty-amp fuse to the hot water heater in the panel box as directed by his best friend and roomie, Jackie.

Theta plugged in her hair dryer and combed out the strands with the bathroom door opened. Billy stopped to admire her gorgeous figure from the rear as she swayed back and forth from one leg to the other trying to blow her hair dry. She instinctively knew that he was watching.

She turned off the hair dryer while turning to Billy.

"Did you like the show?" she asked. Before he could answer, she added, "I hope so because what you see is yours and has only been yours. I truly hope that it will always be yours."

"Theta, I am totally mesmerized. I have to take back something I said earlier that was verbalized backward. I love you for who you are. Though it is very hard to get past your body, I realize that it is your soul that I am in love with. I didn't realize it fully until yesterday. But I will leave this weekend sure of it," Billy stated.

She came to hug him again. Theta then suggested that they finish cleaning the place up. She giggled as she pushed him away.

"We'll have plenty of time for more nakedness later. Let's be naked in Atlanta. Let's be naked in Charleston. We can find a whole world out there to be naked in," Theta chided.

Billy lugged the full hefty bag of trash to deposit at the can outside of the gate. He returned, wiping his bare feet on the porch mat.

Each time Billy would compliment Theta, she would deflect his appraisal. Theta was honest in her mindset of her self-assessment. She was self-critical and extraordinarily humble. But to Billy, there could be no more beautiful creature ambulating the meadows and shores of creation. Her humility made her much the more perfect in Billy's loving evaluation.

"Theta, you're a ten. I cannot imagine anyone more attractive inside and out. We're leaving in a moment. Can we just sit on the bed for a while and let me admire you for a few moments longer?" Billy begged in a most sincere tone.

They sat at the bare bedside. Billy hugged her tightly. Theta was waiting for the sheets and pillowcases to dry from their last cycle. They stared and caressed as the sheets tumbled vigorously in the dryer.

"The creaky bed is naked too," Theta suggested. "I've never experienced a lot of things I've done this weekend, Billy."

She looked downward. "I've never slept without pajamas, I've never bathed naked in a waterfall, and I've never kissed a man sleeping next to me good night."

They spoke within their never-ending conversation until the dryer buzzed. They retrieved the warm bedding sheets. Billy helped her to make the bed. He then checked the refrigerator for anything left.

They met for departure at the screened porch door.

They walked out together and placed a few items into the back seat of Billy's old blue Toyota. They strolled back, perusing each other with a knowing devotion. Billy positioned the cabin key under the porch planter. They were still entirely and unabashedly nude. The sun was bright and warm.

"You wanna know something, Theta? I never expected anything like this could ever happen in my life. It's a memory I know that will always remain," Billy said with melancholy. "Let's never forget this time."

"It's the greatest moments of my life, Billy. No regrets. I now have a secret that I cannot tell anyone—ever," Theta stated modestly.

She added, "I would not have imagined this ending when we showed up in the rain on Friday. I was my own adversary for such an event. I'm with the man I adore. The nudity is a revelation of physical truth and companionship comfort. And I am no longer waiting for the right man to deflower me to society's most appropriate timing. We found each other, and that timing was perfect."

"We wouldn't even be able to tell our grandchildren this story," Billy added. "It's too juicy for anyone but us. It's our secret only. Deal?"

"Deal," Theta confirmed.

They had chiseled away their inhibitions like a patient ice sculptor would create a swan at a banquet. They conjured four truly memorable lovemaking sessions—three times in the Eden of the waterfalls and the exciting midnight liaison.

"Why not add the cherry on top?" Theta offered. "Let's dress each other back from head to toe. Grab what you wanna wear home, and I'll do the same. We'll dress each other—slowly so that we can remember it always."

Her spontaneity was wonderfully timed and romantically surprising to Billy.

The last challenge was both methodically choreographed and consensually mesmerizing. They chose their outfits and placed them in two piles on the porch swing. No words were spoken.

Billy slipped Theta's sea-foam blue-laced panties across her sun-pinked thighs, again kissing the unadorned skin. He gently pulled them to her waist. The slowness of this first dressing action set the tone for the entire exercise. It would be tantalizing and titillating. Theta then pulled his Yellow Jacket emblem T-shirt over his damp and wavy dark hair. She reached purposefully around Billy's neck to place the label on the back of the neck downward. In doing so, she planted a soft kiss upon his jaw. She then reached to the swing to retrieve his folded boxer shorts. She bent down, still only adorned in her panties, to place his boxers over his ankles slowly and assuredly, patiently slipping the waistband over his genitalia carefully. She straightened them sensually.

Billy grabbed her matching sea-foam-laced bra next. But Theta insisted on remaining topless to amuse him as she slid his jean legs over his feet. He held the bra down to his side, submitting to her command. She zipped his jeans up slowly as if to delay a sad good-bye. Billy paused before the next article of clothing was to be added. He kissed her perfectly shaped breasts passionately. Theta reacted by placing her hands on his face and applying another long passionate kiss.

Billy positioned the bra clumsily. Before its placement, he studied each upper torso freckle for its originality in the cast of light. He then hooked it in the back as Theta turned to allow his dexterity a better avenue. Theta pulled the bra adroitly over her tender breasts to straighten it. Billy looked forlornly again into her emerald eyes. Her countenance was to be indelible in his mind view of the highest level he would forever recall as classical splendor.

Billy placed her white shorts past her thighs and buttoned the front slowly so that both could enjoy the moment. She giggled at his attention to detail. Billy massaged her calves caringly as he placed her flat tan shoes on her softened feet. He buttoned her light-pink shirt from bottom to top, stopping only to stare yet again into Theta's loving eyes as they glistened in the sun.

Theta shuffled Billy's loafers onto his waiting feet. Last, Billy stroked her long, dark red hair back behind her ears. With her hair still in his strong and purposeful hands, he drew her lips to his. It would be the kiss of forever. She surrendered her shoulders as if this was the moment of total submission to their future together. The kiss was long and deep and bestowed the passion of the past twenty-four hours into a sense of happiness they could never suppress or surpass.

"That was the best kiss I've ever had with this many clothes on," Theta chided.

Billy laughed. "And that was the best kiss I've ever experienced with or without clothes. Let's always make sure the kiss signals our passion for each other."

Theta swooned and placed her hands up to her heart. Her eyes were misty within that short moment. She nodded lovingly. She was crying softly, holding the moment to her breast.

They embraced again in their newly adjusted outerwear. They glanced at the cabin. Neither knew if they would ever see that riverside cabin again. But it was sure to remain vivid in their future lives together. The car was loaded. He opened the passenger door for Theta as she sat and turned forward. After closing the car door, he walked back around to the driver's side and got in.

The sun was out—much as if the sky was warming to their pure and natural love for each other. The enchanted new couple left with just one curt warning spoken simultaneously as Billy turned on the ignition to his Toyota SUV.

"Seatbelts!"

CHAPTER SEVENTEEN

Hal Butters

SID RECEIVED NEW guests at booth 14 often. It seemed that they appeared by providence. He did not operate on a referral system because most of the visitors who came did not want to admit that they were seeing a stranger about conundrums that were all too personal. He arrived at the booth daily to be available for his deeply embedded sense of duty. Somehow, he knew that his "clients" would find their way.

Hal Butters had just returned from the Mount Pleasant Clinic, where his wife was receiving her initial treatment of chemotherapy. He ordered a full-sized coffee from Callista and clutched a medical journal periodical from the Daily's Section of the Bib and Bibliothéque. The rough-hewn black man sat down and thumbed through the journal, looking for advertising panels instead of informational articles.

Hal raised two daughters and assisted his five grandchildren. A veteran of Desert Storm, he has struggled through life by the confrontations of duty divided by bigotry, blue-collar wages, and the eternal expectation that things will improve over time. His latest drudgery is the worst he could imagine. His wife, Viola, is dying. She has the worst cancer of them all—pancreatic.

The wrinkles on Hal's face and the graying temples could tell his story without a table of contents. Hal Butters portrays a most uncommon man. He expects adversity as a constant, and he expects to defeat it constantly.

He turned to page 17 after a few sips of the jet-black java to see an advertisement of the Cleveland Clinic. He does not trust that the local physicians know everything about pancreatic cancer. Though Viola Butters has resigned herself to the quickened pace of the acute disease, Hal Butters has hope. It is because his life has survived on thin threads of hope for its entirety.

He returned to the café counter to find a pen so that he could write down important telephone information of a vendor advertisement.

"Ma'am, could I trouble you to borry yo pen?" he asked in his barrier islands brogue. "I jus' need to write down a numba."

Callista only had the one marking pen to write names on the cups. She knew that she could not let it get away. The few people who were in line to place orders would not wait for Callista to be even minimally accommodating.

"Sir, I only have the cup-marking pen, but you see that old man over there?" She pointed to booth 14. "He has a plastic pocket protector and at least two pens at all times. His name is Sid. He's just taking up space and using our free Wi-Fi."

Hal noticed the sarcasm. But he had other priorities on his mind. He wanted to call the Cleveland Clinic. He took the medical periodical with him to booth 14, leaving his small coffee at another table.

"Mr. Sid," he began, "that young miss there told me I might be able to borry a pen from you to write down a numba."

Sid looked up from his iPad. He had been studying the impact of the Columbia Ice Field in Alberta, Canada. He was fascinated by the photographs of its rapid recession over the past ten years. But daily life trumped his research of ice decades.

"Why, absolutely. I have a green one I use for the good things like birthday card reminders, red for the bad things like dental appointments, and blue for everyday things like living necessities to pick up at the store. Your choice," Sid offered.

"Red, please?" Hal asked.

The Boracle immediately noticed the medical periodical. He reached to hand Hal the red pen from his plastic pocket protector. He studied the furrow of his brow and the faint scent of black coffee.

"You've been up all night, my friend. You're deeply troubled. But it's not about you. It's someone else. Is it your wife?" Sid asked.

Hal was stunned. He looked down at his folded brown napkin as he wrote the number to the Cleveland Clinic.

"You a psychic or sumthin'?" Hal asked.

"No, sir. The psychics get paid to tell you the obvious from the general. But they make it sound specific enough that one would think they could actually tell the future. It's a ruse. Besides, I don't charge. I just try to help people if I can," Sid explained.

Hal hesitated to absorb the differentiation and the offer of kindness. He was in no position to pass up any avenue that might benefit his wife.

"You got a minute?" Hal responded as he slipped into the booth. He left his coffee at the table several paces away.

"My wife has pancreatic cancer. Dey givin' her chemo but only to shrink what dey know is goin' to still kill her anyway. Kin ya help me get past dat?" Hal asked it in a voice of both inquisitiveness and dramatic impact.

"My friend," Sid began, "there are no guarantees that I can help, only the assurance that I will give it my full attention and help you to decide upon the variables that matter. I do not work miracles, but I have seen a few over my seventy-six years."

Hal Butters had no idea that he had stumbled upon the "luga-byte source" of all research on all cancers. When Sid's wife, Ida, died of pancreatic cancer nearly thirty years prior, he never remarried. The experience changed Sid's entire attitude about life. It was Ida's death that seeded the sense within Sid that every problem had a find-able answer. But that answer may not be received in the time required for its resolution.

"Sid Toile, at your service." Sid extended his right hand.

"Hal Butters."

As they shook hands, Sid noticed the roughness of Hal's palms.

"You're a brick mason, Hal?" Sid asked.

"Yessur, dat's right. Been doin' bricks fo' twenny-eight yea's. I do new, patch, arches, Flemish bond, fire pits, walls, anythin' you can think of."

"Brick masons are builders, and by that very nature they are optimists, Sir." Sid detailed. "They are the resolute architects of stability and safety, as well as longevity. Your choice of a career can be said to have a lasting consequence as well as an enduring impact upon all of mankind. The Great Wall, the Pyramids, Angkor Wat, and Machu Picchu attest to your craft."

After complimenting the worried gentleman, Sid diverted his attention to the man's immediate need.

"Your wife has a mighty bad break. The Cleveland Clinic advertisement you looked at may be the right place. They do great work. Where is she now?"

Hal hesitated, looking down at his borrowed periodical.

"Da East Med Oncology Center at Mount Pleasant Clinic. Da doctors ain't givin' me no signal dat she'll live," he answered. "No signal, man. Nothin'."

"Hal, my wife died thirty years ago. Pancreatic cancer," Sid began. "I miss her every day."

Hal looked up. The commonality of their circumstance earned his full attention.

The Boracle continued, "Since then, there have been a lot of new treatments for neuroendocrine tumors—or what the doctors call NETs. Besides chemo, developments include a newer look at intraoperative radiation therapy and even a new procedure done with less invasion—performed laparoscopically."

"Do wha'? You a docta? Howja know dat stuff?" Hal asked.

"No, I'm not a doc. I'm just a guy who had to know the options myself. Even with what I knew then, I couldn't save my wife. But your wife has a much better chance," Sid forecasted. "There have been many breakthroughs."

"I ain't got no way of getting' her up dey ta Cleveland but takin' her in da truck. Ya' think dade take her?" Hal asked in desperation. "I'll leave t'day."

"No, Hal. We need more information. Let's go see your doctors. I'll go with you. Then we'll do research together. I can't promise you anything. But maybe we can chart the best course to keep hope alive," Sid explained.

"You get an appointment with the doctor for a consult. Just ask for it in the next twenty-four hours. I'll be available. Here's my card. And I'll go with you. If they ask who I am, just say I'm your cousin."

Hal smiled at the absurdity of an old frumpy white cousin. He took the simple card with just a name and a cellular number. He got up hurriedly.

"What's her name, Hal?" Sid asked.

"Viola. Viola like the musical instrument. Viola Butters. She's the love of ma life, Mr. Sid," Hal continued. "I'm goin' over to dat clinic right now. I'll call ya. You can bet I'll call ya."

Hal extended his right hand to shake Sid's. "And thank you!"

The brick mason had no way of knowing that Sid did not like to be thanked. Sid just looked down as Hal extended his hand.

Hal left for the clinic immediately, leaving his lukewarm cup for Callista to dispose of. She was not happy.

"Sid, you sure know how to ruin my day," Callista started as Hal left hurriedly. "I gotta clean after you already. Now I gotta clean different tables around you. And for no tip again."

Her attitude and sarcasm were a matter of course and a constant barrage to the Boracle.

"Callous, I'm keeping a ledger. You stay here long enough and learn to respect your elders, and you'll get a tip. Have I ever lied to you?" Sid reminded her.

"Just the first lie on the first day you came here," Callista responded. "It was when you said you wanted to be alone. You have not been alone since that day."

CHAPTER EIGHTEEN

Heartfelt Letters

(As It Happened, Eight Years Earlier)

THETA ATTENDED TO her harp practice at the Scott College Auditorium. She returned late enough that she was unable to change from her pink top and white shorts she wore from the Guntersville weekend.

Theta couldn't wait to return to her loft bedroom at Watters Hall. Her roommate, Jill Honeycutt, had returned to campus from Meridian, Mississippi. Jill had been an exchange student and spent the summer on a culturally pleasant academic session at Melbourne Girls College in Australia. She was set to arrive that evening but was not present when Theta got in from her tepid Guntersville weekend. Theta and Jill had written letters every other week with tidbits of life's idiosyncrasies both up above and down under. Both Theta and Jill enjoyed traditional penmanship communications.

Theta returned from the symphony practice when Jill was unpacking. They hugged in the glee of seeing each other after several months. Theta helped her place her things and listened to the Aussie adventures and the description of the long flights back to Atlanta through Tahiti and Los Angeles. Both sophomores were yawning in sets—the yawn from one triggering the yawn from the other. They decided to address the stories of their separate adventures in the morning. Theta didn't spend twenty-seven hours on airplanes as Jill did, but her desire for sleep was easily the equal.

The idyllic and romantic weekend with Billy eased its way into Theta's sleep dreams. She awoke the next morning as if her life had been emotionally fulfilled with the overflow as fuel for the coming day.

Monday began in preparation for the initial classes of the fall semester. Syllabi were distributed. Books were procured. In between, Theta caught up with Jill to learn of her many excursions and insights. She had left an Aussie boyfriend she described as a good companion but not a "mate," as they often are called in Melbourne. She and Christopher Calder would remain as pen pals. Jill never asked Theta about her summer, and Theta was content to refrain from any mention of her torrid rendezvous with Billy Grayson. Her reputation as a very private person always gave Jill a sense of reticence. She knew that Theta would only volunteer current dating information on her own terms.

Theta was still excited about the most wonderful weekend imaginable and her amazing lover, Billy. She called him at eight fifteen on Tuesday evening knowing his soccer practice was over. The conversation was still in their pre-weekend genre, both enjoying their routine of highbrow humor.

Since Theta found talking about others to be appalling and unkind, she did not mention Jill's return or adventures with the Aussie boyfriend. She only noted that Jill was back and still jet-lagged. Billy spoke about soccer practice and the need to fill up his Toyota soon.

Theta paused. She thought that the conversation should reach the central commonality they shared instead of the minor comments.

"Billy, we can dance around topics and humor each other or we can talk about waterfalls," Theta interspersed into the small talk. "Which option would you think I would prefer?"

Billy found the conversation change to be an endearing way of saying that Theta wanted to talk about the new happiness they shared.

"Theta, a caveat . . . I will never ever divulge to anyone any small detail about our waterfall weekend." Billy sensed that Theta needed the private reassurance. "But I wanted to tell you again that if I died today, I would die knowing that I lived the greatest romantic experience imaginable with the most loving and gorgeous person I've ever known."

The transition became deeply serious.

"And before you think it was just physical frolic and fun, you should know that I love you. I will always love you," Billy added.

Theta gulped from the surge of emotion from hearing Billy's words. Her voice was choked in the response.

"I love you," she struggled to reply. "You have changed my life for the better."

Billy sensed that she needed a moment of composure. He volunteered a tangent thought.

"It will forever be our vaulted secret, Theta. I know that I didn't need to tell you that I would never utter a word to anyone, but it's kinda sexy having a secret together," Billy assured her. "It makes me feel as your confidant and your most trusted companion. That feels thrilling to me."

Billy assumed that Theta never boasted to anyone about her commitment to remain a virgin. But she was proud of her commitment to her virginity to Billy since high school. Billy wanted to assume the elevated responsibility of keeping their love life confidential, even to his roommate, Jackie.

Theta only spoke of her virginity to those that she felt needed to know—her roommate, Jill, and a handful of high school girlfriends that had probably forgotten. She also told her father. She hid nothing from her parent-mentor. Their frank, respectful, and honest relationship was paramount to Theta. She had no similar relationship with her mother. She had not divulged the traditional role reversal of these understandings with Billy yet. Being comfortably forthcoming, she had not thought to discuss the subject of her parents.

For now, Billy wanted to talk about their new discovery—each other.

"How can I possibly put into words—even with the help of a *Roget's Thesaurus*—to describe the complete and precious experience we shared, Theta?" Billy started. "I've thought about it last night and all day today. I am not capable of uttering the full scope of how I feel. I can only hope that you see and feel me in your future so that we can be together always. That period of total joy sets us on a hopeful course of lifetime devotion. It's so clear to me. I hope you feel as I do."

The thought of a lifetime with Billy was both settling and coveted. Tears welled up again in Theta's shimmering green eyes.

"I would trade the world just to kiss you again," Billy added.

Theta sobbed.

The conversation lowered from the initial voices of excitement to the tone of insight. Theta continued to cry quietly, trying to compose herself to say something she felt. She knew that Billy had exposed what she also felt during the past twenty-four hours without him.

"Billy, I am so emotional. Please do not think I'm a silly fool with all these tears. It's because I'm so happy and because you touch my heart. I love you more than any words. When can I see you again?" she asked warmly. "Where can we go to be with each other?"

Billy replied, "I am longing to see you too. This week's schedule is difficult. Coach Harmon is bussing the team down to Statesboro tomorrow for a scrimmage. We open with Auburn on Saturday. He says we're not ready. We have another scrimmage here against Valdosta State on Thursday. With classes and the travel, we can meet on Friday or Sunday. What's your schedule, Theta?"

"It will have to be on Sunday afternoon. I have the first performance at the pavilion on Friday. It won't be over until ten fifteen," Theta offered. "But I just cannot bear to wait for Sunday."

She added, "I want to see you now, tomorrow, and forever. Can I come to you on Sunday? I just want to be with you, Billy. It will be a dangerous time for anything physical until I get on the pill. But I have to get an appointment just to do that. I can't imagine how I could explain this to Dad."

"Your dad?" Billy asked.

"Long story, Billy. I'll tell you this weekend," Theta began. "My family is backward. My life's mentor is my dad, not my mom like most girls. But can I explain it to you when I see you?"

She continued, "Church is out by ten-fifteen. I can drive over there by eleven thirty. We can go to Buckhead or over to Decatur and get a pizza maybe."

"Let's leave it open and decide on Sunday," Billy responded. "I yearn for you so much. I wish that Sunday were tomorrow. Meanwhile, let's call each other like this."

"I like hearing your voice, Billy. You've opened my world in so many ways, and seeing you will make us both feel better," Theta retold. "I want you more every minute. Please be the Billy from last Sunday next Sunday!"

Her lilt was its own inducement.

After they concluded their conversation, Theta was enchanted. She knew that Billy loved her and had just heard his voice. She was excited. She knew that she needed to do something other than fall off to sleep.

She did what she did well. She pulled out stationery to write a letter to Billy. She was an elegant and expressive writer. Her penmanship was precise and flowing. She could paint a portrait with carefully chosen words. She began to write down her innermost thoughts. The sensual composition would take nearly a half hour. She described the realization moment from their prior weekend together as the centerpiece to her heart's flutter and her mind's devotion.

> *My Dearest,*
>
> *You have me here by you. I am warmed in the glow. The fragrance of the midnight shower rides upon the furtive gusts of the nearby forest. It is a misty trace of tenderness we share. I shall never witness a nighttime rain again without conjuring your*

touch in my ardent dreams. I have given myself to you alone and completely. It is the surrender and trust of love.

You rest in the calm. My heart is swollen in the love of you. Could I ever be any happier? Could I ever find a greater peace or a more wholesome joy? The breeze brings my spirit into you, and yours into me. There is a secure delight to be awake while you sleep. I can admire you without the awkwardness of your waking perusal. In this, I am most contented.

We spoke of a never-ending conversation. Let us also cherish a knowing silence. Let us embrace a bond of gladness, a tie of kindness, and a pledge of adventure together. Let us remain as ourselves individually but as one together. There could never be a vision so vivid, a wish so vibrant, or a desire so wanting as the delectable trance of your companionship. I shun my doubts, my fear, and my vigilance in the face of the fully effervescent sunlight that will warm our future. It illuminates a new and glorious world. You have me here by you. I am warmed in your sunglow. I will love you forever.

Theta

She took the letter to the Scott College administration building on Wednesday morning. There, the faculty and staff heavily utilized a centralized postal receptacle. She kissed the personalized envelope to allow a vestige of her poppy-red shade lipstick to hint of her fervent wishes. She lovingly deposited it into the mail chute.

Simultaneously, Billy began typing on his laptop. He was exploding within his nineteenth-century-centered romanticism to express a literary shrine to Theta extolling the best day of his young life. Their love for each other was mad, meaningful, and inspirational. Mount Vesuvius had lesser temperatures and more control than Billy Grayson. His creative literary abilities would command the enterprise. He would compose an epic tribute from his elevated wanderlust intended for the goddess of his dreams.

It was going to be a process for Billy that would take a few days to compose perfectly. It was to be the marriage of his love of poetic form with the still-verdant memory of Theta from the prior weekend. He would complete it and mail it with the inherent glee that it would please her and certify his newfound passion.

Theta's letter landed in Billy's campus mailbox on Friday afternoon. He checked his mail that morning before the letter's delivery. The timing of Theta's handwritten love letter arriving on Saturday afternoon would be fortuitous.

Billy took time to perfect his coded literary "toast" to Theta. Ever patient and diligent, the carefully crafted prose was calculated to a lettering sequence he had placed within it. He would not print and mail it until he was certain it was flawless.

They made cell phone calls to each other daily. Billy pointed out on Friday that his special tribute to her was complete. He mailed it to her on Saturday morning.

"Did you receive mine yet?" Theta asked on Friday.

"It wasn't there this morning, but I was there before ten. I'll check back either later today or after the game tomorrow. I can't wait to get it," Billy responded with genuine curiosity and excitement. "Don't expect my letter to be anything but my sincere feeling for you. It's nearly ready. I hope you enjoy it."

"You should know that I hesitate to send mine to you. It's not a letter but a stab at free verse," Billy told her. "But, Theta, I'm having so much fun doing it because each line seems to take me to a different thought of you and our crazily-timed love. I was lucky not to be sleeping on the floor in the den that last night. That first kiss! I was thinking you were going to whop me. That was the moment. I'm so grateful that you did not push me away."

Billy was humbled that Theta had already mailed a thoughtful and sensitive letter to him. He knew that his poetry was not only a love letter but also a work of enduring art. He felt that their relationship was the beginning of a permanent dream.

Theta assured him that she could not be disappointed.

"Now, Billy, if you were to send me drawings of stick men and scribbled captions, I may have a different view," Theta chided. "But if you send anything as lovely as you wrote in our high school yearbook, you can bet I will frame it."

"I should finish it tonight," he assured her.

Billy changed the subject to agree upon their next meeting.

"Would you mind if I came in sweats from practice? Otherwise, I might be another half-hour late?" Billy asked.

Theta, ever looking for a light response, returned the question.

"So you're asking if I want to see you smelly and sweaty, or wait a half hour more to hug you endlessly fresh and clean?" Theta posed. "That's a tough choice, Billy."

She added, "Can you wear the Versace Dylan Blue so that I can be reminded of last weekend?"

Billy would be arriving a half hour later.

After Billy hung up, he immediately went back to the verse to finish it. Having just heard her voice and observed her inherent sweetness, the words for finishing line came naturally.

It had taken Billy three days to compose the prose given the interrupted delays of college athletics. There were bus rides, weight room activities, and the first week of his class schedule at Tech. The warm thoughts of Theta and their exquisite weekend together invaded his mindset like migrating caribou on the tundra. The feelings were pleasant and blissful. He wanted to author a classic. The last comments on their phone exchange lifted his creativity even more.

In his prosaic effort, he assembled the coded drift of a delectable memory within an irregular rhyme scheme. The lines would separate the stanzas as needed by his metered hidden message. He intended to reassure her of his love through what had been a life-changing decision for her—the loss of her virginity. He treated the subject with the utmost delicacy. His Cambria scripted issue of the composition was printed and sealed in a plain manila envelope. It was mailed to Theta s promised. Billy hoped she would get it before they met on Sunday afternoon.

Billy's prose built in the cryptogram he wanted to simplify. It was a code of advancing clues—the first letter of the first line, the second of the second, the third of the third, and so on. The secret message was made easier by the irregularity of stanzas. It read as a toast, as

DISAFFECTIONS OF TIME

hinted within the wine theme of the prose. The twenty-three lines had twenty-three corresponding letters. Twenty-three was Billy Grayson's soccer number. It was also the number of paces it took to carry the protesting Theta from the cabin to the brook on the morning they left Guntersville. It was a memory they would share forever, Billy supposed.

Chance upon a Dusky Dream

*To the glimmering glass of life's romances,
alizarin nectar, and circumstances;
Wondrous hopes—like rare aged wine, enhance
the journey—they intertwine.*

*No triumph of greatness can trace its cheers
To the barren groves of fruitless years.
Fervent blooms of bliss grow within a damnable depth of discipline,
Cannot joy and rapture guide your heart
'Til we mark synchronous lines on a chance-drawn chart?*

Is this time of ceaseless want—a time to dare, or a time to daunt?

*The wasteland extends from reality to sublime,
For it has no measurement for passing time.
Our cynical view of its void—fate, too often, has enjoyed. And
nothingness rolls onto its empty shore in whispered waves of yester-yore.*

*As in the sleepy dusk of past romances, by
moonlight cast on stilled advances.
No cloistered columns reach with stone to
hold what is dear or what is gone.
Melancholy the muse that once directs the
vigilant soul that virtue protects.*

Fervently dwells in boundless space the love-filled joys of another place.

Holding dear the tender eyes—embracing what life glorifies!
The defeat of conscience nobly fought, thus betrayed by honor wrought.
The candles glimmer near the gate, and
shimmer in shadows of shifting fate.
As rain-washed dusk heeds the dawn, pure passion pulsates on.

Allow thy soul to cast thy youth to find the light of naked truth
And I, to last, shall toast to thine—with
mysterious, though enchanted wine,
Fragrant with a mellowed musk, vintaged near a shared and sleepy dusk.

Love,
Billy

CHAPTER NINETEEN

Penalty Kick

(As It Happened, Eight Years Earlier)

IT WAS AGAINST Auburn in the final period that Billy Grayson dodged a defender and executed a deft kick that sprung out a teammate for what appeared as the winning goal. Only three and a half minutes remained, and the Yellow Jackets took a 4–3 lead. But that is not how the game ended.

From a corner kick in the final minute, Billy and an Auburn defender, a Scottish recruit named Wally Bailloch, converged for a header. Billy was knocked out cold. The officials called out the trainer and the medical supervisor. Billy was not moving and barely breathing. As they worked on him trying to revive, Coach Norman called the team together next to him. They encircled the coach. He knelt to say a prayer for Billy.

The Auburn coach had his team on the sideline for these death-warned moments. They prayed as well. However, Wally Bailloch disappeared.

The left side of Billy's head above the ear developed a large blood-filled lump. The impact had cracked his skull and caused his brain to hemorrhage. Billy's eyes were staring out until Coach Harmon closed them. He assumed that Billy would die from the sudden trauma. His brain would not be able to signal other functions to his listless body.

Within ten minutes, an ambulance arrived. They rushed Billy Grayson to the Atlanta West Parkway General Hospital. They knew he had a brain contusion and feared he also had a broken neck.

The game did not seem to matter. Neither team wanted to continue the game, but the game officials insisted that the last minutes be played. Auburn scored near the end and won the contest on penalty kicks.

Billy had suffered the severe head injury that no family would want to be informed about by phone. His family came immediately from Mount Pleasant. Theta, who had been in classes at Scott College, hurriedly came when she heard the news from Jackie Mann. She was told the dire details at the hospital and became inconsolable. Within minutes, one of the doctors came out. He relayed the more distressing news.

A nurse from the operating room gave the report. "Dr. Michaelson has done all he can for now. It's touch-and-go. The patient's heart stopped for about forty seconds about a half hour ago. He flat-lined. But Dr. Michaelson was able to revive him. We do not know what damage this may entail. We're trying to stabilize him."

Theta placed her head into her hands and sobbed in the waiting room chair. Jackie tried to cheer her up by telling her about Billy's workout routine and optimistic outlook on life. He knew them to be close friends from their interaction during the weekend before the accident.

"Theta, he's going to be fine. You'll see. He's a fighter. He'll get through this," he said. "He'll be back out there in a few weeks like it never happened."

Jackie had no basis for his assurances. He hoped that his roommate would get a few stitches and then walk out looking for a ride home.

Coach Harmon arrived directly from the soccer match. Jackie apprised him of the dire situation.

The emergency operation took nearly six hours and two of Atlanta West's top neurosurgeons. The blood loss required nearly constant hemoglobin supplies. The neurosurgeons applied pressure constantly to try and halt the blood seepage. Billy never regained consciousness from the point of injury to the surgical procedure. He had to be induced to a comatose state because of the excruciating pain and the use of morphine. The nurse reported that Billy's prospect for survival during the intense hours of surgery was less than 20 percent. Coach Harmon, Jackie, and Theta were stunned. At another stage, Billy had flat-lined again for nearly a minute. The trauma would engage the emergency room crew and the skills of Dr. Michaelson anew. A faint pulse was strengthened by medicine, expert medical procedure, and divine providence.

Billy's parents and little sister were stuck in traffic coming into Conyers on Interstate 20. They had no idea that Billy had died twice.

Jackie absorbed the reality at the last intern's report.

"Oh my god. He can't die. He's gotta pull through," he responded to the ominous report. "God save my buddy."

Just as the Grayson family parked the SUV to run into the hospital emergency room, the surgery was complete. Billy's head had enlarged from the swelling, and other medications were being pumped by intravenous means. His entire system was on life support. The consulting experts were waiting for the parents.

Dr. Michaelson came through the double-doors from surgery immediately prior to the Grayson parent's arrival. He reported on the procedure.

He spoke to Jackie with Theta listening intently by his side. Coach Harmon stood by, distraught at the troubling news.

The doctor advised, "Your friend is fighting, but the prospects are not good. If we can get him through the next hour, he has a chance, but every indicator is working against his survival. My best advice is to pray."

Theta was overcome with sorrow. She turned away. Jackie consoled her. He said, "Billy will make it. He's got to. Believe it."

Coach Harmon remained stunned by the revelation. He went to the hallway to call the college's athletic director.

Lucy, Mathew, and Carla Grayson burst into the waiting area. Jackie and Coach Harmon filled them in with the awful details. Billy was considered by the experts to be on death's door. They were all helpless.

A staff member took Mathew Grayson to a desk to get the vital information and treatment authorization. Among the papers she presented were two frightful forms—an organ donor sheet and a DNR—do not resuscitate. Mathew was taken aback at the starkness and timing of the decision. He declined to sign either without speaking with his spouse, Lucy.

From postoperation recovery, Billy was taken to intensive care where the permanent monitors of his heartbeat, pulse, and oxygen could be viewed. It would take another ninety minutes before the hospital allowed Billy's parents and his sister, Carla, back.

After the family returned, Theta went in to see Billy with Jackie for only a glance. Theta was frantic in her despair. She broke out crying and had to leave.

Billy's head was thickly wrapped after the emergency surgery to compress the blood vessels inside his cranium. He was correctly diagnosed with an acute subdural hematoma. His neck was sprained but not broken. However, Billy faced very difficult prospects. He struggled to maintain his breathing without artificial assistance. There was no hurry on anyone's behalf to measure brain activity, since the surgery was still unassessed.

"I can't bear to see him like this, Jackie. He is my best friend in the world. I'll never be the same. He's gotta pull through," Theta cried out.

Jackie's eyes were wet as well.

"He is a crocodile, an elephant, and a lion. If anyone can survive this, Theta, it's Billy. He has already beaten death twice. I don't care whether they say 20 percent or two—he's recovering, and he's going to walk out. I just know he will," Jackie assured her with his baseless optimism.

Dr. Michaelson came back to reassess the situation to the parents.

"More than half the patients who have to endure this painful skull-invasive surgery die within forty-eight hours. And even then, there are complications. If he makes it, we will still have a long road ahead. Please forgive my directness, but I have to be direct and pragmatic. I will do all that I can to save your son, but much of this is out of my hands," he advised.

But Billy would not die that night or the next. Minimal brain activity was detected on the third day. He was among the scant 39 percent who survived a full week after this delicate surgery. Of that small number, only 14 percent would return to a normal life.

The brain swells, and the subsequent drainage is excruciating. Clots are the enemy. Questions remained if he would awaken, if he would walk again, and if he could recall his past.

Billy remained in an elongated coma. Not much would be known until and if Billy emerged from the blood-filled brain injury and out of the coma. The Grayson family remained vigilant at Billy's side.

Theta was ever present. The Graysons knew that she and Billy were admiring friends. They had no idea of their new and exciting relationship. Theta felt it best to remain reserved on the matter. She knew that Billy had not intimated details to anyone.

Doctors and nurses came in regularly. They were trying to assess the full damage. It would take time. A departure from life support was still not out of the question. Theta hoped that the DNR form remained unsigned but was afraid to ask.

Billy's prose letter arrived on the Monday after the accident. She placed it in her purse and read it for the first time while sitting in the hospital waiting room. Billy had not been out of surgery for forty-eight hours yet. She sobbed.

She read the meaningful prose repeatedly upon her daily hospital visits. She kept it pressed in her notebook and shared it with no one. She cried so often that her eyes reddened by their lack of ability to produce more tears. Theta attended classes by day and then went to her apartment to shower and change only to return to the waiting room until midnight. She waited for Billy to come out of his coma.

Billy's only sibling, the fifteen-year-old Carla, became curious about Theta. She not only knew that Theta was Billy's high school friend and prom date but also knew that they did not date in college. Billy never mentioned Theta to her. Other than Billy's formal prom photograph, the Grayson home had no photo of Theta.

"Theta, did you love Billy?" the precocious teenager asked.

Theta turned to Carla, not knowing what to report and realizing that the question would have to be truthfully answered.

"With all of my heart and soul, I love your brother," she responded.

Carla's eyes lit up as if she had happened upon a secret discovery.

"Did he love you too?" Carla followed.

"I think so. When he comes to, you need to ask him. If he says yes, I will be very happy," Theta said. "But I will be happier if he comes to—than if he loves me. The first thing is bigger than the second."

Carla was encouraged. She felt like she had a new big sister. For the coming weeks when Carla and Theta were at the hospital together, they would always take time to go to the cafeteria and get a glass of sweet tea. Theta never told Carla much more than that she loved Billy. Carla knew that they discontinued dating in high school. But she wanted her brother to wake up and take Theta's hand because she admired her new best friend.

Carla was much like Billy in her subtlety. She was unassuming, quiet, and yet confident. She was a fine girls' basketball player—and quick at five feet four inches. She was athletic and worked hard playing against Billy in the driveway. Her short hair was dark, and her blue eyes were determined. She was not the academic that Billy was, but her discipline helped her to achieve better than average grades. She feared that she was soon to become an only child. But Theta seemed to calm her despite Theta's fearful misgivings.

"Don't worry, Carla," she would remind her. "Everyone knows that Billy's a strong athlete and will never give up."

Theta said it as if she was assured of a positive outcome. But deep down, she wondered.

It was on the twenty-third day that Billy opened his eyes for the first time since the life-saving surgery. He had no idea where he was. The doctors and therapists began a regimen. He could not speak and did not seem to recognize his parents, his sister, or Theta.

At first, Mathew Grayson surmised that it was the morphine that had his son, Billy, dazed and unable to recognize anyone. But as the weeks wore on, his cognitive abilities did not improve.

The Graysons were impressed that his high school prom date came to the hospital so often. They liked Theta and tried to calm her when she began to cry. Mathew thought that she was overemotional and needed to not come as often so that she wouldn't be so upset. Theta wanted to be there when Billy awoke. Although she was elated that he would live, she was disappointed that he did not know her. She realized that his survival and awakening from the coma was an answer to her nightly prayer. She accepted the consequence of his amnesia.

Theta stayed until midnight for several more weeks. Her routine was established. She left for her dorm room and unfolded the prose letter at her desk. Tears followed. He would live. The prose became the last insight into Billy's heart before the horrific accident left him fighting for his life.

Theta was in the throes of an anguish she kept inside. She remained committed to her forever lover but was slowly realizing that Billy might not emerge from the trauma physically, mentally, or emotionally connected to her in any way.

She had deciphered the cryptogram in her handwriting below the prose. It brought on other difficult feelings.

To Theta,
I love you.
I need you.

She cried in unrelenting grief over the hidden message. How would he have known that she'd be there? He needed her. She needed him as well. She read it over and over again—distraught that, though he would live, she would lose the only man that she could ever love. In this mindset, she folded the poem and placed it in a plastic storage box in her dorm closet. She would not read it again, as it brought too much pain and anguish.

Her despair was immense. She cried herself to sleep nearly every evening. On this evening, she would be thankful to God for his life. But she realized that she could not bear to read the words he had written to her, as she may never know that gentle and amazing man ever again.

Her roommate, Jill, had often been awakened. She tried to console her. But there was much that Jill did not know. Theta was reticent to tell anyone of her whirlwind twenty-four hours with Billy. It was their secret and theirs alone.

One rainy afternoon, Theta arrived at the hospital just after her three o'clock class.

"Theta, you are so kind to come here every day for Billy. He would be touched that you cared so much," Lucy Grayson told her. Lucy had updated news to tell her.

Lucy would have no idea of the intense affection Theta carried for her son. She admired that Theta was a person of great care and concern.

Lucy began, "The doctor consulted with us this morning."

"Will he talk again? Will he walk, Mrs. Grayson?" Theta asked with tears streaming.

"The doctor says that it's still up to God and time. He'll stay in intensive care for a while. They do not know enough about the brain damage yet. He had so much swelling before. It's still receding. They'll have to wait. But, God willing, my boy is tough. He's such a fighter." Lucy said this as much to be self-assured as she intended to assure Theta.

Lucy added, "The doctor said this will be a very long road."

Her words were prophetic. The assessment of his injury was developed more fully over the weeks of assisted recovery.

"He might never walk again because of the swollen brain's impact upon his central nervous system. The consulting neurologists were unsure of his memory, his motor skills, and other key indications to signal his progress. Billy's strong symptoms of rapid brain activity are a promising sign for a modified recovery," she continued.

The next news item surprised Theta.

"As Billy's brain swelling receded and he showed other physical signs of recovery, the medical team recommended that he be transported to a neurological center in Houston where Billy might gain other advancements," Lucy advised.

Theta was devastated by the news. But she had other reasons that she would need to discontinue her visits.

Billy left the Atlanta West Parkway Hospital after eleven weeks, awake and confused. Theta Barnwell had visited him every day, though he did not know her. The Graysons stayed at a local hotel and came daily. Jackie Mann came in three days a week.

As Billy began breathing on his own and slowly regained movement skills, he did not recognize anyone. He began to become reacquainted with his family. His verbal skills had not returned.

Billy's father, Mathew, was a civil service employee who loved fried foods, IPA draught beer, and Clemson football. He had just turned forty-seven and was under a nephrologist's care because of kidney disease and high blood pressure. He lived for the moment because he knew that he would eventually require a dialysis regimen.

Mathew took Theta aside to inform her of the family's decision to move Billy to Houston the day after Lucy divulged the new prognosis.

"Theta, we'll never forget your kindness. You were here every day," he began. "The chief neurologist said that they could not help him further here. He suggested the Houston Methodist Hospital and the Dade County Center in Miami. Houston seems to be the best option for now."

"Will he ever walk again?" Theta asked.

"Maybe. That's part of it. The doc tells us his brain swelling impedes the assessment to all of his other functions," Mathew explained. "Much depends upon the relief of the swelling, scar tissue, trauma, and so many other unknowns they told us about. So he might walk. Billy is strong. I believe he will walk. They say he may never be able to recall the past. That's another issue. We can only pray for what's best for Billy."

Theta cried softly as she took Mathew's words in.

"Dear, dear," Mathew followed. "We've all cried until we cannot cry anymore. One day, Billy may walk again. He's already breathing without help. He might talk again. He may write letters again. That's what we have to pray for now."

Mathew had no reason to know that Theta was crying because she and Billy had professed their love for each other just six days before the accident. She was much more than a friend to Billy. She was the love of his life. And she knew she could never love someone as deeply ever again. Theta knew the circumstances and realized that she would not be able to stay by his side in Houston. She was suddenly the past. He would likely never know her again even if he pulled through to lead a reasonably normal life.

"Theta, dear, Lucy or I will call you once Billy gets settled in Houston. We'll keep you informed like you are part of our family. You deserve that for all you have done," Mathew advised. "You have been a sweet angel to all of us."

Theta also knew something that she could not tell Mr. Grayson. She was several weeks late waiting for the onset of her menstrual cycle. She sensed that she was pregnant, though the excitement and emotional distress, she rationalized, could delay a healthy woman's cycle.

Thanksgiving break was near. She would wait and see her gynecologist back home in Mount Pleasant. Her high school biology courses and the sense of the timing she knew refuted the likelihood that she could be pregnant. But other signs indicated the reality.

The Grayson family accompanied the unwieldy transport of Billy's struggling body to the Houston Medical Center the next morning. Billy would have a small chance of becoming self-sufficient and live independently if fate played a promising role. Fate would take many months to develop a way forward.

Theta did not return to the Atlanta West Hospital on the day of transport. On the Monday before Thanksgiving, she packed her car from the dormitory room and went to the administration building to inform them that she had a personal emergency that would preclude her finishing the semester.

She had lunch with Jill Honeycutt before leaving at the Scott College cafeteria. Jill could see that she was quite upset. Against her parents' and Jill's advice, she forfeited her semester's work.

"Jill, my concentration and my energy have been away for weeks. I cannot think of anyone but Billy, and he'll never be the same. I have to get away and clear my mind," Theta explained.

"But why not finish it out to December 10 and at least get your credits for when you return?" Jill suggested.

"It's because nothing seems important right now. Prayer is important. Hope is too. But I cannot even imagine what the Graysons are going through. Billy could've been the one person I would have loved forever. But he'll never be the same. It is unlikely that he will ever regain his memory. I'd take him in, wheelchair, respirators, everything. But he doesn't know me at all," she revealed as she held back an avalanche of emotion.

"Theta, do me this solid. Just go home and find a new direction and then come back. They'll take you. Your grades are the best. They like smart at Scott. I'll keep you informed of what's going on here and send some photos. You just get right," Jill implored.

Theta began making her rest-of-her-life plans by giving Jill much of the dormitory leftovers. She was too depressed to think about it. Besides, she couldn't pack it all. She left the small flat-screen television, her sheets and towels, and many classroom supplies.

Theta and Jill arose from the table together. They hugged.

Theta walked away through the cafeteria doors and down to the parking area never to see the stoic and serene Scott College campus again. She drove herself back to Mount Pleasant.

Several of her classes posted A's for the semester as if she had completed the work. The grades were transferable. She had never missed scheduled classes and would have exempted each exam. She retained essential class credits for the semester despite the personal distresses. This circumstance would assist her transition into the next stage of her life without Billy.

She had a pressing and secretive appointment set with her gynecologist set for the Monday after Thanksgiving. She was six weeks overdue for her menstrual period and realized that she was pregnant with Billy's child. Yet the idea of an untimely pregnancy made her glow with contentedness.

CHAPTER TWENTY

Pablo Gutierrez

ANSON BROTHERS ROOFING Contractors had a fine portable tar hot-mix expert in Pablo Gutierrez. It was a job nobody else wanted. Yet these are the occupations that even the chronically unemployed will not accept because the arduous and repulsive work fails to surpass one's self-esteem and dignity. The line for food stamps is easier to negotiate.

Pablo was punctual and efficient and earned bonuses from the benevolent and thankful brother-owners. Pablo had been working at Anson Brothers since he illegally crossed the Texas border near Juarez seven years before. He was only fifteen then.

Fate changed everything. Pablo's younger sister, Valeria, had come to America two years earlier with Pablo's brother, Juan. But Juan returned and left Valeria with Pablo. When Pablo and Maria Delgado married, they offered to have Valeria move in, but she wanted to make it on her own. She found a promising job at the Chalk Wright Drygoods Warehouse in North Charleston.

Valeria was pretty and had continuously rejected the inappropriate advances of her belligerent coworker Sammy Clinton. Sammy was as obliviously predisposed to overt sexual harassment as a herd of sheep would be oblivious to drifting into rural intersections. In both cases, a tragedy became imminent. It seemed that the rules never applied to Sammy. Valeria withstood the unwarranted advances so that she would not draw attention and possibly lose her job or become a target for deportation.

On a Friday, Sammy again became aggressive and made an inappropriate physical advance to Valeria in the warehouse. She became cornered in the rear quadrant where others could not see the confrontation. Sammy came from behind her and clutched her by the waist. Valeria turned and instinctively kneed him in the groin. Sammy keeled over in pain. After recovering, he assumed that Valeria might report his wanton misconduct to his superiors. He had to cover his tracks.

Sammy found Valeria's personnel folder in the small office file cabinet. He informed the local Immigration and Naturalization Service officials of Valeria's citizenship status and her rental residence location.

In an unfortunate consequence of timing, her brother Pablo was visiting Valeria when the INS officials arrived. He had no identification that would prevent his deportation with hers. The INS was running low on their monthly report and needed a "score" to prove their worth.

Pablo and Valeria were both picked up in the early evening raid. As suspected illegals, they were transported to a detention center in North Charleston. Maria Delgado received the ominous call. She knew that the destitute neighbors would later raid the rental property and steal Valeria's personal items. She called Sid immediately.

"Mr. Sid, something terrible has happened to Pablo and Valeria. They have been arrested and are to be deported," she related, frantic in telling the news. "Pablo called me from the detention center."

"Maria, we have to go to their place immediately. I'll pick you up in fifteen minutes. Meanwhile, I'll try to contact Pablo or a judge," Sid advised.

Maria had gained citizenship only months earlier through Sid's diligence. Pablo's paperwork was delayed. Sid was unsure that he could resolve the deportation for Pablo or Valeria. He would have to talk to Pablo at the detention center the next day. His immediate concern was to preserve Valeria's personal property.

Sid pulled to the corner of the dead-end street and turned the ignition off in his Volkswagen Beetle.

"We should go inside, Mr. Sid, and pack her valuables," Maria prompted.

"No, let's wait a minute. There's a car there now. It may be another INS team. Let's see what they're up to first," Sid suggested.

The INS had already left the area after searching Valeria's home for contraband. A silver Ford sedan that the neighbors may have assumed was part of the federal authority team was in the driveway. Sammy had waited until the INS left to raid Valeria's home. He was capitalizing on the incident that he had maliciously engineered. Sammy was going to steal his victim's personal effects.

Sid and Maria watched as Sammy entered Valeria's small clapboard home. Sammy had tied crime scene tape across the porch columns to fool the neighbors into thinking he was performing the INS protocol. He took many of Valeria's household items and placed them in pillowcases. He could pawn her small television and other smaller items. His detestable revenge was without remorse.

Sid watched as Sammy brought items to the trunk of his car. Maria took photos with her cell phone from the distance as daylight began to fade into the dusk. Sid wrote down the license plate and waited. When Sammy came out with the last load and began to leave, he decided to follow him. Once he arrived at Sammy's residence, he called the North Charleston police dispatch to report the theft, the license tag, and the home address. He reported that the suspect had a stolen handgun. No gun was visible. But Maria knew that Valeria kept a small handgun in her nightstand. He deduced that Sammy had placed it in the "booty bag."

Sid gave his name as a witness, along with Maria's. They waited near Sammy's home until the police arrived.

Within ten minutes, police cars swarmed the home of Sammy Clinton. He was arrested on charges of grand larceny, illegal possession of a stolen weapon, child pornography, illegal drug possession, impersonating a policing authority, and other charges that would follow. They read Sammy his Miranda rights as Maria watched them apply the handcuffs. She took more photos from Sid's car window. Sammy was taken away. The police car rode past Sid's Volkswagen. Maria stared at the culprit with disgust.

The evening's events were an unexpected ordeal. Maria cried in anguish as she rode in Sid's car back to her home. Sid turned to her.

"Not to worry, my child," Sid reassured her. "We will contact Pablo tomorrow at the detention center. He may want to be released immediately, or he may opt for a free trip home. In either case, you will have him back here in short order."

"I do think Valeria wants to go back home. She has told me as much," Maria reasoned. "But Pablo has me and our children. I'm legal. Can't he be released?"

"Let's wait until tomorrow, Maria. I wouldn't figure that Pablo will let Valeria make the trip home by herself," Sid said. "Let's get the facts and then plan a solid solution."

"Mr. Sid, do not let them take my husband from me, please." Maria cried. "I have no life without Pablo."

"You will have your husband back. I promise," Sid countered.

Before returning with Maria back to Mount Pleasant, Sid re-inspected Valeria's apartment. The vulture neighbors had not waited long before descending on the prize. All of Valeria's clothing, supplies, and food were taken. By the next morning, the ruddy pink clapboard rental unit was ready for its next tenant. But the valuable items that Sammy had pilfered saved Maria and Sid the trouble of retrieving. They were in police custody and being cataloged. These would be returned to Valeria or her family safely after Sammy Clinton's guilty verdict.

Pablo was sequestered to an eight-foot-by-six-foot cell with a double bunk and a distraught sixteen-year-old roommate from Guadalajara. The disgusting open-air commode was in the corner away from the cell door and had no toilet seat. He was treated more as an animal than as a human being. Even so, he took the time to calm the teenager being deported with him.

The young illegal looked at Pablo quizzically. Pablo had an obvious congenital birth defect. He had no right hand. Where the hand should have developed was simply a nubby end to his right arm.

"¿Qué le pasó a tu mano?" the boy asked.

"Defecto de nacimiento," Pablo replied.

Pablo went on to explain that he was fifteen when he left Puerto Angel with an older brother to find fame and fortune in America. Their parents encouraged them to build careers. Once they established permanent jobs in manual labor, they sent money home to assist their younger siblings. A third sibling had turned fifteen and came to join them later. Their living conditions in Puerto Angel were quite impoverished. His father grew lemons on a two-acre tract to consume and offer to sell for two pesos each. They subsisted on fish and crabs from the seashore.

The beachside town had no tourists. Raids from Guatemalans occurred during his childhood. The Guatemalans were even poorer than the Mexicans. The Guatemala border was only six miles south of Puerto Angel. People were often shot in these occasional raids, adding impetus for Pablo's mother to have them leave home to take a chance in America—even knowing she might not see her children again.

He told the boy inmate that he learned English at night from a Catholic mission on John's Island. Our Lady of Mercy Community Outreach also taught him how to budget and to learn a trade. He loved the Sisters of Charity. They had changed his life.

Pablo became a carpenter because he learned that Jesus was a carpenter. The fact that he only had one usable hand never deterred him. He could frame houses, build custom cabinets, install trim, or add a deck to an existing home. He had done it all. No person that hired him for weekend jobs had ever rejected his work or the time that it took him to complete it with only one hand. But contractors would not hire him for carpentry work because they prejudged him by what they considered a severe disability.

The only thing Pablo couldn't do that troubled him over his lifetime was to shake hands. He had a natural reticence to offer his nubby extension to anyone who might not know of the birth defect. So when people began to shake hands, he always offered his left hand instead.

Since Pablo and Valeria were siblings, they would be transported back to Juarez, Mexico, together. They were allowed interaction in the detention center. Valeria wanted Pablo to stay because of his two young sons, the "anchor babies." They were able to speak with guards present in a holding area. Pablo decided to speak in English, realizing that all that was said was monitored and translated anyway. He would make it easy on the security force to know their intentions.

"I will not leave you alone. Maria knows that. So does Mr. Sid," Pablo began. "I'm certain Mr. Sid is working on a plan to get me back to my family, but that will have to wait."

Valeria was misty-eyed. She had been crying.

"Are they treating you OK?" Pablo asked.

"Yes. I did not mean to cause this," Valeria said. "Please forgive me. It had to be because of what I did earlier today. A coworker had been threatening me and was making advances. I finally kicked him and ran away."

"Who?" Pablo asked. He was not able to do anything but figured that he could tell Sid the name.

"It doesn't matter now. I'll never be back," Valeria related. "You should show the judge your children from your wallet."

"They took my wallet," Pablo countered. "They took my cell phone and my keys. But Maria has the spare and will get my car from in front of your house."

The security guard interrupted.

"Wrap it up, *amigo*," he ordered.

"Yes, sir," he turned to reply and then turned back to Valeria.

"Let's go see *nuestra madre,* and then I'll depend on Mr. Sid," Pablo said as he stood. "He'll know what needs to be done."

They were led away from the common area. Valeria looked back, still upset at the circumstance.

Pablo and Valeria had no idea that Sammy Clinton's evil act of vengeance was already being answered by Sid's sense of propriety.

As Valeria and Pablo parted, Sammy was transported to a waiting jail cell across the lot from the detention center. After getting his fingerprints, he appeared for a preliminary hearing. Sammy had two prior petty larceny convictions. The handgun theft, child porn evidence, and large drug discovery made the arrest rise to the level of a federal crime. As a repeat offender, Sammy Clinton faced up to thirty years in federal prison. Within seven months, his trial and sentencing upheld the three-decade punishment.

Maria and Sid approached the crime scene police officer in charge and arranged to secure all of her sister-in-law's personal effects from the authorities.

It was Sid Toile that reminded Pablo of a most insightful perspective.

"Pablo, you were lucky to be born in Mexico. If you had been born in America, someone would have told you and your parents that you were disabled and entitled to lifelong benefits. You would have fallen into the crevasse. They would have kept you from making something out of yourself and building your self-esteem. They would have convinced you that you were not a full human being. No houses would have been built, or decking added that had your special abilities. You would have been given something free in exchange for your pride."

But now Pablo was separated from his children and wife. He would not divulge their existence to protect the American dream for his children. He knew that he would return. He trusted that Maria would inform Sid of his deportation and that Sid would resolve all to make the world right again. It was because Pablo knew that solutions were what Sid delivered.

Prison guests that came to the detention center had to register twenty-four hours in advance. Pablo was allowed one guest per day. Maria carried her citizenship papers with her and visited Pablo and Valeria daily at the center. She placed Sid's name on the docket to visit Pablo before he was to be deported.

"Pablo, are you doing OK?" Sid began.

"Si, Mr. Sid, I hate that you have to come here," he responded.

"Maria told me your plans. It makes sense," Sid affirmed. "You know that I cannot hand you anything. But I have made an arrangement. The immigration officer said that they have to give back your personal effects they collected in a large yellow envelope when you reach Juarez. Call Maria then. She'll have instructions for you. Once you are home for a while and are ready to return, you'll have bus tickets to get to Oaxaca. You'll fly from there to meet me in San Jose, near Cabo San Lucas. You OK with that?"

Pablo was momentarily stunned at the detailed plans.

"Just remember three things, Pablo. (1) I'll watch after Maria and the boys until you return. (2) I'll be in touch through Maria's number at an agreed day and time with details once you've visited your folks in Puerto Angel. (3) You'll get tickets to meet me in San Jose. The rest will be up to me," Sid instructed.

Pablo had no concern that he would not return. He knew that Sid would protect his family and, somehow, this incident would never happen again.

"Will Maria have all the travel information?" Pablo asked.

"Yes. Now you take care of Valeria and say hello to your mother from your uncle Sid," the Boracle smiled.

He knew that things would be fine in another month or so.

Pablo and Valeria were held in the North Charleston detention center for ten days before being shipped to Atlanta by a school bus with steel grated dividers. He waived his option of a lawyer since the cost would have been prohibitive. His case came up at 8:30 p.m. and lasted ninety seconds. He pleaded guilty as an illegal immigrant. The judge took no note of his "anchor" children, never allowing the conversation to begin. Pablo did nothing to bring attention to himself, as he wanted to get the ordeal over. He followed directions in the herding activities that the prison guards demanded.

The sixteen-year-old boy who shared Pablo's cell was picked up from a small auto accident in a grocery store parking lot. With no driver's license, the boy was handcuffed and taken to the detention center the same evening as Pablo's arrest. Pablo served the role as mentor to the young illegal immigrant. He could see that the boy feared the unknown. He assured him that he would assist him to get back to his Mexican home. When that day came, Pablo and Valeria went with the boy to his home in Guadalajara before continuing the long journey down the length of Mexico. They all enjoyed the use of a late-model Chevrolet Tahoe that was waiting for their arrival at a Juarez dealership. It was another solution that Sid had arranged.

The deportation experience lasted six weeks.

Pablo spent three weeks with his parents and younger siblings in Puerto Angel. His father, Luis, worked daily at a small factory in Mazunte. He hosted a celebration at the Gutierrez home three nights after Pablo and Valeria arrived. Valeria stayed with the family, undecided on whether she would ever leave her parents again.

But Pablo knew he needed to return to Maria and the boys. They were his new life. He gave the gifted Chevy Tahoe to the family to use. Valeria was sure that she could use it for a taxi since she was bilingual and could speak with the eco-tourists that began to come to the port town.

On the appointed day and time, Pablo called Sid.

"*Buenos dias,* Mr. Sid," Pablo began.

"*Buenos dias,* my friend," Sid replied. "By now, you have Maria's photos of the idiot who caused your deportation. Let Valeria know that he's going to be in jail for the next thirty years. And tell her that Maria has her personal items here safe and secure. We can FedEx down anything she needs."

"OK, Mr. Sid, I'll tell her. She thanks you for the car. She is using it as a taxi here and making good money," Pablo reported.

"Good for her! That worked out well. Now, down to business. Pablo, I have purchased airline tickets on Aero Mexico flight 196 from Oaxaca to Los Cabos on August 8. It leaves at eleven. Can you make it?" Sid started.

"Yes, Mr. Sid," he replied. "I can even come earlier."

"Good. Let's do this on the eighth. I'll FedEx these tickets to you," Sid confirmed.

"Now, there's been a slight change to get to Oaxaca. It's six hours over the mountains by bus. I wouldn't do that, so you shouldn't either. Take Valeria's taxi or the local bus to Huatulco. Your flight there the night before at eight forty connects to Oaxaca. The ticket will arrive with the others," Sid advised. "And bring something nice for Maria and the boys."

"What identification should I bring?" Pablo followed.

"Bring a current photo, your driver's licenses from Mexico and the U.S., and anything else you might have that you want to keep here," Sid reminded. "We will take care of the rest when you get to Cabo. The airport there is actually in San Jose, more than twenty miles away."

Sid told him how the two boys and Maria were doing. He reported that they were thrilled that he was coming home.

"I should arrive from a Houston flight an hour or so before you get there. If not, wait for me at the airport," he instructed. "I'll have a rental car there. Everything you bring has to fit in the plane's overhead carrier coming back. Can you do this?"

"Yes, Mr. Sid. I have a smaller carry bag already," Pablo confirmed.

"Good, then I plan to see you on August 8 at about 2:30 p.m. at the San Jose Airport. Maria and the boys can't wait to see you again," Sid added. "Be careful, *amigo*."

"How can I ever thank you, Mr. Sid?" Pablo asked.

"Bring me a lemon from your parents' grove in Puerto Angel. I'll treasure it. That will be plenty," Sid stated. "I'll see you on the eighth."

CHAPTER TWENTY-ONE

Recovery Discovery

(As It Happened, Eight Years Earlier)

BY JANUARY, BILLY had shown slow cognitive progress in Houston. He still could not read and recognize numbers. He had encountered seizures, but the pattern of seizures was becoming less frequent. His blood pressure was stabilizing, and his breathing became normal. The staff could begin a regimen of physical therapy.

His body was frail from atrophy.

By March, he had partially reconnected much of his grade school rote learning. His cognitive abilities were still amiss. He knew no one. He was a classic amnesiac.

His sister, Carla, came and stayed by his side at the hospital for four days over Christmas while visiting a family friend. The Graysons flew in to stay for another week, and Jackie Mann came in for two days. Theta never traveled to Houston. She was focused upon her own ordeal.

The player he collided with, Wally Bailloch, came to the hospital often but never came up to see Billy. It was an eerie response. Wally checked at the information desk and then went to the canteen for a bite to eat before leaving.

The Graysons received a promising report from the head of the Physical Therapy Department. They felt that Billy was a good candidate for learning to walk again. Lucy Grayson was overjoyed by the report.

"Praise God. Billy's gonna walk outta this place," she declared. "Billy, you hear that?"

"One day, he'll come home, Lucy," Mathew added. "That boy has a good heart. He'll make us all proud."

"Let's not get ahead of ourselves yet," the therapist reminded them. "This may take a miracle and a lot of patience. Time will tell."

In the coming days, Billy was hooked up to an apparatus in the therapy center. They moved his legs and measured his response. The days were challenging, and Billy regressed into moments of despair. But he never gave up.

By late March, his reflexes were improving, and his atrophied muscles began to respond. His ability to speak was progressing as well.

On April 30, while he was performing motion exercises in the pool, his mother and Carla arrived. There was something they wanted to tell Billy in private. Mathew Grayson had suffered a massive heart attack the week before. His funeral had been held the day prior. Knowing that Billy could not travel and would not know anyone, they waited to tell him. Billy responded with a perfect sentence in stunted words for the first time.

"M-Mother, I-I know that he-he loved you-you . . . and he-he loved m-m-me."

Billy looked down. He was saddened. He realized that his mother and sister were very sad. He knew that much of his support system was taken away. He wanted to walk more than ever. Billy quit feeling sorry for himself. He began to rehabilitate with purpose because he knew that others needed him.

By June, ten months beyond the accident, he had acquired an affinity for musical notes and their sequencing. He knew food groups and animal kingdom species. He was reading books at night from the center's small library. Billy still did not recognize a single human being from before the accident and the subsequent surgery.

After sixteen months of rehabilitation in Houston, he was still not responding to the few Grayson family photographs and videos showing his previous life. His mother and sister had become more familiar by their constant presence. He knew more of their past by the photographs that indicated to him that he had a happy childhood in Mount Pleasant. Back in South Carolina, Carla attended counseling sessions intended for those who suffer great trauma. She had lost a father and the familiarity of a brother within eight months.

Jackie Mann remained vigilant in his assistance to the Grayson family. He visited Billy in Houston often—building what was to Billy a new friendship.

Though Theta prayed every evening for Billy's recovery, she was not able to visit. Her life had become quite complicated. Nonetheless, she raised money to assist the financial shortfall his parents were experiencing in paying his exorbitant medical bills. Theta did not return to see Billy after those first seven weeks because of his transfer to Houston. Her smile when Billy was awake belied her emotions for the fortnight she remained at his side. But she knew that she would have to face the challenges of the rest of her life without Billy. Her love for the Billy she knew before sustained her in her mission. She lamented that Billy's father had passed suddenly and felt a pressing need to assist. Her fund-raising mission was initiated by phone and e-mail. In time, she sent mail-outs to neighborhoods and to small businesses.

Jackie Mann, the friend whom she had only met once prior to the mishap, became her contact by e-mail updates. Jackie had no idea of Theta's passionate relationship with Billy. Jackie only reached out to Theta out of empathy. He was impressed that she came daily during Billy's early recovery weeks in Atlanta. He informed Theta that Billy would never make a connection to know her or anyone else ever again. He could only recognize those of his present life.

Frieda called Theta to invite her to an engagement party. But Theta had to decline for reasons she did not want her or Jackie to know.

Jackie intimated that Billy thought Theta was a nurse from her mention in his early recovery. Theta was initially understanding of the e-mailed sentiments but soon realized that Billy was a part of the past that would not serve the responsibilities of her future.

All public appearances were curtailed, even the Mathew Grayson funeral, because of Theta's obvious pregnancy. She had shied away from events that were likely to invoke hurtful whispers of innuendo. She knew these whispers and the condemnations as well.

Once Jackie reported his progress, she prayed ever more diligently. Hers was a prayer of silent thanks. She hoped that she'd see Billy at home one day soon and he would know her—just as he had back during that last weekend in August. After the weeks rolled into the months, she simply asked God to restore Billy's health and let him live in normalcy, even if she was the sacrifice that would be missing from his past and his life beyond recovery. She repeated the sentiment when she prayed daily. Her father, Simmons Barnwell, often overheard her in solemn prayer.

"Dear God," Theta began, "give Billy hope and allow me the strength to accept your wishes well beyond self. I only want You to be glorified in Your plans for this wonderful man. Please provide Your holy guidance to me and Your miracle that Billy will find a new life of great joy."

She prayed this prayer over and over each evening. Though she was living the angst and the pity, she exhibited a strength of will that would propel her. She humbly accepted the circumstances of reality.

She would always love Billy. She called his name in periods of despair when she'd awaken at midnight. Her life had descended to depths of sadness she could never reconcile.

She attended the Episcopal service each Sunday, forsaking the ten thirty Mass for the early seven thirty instead. This was the Mass that attracted the elderly. Nobody her age got up that early to attend church services. But even the older parishioners asked questions.

"Where's your husband this morning, dear? When's the baby due? What are y'all gonna name that little fella?"

Theta just smiled and said, "Good morning," never offering an answer. She would then enter her car and start it up, trying not to burst into tears.

As she approached the expected date of delivery in May, her father came with her. He would defer the questions and comments politely. Theta and Simmons both knew that half of the congregation figured that she was an unwed mother. Yet the Grace Church setting promoted a Christian sense of nonjudgmental understanding.

When Theta began feeling sorry for herself, she thought of Billy's plight. She would divert her feelings to pray for Billy. Praying for Billy Grayson was a mantra that delivered Theta Barnwell through her pregnancy.

Billy had suffered more than seven months of seizures and the constancy of severe headaches. Both eventually subsided. Though memory loss is more prevalent in older victims, Billy's amnesia was clinically established and had no signs of repair. He had been robbed of his academic pursuits. But he benefitted from the experimentation of three coordinated national research institutions since the rare medical setback.

In truth, Billy Grayson did not know very much about Billy Grayson. His day-to-day world was medically enhanced. He accepted that his mother, sister, and Jackie would become his baseline of knowledge, but he did not remember their past either. They never gave up on Billy.

Accelerated progress in Houston began after his father's passing. His speech patterns were returning. He learned to communicate in unstuttered sentences. Eventually, he even began to sing. It helped him to put sentences together without stumbling. The hospital professionals were becoming increasingly hopeful since less than a year had expired since the life-threatening brain injury. He was going to build a new and normal life, they believed. But it would have no basis of experience from the past. Few made it this far. Billy was very much the exception.

Theta prayed daily from afar.

CHAPTER TWENTY-TWO

The Other News

(As It Happened, Eight Years Earlier)

THETA WAS EMOTIONALLY devastated by the tragedy of Billy's soccer accident. She realized that nothing in her life would be the same again.

She had no confidant other than Billy and her father. Her closest female friends were not predisposed to protect secrets or impart wise judgments that suited Theta's elevated standards. She had come to terms that if Billy survived the accident, he would never know her or their past again. She remained insular and reserved about the relationship as Thanksgiving weekend approached.

Before she returned to Mount Pleasant, Theta had been experiencing morning sickness. She suspected that she could be pregnant, though her calculations of her cycle would seem to preclude that possibility. She had told no one—not because of shame but because of Billy's circumstance.

She arranged an appointment with her gynecologist, Dr. Maureen Inabinet, for the first Monday after the holiday weekend. She would be transitioning the doctor's expertise to obstetrics. She felt sure she was pregnant but, at nearly ten weeks, displayed no radical physical changes.

Theta couldn't help but wonder if the baby's father, Billy, would ever know of her or the life she wished to share. He certainly would not have known of her pregnancy or the miscalculation she had made over that extraordinarily romantic weekend in North Alabama. It was then that biological aberration had fooled spontaneity.

She thought back to the calculation of days. She had completed her repetitive menstrual cycle just days before going to Guntersville. Her grades in high school biology class were excellent. She suspected she had nothing to fear in her unforgettable tryst with her lover. Every textbook reveals that this is a woman's least likely time to become pregnant.

Theta revisited those general rules after she was seven weeks late. The word "rare" did not protect her. She visited the female doctor with trepidation. Her parents had no idea that Theta was impregnated. The biological fact was delivered from her doctor in a sterile room without others present. Dr. Inabinet confirmed that she was expecting. Theta was choked with tears even though she strongly suspected the result. When Theta explained the unusual timing, Dr. Inabinet simply nodded.

"Theta, the rhythm of menstruation is tricky," she began. "Everything we think we know suggests that in the first week, pregnancy is unlikely. But it does happen."

Dr. Inabinet only knew the nebulous circumstances as Theta outlined. An unnamed lover she was loath to reveal would not know her condition. But she would honor him by delivering their child. She further explained the uproar that would be caused by Theta's society-conscious mother. Theta asked that the doctor remain mum on the test results. Since Theta was twenty, she was legally protected. The doctor felt it necessary to go beyond the clinical diagnosis.

"Theta, I repeat myself often. But I'd feel better if you knew what I try to assist others to realize," Dr. Inabinet explained. "Having a baby is not a disease. It's a phenomenon. It's a natural progression of life and—in almost every case—a benefit of love endowed. Yet so many who find themselves pregnant are presented with a modern-world dilemma. Is this a good thing or a bad thing? Does it fit my lifestyle? Is it incredibly inconvenient? Should I deliver or abort? You may have your own thoughts on the subject as I do."

Theta was focused upon the doctor's mentoring advice, wondering if she was suggesting that she give up the baby by procedure or adoption. Theta cocked her head slightly as Dr. Inabinet continued. She didn't quite understand.

"I have built my career on what I feel are principles I am compelled to follow because those principles are part of who I am. A little person is developing inside of you. That little person consumes your diet and suffers should you deviate from what is wholesome. He or she has no choice except for what your choices are—and what choices you require of yourself. You are carrying a responsibility that may take nine minutes, nine months, or ninety years to relate to your life. I am a doctor who chooses life. I choose it every day. Should you feel as I do, then I will assist you to the best of my ability to make sure that responsibility you have has the best start possible in a life you provide."

Theta's eyes welled up. She felt compelled to tell the doctor of her insight.

"Dr. Inabinet," she stated while holding back tears, "I have no intention other than to deliver this baby. I have no concern of what anyone else thinks. It's my choice. This baby represents the love of my life but a man who is gone from me forever. I will have the baby and cherish this new life."

Theta began to cry and then went silent. Dr. Inabinet consoled her.

"Oh, my dear, you will have my full attention, and I pledge you my utmost care," Dr. Inabinet whispered.

Dr. Inabinet did not need to pry into a patient's personal life but felt compelled to assist someone she felt was stressed over the result.

After the confirmation visit to Dr. Inabinet, Theta knew that there was, but one course to follow and decided to go to her father's office to tell him the entire truth about her and Billy. She felt a sense of calm in revealing the truth and circumstance to her father because she knew he would always act in her interest instead of his own.

She drove straight to his downtown office on Broad Street. She told his receptionist, Mamie Legare, that she would wait until he was not busy and sat patiently for ten minutes. Her father walked a client to the door and saw Theta. He knew something was serious.

Simmons Barnwell was a fine lawyer and an upstanding member of the community. His specialty was loss mitigation representing large corporate interests embroiled in class action lawsuits. He made a comfortable living.

"Theta, what a pleasant surprise," Simmons began. "Everything all right?"

"Dad, I need to speak with you about something really important. Do you have a few minutes?" she asked.

"Mamie, please hold my calls," he directed to his receptionist. He then led Theta into his office, closing the door behind him.

They sat on the corner sofa by the coffee table. Simmons was concerned and sat down. They faced each other.

"Dad, you know everything about me and my life. I have never hidden anything from you and never will. But something happened that I've had to keep to myself for weeks on end," Theta started.

"Theta, I hope you know that you can tell me anything. My concern will always be you and your happiness, my child," Simmons responded.

"Dad, this is a difficult one. You knew about Billy Grayson and the accident?" she asked.

"Yes. Theta, is he still recovering from the coma? I know that you were very fond of him in high school," the doting father noted.

"Dad, he is struggling to breathe and may never walk again. If he makes it, he may have severe brain damage. I am distraught," she intimated as she held back tears.

"Honey, there is a benevolent God who will look after Billy. You have to have faith. You must continue to pray," her father shared.

"Dad, I love Billy."

Her words drifted as she paused to compose herself.

"The weekend before the accident, I lost my virginity to Billy."

Simmons Barnwell was slightly taken aback, sensing that there was more information to be disseminated.

Theta began to sob openly. "I just came from Dr. Inabinet's office, and I'm pregnant with Billy's baby. It was not his fault. It was all mine."

"Theta, you poor girl. You've been carrying this information inside all this time. You have been on edge about the accident. I've heard you praying. You've included him in nearly every conversation since you've been home. It is evident that you love him."

Her father was scrambling for words of reassurance. He was thinking about all of the ramifications of her pregnancy.

Theta lamented momentarily. "I should have saved myself for marriage as I always planned. I know that. But I fell so deeply in love with Billy, and he never pushed the issue. I did. Then when he nearly died, I went there to be with him every day. I prayed that he would live no matter what would happen to me."

"So he would have no idea that you're with child. What about his parents?" Simmons asked as he considered the implications.

"They were there with Billy too. And his little sister, Carla," she began. "They are despondent already. When I assumed that I might be pregnant, I really wanted to let them know about our relationship. But then I thought telling them would be selfish of me. They had too much to pray over already."

Theta thought about the consequences of the information she had just shared with her father. She wanted to convey the importance of keeping the biological father's name confidential.

"My pregnancy wasn't confirmed until about an hour ago. Nobody knows but you," she stated.

She added her concerns. "Nobody can ever know who the father is, not even Mother. Why would that identification matter? Let the rumors swirl. I want to have this baby. As bad as this may be for others, I know that I love Billy and he loved me. If we never found each other again in this life, we found true love, and I want to keep our baby."

Theta continued to cry. Simmons became concerned that his executive assistant, Mamie, might overhear her emotional confession.

Simmons was immediately fond of Billy because Theta lifted his character to the pinnacle. It was an unconventional twist of circumstance that a father would immediately embrace the persona of an unwed daughter's lover.

Simmons clutched her hand and looked into her wetted eyes.

"Theta, you will have the baby. I will be there for you. You're right. We cannot let anyone know the name of the father. But you have to be prepared for the onslaught of busybodies that will pressure you to know that information," he advised, "especially your mother."

"I regret that you have not gotten to know the man that I felt was most like you," Theta told her father. "He is honest, a gentleman, and very bright. I just hope he can pull through. Please never blame him for what will be a blessing for both of us. I promise to be the best mother ever. I can handle this."

He released her hands and stood up. She looked up at him lovingly. He turned and walked to the closet next to his private bathroom.

"Sit a while dear," he directed. "I have something."

Simmons opened the wall safe in the closet and pulled out a small wooden box. He removed the contents and replaced the box. He closed the safe and brought something mysterious to Theta in his left hand. It was an heirloom amulet on a silver chain. The nearly clear stone was tinted lavender. She had never seen anything like it.

"You take this and wear it. I have had it far too long. It belonged to a relative many years ago, and it was passed down in the family over the generations. I have no idea of its value, its origin, or its meaning. My grandmother told me to give it to the person who needed it most. When I asked how I would know who that was, she just said 'You'll know.' Simmons declared in a low tone. "Until now, I had no idea that that person would be you."

Theta was intrigued by the mysteriously tinted Barnwell family heirloom. It had a medieval clasp and a sculptured silver setting to affix the stone. She placed it around her neck, locking the clasp below her chin before swinging the walnut-sized stone to the front. She wore it as directed but wondered what the stone had to do with her predicament.

"I have no idea what it represents. But I am convinced that it is a protection that will shield you well beyond my earthly years," Simmons instructed. "MaMa seemed to think that this stone had magical powers and saved many lives. I only ask that you do not ever surrender it until you know deep in your heart who to pass it to and when. It has meaning beyond life. Never lose it."

"Are you sure I am the right recipient, Dad? I do not feel deserving of anything right now. I will bring you and Mother so much embarrassment. How can I live up to the standard that you have set and lived? I feel so awful now."

New tears streamed across her reddened cheeks.

"Dear. Dear. No reason to be upset. I will have a grandchild. You will have a child. It is a time to be happy, not sad. There is no reason to spend time in sorrow.

She thanked him and apologized for any hurt she may bring into his life. Theta hugged her father.

"Theta, I want you to think about something. Suppose Billy had not had the accident? Would you feel the same way?" Simmons asked.

"If he had not had the accident, then my foolish pursuit of him would have ended his soccer career, his free education, and maybe his direction in life. I would have caused him to miss out on all that he deserved. And he might have felt robbed of so much later in life," Theta related. "I've thought about this while I was sitting in the Atlanta hospital every day. Dad, that situation could have cost me his future devotion."

"Theta, you are smarter and wiser than I knew," Simmons said. "I want you to know that I am proud of you always and especially proud that you do not make excuses and take personal responsibility.

"Be prepared, dear. Your mother will have a very strong opinion. Just deal with it and know that you should do what is in your heart. Have the baby. I have your back," Simmons said. "We'll find a way."

Simmons walked Theta to the office door. He hugged her again. Theta left. She would go directly home to report her new information to her difficult mother.

Theta's mother, Martha, was not as understanding. She envisioned Theta to be the debutante and social success that she had been. She had mapped out Theta's future to join the Garden Club, the DAR, and the church auxiliary. She was to participate in the seasonal cultural events on the Charleston calendar as Martha's amazing daughter, formally educated as a Phi Beta Kappa at Scott College. She had presupposed that Theta's wedding would be the most exquisite showpiece wedding of the year and that Martha's friends would talk about it for its beauty and perfection.

The ensuing conversation was difficult, and the reaction was much as Theta had calculated.

She came into the house with a sense of conviction, knowing what was to come. She knew that the conversation would not be pleasant. She found her mother thumbing through a design magazine in the kitchen.

"Mom, you have a minute?" Theta began.

"What now, Theta?" she asked looking up from the magazine article.

"I just returned from Dr. Inabinet and found out that I am pregnant," Theta blurted out.

Her mother was stunned.

"What? Who? When?" Martha asked in a loud tone.

"I'm pregnant. It doesn't matter 'who' because I'll never even let that person know. I have no marriage plans, and the man is out of my life. I'm due in late May," Theta followed.

"Young lady, you have no idea what you're doing. You're not ready to be a mother. Nonsense. Does your father know?" Martha pressed.

"Yes, he knows. He said he'd support me in any way I need," Theta added.

She felt a small sense of vindication in letting her mother know that her father handled the news very well. She knew that the household would be divided.

"Theta, how many weeks?" Martha asked. "You must be in the first trimester."

"Seven. And don't even think about it. I'm having the baby. I'm twenty. It's not your decision," Theta declared.

"You have no idea. A single mother! No college degree. Use your common sense. Your life will never be normal again," Martha insisted. "You can get an abortion and go back to a normal life—especially if the father is not of consequence. There is so much ahead for you. Don't do this to me!"

"Mom, my life is normal," Theta explained. "And since when is my pregnancy doing something to you?

"I have an abnormal circumstance, that's all. The father will never even know he's a father. It is no fault of his but is all mine. I take full responsibility. But I'm normal. I know my heart. I know my feelings. I will do everything I can to make sure that the baby will represent who we are as a family. Terminating this pregnancy will end my hope of being normal. It will make your life more convenient, but can't you see, Mother, it will ruin mine? I cannot even stomach the thought. I'm having this baby, and that's that."

The argument initiated a vast chasm. Both women left the room. Both cried but for different reasons.

Martha Barnwell retreated from society as if her gorgeous child, Theta, was now her life's most significant embarrassment. Theta and Martha had broken entirely from the mother-daughter relationship. Theta knew that the relationship was strained over the past decade. They had little in common.

Conversely, Simmons Barnwell was proud of Theta. He knew her resolve, and he championed her independence. Theta had a quiet confidence that circumvented the apprehension of the unknown. She was smart and resourceful and radiated bravado within a moral value system. To Simmons, the course that Theta had set for her and the unborn child made him more proud of her by the day. He told her of his pride often.

After Theta told her mother the harsh reality of her pregnancy, Simmons Barnwell took Martha's emergency call at the office, predicting the purpose she would promote.

"Mamie, go ahead and patch her in," Simmons instructed his assistant.

She was vehement in advancing the idea of an abortion for Theta.

"Martha, you're doing it again. You're imposing your sense of status upon our daughter. She is of an age to make her own decision, and she has made it. Accept it and respect it. I will hear no more about it." He angrily hung the phone.

Simmons chose supportive words to deliver when he came home that evening. At first, he gave Theta the advice to think about finishing the semester at Scott College and taking a break from school before resuming the following fall.

"Dad, I know that my academic work is much more critical now. I promise to finish college. But I cannot go back now. Billy's teammates or my roommate will know that I am pregnant. What if his family finds out? His roommate, Jackie, would figure it out too."

"I understand. Then, let's find a way to rework schedules. You could finish your academic work at the College of Charleston," Simmons suggested.

Her father transitioned to make another observation.

"Theta, lesser people do lesser things. It is the moral character that wells within you that manifests as the greatness of a life lived with purpose. I admire you beyond what you may ever know. And you should hold in your heart that I admire your principle," Simmons professed. "Don't hate your mother. She'll get through this too."

"Dad, you know I get my convictions from you," Theta replied. "I do have your iron will. And Mom hates me. I believe that once the baby arrives, she might come around. She'll love being a grandmother. I still think of Billy as the perfect gentleman with whom I fell in love. I realized that I had found my perfect match. He felt the same way. And in a flash, I do not have him. I may never know true love again."

Theta paused as she wiped the tears away.

"But I have the chance to have our child. Dad, I will never know the life we would have had together. But I do know that Billy lives deep in my heart and that this baby will be a gift. I am not embarrassed like Mom is. I am proud to have had the honest love of Billy Grayson and the experience of knowing that true love fell into my life, if only for a short time."

Simmons immediately consoled his sobbing daughter; his arm wrapped tightly around her shoulder as he pulled her to him. "Theta, keep that point of view as hope. Your life is special. You are charmed. You will find great happiness again. Be diligent, but be patient, my dear."

Dr. Inabinet delivered more good news to Theta during her follow-up visit. Just nine weeks into her pregnancy, the ultrasound detected that she was carrying two embryos. Theta was elated at the news that she would deliver twins. It was providence.

The months of Theta's pregnancy became a building dam of rumor and innuendo. The swell of fiction, like the rising floodwaters, was e-mailed back and forth between erstwhile friends from her high school. Would the dam hold?

Some guessed that she had a wealthy lover who was already married. Some speculated she was a surrogate mother for a couple wanting a child. Some imagined that she had been raped at college. Others assumed that she had gotten pregnant at a party and rejected the suitor.

Friends hounded Theta for the detailed cause of her condition. She simply sidestepped the queries. Some of the approaches were anything but subtle. Other female friends tried to win her trust just to ascertain the information. Theta was resolved never to indicate the father or the circumstance. She answered all of her blatant questioners by the same pat answer.

"The father will remain anonymous for the benefit of all concerns. As a friend, I ask you please do not pursue this any further," she consistently replied.

Sadly, the pregnancy shattered many friendships from her high school years. Theta was both determined and contented in spite of the social uproar. She knew that she would resume her coursework at college in the fall semester. Her father had recommended that she study something that she enjoyed and that would have employment possibilities beyond her degree. He wanted her to think about attaining her masters or perhaps even a doctorate. Theta spent the months in quiet and insular preparation of her new children.

By her next visit, the sex of the twins had been determined. She would deliver daughters. She looked through library sources for parenting articles, nutritional insight, and for naming ideas.

Buoyed by the exuberance of her father and the special care of her doctor, Theta endured the morning sickness, indigestion, and swollen ankles associated with her pregnancy. She braved the snarky remarks and the odd stares from friends she had not seen. The most challenging obstacle before her was not physical or social. It was her knowledge that the children she would raise would never know their father. He was the man she had loved with devotion and completeness.

Her father had recommended Theta to a friend for a part-time job in a travel agency. The friend hired Theta on the strength of her father's community reputation despite Theta's burgeoning girth. She worked hourly for four months without health benefits prior to her water breaking.

The twins came early. The natural delivery she had planned would have to be altered in favor of a Caesarian section. Nurses scurried. The two newborns had a risk of an umbilical entanglement. They were born without other complication at thirty-four weeks. Theta prayed that they would be healthy.

Their postnatal care at the Regional Children's Hospital was superb. The maternity staff recorded their Apgar scores and registered their respective weights. The babies received their identification bracelets.

As the babies were brought back wrapped and tucked, Simmons Barnwell was allowed in. He came forward and kissed Theta on the forehead. He kissed his new granddaughters similarly. The tall, thin barrister proved to be a paragon of the Charleston community. His benevolence was only exceeded by the gentleness of his soul. He was diligent yet patient. His only child had become his most trusted sounding board. They were much alike. He pledged his financial and moral support to Theta.

"My darling daughter," he started, "you have exceeded my every expectation. You are at my highest level of honor. You may never have a day that will make me more proud of you than this day. Now rest and enjoy the future."

Her green eyes stared fixed upon her doting father, a man unlike any other. She knew that she had made him happy.

Theta's tears—tears of utter joy—began anew.

Martha Barnwell did not come to the hospital.

Theta remained deeply in love with the memory of the man who was their father but whom she doubted would ever function normally again. She never told Lucy and Mathew Grayson that they were grandparents. Yet she would list them as grandparents at delivery that first week in May. The father that Theta listed was William Reynolds Grayson. By Theta's agreement, the birth certificate was modified for the public record. Her father had this part of Theta's privacy altered before she left the hospital.

Theta would have preferred having a trust relationship with her mother and letting her know the name of the twins' father. But Martha Barnwell could never keep a secret. Secrets were Martha's favored currency for acceptance into her wide social circles.

Martha assumed that no one knew the father other than Theta. She used the excuse of this family mystery to explain her division of sympathies with her only child. It was also because her mother wanted her to abort the child, as the pregnancy would pose untenable complications related to her societal standing.

The newborns would complete the wishes of a grandfather, the hopes of his daughter, and the blatant disapproval of Martha Barnwell. The rift would become profound. Theta would be entirely responsible to the two girls without the assistance of her mother. Her mother had hardly acknowledged that the miracle and joy of two related births had occurred.

Theta and the babies left the hospital in three days because of the Caesarian complication. She named them Leah and Mia. They were fraternal twins. She could see that Leah favored Billy, but the resemblance would remain her secret.

The rest of her life would begin when she arrived home. She was mentally ready for the myriad challenges—the feedings, the finances, the sleepless nights, the rumors, and the sneers of her mother. Martha offered little help to Theta.

Theta took her father's advice and required only two years and two summer sessions to gain her degree in marine biology. She was able to work part-time at the travel agency. She juggled schedules and left little time for herself. By the time the twins were three, she had a degree and a full-time job at the travel agency. She stayed at the agency because she could build other income from commissions and bonuses.

Her sole work friend, Rosie Callahan, had convinced Theta to come to after-hour functions from the office on occasions. She gave her cards out at monthly Chamber of Commerce meetings. Those that noticed she did not wear a wedding ring called as dating prospects. Some diverted their plans immediately when told that she had to get a babysitter. A few that she dated to events like Christmas parties and company outings were fine gentlemen but not of the ilk of the man she used to know and couldn't dismiss. She showed no interest. She went on three dates with a young minister but could not recapture what she internalized as the "never-ending conversation." They remained friends.

Theta focused her efforts to her priority—providing for Mia and Leah. She knew that their apartment-living childhood would need an upgrade and saved meticulously for a small home. Her father continued to mentor her and would have extended funds to assist a home purchase had it not been for a devastating ordeal. His cancer worsened. Treatment options dwindled. His welfare in his last few months became Theta's obligation and honor.

CHAPTER TWENTY-THREE

Providence

(Two Years after the Accident)

P ROVIDENCE IS A catalyst for happiness.
Socially, Theta had no one to tell that she was the virgin who became pregnant. Even her best friends pushed away from the lovely Theta, a would-be virgin who had become a phony in their eyes. They had no idea about the deep and abiding love that existed between her and Billy. Cruelty has no bounds.

Concurrently, by May the following year, Billy's visit to a neurological rehabilitation facility in Houston meant that he would not be there or even know of Theta's delivery of the twins. He was recovering by inches and millimeters.

Jackie Mann had not been apprised of Theta's pregnancy and delivery. Before Billy transferred to the Houston Rehabilitation Center,

Jackie visited frequently. Others visited. Coach Harmon and many of Billy's teammates saw him in the early days, but none came after six months.

Theta was at the hospital daily until the fear of her pregnancy showing required her departure. When Theta quit coming before Christmas, Jackie assumed that she had either given up or began dating someone. Jackie never thought to get Theta's number in case Billy made progress.

Months of critical attention delivered Billy from death's door to ambulatory rehabilitation. His verbal skills improved rapidly. His atrophied physique began to build mass again. Theta continued to pray for Billy every day.

The long chasm of noncommunication with all those he knew was secondary to Billy's memory loss. Everyone he saw who were in his life before the accident appeared to him as a stranger. With the breakthrough of communication exchanges, the total rehabilitation process gave minimal hope for his memory to return. Billy was taking dangerous steroids to repair damages. He could not take them for an extended period for fear of other debilitating effects. He was on blood thinners, antibiotics, and—for much of the time—life support mechanisms. His total bill exceeded the college's million-dollar catastrophic coverage policy for athletes.

Cooper High started a fund-raiser. Georgia Tech did the same. Billy had no idea of the financials or the people who donated. Theta Barnwell was the primary catalyst in Charleston. Jackie Mann raised funds in Atlanta.

With progress in Houston established, Billy moved to the Bryson Clinic. It happened that the Bryson Clinic for Neurological Disorders included a cutting-edge discipline of creative enterprise. There, Billy learned to walk again, to whistle, to laugh, and to write. Month by month, his progress was encouraging. Dr. Vogel, an enterprising therapy superstar at the clinic, introduced Billy to the guitar. It was propitious.

In five more months at the clinic after the progress in Houston—and only twenty-four months after the traumatic accident—Billy had navigated the entire medical transition episode. He left the clinic under his own power. He flew back to Atlanta. Jackie Mann met him there to help set him up in a new apartment. He and Frieda had recently married. They were so happy for Billy.

To Billy, he had befriended Jackie after the accident. He knew of nothing prior. He didn't know Frieda. His world was new every day.

Jackie was surprised to see him carrying a guitar case into the flight arrival waiting area. He was amazed to see his gait and his ease of movement.

"Whose guitar is that?" Jackie asked.

"It's a gift from Dr. Vogel," Billy replied.

"Wait . . . you went to Houston unable to even talk, and you come back with a guitar," Jackie vocalized. "Can you play it? You never played music before."

"Jackie, I have no idea whether I played music before. But I can now," Billy observed. "And the funny thing is that it comes to me easily. I don't really think about it. It's second nature. And I love it!"

Billy had spent nearly two years in hospitals and clinics. In that time, his patience for all things was enhanced. His strong figure had atrophied. His mind was bereft of all details from his past. The rise from the bottom was steep. He was nearly back to his imposing athletic physique. He was discovering new things about himself daily, and he had clearly become a musical ingenue. He had high-level skills that his mind tapped into—dormant before the accident.

When Billy asked Jackie if he dated anyone, Jackie told him a handful of girls that he used to date, the last being Theta Barnwell.

"But, Billy, you and Theta were not really dating . . . just friends. She was nice and wholesome but was the Antarctic's largest floating iceberg. You had nothing going, trust me," Jackie assured him.

Billy was convinced that he was particularly unattached with no current romantic prospects at the time of the injury. It simplified things.

He told Jackie that he had gained a deep-seated aspiration to write songs.

"Songs are in my head, trying to get out to my fingers on my guitar," Billy told Jackie. "And I have energy to pursue this that I cannot explain."

Miracles happen. Billy was nearly fully recovered. He could now read notes, write lyrics, and sing well enough to attract listeners. Life-threatening and traumatic experiences like Billy's have had similar transitional results recorded in medical journals.

There was a physician in Michigan who was struck by lightning in 1994 while at an outdoor phone booth. Dr. Joey Cicado was nearly killed but miraculously survived. His skills as a doctor remained, but he acquired another skill previously foreign to him. He became a concert pianist. Oddly, he had no abilities in that area of culture before the lightning strike.

An interview on YouTube detailed the moment. "I experienced total calm and peace in that flash moment as I gazed into a crystal-blue cloud. I redirected the new force that flowed through me," Dr. Cicado recalled. He became a concert pianist overnight and even produced a landmark piece that he named, aptly, "Blue Lightning Sonata."

In 2002, a Welsh plumber had a similar experience. Hugh Lawson had an aneurysm while getting ready for work one morning. He was in surgery for five hours and nearly died. He fully recovered several months later, but his brain worked differently. He could paint very colorful canvases of faces he saw vividly. These were souls crying for help within his life-threatening trauma. His obsession with the painting process took him to a level of energy that had him filling canvases sixteen hours per day. Though he had no formal training, his works were in demand. The sudden aneurysm changed his life.

Billy Grayson not only recovered after his ordeal but was also experiencing the Cicado effect. He had become a musical genius in both his timing for note sequence and as a lyricist. He saw music clearly and felt the pace and concordance of lyrics instinctively. Billy had written a seven-stanza song on the plane between Houston and Atlanta. The music was compelling. It was his new beginning. It cemented his future. He had no past to otherwise consider. Jackie Mann marveled at the new Billy. Billy's guitar playing led to his confidence to sing out with the lyrics he had written. Billy was an undiscovered singer-songwriter whose skill set rose to a professional standing in less than ninety days. He needed this conduit to bring him to a new and exciting career.

The medical journals recorded the transformation. It was eerie. A man who almost died and had to learn to talk without stuttering was playing new and brilliant melodies. His uniquely suited raspy voice was the finishing asset. He was different. And he could write lyrics as well as he could play the notes.

CHAPTER TWENTY-FOUR

Requiem

SIMMONS BARNWELL HAD an unselfish wish. He wanted to die suddenly. He had prepared himself for the moment. But he had not prepared others. He did not want his family to suffer the daily impairments of an extended illness.

Simmons bought a burial plot in the Magnolia Memorial Gardens. It was near a small oak that bordered the back marsh. The shade was for his fair-complexioned daughter, Theta. He had arranged to place a marble bench there that matched the coping. He planted azaleas and gardenias—plants that could survive the hot Charleston summers in the indirect sunlight under the oak. The stone bench faced away from the small mausoleum he had installed. Simmons knew that the time that anyone spent at his grave site would be better spent in the marsh view of the Ravenel Bridge. It was the highest fixed span bridge in the Western Hemisphere.

Besides, Simmons thought, who would want to look at something depressing when there was something beautiful in the opposite direction?

Simmons's wife, Martha, and daughter, Theta, had no idea that the plot, the mausoleum, and the view even existed. They would find out when its use became necessary.

Detailed exit plans never seem to follow a script. Some unforeseen obstacle always trips the retreat. When Simmons Barnwell had to retire as the effects of non-Hodgkin's lymphoma reduced his abilities, everything changed. He confided in Theta. His will transferred everything to Theta's mother to resolve debts and the considerable medical bills as well as provide her living expenses. He reserved a small trust for his granddaughters, Mia and Leah. It had a $40,000 corpus deposited for their formal education, administered by Theta. He also gifted $70,000 to Theta to place a down payment on a home. She had been a renter for over two years.

Other limited funds were set aside for the funeral, for several of his favorite charities, and for his beloved church's building fund. The Grace Church would host his final services.

As death approached, Theta worked daily, took the twins to a student neighbor's apartment, and visited her father in the evenings. He was much more than a father to Theta. He was her most admired mentor and confidant. Without him, her world should inevitably regress. She had to be strong.

Martha Barnwell was scarcely able to repair the relationship she had banished in favor of her social standing. Her wine-wetted lunches turned into multiple cocktail evenings. She never reconciled when Theta divulged that she would be an unwed mother. Martha was further distanced because Theta would never allow her the secreted knowledge she demanded—the name of the children's father.

As Simmons's disease progressed, the family was called in. Simmons was placed on a drip solution of morphine to ease the pain. Hospice reacted in their most accommodating and expert coercion to the end. Theta cried for days. Martha drank her time away until the funeral.

It was during the intensity of the final days that Martha came in the evening. She was slurring her words and thoroughly drunk. She stopped Theta at the door as she kissed Simmons's forehead as he dozed and attempted to leave.

"This is all your fault, young lady. You brought the stress and his cancer. You caused the drinking. You and those bastard kids," Martha charged. "All you had to do is terminate the pregnancy, but, no, you wanted to bring me this pain."

Theta looked at her mother, shook her head, and forced her way past her, never saying a word. At four o'clock the following morning, Simmons Barnwell passed away.

Grace Church coordinated the services with Alford's Funeral Home. Theta was to sit in the first pew with the twins separating her from her mother. It was for public show. The twins were only six years old. Martha wore her traditional black. Theta wore a melon-colored dress with a shawl for the November chill. She volunteered to perform a biblical reading by reciting the Apostle John (14:1–6).

> *Do not let your hearts be troubled.*
> *You have faith in God; have faith also in me.*
> *In my Father's house, there are many dwelling places.*
> *If there were not, would I have told you*
> *that I am going to prepare a place for you?*
> *And if I go and prepare a place for you,*
> *I will come back again and take you to myself,*
> *so that where I am you also may be.*
> *Where I am going, you know the way.*

Theta performed the pace of the reading expertly, never looking up to see the full audience of mourners. She wanted Mia and Leah to hear the words much as they would listen to a dramatic reading of a fairy tale in the Bib and Bibliothéque on Saturdays. She wanted to commemorate the special relationship she had with her father bravely. Her performance was admirable given the hours that she spent in the despair of his passing. Her father loved her, she knew. He loved the mannerly twins profoundly.

The interment ceremony was different. The funeral stretched nearly a mile down Wentworth Street to Coming to East Bay, Morrison, and, finally, to Cunnington Avenue, where the old Charleston families were buried. Gravestones dated to the early 1700s from the four cemeteries that abutted the area.

Theta symbolically placed a carnation on the top of the casket before the exercise of sliding it into the permanent enclosure of the mausoleum. After the ceremony, she rode back to her apartment with the twins in hand.

She never saw her mother again.

Her father's last cogent words to her rang out.

"Life is a wilderness. We encounter a variety of fellow travelers to make the journey seem secure. The other end presents a new wilderness where our familiar travelers leave us. That is where we will be most secure."

The thought of her father's perspective warmed her. She found peace in his sense of an ultimate destination. Simmons Barnwell had taught her to travel life unafraid.

Theta, now alone in a challenging world, injected more into her travel agency career. Before the year's end, she was promoted to assistant manager. Because of her sincerity and keen organizational skill, her customer base grew. It allowed her to gain the income necessary to fit a bank's stern lending guidelines.

She found a three-bedroom home in a neighborhood close to the twins' school. She calculated that she could afford it and would stay there until they began college. It had no frills. There was no fireplace or crafted woodwork. The counters in the two bathrooms and the kitchen were of pink tile. The driveway was cracked from tree roots, but the roof was good, and the fenced yard had plenty of play area. Besides, she would need to build an equity fund to handle the unknown emergencies that could happen as she raised Mia and Leah.

Theta remained diligent in bringing the girls to church and Sunday school. She also enjoyed the academic and cultural advancements of Saturday mornings at the Bib and Bibliothéque. The price was perfect—free!

She missed her father. She lost Billy Grayson. But she had her twins. They depended on her vision, her effort, and her choices. The three of them would face the world ahead alone.

CHAPTER TWENTY-FIVE

Chance

ASHTON GRAYSON WAS unusual for a three-year-old. He never walked anywhere. The toddler ran. On this muggy Saturday, he left his father, Billy, to run into the reading emporium. He wanted to arrive in time to play with the Legos before the dramatic reading of *Hansel and Gretel*.

As Ashton turned past the overstocked display of books on Renaissance art, he ran into Theta Barnwell hard enough to propel him to the floor. He was stunned but did not cry. Theta reached down to help him up, hoping that he did not break anything. Her demeanor was soft and apologetic as if she were responsible for the collision.

"Oh, my heavens! Are you OK?" Theta responded as she reached down. "You really pack a wallop, young man! And look how strong you are!"

The softness of her voice and the motherly instincts seemed to calm Ashton. He was immediately unaware of any pain from the stunning impact.

Just as he was lifted by his underarms back to an upright position, Billy appeared. He was concerned that he had heard Ashton fall.

"Ashton, are you OK, buddy?" Billy asked. He was simultaneously surprised to see Theta.

As Theta placed him down, he immediately ran to his father. Billy bent down to hug him, though he still did not let on that he was stunned or hurt.

Theta noticed that Billy was thinner and that his hair was longer. She knew that he had been through a grueling rehabilitation and recovery over the past eight years. Though he still commanded an athletic appearance, he was nearly twenty pounds lighter.

"I see that you have a very grown-up little boy. We collided quite hard, him bouncing off of the rear of my leg," Theta reported. "But he seems all right, and I'm fine too, Billy. This must be the little tyke you told me about a few months ago."

"Yes. This is my little buddy, Ashton. Sorry that he ran into you. I know he was not walking. He developed from a crawl to a run. There was no walk in between. He never walks anywhere."

Theta noticed how cute Ashton was and how much he was attached to Billy in an unsure moment. Billy whispered to Ashton and rubbed his head, and off he went at full speed to the reading emporium.

"I'm glad I've found you, Theta. I called and left you a message a while back. Then I had to travel to Nashville," Billy began.

"Sorry, Billy. I should have called you back. I have an aversion to getting involved with the dating scene. I have the two girls, and they take my entire time. Once guys see the instant-family future of two precocious little girls, they are not apt to have an interest in dating anyway," Theta explained. "In a sense, my hesitance saves them the walk into the wall of reality. I live for the twins."

Billy nodded and then acquiesced by counterproposing something different.

"Theta, I have an identical commitment but have to juggle my travel with my mom—who helps me raise the 'Roadrunner.' So let's establish that we will not date. That way, we can't possibly sacrifice our priorities. Instead, let's plan on seeing each other as time allows right here—when we both have the kids at the emporium," Billy suggested.

"No dates, no schedule, no hassle. We operate on a sense of serendipity. If I come on Saturday mornings to bring Ashton and see you, then maybe we can have a short cup of coffee or a bagel. And vice versa. Look for me when you come. If I'm here, let's at least take a few minutes to chat. I'd like knowing that you might be here."

Billy had no idea that Theta longed to see him but had avoided him for the pain that would revisit her all too often. She brought Leah and Mia to the reading emporium with the repressed thought that Billy might be back in town.

"Ashton begs me to take him here," Billy conceded.

Billy had built a curious interest in the girl with the twins that raised money for him without a need to be thanked. She always dressed conservatively. Her grace and humility were attractive. Her emerald eyes were sterling and much like his, though his green eyes were gray-shaded.

"You are a good father, Billy. Too many parents let their careers get in the way of their parental responsibilities these days," Theta stated. "I must remind myself of that important balance often."

"Thank you for saying that, but you just wouldn't believe the dilemma that I am presented with—always related to my career," Billy answered, wanting to expound upon the concerns he shared with Sid Toile.

"Ashton is comfortable with Mom, but I have to leave sometimes for a week or so. I had considered moving to Nashville so that I wouldn't ever need to leave him, but I would have to leave Mom and my sister, Carla, here in Mount Pleasant. I'm still struggling with it. Ashton has never known his mother. I'm all he has, and when I'm away, it places too much on my mother. I have to work on a better solution."

Theta was mesmerized by the parallels in their lives, knowing that Billy was at the B & B with three children he had fathered, not one. Nonetheless, she could readily see that he was a kind and sincere man who had not allowed the trappings of celebrity to devour his sense of responsibility.

"Billy, I have been able to juggle my life for my daughters by using the B & B's emporium wisely. They come here for entertainment. While they hear a fairy tale or watch a puppet show, I search the travel section for information about places I recommend to clients in the travel agency," Theta explained. "The more knowledgeable I become, the better the agency that I manage. That travel agency allows me to raise the girls on a single income."

Billy nodded, just realizing that when he had seen Theta at the B & B, each time she was near the travel section.

"Could I speculate that you also have a great interest in travel? If not, you would not be successful, correct?" Billy asked.

"Billy, I would love to go to the places that I recommend to others. As it is, I've only been engaged in travel a few times. There was our senior trip to Miami ten years ago. Well, maybe you wouldn't know. Sorry."

Theta mentioned the trip knowing that Billy was on that trip just before they dated that spring. But she realized he would not recall the activities or the circle of friends who attended.

"Did I go?" Billy asked.

"Yes, you did. But we hardly knew each other. I was always the quiet one. But I think you were a bit shy as well," Theta answered.

"Where else have you traveled?" Billy followed, hoping to continue the warm conversation, as he was enjoying the reserved and mysterious lady of substance.

"You'd be disappointed to learn," Theta began. "I've only been to six states and have never left the country. Imagine that with my career! That's why I read so much about the places people want to visit."

"Any favorite places?" Billy asked.

Though Billy was asking about the places that Theta read about, Theta took the question as directed to the places she had been. Realizing that Billy had no memory of the past, she still wanted to tell him about her fondest memory.

"That's an easy one," Theta spoke from the glow of memory. "I once went with friends to a neat little place in North Alabama that was next to a beautiful waterfall. To me, I still think of those rocky waterfalls with the ten-foot drop as a piece of heaven."

Theta somehow hoped that Billy would know this place in his subconscious and make other yearning connections. She sincerely desired that he would suddenly know her as his lover and know her children as his daughters.

Billy admired Theta's way of describing a simple place. Though he was expecting a research reference to Hawaii, Paris, or the Caribbean, he was taken with the simplicity of a place of great peace Theta described.

"Perhaps you'll return there one day," Billy added. "Maybe you'll go to places you send your best clients to as well. I do hope you'll have your personal travel map enlarged."

"How about you, Billy?" Theta inquired.

"It may sound silly, but since my recovery, I have had a whirlwind. I've been to London, Prague, and Copenhagen. Our band, *The Pals*, went on a European tour for ten weeks. Rome, Barcelona, Madrid, Florence, Paris, Amsterdam, Lisbon, Munich, Vienna. I saw them all. My favorite travel moment each time is getting my luggage from the conveyor upon my return to the Charleston airport. Silly, I know."

"No, not really. Hard to argue with home," Theta added. "Besides, we don't have the traffic, the crime, the pollution, the unemployment, or the harsh winters like you'd find in so many destinations."

As Theta was responding, Mia and Leah came to her. The dramatic reading of *Hansel and Gretel* was over. Ashton was just behind them.

"Billy, I have promised them lunch at Chick-Fil-A," Theta interjected. "I sure enjoyed talking to you. I'll look for you next time."

"I hope to be here. If so, please consider a cup of coffee. I'd enjoy that," Billy added. He was smitten by the fresh and wholesome face of a girl who did not treat him as a rock star.

With the children's prompting, Billy and Theta had departed from the most intimate conversation they had engaged since the last weekend of August eight years earlier.

Theta said good-bye to the person who looked like the only man she had ever loved. Billy had bid adieu to an intriguing woman he would like to get to know better despite her reticence to dating.

CHAPTER TWENTY-SIX

Little Ashton Grayson

A WEEK LATER, BILLY Grayson came by booth 14 to see Sid with his three-year-old son, Ashton. He wanted Sid to enjoy the exuberance of youth as he did. Ashton was antsy. He had recently "graduated" from diapers and liked to play with his matchbox-sized cars on the floor. Detaining him was useless. He placed Ashton down and watched as he immediately engaged in toddler play.

"He's all boy, Sid. He loves the cars you gave him last time, as you can see," Billy started.

"Are you here to tell me you're leaving, Billy?" Sid asked.

Billy was caught off guard by Sid's abruptness.

"Yes and no," Billy replied. "I'm writing music and lyrics from home, but I just landed a deal in Nashville. I'm just going for a week to record a crossover album. They'll market test it from Blackbird Studio. If the numbers support it, they'll set up a gig at the Ryman Auditorium there within two months. It's a layover recording. In other words, I do it in three or four parts with studio musicians added as needed."

Billy caught himself in midsentence defining a music industry term that he realized Sid already knew.

"That's not why you're here, though?" Sid led Billy on.

"No, Sid, it's not. You know stuff before I do, it seems! My mom has been great at keeping Ashton for these little gigs. I like being here with Ashton. He is my life. You were right. That little guy looks to me as the avenue to make his way to adulthood. I have no other companionship. And I don't want to introduce any woman to Ashton unless I suspect that I have found the right one. It's too unstable for a child. Mom agrees."

"Billy, my friend, that particular unselfish commitment might take years. Are you prepared for that?" Sid asked.

"Absolutely. I know that now," Billy said.

"But, Sid, I am looking for advice to clear up what I may never know. Mom and I have been looking through my yearbook from Cooper River High. I do not recognize anyone. Mom pointed out a handful of students with whom I began the first grade. I marked them. She circled the girls I dated from my sophomore year on through—seven in all. Katie Abbot looked like my type. Mom says she got engaged, married, and moved away. One of those I dated for two months got married to another girl and lives in Hawaii. So I suppose I was not her type! Three others moved away. Another, Theta Barnwell, had two kids. I don't know her circumstance, but Mom said she never married. Last, there's Lois Epperly. I went out with her two weeks ago. She's a sweet person and a divorcee. But she's a bit hyper. Not my type. I can't figure why we even dated in high school. But she did say that she thought that Theta and I made a perfect couple. But Jackie Mann insists that we were just friends at best."

"What do you want, Billy? My permission to call Theta Barnwell? That's a leap, even for you," Sid began.

"I know who she is because we met by chance the other day. Her two daughters come here some weekends for the children's emporium program. They were just here last week for the marionettes. Theta appears to be a good mom. I've never met the father that I know of, and she appreciates that her personal life is none of anyone's business. Those two little girls are very well mannered. I believe they are the attorney Simmons Barnwell's only grandchildren. Anyone can see that Theta has a vaulted secret, but my senses tell me that whatever it is, it has only made her a better person."

"Yeah, Sid. Theta is a leap for me," Billy continued. "She's dedicated. She's not hard to look at, and she seems so sincere. She's nice but is very distant, if you know what I mean."

Sid nodded as he anticipated that Billy would continue the thought.

"Forget it. I feel like both of us are devoted to being single," Billy continued on his soliloquy.

"Jackie Mann roomed with me at Tech. When I had my injury, Jackie said I was dating someone else in Atlanta. Whoever that was abandoned ship. I don't blame that person. It would not have been Theta; I found out. She came to visit regularly. Everything I've put back together tells me that Theta wasn't the dating type. She was the career type. So it doesn't feel like I even knew Theta that well before the accident. He said that Theta was nice as a friend but not as a serious person to date.

"He mentioned a girl I liked named Georgiana. He said that I was nuts over her. But Georgiana never visited me. Theta did. Why would Georgiana leave me in a time of need? And, Jackie contends, Theta showed up to help and took my injury to heart. She must've been a more genuine friend than Georgiana."

Sid acknowledged Billy's thought process. "Go on."

"Sid, the best way I can describe my memory of things is that I know absolutely nothing from the past. I have to piece it all together again. Or I don't need to do anything and just live without ever knowing who I once was. Would that even matter now?" Billy asked rhetorically.

Sid felt he should respond nonetheless.

"You are who you are now. You have a gift. It's the gift of not knowing. Whoever you were should never matter to who you are," Sid instructed. "Enjoy the gift that few will ever have—the innocent gift of never knowing."

Billy absorbed the Boracle's advice as it resonated with what the therapists and his family had reinforced over the past few years. It was as if the first twenty years of his life didn't count.

"You're right, Sid. Until I was about two years past the accident, I didn't know squat. My life was all about attaching a memory to a face or an event. There was nothing. It was hard enough trying to grasp what they were trying to reteach me. I couldn't walk. I couldn't read. I couldn't even dream. I was in and out of reality. The coma should have been the end of me. I had major rehab. I had strange people and strange faces telling me they were somebody I should know—my parents, my best friends, my doctors. I didn't know me well enough to ever know them."

Sid listened attentively to extract all critical information from Billy to assist him. Billy explained his process from a vegetative state to a musical talent admired by fans across America. He told him of his despair, his loneliness, and his frustration at the pace of his physical recovery. Billy further detailed his state-of-mind in the process. Sometimes he wailed at night. Many times he almost gave up. The entire process taxed him emotionally and wore him down physically. Some days he wouldn't eat. Some days he didn't take visitors. Other days, he refused to take his medications.

Billy described the macabre world of just having eyes that searched the ceiling tiles of hospital intensive care centers for hours on end. He described people who came and went, never attaching whether they were clinicians, soccer teammates, family, or friends from a distant past. He told Sid about the four-inch diameter black and white television that was attached to a mechanical arm and set to one channel. It stayed on daily for months. He hated that TV. Moving from Intensive Care to a private room gave Billy a morsel of hope. He began to develop movement. Then speech. He began to be fed spoonfuls of regular food. His favorite was cold unsalted string beans. They were like ice cream.

Billy chuckled. "One day, early on, a rabbi walked in. He must've figured that I was Jewish. I had no reason to believe I wasn't Jewish. He began to pray a prayer called the Mi Sheberakh. I mumbled to him that I had forgotten the words and that he would need to remind me. I started faking the words he prayed in a delayed manner with an accent. He came back a few times. One day, about halfway through the prayer, a nurse came in to tell the rabbi that he was in the wrong room. The little guy just looked at me as if he just knew he hadn't wasted his time. I struggled to say, 'Rabbi, let's finish. If I'm not Jewish, what would it matter anyway?' And we finished the prayer. That rabbi continued to come by twice a week.

"One day, he came in when my very Christian mother was visiting. He introduced himself. My mother fell out laughing. Then the rabbi laughed. After it all quieted down, the rabbi put his hand on my head and said, 'Yahweh, make this man whole again, and then we can all have a shot at his soul!'"

Sid laughed at the episode. He was happy that Billy had fully recovered and had set his life toward a positive human consequence. Then he offered his view.

"You have two things to do, my friend," Sid began. "You have to reach into that soul the rabbi mentioned to find who you want to be and become that person. Then you need to find an approving accomplice. What I mean is that you are alone in your soul quest. Recruit a trustful companion. This person will eventually help you to define yourself."

"Sid, you're suggesting that I call the girl that helped me . . . Theta, right?" Billy questioned with hesitation. "Am I reading this right?"

"Just exactly what do you have to lose, Billy?" Sid postulated. "You and Theta are both single parents of differing but odd circumstances. She knows you, but you don't know anyone from before your accident. So she may know more about you than your college roommate but less than your mom. You're filling in blanks that may be embarrassing for you to ask others. But they understand, my friend. So write down the questions and make them count. Like I said, what do you really have to lose? You're an orchestra practicing on a clean sheet of notes that no one has heard before. Make it a classical piece for the ages."

"I left her a message before that she did not return. Then I saw her here. She told me that her girls are her focus and that she does not date. We agreed to maybe get a coffee one day. But I'm not sure she wants to get involved at all," Billy reported.

"What I'm hearing from a guy who beat death away with a stick is that he is giving up a noble pursuit because of an initial setback," Sid summarized to Billy. "You're made of much more, my son."

Ashton rose from the floor by the booth and whispered to Billy that he needed to go to the potty. Billy smiled. The training had worked. He excused himself from the booth and picked up Ashton to take him to the restroom.

He looked at Sid with conviction. "I'll shorten my trip to Nashville and call Theta when I return. You have my word."

CHAPTER TWENTY-SEVEN

Beauty Within

A CHILLY SATURDAY MORNING visit found Eliot S. Toile at his booth. It was as if he were there waiting on someone. He was. As the reading emporium opened and nearly a dozen young minds gathered for a pantomime performance, a most impressive woman appeared over his right shoulder.

"Mr. Toile, I'm Theta Barnwell."

With that short introduction, a life was changed.

"Yes, Theta. We've spoken before. I never forget a face. I've seen you here over the past two years with your twins. We met once by the front entrance a few months back. I remember the little girls too. They're fraternal and well-mannered. I'd bet they are near the age of eight. One is much like you, the other like her father."

Theta smiled. Sid Toile was apt to hint of what he knew as an inducement for those he hoped would sit down.

"Please join me, Theta," the Boracle started. "Can I order you anything?"

"No, sir. I'm fine." Theta began in a hesitant voice while looking down at the table.

"I'm not sure why I'm here to see you, but I know that you sense things that others do not. I have a great career managing a national travel agency here and have stayed focused upon providing my twins the best future I can."

"Got it, Theta. I'm following," Sid assured.

"The girls have never known their father, a man I loved deeply. But that man no longer exists." Theta's eyes welled up in the beginning of tears. She paused and drew the courage to explain.

"At least he does not know of these girls, or me for that matter. A tragedy occurred. Since then, I have not dated anyone. I'm twenty-eight and feel strongly that my first duty is to my children. The men that have pursued me have all seemed to be shallow—and my instant family, understandably, would turn anyone off. I shun everyone away, and I just don't know why except that I have a strong sense of motherhood. I feel that is my only destiny."

Theta smiled, hoping that the old thin and bearded man could set her upon the winds of providence. She was seeking the magical, mystical course of fate.

"Theta, maybe someone told you differently," Sid interjected. "I'm a synesticist, not a clairvoyant. I do not know your future. I simply try to solve the present."

Theta nodded.

"I gather that you can help. My issue is not so much of the future that I have concern but the present as well. Can I tell you a few personal things in the strictest confidence?"

"You already have, my dear girl. And you may continue as you wish. I do not let anything out of this booth. Your thoughts and concerns remain between us," Sid confided.

"The girls are getting older. I have lied to them and told them that their father was lost in an accident. That part is true. But they believe that the word 'lost' is the same as 'died.' Their father still lives, but the accident has indeed taken his life from me and from the daughters he never knew that he had. How will I reconcile this to them?"

Sid had already searched his "Luga-byte cache" of all things and connected the seemingly unrelated trivia. The Billy Grayson accident surfaced. He knew that Billy Grayson was the father of the twins without prying for more information. But he did not want to raise the facts beyond Theta's explanation and request for fear of startling her.

The conversation began like an admonition in a church confessional. Eight years of an electrical circuit board that needed extensive soldering had been laid out. Theta was not sufficiently confident that she wanted it fixed.

After the meaningful personal information was laid out to the Boracle, he paused a few moments and then responded.

"Theta, nearly every tragedy that I have encountered had a pain, a disdain, and a refrain," Sid offered. "You have passed through the first two and are mired in the third. You have come at precisely the right time to move to the important and beneficial fourth stage, one that you have not fully considered."

He continued, "Your daughters look to you to know the world. They go to birthday parties, and Christmas plays. There, they see their friends with parents in twos. So they already know that you are someone special serving a life that demands two parental responsibilities. Shall I go on?" Sid asked.

Theta adjusted in her seat and nodded. She was in awe of the simplicity.

"They also know that you are lonely. Your natural expressions of happiness are the surface. They will realize this as they mature," he explained, knowing he would need to address the sadness of Billy's amnesia.

"Your question is from a deeper series of questions you have, Theta. There is much more. From that long, lingering stage of refrain, you must rise. You harbor a sense of unfairness that overwhelms your sense of propriety. You believe that your life has hit its apex when in reality there is such happiness just around the corner. You will need to be decisive about finding it or avoiding it. The avoidance viewpoint is borne out of caution. You were without caution when you were most happy. Now you believe that caution is your most trusted ally. It is certainly not. Your most trusted ally is the natural God-given inclination that all humans have. It is the need to fulfill your soul."

Theta readjusted herself again in the booth. She had been visually uncomfortable since the admonition that her suitor lived beyond a most horrific accident. She was simultaneously intrigued that the Boracle knew so much of what she had experienced. She did not want to share the other details that her mother abhorred. She didn't need to.

"Theta, most of the beauty in this world is barely seen or noticed. It is the beauty of a pleasant thought, a soft evening light, a breeze from the river, the scent of honeysuckle, the sound of waves rolling to the dunes. There is the science that God gave us to treasure—childbirth, a cry of joy, laughter, and remembrance. There is a wholesome smile within your heart. You know this. You come back to it from time to time. It is vivid to you. It is beauty and rapture—and a constant that will never leave you. But your sense of caution has penned it up and left it lit by a dim forty-watt bulb. You need to take a turn from the highway to find this side road again. I cannot do it for you. You have to do this on your own."

Theta exhibited a slight smile indicating that he had immediately resolved a lengthy and burdensome conundrum. The Boracle had soldered the circuit board. Her eyes moistened as she listened. It was the revelation her soul craved.

"Theta, I connect things sometimes that I hesitate to connect because they sometimes lead to chaos—or something worse than they were as unconnected. There is no certainty in life except that everything is uncertain," Sid detailed. "I know that you went to high school with Billy Grayson."

Theta was astonished. She squirmed. Sid was about to tell her about her entire past.

"All is confidential here, so do not become defensive. It appears that you and Billy knew each other before his accident, perhaps as confidants with a special bond. Billy saw me recently. Like you, he has a parental responsibility. You have more than that as a commonality," Sid retold.

Theta was satisfied that the Boracle knew all. She was suddenly reserved and insular in her thoughts, reverting to her overcautious demeanor.

Sid noticed the change of mood.

"I hope you do not mind my insight, Theta. Billy knows nothing of his past. He cannot recall anything before his accident, as you well know. It was my idea that Billy at least tries to involve people he once knew to find his way. He will not likely regain his memory, but if he remains true and genuine, he can regain his friendships. Do you agree?"

Theta blushed. She found the conversation daunting and felt that if anyone could drill down to truth, it was the Boracle. She resisted the confrontation of the long-ago pain.

The Boracle sensed her immediate recollection of the accident's aftermath. He felt he needed to divert her thoughts.

"What you see as pain is an apparition. It is like a mirage. It must be approached for it to disappear," Sid advised.

Theta instinctively sensed that the old man in front of her was not of this world. She deduced that he must know that Billy was the father of the twins. She did not want to concede this, even to the savant.

Theta spoke up.

"I knew Billy. He was everything you said. He was honest and genuine. We were friends. When I found out he was in need, I started a phone campaign to raise money to help him. But we only raised $16,000. It wasn't much help," Theta offered. "But my dad kicked in another large amount and got most of Billy's bill caught up. I don't think Billy will ever know what my dad did for him."

Sid remained noncommittal to the facts he had connected.

"I supposed that you and Billy were close because of the work you did leading the campaign to raise the $16,000. I noted, too, that it was a call campaign." Sid added as he connected the insight that Theta was fully pregnant at the time.

"Yes, I set up a PO box and a checking account. Dad also helped with the deposits and correspondence to the Atlanta Regional Medical Center," Theta divulged.

"Theta, can I ask you something personal?" Sid followed.

Theta stirred again in her seat, nodding. But she was uneasy about what was to come.

"Did you love Billy Grayson?" Sid asked poignantly.

Theta looked down and back up, her green eyes shining in the saturated hue. She responded honestly, "Yes."

"Your secret is safe. It's OK, my dear," Sid assured her.

"Did Billy ever know, before the accident, that you were pregnant?" Sid pried further.

"No. I didn't even know," Theta whispered in a barely audible tone. Her voice cracked at the revelation.

"Do your parents know who fathered your twins?" Sid spoke lowly.

Theta knew she would need to explain. "My mother is alive and has never known. My father passed away—September—a year ago. He knew everything."

She began to explain the dynamic in a very soft voice as if she were being recorded.

"No living person other than me knows the father of the twins," Theta conceded, "until now."

"It will never be told by me. And I presume, then, that Billy does not know?" he added.

Theta turned away. She put her half-clenched fist up to her chin and looked toward the serving counter. She did not need to report the answer. Sid knew that Billy Grayson was the father of the twins, Leah and Mia, but that the amnesia absolved the predicament. Billy did not know of my condition before the accident. He had no reason to know afterward.

Theta had full tears streaming again. She turned back to Sid. She wanted to explain her intensified feelings.

"Was it necessary to attribute the girls' fatherhood to a man I thought would not even live? Billy came out of the coma and survived by a miracle. I prayed for him daily. By all accounts, he is back to normal, except that he knows of no past and would never even guess that we were lovers. What would it benefit anyone if I were to confront him with this information and order a paternity test? For what reason?

He'll never be the Billy Grayson that I knew before—or the perfect gentleman I loved honestly—who fell in love with me.

"He's a stranger to me, and I am even stranger to him. His life has been harder than mine. He will never get his prior life back. He will never remember how much we loved each other."

She paused to reflect upon her decision to have the twins.

"Had Billy not had the accident, it would have been an even bigger dilemma. My father knew this, so he felt like there was some silver lining to the situation. Had Billy not lost his memory, he would have had to change his life, his soccer career, his education, and much more because I did something stupid. The pregnancy would have stressed and maybe even ended our relationship. And it would not have been his fault, though knowing him then, he would have accepted full responsibility," Theta explained.

Theta wanted to broach the subject of the current state of affairs with the new Billy.

"He was suggesting that we reconnect as if we hadn't seen each other since high school. He has our prom photo as his basis. He has no idea about his daughters, and they have no idea about him.

"Billy called me and left a message asking me to lunch two weeks ago, Sid," Theta explained. "It was on the recorder. I was afraid to answer. The timing was awful for me. I had not come to terms that I could sit at lunch with the man I had never known in his present world but wildly in love with for who he was in my past. The love I had for that Billy was boundless. I can only bring him pain now. And I realize he cannot take away my pain because he is not the Billy I knew."

Sid did not speak, expecting that Theta would add to the response. He was hoping that she would have called Billy back. Theta gathered other thoughts.

"I know that he was hurt. I didn't respond. I didn't know what to say, and I didn't want to tell him a white lie either," Theta retold. "I believe that I have shut that door forever. I'm not sure that he ever read the letter I sent to him that told him I would be a part of his life forever. If he had that letter beyond the accident, surely he would have already connected the dots. Right?"

She was hoping that Sid would follow her line of thinking.

"Maybe the accident happened before he was able to retrieve it from the post office, and the letter was unclaimed and lost forever. It was luck or fate. Maybe it's better this way," Theta explained.

There was more information than anyone knew that Theta kept inside these many years. Much less was said to the Boracle than Theta could muster the courage to reveal.

Sid looked up to Theta, his azure eyes affixed to hers. His synesticist reception was acute. Theta loved Billy more deeply than one life could hold. But Billy Grayson had two lives.

He was about to utter the profound words that he was sure would cement a connection.

"Theta, dear, your life is just like his life in this way. It starts in the forward mode. You cannot look back every time you see Billy. You have to view the road ahead of you for your sake and the sake of the twins. I cannot predict that you will see Billy in that view. But if you keep putting your life in reverse, you will surely back over Billy. He will have the pain of two grave accidents, and so will you. Look forward only."

The savant had spoken.

CHAPTER TWENTY-EIGHT

Dr. Ramsey

SID MET HAL Butters in the lobby of the East Cooper satellite hospital to MUSC. The oncology clinic was across the parking lot. Hal had set up an appointment with the resident head of Oncology, Dr. Rich Ramsey. They waited an inordinate time before the doctor finished his rounds at ten twenty and called them in. Dr. Ramsey was skeptical of having the nonfamily member attend the meeting.

"Sorry for the delay, Mr. Butters. We had a few matters to attend that required my attendance this morning that could not be helped," Dr. Ramsey began.

"Yeah, doc, I sure understand," Hal began. "This is my friend Sid."

"Sid Toile at your service," Sid followed.

"Mr. Toile, good to make your acquaintance. Are you a lawyer or a cancer specialist?" Dr. Ramsey asked.

"Neither. I'm just a friend whom Hal has asked to attend the meeting. Not sure I can help you, him, or his wife, Viola, but I'd like to know more and help Hal through this," Sid explained.

Dr. Ramsey became defensive at first but then realized that the old frumpy man would be of no concern.

"Mr. Toile, this is among the finest facilities in the region. We are a research hospital. We are pursuing the tracks of treatment that have the best percentage outcomes and lowest invasion options to the patient," Dr. Ramsey offered with a voice of authority. "We are quite upfront with the diagnosis and treatment path for the patient and family members."

Sid noted the initial defensive posture. He was afraid that the conversation could divert into confrontational tangents that should be avoided.

"That's all we needed to know, Dr. Ramsey, and all we can ask," Sid responded kindly and humbly, assuring the doctor that his presence was innocuous.

"Hal and I will be around for any other needs that Viola may require. We're going to step out and see her now. We thank you for your time," Sid offered. "If we need a few minutes in your schedule later, should we just call your office?"

"Of course, and I will be happy to see you," Dr. Ramsey stood.

Hal was confused. He expected Sid to challenge the treatment and work a miraculous turnaround for Viola. He reluctantly stood to say goodbye to the doctor.

"Yeah, doc," Hal added. "We gonna go see my wife. Thank ya, sah."

When they reached the outside hallway, Sid began the conversation because he knew that Hal was disappointed with the meeting.

"Hal, that was a good meeting. Here's what we found out. They have a set plan of treatment. The treatment may be inflexible. They will not adapt to something outside the lines. The doctor initially thought I was a lawyer and took a legal route, telling us very little outside of the generalities. Dr. Ramsey is not likely to change if change is a determination we make. We will not know that until we see Viola," Sid summarized.

"Huh? You ain't goin' ta change her meds? We ain't movin' her? You acceptin' what dey doin'?" Hal asked.

"On the contrary, my friend," Sid replied. "I'm here to try and save her life. The most important part of that plan is to see her. That will tell me more than the doctor will. From there, we'll look at all the data and make the best determination possible."

They walked across the parking lot and into the oncology clinic. Viola's room was on the third floor with a window view of giant HVAC units. It was a subtlety expressed. Terminal patients wouldn't need an optimum view since they were destined not be repeat customers.

When Hal walked in, Viola was still on her back sleeping. She had a finger monitor for her pulse and a drip solution via arm injection for her medications. The television was low as a midday game show played. Hal started to wake her, but Sid admonished him to let her sleep.

Sid walked to the window to follow the natural light to Viola's thin and slightly emaciated body. He made mental notes of her visible vein patterns, her posture, and her pace of breathing during her sleep. He looked at her fingernails closely. He was bent over looking at her wrist when she awoke.

She saw the strange man before seeing Hal standing at the foot of the hospital bed. She was immediately confused.

"I assume this man is not the undertaker, Hal?" she inquired in sarcasm.

"No, dear. This is Sid," Hal answered, looking at Sid as he stood back straight.

"Sid Toile at your service, madam," he immediately responded.

"You ain't from hospice, are ya? I ain't ready for dem yet," she asked.

Before he could answer, she added, "Hal, you'd tell me if we at dat point, right? I know you'd tell me."

"Ma'am, I'm just a new friend of Hal's. He asked me to help research your condition and maybe see if it's possible to help you to feel better," Sid offered.

"So you another doctor. I seen twenny docs. Ain't none of dem know de udder one," she said in a surly tone.

"Ma'am, I'm not a doctor. I'm not from hospice. I'm just a person that Hal has asked to help. I have helped others. So I thought I might help you. Are you OK with that?" Sid implored.

"Man, what I got t'lose? Whatcha need from me?" she consented.

"I just need a few things from you. When you sit up, do you breathe better or worse?" he started.

"Betta."

"You have abdominal pain. Can you place your hand where it feels worst?" he followed.

"Right chere."

She placed her hand near her lower ribcage. "But you ain't got no chart, man. Ya gonna 'member all dis?"

"You bet. Now, last . . . how often do you take water or any liquids?" Sid asked.

"Not much. I ain't thirsty like I was before I got sick. Should I try ta force mo watta down?"

"No, ma'am. Not yet. I've got to work on a few things, and I'll get back with you tomorrow," Sid stated. "You rest. Visit with Hal. Drink water when you want water. I'll wait in the lobby."

He placed his hand forward to shake hers. She reluctantly lifted hers. Sid departed to the lobby.

After he left, Viola looked at Hal quizzically.

Hal felt he needed to explain.

"Sweetie, he's like a really smart man dat people go to fa ansas. I ax him fa help. It can't hurt. He met Dr. Ramsey too. Just relax and we'll see if Mr. Sid comes up wid sumthin'. Can't hurt, sweetie. Can't hurt."

Sid waited for Hal in the lobby. It happened that Dr. Ramsey walked out from the cafeteria. Sid stood up as the doctor walked nearby.

"Dr. Ramsey," he spoke up.

The doctor stopped to answer.

"I'd like to get ten minutes with you tomorrow," Sid began. "And before you make up an excuse, it's important. My wife died from pancreatic cancer thirty years ago. I miss her every day. Hal's got a tough road. Hal's in with Viola now. I was just there too."

"Mr. . . . ?"

"Toile, sir. Sid Toile. Call me Sid," Sid answered.

"Mr. Toile, you probably know that I cannot discuss patients with anyone other than family members. It's the law. So I'm sorry . . ."

"Oh, doc, we will not discuss any patient, my promise. I just want ten minutes to discuss pancreatic cancer," Sid offered.

Dr. Ramsey looked at his watch as if he were late for an appointment. He looked back up.

"I'll tell you what. Ten minutes, and that's the end. Tomorrow at my office at two thirty. If you bring up Mrs. Butters, I'll have to ask you to leave then and there. Got it?" Dr. Ramsey directed.

"Got it, doc. I'll be in and out before ten minutes expires. See you then." Sid did a slight bow and offered his hand. The doctor shook it quickly and left.

CHAPTER TWENTY-NINE

A Dark Reappearance

AS SID LEFT the medical center, a white pickup truck with Tennessee tags sat across the lot. Arlo Crutchfield had spotted the old man. Arlo had a scheme that would rid the world of Sid Toile. Arlo was a now-retired farmer with a blind view of reason. He had sworn vengeance upon the man who robbed him of his sister. It had taken him many years to find Sid. The cagey savant had escaped Arlo's grasp on prior occasions. He only needed to develop the opportunity to perform the deed of his gnawing compulsion.

He followed Sid to his condominium home and noted that the domestic assistant, Maria, left immediately. As she drove away, Arlo got out of his truck and inspected the area around the complex. He did not go to the elevator area or to the front marsh view. He was cautious and deliberate. Arlo had the weapons and the instinct to break into Sid's home and shoot or stab the defenseless old man. But he did not want a violent death to be publicized as a mystery to a media-hyped martyrdom. He had chosen poison as the catalyst of Sid's demise. He could make his death appear to be from natural causes.

Arlo knew the home but needed to record the timing and habits of the victim. It became much like the mode that Arlo used to trap foxes back in Sparta.

He stayed in Mount Pleasant for three weeks, noting the habits of the housekeeper along with the route of Sid Toile to the Bib and Bibliothéque. He noted the delivery of a latte each morning by the wildly adorned café clerk. He could not fathom an opportunity to poison the cup.

He decided upon another avenue. He would poison something at Sid's home. He could do so by stalking the housekeeper when she went out for groceries. She drove to the store every Thursday for fresh fruits, a quart of milk, lettuce, and a variety of whole grain products. She always bought a week's supply of refrigerated yogurt.

Arlo decided to inject the yogurt with a deadly dosage of an arsenic-based concoction. The concoction would take several hours to sicken the victim before stopping his heart. To make the switch, he would have to gain a brief moment with the target receptacle—a serving of yogurt.

He prepared a cache of the liquefied arsenic laced with other deadly ingredients. He had already mixed them to a disulfide form. He would find a moment to introduce the poison into other medium. Yogurt would be a virtually unintelligible carrier of the toxins.

Arlo was already at the large grocery store where Maria Delgado shopped for Sid the following Thursday. He had scouted the brand, size, and flavor of the yogurt Maria bought each week. Arlo placed a four-pack of the predicted strawberry flavored brand into his cart and doctored the contents with a poisonous concoction through a hypodermic needle. He stayed near the dairy aisle until Maria came to select the yogurt. He would switch the two when Maria turned to get the milk and orange juice. He stood near the dairy products aisle looking as if he were reading a label for caloric content.

Maria arrived and placed the yogurt in the small upper portion of the cart. As she turned and reached to gather the other dairy products,

Arlo made the switch undetected. It was a perfect programming sequence to a devious murder plot.

The man that Arlo Crutchfield had pursued in his caldron of vengeance was now going to pay for his sin. Arlo would make sure that Sid Toile was going to die. In his demonic pall, he would stay until he knew the deed was completed. He had waited thirty years for the revenge. He would not miss its finality.

Arlo followed Maria back to the condominium and saw her take the groceries to the elevator. He felt like an exterminator putting glue traps in the path of rodents. Something was bound to happen. He just needed patience.

Sid depended upon his dreams to guide him. They had never let him down before. That brilliant cerulean light that guided him across a lake when he was not quite ten was still beaming into his old age. The blue light dream would return.

CHAPTER THIRTY

The Fixers

SWEATY AND NERVOUS, Joey Preticos came in early Monday to see Sid. He was wearing sunglasses and a gray windbreaker with the collar up.

"Sid, I'm in trouble. Two of Tony the Blade's guys are in town looking for me. I can't go home. They're parked down the street from my house on Elizabeth Avenue. I had to call my neighbor to feed the cats," Joey began

"Can you sit?" Sid asked.

"I'd rather stand with my eyes to the door, Sid. These guys are not to be trifled with. I walked here. I'm afraid to crank up my car. I owe them money, and they are past the promises and into the second phase of collection. There is no third phase, Sid. I've gotta disappear long enough to get the money."

"How much, Joey?" Sid was hesitant to ask.

"I'm into them for a hundred and six grand. They'll want interest too," Joey admitted.

"Joey, if you paid them a hundred and twenty grand, where would the repayment of that money come from?" Sid asked even though he knew the troubling answer.

"I've been on a bad streak, Sid. It's never been this bad. My luck will turn. I just need a decent stake and some time," Joey stated as he scanned the people milling beyond booth 14.

"Joey, I knew the answer before I asked the question. I'm not going to lecture you as much as I will try to solve the problem," Sid assured the chronic gambler.

"You like college basketball, Joey? You follow Tulane, Boston College, Northwestern, Kentucky, NC State, or Iowa."

Joey nodded at each mention of a college team. "Yeah, those are big league programs—SEC, ACC, Big Ten, Big East—well, except for Tulane. They play the big boys but are in a smaller conference."

The Boracle set the trap and then continued.

"Each of those colleges were defrauded by their own players in point-shaving scandals that tilted the numbers to pay off big bucks to crime-related entities. The colleges were left with the damages. The players moved on.

"The player with the most hits in baseball history was banned for betting on games, likely his own team—when he had reasonable control of the outcome. An NBA game referee went to jail a number of years back for point shaving. The 1919 Chicago Black Sox rigged the World Series despite being overwhelming favorites to win it. It's happened in pro football as well.

"My point is this. The professional odds makers know the weather, the players, the coaches, the injury report, the history, the field and track conditions, and the various other factors. They set what is a pretty accurate spread. You disagree on either side of that spread as a gambler without even considering the last factor—insider cheating. Billions are wagered. Somebody wins. Somebody loses. But in the end, everyone loses. This is the point you've reached, Joey. What asset you have left is your life and your future to do something else contributory to society.

My question to you is, are you ready to place your very last wager? Will you gamble on you?"

Joey Preticos's eyes got big. Sid Toile was offering a life solution if Joey could decide to start all over. He was as much desperate as he was attentive to the lesson. In his heart, he wished he had never bet on his first football parlay at the age of seventeen.

"Sid, I have no skills. I have no money, and I have no place to go home to. At the very least, Tony the Blade's guys are going to rough me up. They may break my legs. Or they may just waste me," Joey explained. "You're asking me that if I could resolve the present, would I commit to a different future?

"I'm under a lot of duress right now. I can't think. What would you do?" Joey asked. "How can I find a normal life from this mess?"

"Joey, avoiding decisions under duress is like frying eggs on a cold stove. It's the fire underneath that motivates decisions. You need to decide and then follow the decision without looking back. *Capisce?*" Sid reinforced.

"If I woke up tomorrow without gambling, without debt, without my cats, what would I do?" Joey began questioning himself.

"Sid, I'm all in. I swear on this cross around my neck that if I could start all over, I will never return to gambling. But how do I avoid the thugs who are here from South Philly to destroy me?" Joey's voice rose up.

Sid heard what he sensed as a true commitment. "I think there could be a way. Give me some time to write down the formula, Joey. This is going to be like a doctor's prescription. You must follow every step carefully without deviation. If you do not, the consequences will be your annihilation. For now, find a book here on hydroelectric power. Here's twenty bucks. Buy it. Walk the backstreets. There is a large remote garden behind the Catholic Church off Coleman. Go there and sit on the bench. Read all you can in the book. I'll meet you back here after lunch. Let's meet at two thirty."

With the Boracle's comforting advice, Joey left to find the career section of the bookstore.

Joey had no way of knowing that Sid Toile had lived in many other communities over the past thirty years. He knew people. He helped people everywhere. He had become a frillionaire well before he arrived in Mount Pleasant.

There were more-difficult solutions presented to Sid Toile than Joey could imagine. Sid was not averse to failure. As a synesticist, he could assess the true odds—something that Joey Preticos could not fully understand.

He could read people as well as he could understand their intentions. He was rarely incorrect. He felt strongly that—with time to devise a plan—he could redirect a wasted life.

CHAPTER THIRTY-ONE

Who Is Charlie Landon?

THE BORACLE HAD a printed outline in a folder. The folder was titled "Charlie." He had composed it and made the necessary arrangements in less than three hours. In that time, Joey Preticos scanned most of his hydroengineering book in the church garden. Joey couldn't help but wonder how this old man could help him evade certain pain and maybe an execution. He wondered why he was reading about turbines and dams.

At two twenty, Joey Preticos moved over by the last shelf of new publications. He hoped Sid would see him. He did not want to walk into a trap. Sid sensed his presence, though Joey was behind him. He half turned his torso and waved him toward booth 14.

"Joey, I think I have a solution. It's very detailed, but it will save your life. I have a plan I will follow to take care of the cats and release your home for rent without interference from the fellas you have attracted from South Philly. To do this, you will have to trust me implicitly. You need to sign these two power-of-attorney documents first. Are you following me?"

"Yes. You'll take care of the cats. You'll contact the landlord. What about protection? Do you have a gun? Mine is at the house under the bed," Joey considered.

The Boracle listened to Joey's concerns and then continued. "This file is for you. Read it now and follow it carefully."

The Boracle had pieced together a very workable plan of immediacy.

"Do not deviate. Do this precisely as written," he instructed.

Sid turned to Joey to offer very stern warnings. "You will have others that report to me watching you. If you ever place another wager—even buy a lottery ticket—I will discontinue my assistance. Do you agree to this?"

Joey was still wondering how he could escape this nightmare he had self-inflicted without damage or death.

"Sid, I swear I will never gamble again. If I can get out of this and find a whole new way of living, I will be the happiest balding Greek man you've ever met. I'll sweep floors at McDonald's, shovel horse barns, whatever. Just get me to a way out of this, please," Joey implored.

Sid cited the information that he found from sources outside of the Wi-Fi signal.

"The Wilkens brothers are affiliated with Anthony Giancone," Sid noted. "Giancone, or Tony the Blade, is the just part of the enforcement arm of the Vizano and Benedari families out of Palermo. These are large Sicilian Mafioso families. The Mafia! You cannot evade these people without a perfect plan. I believe I have that perfect plan. In fact, I'm betting your life that I do."

Sid had gotten Joey's full attention.

"Sid, you're saying that they'll find me soon. Maybe even today?" Joey asked in an elevated tone of desperation. "I've got to disappear. If you're asking me if I'll ever return to this life, well, I hope you know I wanna live. I'll do anything to change. You name it."

"Joey, you cannot return to this life. You'll be dead in days. So if you're sure that you can kick the habit, the plan will work," Sid assured.

"I swear to you, give me a new chance, and I'll never come back to this hellhole career," Joey pleaded.

Sid Toile found this conversation to rise to his expectations, and he truly believed that Joey Preticos would never gamble again. So he proceeded with the plan.

"Joey, I expect nothing in return from you except that you will never contact me. Should you need to be contacted for any reason, I will contact you," Sid began. "This folder is your life. Do not misplace it or lose it. Follow ever detail. Now sit and read it so that if you have questions, I can answer them now."

Joey opened the folder and began to read with heightened interest.

1. *You are never to wager a bet, serve as a bookie, or gamble in any form from this day forward. Any breach of this rule will be detected, and your protections will cease.*
2. *You are not to drink or smoke. These are the most dangerous identifiers that your enemies will detect. A breach of this rule will have dire consequences as well.*
3. *All remnants of your life here will be erased entirely. If you follow instructions diligently and do nothing foolish, your new life will prove to be much better than the one you will leave behind.*
4. *You are never to return to this area. You are never to contact anyone from your past life here. Even if you feel that a direct contact back to this source would be deemed necessary, you will not contact me. I will contact you as needed through a chosen intermediary.*
5. *Here's your new cell phone. It's in your new name, Edward Charles Landon. You go by Charlie. Your phone password is set as HAaron75576 (Hank Aaron hit his 755th homerun in 1976).*
6. *Next Thursday, download a new untraceable app called 24Rhino. It will eliminate the need of a password while simultaneously erasing your electronic signal by a cyber scrambling device. No person will be able to trace your cell phone.*
7. *Go to see my friend Gerald Browning at 11 South Battery this evening at seven o'clock. He'll be expecting you. Take the six ten City Center bus from Loop Road Mall five blocks from here. It*

takes you to King and South Battery. Keep a very low profile. Speak to no one. Give him one of these two small brass medals of Joan of Arc. That's the verification. Mr. Browning will change your social security number legally and get you a new passport. The new social security card will show that you have changed your name as well. Just sign the paperwork he will have prepared and ask no questions. A federal judge will seal the identification change documents tomorrow.

8. Gerald will drive you to the Country Suites Motor Inn. Your room is 1120. He'll give the room key to you. Do not leave the room for any reason. There will be a boxed meal, bottled water, and new toiletries for you there.

9. You will have two new suits; size 44 short, pants tailored 42 x 27, all will be hanging in the closet. You will have a new box of oxford white dress shirts and an assortment of ties as well. Cole Hahn lace shoes, size 9w, are also in the closet. Leave your signet ring and chain necklaces in the nightstand drawer. A digital Seiko watch with an oyster face and a kelly green leather band is there. Wear it. It is an identifier for those that will help you. When you are not sure if someone is a stranger or a friend, look at your green-banded watch. It is part of the identity switch. The watch gesture will be the safe approach signal.

10. The suitcase that has your socks and underwear will have three essential books about how dams, release valves, and turbines work. Know these books inside and out. There is also a debit card for gas and necessities. A new driver's license will be there too with your current photo, doctored to show you without the dark sidewalls of hair you have now. Shave the sidewalls off. Keep your face clean-shaven.

11. The side pocket of the suitcase has car keys for a dark blue Ford Taurus. It will be parked directly across from your motel room door. It has no traceable identification or electronic detection devices. It belonged to the FBI. It is in perfect running order, filled with gas, and registered to Edward Charles Landon with Alabama plates. The keychain also has a PO box key. You'll need this later.

12. *A college degree certificate in engineering with the Landon name from Rensselaer Polytechnic in Troy, New York, is rolled in a tube next to your socks. The college has verifiable records of your attendance. You never say 'Rensselaer.' You call it RPI. Your fictitious employment, health, and credit history are listed in the other documents. Memorize them.*
13. *You leave at daybreak tomorrow for Birmingham, Alabama. Never leave Interstate 20 after Columbia except for gas or food near an exit. A map is in the glove box to your temporary quarters at 3194 Highland Drive near the Birmingham airport. You will be there for three weeks. It has a one-car garage. Keep it closed. It's furnished and has everything you need, including food supplies. Do not leave this house until I contact you.*
14. *Once contacted, you are to proceed to the zip code 35005 post office to pick up your new passport in box 19061. Get the passport and the other envelope out. Leave the PO box key in the box.*
15. *The other envelope will have a second debit card in your name with $750 in Canadian dollars from the Bank of Toronto. It will also have an airline ticket for a flight to Ottawa, connecting through Chicago's O'Hare.*
16. *Leave the car at the long-term parking at the Birmingham Shuttlesworth Airport. Place the key in the glove box but remove the registration. Leave nothing else in the car, even wrappers or newspapers.*
17. *When you arrive at Ottawa, you will be met by Charlton Fleming. He'll know you. Check your watch at the moment baggage starts coming down from the flight. Give him the second Joan of Arc medal.*
18. *He will take you to a furnished apartment in the Grove where you will have your first four months of rent paid in advance. You are safe in Ottawa. A late-model Subaru Forester all-wheel drive will be there and registered in your name. The key will be in the nightstand again.*
19. *You will work from eight o'clock to four thirty at the Chaudière Falls Hydroelectric plant. Charlton is your immediate supervisor.*

You will learn on-the-job duties from him. He will become your best friend, but he will have no knowledge of your past. He will never ask.

20. *In six months, you will receive completed dual citizenship papers in the mail. Only the Canadian tax filings will be necessary. You will make about $54,500 per year as the assistant to Mr. Fleming, or about $66,000 in Canadian dollars.*

After perusing the instructions, Joey looked up in awe. All of Sid's planning was accomplished while he was reading in the church garden.

"Joey, the first rule of a new identity is to extinguish the old one. You are to dress nicely every day, refrain from harsh language, be punctual, and, most importantly, remain quiet and reserved," the Boracle suggested. "Keeping a low profile is your daily mantra. No bowling leagues, no parties or receptions, no funeral visitations. Never be where others gather."

"Order deliveries, even for clothing and food. Any shopping such as drugstores and groceries should be done at off hours. Never invite anyone over. No social media. No e-mail exchanges. No Twitter or Instagram. Pay all bills online. You can go to church but not to the Greek Orthodox Church. Go early or late when fewer people attend. You can volunteer at the library or at the junior college, but not where you would see more than a handful of unfamiliar people. Never speak about your past or your college or your family. If it comes up, you're an orphan. It is too easy these days for someone to detect fraudulent information. Got it?" the Boracle asked.

"Yes, sir," Joey snapped. "But, ah . . . Well. How did you do this? How can I thank you?"

"The less you know, the better off you are, Joey," Sid started. "I like a challenge. You can thank me by following the instructions to the letter. You can only make this a worthwhile endeavor by changing everything—your name, your appearance, your habits, and, most importantly, your goals in life. You're a college-educated hydroelectric engineer. Act the role and enjoy the consequences. My friend Charlton Fleming will look out for you. The most critical time for this transition is the next twenty-four hours. Follow each instruction carefully. Leave no clues behind."

Joey gathered the file and began to walk away. He turned to announce his thoughts.

"You can bet I'll do everything just as you asked. And you can bet that I'll never bet again."

CHAPTER THIRTY-TWO

Police Escort

FOUR DAYS AFTER Joey Preticos left to drive to Alabama, two strangers came into the Bib and Bibliothéque. It was apparent to Sid that these were the thugs out of South Philly looking for Joey. They came over to booth 14 as if they had a flight to catch, not wishing to wait to see the busy synesticist. Sid saw them and knew that the moment had arrived.

As they approached, he asked Evelyn Rhett for a private moment with the interlopers.

"Evelyn, I'll be about five minutes only." Sid motioned to her. "Could I take care of these two coming and get back with you just after?"

Evelyn grabbed her Etienne Aigner designer handbag and rose to go have her latte refilled. Just as she left, Jocko Santo and Myles "Tort" Tersini slipped in the vacant seat.

Jocko was a heavy person with a ruddy face. He was winded when he sat down. Myles Tersini received his nickname Tort from Tony the Blade Muzon because he had invented more than two dozen methods of torturing someone to extract information. Myles was thinner and taller. They were obviously packing heat.

"Fellas, I can guess who you are, who sent you, and whom you're looking for," Sid began. "And I can give you the best answers that will satisfy all three questions and deliver what you need so that you can be on a flight this evening."

"Where we're from, we don't talk to wise guys. We dispose of them. You're no exception, so tell us what we need to know before we make your head into a lopsided melon," Jocko threatened with intense and furrowed eyes.

"Whoa, fellas. I solve problems. Even yours. You're from South Philly. Tony the Blade sent you. You need Joey Preticos's carcass or his money. Right?" Sid stated.

"Yeah, so what? Good guess, Einstein. Now, where's Joey?" Tort asked with vigor. "Give us that little bastard, and you'll live."

"I've got a better deal. But you decide," the Boracle began. "I have his furniture, his jewelry, and even his cats tied up for a debt he owes me. It's called a chattel mortgage."

Sid placed the papers from his coat pocket on the booth table.

"Read it. It's legal," Sid suggested.

"I also have an envelope in my briefcase. If you take the envelope with you, you can count all $136,000 in unmarked bills on the plane on the way back to Philly. It includes interest and travel expenses to collect Joey's debt and—" Sid was rudely interrupted.

"Yeah, we'll take the money back he owes. But we need to rough him up a little bit, you understand," Tort shot back. "You don't want no part of this, old man. Just give us his location."

"Well, that's the tradeoff, my friend," Sid explained while keeping his hand calmly on top of the large manila envelope.

"You get the money and the amount for expenses plus the interest. But you don't get Joey. That should not pose a problem to anyone. Tony the Blade gets his money, plus some," Sid explained.

Both interlopers looked perplexed, as Sid had commanded control of the forceful conversation.

Sid added an insight for the thugs.

"Gentlemen, Joey is no longer living here and will never be here again. So no matter whose head you threaten to bash, you will not bash his. Besides, when you pick up the envelope, it means we've made a deal," Sid stated, looking directly at Tort.

Both thugs looked at Sid as if he were the most naïve man on earth. They had no idea they were being set up.

"Detective Moore over there at the counter and Lieutenant Powell in the booth behind us know that the acceptance of the envelope will be the sign that this deal is complete. They will signal the others who are watching this booth with great interest. The detective and the lieutenant will then escort you to the airport so that the money is safe. You're on Southwest flight 2191 direct to Philly. It leaves at six ten."

The two underworld enforcers looked around to see there were several law enforcement people positioned across the bookstore. They glanced at each other with sudden incredulity.

"Yeah, suppose we don't do this?" Jocko countered. "Tony has some reinforcements too if you know what I mean. You can't run us out of here without consequences, old man."

"No, you're right. Others could come back to vindicate you. You'll be in our jail here, held without bail by Judge Watson for federal crimes across state lines. My deputy's badge is attached to the satchel next to me. A recording device is there too. You said too many things that will implicate Tony as well. It's your decision. You get the money and the plane tickets. But to do that, your unpermitted conccaled weapons will go in this satchel. Knives too."

Lieutenant Powell stared at them. Detective Moor moved his hand to his vest. Sid Toile had gotten the drop on two hired professional killers.

"Otherwise, your trial might come up in a year and a half. By that time, our energetic prosecutor may find a few more charges. We have usury laws, extortion, threatening an officer of the law, unlicensed weapons, and a few others they can add from the Philly police. The six police cars you see outside will escort the two of you with the money to the airport, or they can take you without the money to Judge Watson's court. You want to call Tony first? Here's my phone with Tony's cell number already dialed in. Of course, if you call him, he can be deemed as an accessory to the fact. Not sure you want that. But it's your call—no pun intended."

The two men both paused before Jocko reached to get the envelope.

Sid held it tight. "Not yet, gents. The weapons go in this bag first. You better dump anything you do not want detected at the airport security."

Jocko grabbed the small satchel and placed his Glock .45 caliber inside. Tort followed suit with his Sturm Ruger 9 mm.

"The rest? We would not want to have airport security involved, would we?" Sid reminded them.

Jocko surrendered his blue lightning OTF switchblade. Tort, the expert on extracting information from suffering victims, surrendered an imposing nine-inch stiletto with a carbon fiber handle. They gave the canvas bag over to Sid while perusing the room, ever aware that they might be arrested anyway.

Sid shoved the manila envelope forward to Jocko.

"Wise decision, my friends. $136,000 cash or a real mess in the court system," Sid summarized. "Leave the keys, and we'll even return your rental car. I believe Tony would have advised that you take the money and fly home free. We'll have a video recording of you doing just that. I'd advise you and your compatriots to stay out of South Carolina. Nothing good can happen for you here. So may I be the first to bid you adieu?"

Jocko and Tort rose from the booth; the envelope went under Jocko's arm. Tort stared at Sid as if he wanted to memorize his old craggy face. A large black Chevy Tahoe SUV pulled up to the entrance, and the rear passenger doors were opened. The two men looked bewildered as they left the Bib and Bibliothéque.

Four police cars drifted up behind the SUV. They followed the thugs to the airport.

As the men left, Callista scurried over to the Boracle.

"What the hell was that all about, Sid?" she inquired. "Why all the police cars?"

"Campaign security, I suppose. One was running for president—the other for the senate. Of course, I didn't contribute. Unfortunately, both your mother and I didn't support the abortion issue. As we talked, it was apparent that both of those guys were against protecting innocent lives."

Callista was unsure whether Sid was telling the truth or humoring her. The inquisitive waitress had no idea that she had been insulted.

Sid had eradicated the life threat to Joey Preticos. Yet he had incited a potential reprisal to himself. It was a calculated risk. With favors due to him from the local policing authorities, he had been able to route a wasted life back into positive human circulation by inventing a motivated hydroelectric engineer from a forlorn and downtrodden bookmaker who was on his way to ruin. The risk for what Sid considered entertainment was $136,000. He always considered money as a rented commodity. The paperwork that Joey Preticos hurriedly signed left Sid with the ability to redirect a life and derail a violent crime.

The local policing authorities were able to contact the Philadelphia Police Department to let them know that Jocko Santo and Myles "Tort" Tersini would arrive at 7:44 on Flight 2191 at Philadelphia International Airport. They would be unarmed. The reward for their capture would be paid to an anonymous informant. The arranged award was $136,000.

Sid had arranged a temporary solution. He knew that he would become a target to the South Philly syndicate. It would take them months to figure it out.

CHAPTER THIRTY-THREE

Remington Reality

EVELYN RHETT RETURNED from the Bib and Bibliothéque restroom. She had been momentarily detained there to by a policeman. She arrived in time to see the police caravan that took the intruders away. She approached booth 14 quizzically.

"What was that all about?" Evelyn inquired.

"Nothing of consequence, Evelyn. The two fellas you saw had to catch a flight, and I knew someone who could get them to the airport safely," Sid responded coyly. "They'll make their flight. 'Parting is such sweet sorrow,' you see."

"Sid, you're doing Shakespeare? Wow. *Romeo and Juliet* or *Hamlet*?" Evelyn was amused.

"From Romeo, act 2, scene 2," Sid related. "And the line gave notice of the thrill of meeting again while departing in sadness. But I'm nearly certain I'll not see my two friends again. My Shakespeare reference was laced with subtle sarcasm. Conversely, I am able to see people of great joy who are temporarily not maintaining the status of joy. Do you know anyone like that?"

Evelyn knew that Sid was referring to her.

"I get your point, Sid. You have a way of understanding life at a level that life should be lived. I have a tendency to worry and to feed my worst fears with my emotions. My daughter sees this, I suppose. She's what I want to be again. Carefree. Composed. Open to the world in front of me. But I can't seem to relate," Evelyn admitted.

The conversation turned from a relationship between a mother and a daughter to a relationship between the heart and the soul. Sid noticed something that matched something from the time he first met Evelyn.

"Evelyn, you are either very clumsy or hiding a deeper secret," Sid began. "I suspect the latter."

He boldly supported the observation.

"The day I met you, you had a bruise on the underside of your left forearm. Today, you have another in a similar place. If you could see it when you brushed your hair, you would've tried to disguise it with your makeup base. The second one is larger. Both bruises indicate blows from a defensive posture. I suspect they came from someone close to you who has an uneven temper."

Evelyn glanced down. She was afraid to reveal the truth.

"If you do not speak the words, you are doomed to the repetition of the past," Sid advised.

"Sid, I cannot change anything. I have to accept some things you wouldn't understand. The episodes are infrequent. The normal is tolerable. Let's leave it at that," she suggested.

Sid looked across the top of his glasses directly to Evelyn.

"Despite my apprehension, I will do as you suggest. But we will come back to this when you're out of options. These things never get better," Sid said. "And I'd bet Anna knows more than you think."

He wanted to extol a higher plateau of Evelyn's sense of living fruitfully. But it would involve more than repairing a daughter's relationship. She had to extricate herself from another darkness.

"Evelyn, you have all that you need and an abundance beyond," Sid added. "But what is it that your soul and heart are missing? You need a North Star. You need to resolve your PHC—your positive human consequence. We're all at a time and place for a reason. Find yours and live it. There are major obstacles that distract you. Meet those head-on."

Sid did not want to drift too far away from the observation despite Evelyn's dismissal.

"Our respect for others stems from our respect for ourselves. We gain that respect because we recognize a reason for our lives that benefits humanity in large and small ways. It is the self-actualization aspect in action. It could be just being a good mother—or finding a cure for a disease or inventing an item needed by a waiting world. We all have to nourish our positive human consequence. It dictates why we were born and the significance of living a cause. Distractions are many.

"Anna sees that you have a set of passions. They may or may not interest her. They could be activities from bible studies to bowling. Is there an activity that you can enjoy together? Shopping? Scrapbooking? Music? Finding a common passion could be the first step. Channeling that passion to something that helps others would be the highest potential result."

Evelyn thought for a moment before offering a few ideas before mentioning a workable common interest. She wanted to divert the apparent concern that Sid knew was in play. She was a physically abused housewife.

"Anna likes scary movies. I know that's crazy, but the thrill of being the next victim or seeing an outline of a face in a dark corner gets her every time. I used to watch the Freddy Krueger movies with her. She just loves being afraid.

"She loves to work out on the Nordic Track at the fitness center. But she goes when there are fewer people there because she is so self-conscious about her body. She works out to old music from the 1980s because the songs have a faster beat. She likes bands like Led Zeppelin, the Doobie Brothers, and a lot of heavy metal. It's what I played on albums growing up."

Evelyn rambled into a revelation.

"We both work out. I guess I could spend more time working out with her," she said.

"Evelyn, you have the right idea, but you'll need to be subtle. Start with a workout or two before you order a *Friday the 13th* movie on Netflix. Don't force it, and it will come to you," Sid advised.

"Use the workouts to intimate a concern that you have that she can help you resolve. Make sure that she knows that you value her judgment," he added. "You'll be surprised at what she already knows, and her insight might help you as well."

Sid felt strongly about advising on the other matter of domestic violence. He felt he could move the daughter conversation forward to open the husband matter anew.

"Your daughter, Anna, is a predictable challenge. Mothers seem to have more issues with daughters than fathers have issues with sons. But both are built on divergent emotions. Anna is normal. She will rebel and repel. But like the person who repels by rope, they push further away to come back faster. She's simply growing up. You are the unfortunate object of her collision with maturity, hormones, social networking, and other misgivings that are unavoidable in the process. She will repel back to a final destination eventually by landing on the safety of level ground. That ground represents gravity. Gravity to Anna is her mother's unrelenting love. You will become Anna's pride and enjoy a lifetime of closeness."

Evelyn mentally embraced the prediction. She knew in her bones that the Boracle was in tune with life and had a patent on outcomes.

"Evelyn, my dear, your own joy must be fully promoted in the present. You alone will shape tomorrow's memory to either despair or delight," Sid continued. "You must confront all obstacles to move forward. Think about the others, and we'll devise a plan for happiness. The failure to act upon the obvious has an impact upon other relationships. Anna wants to see you do something bold."

Sid hoped that his advice would convince Evelyn that postponing action to escape a troubled marriage was impacting her, her daughter and could be perilous. Meanwhile, Sid planned to assist in healing her relationship with young Anna.

The Boracle ordered two exercise gliders to be delivered to the Rhett garage. They arrived by express shipping three days later. He also ordered a Sonos music system to play the music that Evelyn and Anna could enjoy together. They could play anything from any genre from their cell phones.

Within weeks, the exercise and music brought mother and daughter to the same place every day. It was the pure sense of being there that lifted Anna's eyes to see her mother's efforts of brokering a relationship of strength. Evelyn discontinued meddling and dedicated herself to being available instead of being an obstacle. They listened to the Grateful Dead, Nirvana, and Guns and Roses. They worked out regularly. The unobtrusive path worked. They were moving in the direction of a new relationship built on a new foundation of trust. Eventually, they talked when Anna wanted to talk.

In a manner of weeks, Sid's second prediction materialized.

After a Saturday workout, Evelyn and Anna went for a brisk walk in the neighborhood. Evelyn's husband, Horace Rhett, was a successful residential contractor. He left that morning to play golf at the country club while his wife and daughter were out walking.

The sequence of the day belied the sunny weather. The sixteen-year-old Anna felt secure enough to broach a ticklish subject.

"Mom, you are pretty and in great physical condition and have a college degree. You sold real estate at one time. You could make it on your own. Why did you marry Dad?" Anna asked.

Evelyn immediately knew that her troubled marriage relationship was evident to Anna. The conversation began the healing by determining the cause of the pain.

"Because we fell in love, Anna. And because, deep inside, he's a good man," Evelyn added. But Evelyn didn't even believe her own words.

"But he screams at you, and I know he's hit you before," Anna revealed. "That's not the sign of a good marriage."

Evelyn was momentarily stunned that Anna knew about her father's violence. But she remembered that the Boracle had predicted the revelation.

"Honey, when your father drinks, he doesn't think. I have tried to get him to counseling. He is against it. He thinks I badger him. And when he has too much to drink, he loses his temper. I have tried to keep him away from you and from making this situation public. I have been much too protective," Evelyn explained.

She chose her words as if she had been expecting the question for years.

"But, Mom, he hits you. You enable him by allowing the behavior. How can he respect you when you let him get away with it?" Anna asked. "He needs help. You need help more. He might hurt you one day."

Another thought from Anna followed.

"Why not remove all the alcohol? If he doesn't drink, he's not violent," she assumed. Anna had no concept of the deep chasm that alcoholics descend.

"It's not that easy. He can find drinks anywhere. And when I have not bought beer or vodka, he really gets angry. It's a no-win," Evelyn said. "He hasn't hit me in weeks."

"Mom, Dad drinks too much and is often violent. He's moody. He's a dominant male from another age. Reasonable people do not promote that behavior. Why don't you have him enter a clinic or something?" she reasoned.

"Honey, I can handle him for now. If it gets worse, I'll consider taking him to a clinic. But he won't go voluntarily," Evelyn noted. "So let's hope we can get him to stop drinking and he'll be normal again."

"Mom, even I know that hope is not a plan," Anna said. "Suppose he breaks your arm or worse? Don't you read about violent people who come home and shoot everybody? Daddy has his hunting gear and way too many guns for someone who drinks that much. What happens when he goes over the edge? You better talk to someone about getting him sober. Seriously."

The revelation that Anna cataloged her father's physical abuse was uncomfortable to Evelyn. Anna further warned her about the consequences. Evelyn considered that Horace might even harm Anna in a drunken state. Evelyn decided to seek a professional expert. She would go and see Sid the very next Monday. She assured Anna that she would take the first step at the start of the week.

Anna showered and left a note on the kitchen counter that she had bicycled down to her friend Victoria's house. She'd be back before supper.

When Horace Rhett came home after four o'clock, things got out of hand. He had been with his buddies on the golf course and played gin rummy in the clubhouse. He had put over a dozen beers and a few vodka tonics on his tab. Evelyn heard Horace slam the door to the garage. He grabbed a Bud Light from the refrigerator and headed to the couch.

"Where's Anna?" He demanded.

"She's at her friend Victoria's house. She'll be back soon. How'd you play?"

Evelyn changed subjects. Seeing that the conditions present could escalate to violence, Evelyn lied about when Anna would be back. She hoped that Horace would just turn on ESPN and pass out. That had been his routine.

"I lost my ass and then tried to make it up in cards," he slurred. "I'm out four hundred. What's it to you? You don't bring anything in. It's my damn money."

Horace challenged the moment in a forceful voice. His temper emerged. He threw the half-full beer can at the fireplace. It was his vent at both losing the money and her questioning sequence.

Evelyn had been advised by Sid and then Anna to make a definitive change to her approach. She knew that something needed to change.

"Honey, just calm down. I'm not mad about the money. That's your business. Just don't take it out on me. You need to get counseling and not drink so much. I'll help you," she introduced.

"What? You'll help me! Damn. I didn't know you could help poor old me," Horace continued to slur. "I own you. You don't have a pot to pee in without me. How are you going to help me?"

The more Horace protested, the louder his voice became.

Evelyn decided to leave the issue alone and left the room. As she did, Horace yelled, "Hey, get me another beer, woman."

She instinctively reversed and went to get another beer despite his belligerency. She hoped that he would just pass out as he had done before. She brought a new cold beer back with a dishtowel to clean the thrown beer can by the fireplace. Horace snatched the unopened beer and then grabbed her arm. He squeezed it.

"Let go! You're hurting me," she pleaded. "Just let me go."

Horace pulled her to him and ripped the front of her tan flowered blouse. Evelyn tried to get free while covering herself up. Horace backhanded Evelyn across the face with a powerful blow, knocking her completely out. She had blood coming from her nose, and her right eye was swelling. He released her arm and threw her over across the ottoman. He mumbled unintelligible words and passed out.

When Evelyn awoke from the ordeal twenty minutes later, she scurried to the master bedroom bath. She threw her ripped and bloody clothes into the hamper and showered. She expected that Anna would arrive at any time. Her nose was broken, and blood was all over the den carpet and the ottoman. Her eye was nearly shut from the blunt strike. She cried in pain. She did all she could to try and minimize the wounds to her face and arm, but this episode could not be hidden.

She realized that she would either confront the episode with policing authorities or hide it by staying invisible to others for weeks. In her despair, she decided upon a third option.

She dried off, put on her robe, and retrieved Horace's keys from the kitchen table. She went to the spare bedroom where Horace kept his hunting weapons in a glass case. She unlocked it and loaded the Remington Beanfield Sniper that Horace used for deer hunting. She was crying nervously but deliberate in her intention. Evelyn walked back into the den, still crying from the pain and her heightened emotional state. She remembered a blackened eye, a wrist sprain, and too many bruises to list. Horace was still passed out on the couch. Evelyn could take no more of the pain. Evelyn removed the safety lock from the weapon as she stood across the room. She pointed it at Horace's chest.

She hesitated to shoot it, realizing that she would be convicted of a serious crime and serve time even if the circumstances warranted the shooting. Despite the consequences, she decided to pull the trigger. But she faintly heard Anna returning the bicycle to the garage. She panicked. She put the rifle behind the couch and tried to get a towel from the bedroom to cover the bloodstains before Anna came in. Her timing was off. Anna came in and saw the evidence immediately.

"Oh my God! What happened? He broke your nose, didn't he?" Anna cried.

Horace was still passed out. Anna saw the pool of blood on the ottoman.

She took out her cell phone and dialed 911. She reported a domestic incident. Evelyn just sat and cried. She knew that option three was averted and the default option one was now in play. It would be the worst of the three.

Before she left to dress, Evelyn told Anna to take the rifle from behind the couch and put it back in the spare bedroom case. Anna was shocked. She realized that she might have intercepted a murder scene. She wasn't sure who was going to murder whom. She cried even more.

When the police and EMS arrived, they woke Horace and read him his Miranda rights. They took him away. A female medic attended to Evelyn in the bedroom. She was apprised of the violence sequence and all injuries. Evelyn signed a statement. The police took her torn and bloody clothes from the hamper away in a plastic evidence bag. Anna signed a statement of what she knew.

Neither Anna nor Evelyn made mention of the loaded Remington Beanfield Sniper that had been returned to the spare bedroom case.

Anna accompanied Evelyn in the ambulance. She advised her mother to get a lawyer, knowing that her father would be even angrier than ever when he returned. She saw enough television to know that a restraining order was the next step. Anna cried while trying to get her mother to call a lawyer.

Evelyn reached into her purse and pulled out her phone. She instructed Anna to call Sid Toile from her contact list. Anna assumed that Sid Toile was a lawyer and called him immediately. Evelyn was still being attended to by the medical personnel.

"Mr. Toile, I'm Anna Rhett," she started.

Sid feared the circumstance. He replied, "Is your mother OK?"

"No, sir. We're on our way to Cooper River Emergency. She has a broken nose," Anna reported. She assumed that Sid was the person who was going to get a restraining order from a judge.

"Tell her that I will be there in twenty minutes," Sid informed. "Don't worry, Anna. All will be fine. Your father needs counseling. Your mother will get through this."

"Thank you, sir," she replied nervously. Anna hung up.

Anna wondered how the man she thought was a lawyer knew that a case of domestic violence had occurred. She never said what happened or who did it.

Sid arrived at the Emergency Room of Cooper River Hospital. He saw a teenager in the waiting area crying silently. He went to her.

"Anna, I'm Sid Toile—your mother's friend."

"Mr. Toile, thank you for coming. Mom's having her nose worked on. She's hurt badly. Can you get a judge to keep my dad away?" Anna asked.

"Yes, I can. But that is not my decision. It's your mother's. And there are other considerations she must balance," Sid informed. Anna still had no idea that Sid was not a lawyer.

"Mr. Toile, my dad is capable of killing her. He may have passed out before doing it this time. There's no other consideration I can think about than keeping Mom safe."

"Yes, I agree. There will be many adjustments. She'll need to consider your well being. She'll place you first, even ahead of her safety. Then there's the living expenses, the legal costs, the possibility of your father's rehabilitation, who gets the house, the car, and other concerns," Sid detailed. He knew that Anna was bright enough to see the immensity of the situation.

"Mr. Toile, all I care about is my mother's safety. We can deal with the other stuff," Anna countered. "Please help us."

Sid knew that Anna had accepted that she would need to stay close to her mother.

An intern came to the waiting area to inform Anna of the treatment. He said that they had to reset Evelyn's nose and administer to her eye delicately. It was patched. She would need to visit an ophthalmologist within the week. The patch could be removed in the next twenty-four hours. Her arm injury was painful, but there was not a break. She had been given sedatives and would need to be driven home. Rest was prescribed.

Sid immediately offered to drive both of them to their home. The intern went to retrieve Evelyn. She came to the lobby in a wheelchair because of the sedatives and hospital protocol. Sid retrieved his Volkswagen Beetle and drove to the covered portico near the emergency release area.

Evelyn was relieved to see Sid. She reintroduced him to Anna. She never mentioned how they knew each other. She told Anna about his abilities.

"Anna, Mr. Toile is not only going to help us get home. He'll point us in the right direction. I'm sure of it." She was still tearful.

Sid responded.

"Let's get you home. You rest. Anna, here's my phone. Please add your number into my contacts folder. I'll call later," Sid advised. "There's much to discuss, but we should wait until your mother gets some rest."

"But, Mr. Toile, what about my dad?" she asked. "Can't he come back?"

"Not for at least twenty-four hours, Anna. Once I drop you two off, I will go to him and see what course of action to take."

Anna had never heard of a lawyer visiting both sides of a case. But she accepted the statement as if she knew Sid was going to do what was best for her mother.

After dropping off the mother and daughter, Sid called the county sheriff, a personal friend. He explained the situation.

The sheriff contacted the jailer to find out that Horace Rhett had been visited by a bail bondsman and would likely be released by the magistrate on a light bond at ten o'clock the next morning. He had no prior incidents. Sid asked to have his hearing moved to 2:00 p.m. to give him time to see Horace in the morning. The sheriff consented.

By nine o'clock on Sunday morning, Sid was on his way to the county facility. He called Anna to check on Evelyn.

"Anna, this is Sid Toile. How is your mother?" Sid asked.

"She's sitting up and eating eggs I have scrambled. She had a bad night," Anna followed. "She cried a lot, not because of the pain as much as she lamented that our lives would be changing rapidly. She imagined that they would divorce and that my dad's business would fall off because of his alcoholism. She said that she would need to find a job so that we can keep the house."

"Anna, you are young and have so many challenges ahead. This one will not be as difficult as you fear," Sid said in a calming voice. "Stay with her and talk about happy things. Let her know that you will be at her side no matter what. That's what she needs to hear."

Anna responded, "But I have school tomorrow. Should I stay to watch her?"

"No, Anna," Sid counseled. "That will cause other reactions with the school officials and your friends. Keep this confidential. A locksmith named Paul Surratt will be there by nine. He'll secure the house and give your mother the new keys. You will need to have your mother change the alarm code. A lady named Maria will be at your home at eight o'clock tomorrow. She'll know what to do. She's my housekeeper. Let your mom know about Maria coming, and tell her that I'll be in touch later today, please."

"Yes, sir. And you'll let us know about Dad?" Anna inquired.

"Of course. I hope to get him the help he needs," Sid answered. "But he's going to have to come to that conclusion on his own."

Sid said good-bye and hung up. He was in the county jail parking area.

A security guard brought the large beer-bellied Horace Rhett to the visitor room. He was handcuffed. He told him that he had ten minutes.

When Horace saw Sid sitting across in a plastic chair, he asked, "You're the best the county can get me? Are you doing charity, old friend?"

"Mr. Rhett, I'm not your lawyer. And I'm not your friend. I'm Sid Toile. I'm here to save your life," Sid posed sincerely.

"Are you a doctor or a psychiatrist?" Horace followed.

"No, sir. I am just an old man who knows much more than anyone else on the planet about where you and your family are headed," Sid began.

"Oh, really. I gotta hear this. Where the hell do you think I am now?" Horace asked sarcastically.

"Mr. Rhett, you should use the few minutes remaining to listen. Your bombastic behavior will only make your salvation all the more difficult. Let's talk about the root problem, shall we?" Sid began.

Horace was stunned by the forthright demeanor of a septuagenarian visiting a person with a documented violent temperament.

"Now, you're a classic alcoholic. You have gone over the edge to destroy your marriage. You'll likely lose your home. You'll lose your daughter too. Despite your public record, you are a repeat violent offender. That's a provable point. Much of this is available to a prosecutor. You have only one way out. If you do not take this way out, I will not help you, and all of the misery I've outlined will happen indeed. So we have four minutes left. Do you want to take the hard route to save your life or the easy route to destruction?"

"I still don't know who you are and what the hell you're talking about. I get out of here at ten. Then I'm going home to get some sleep. My wife and my kid will be there. And my wife—she'll never say another word," Horace declared.

"Horace, you are not getting out at ten. I made sure of it. But you can eventually get out on bond. Then what? You will have a restraining order. You will be watched like a hawk. Then you'll drink more. You'll get angry again, and you'll get arrested again. You'll lose your business. In addition to the loss of your wife and daughter, you'll lose your friends, and you'll be living on the street. Do you want that?"

"I doubt that. You don't know me. I'm a kick-ass guy. My wife doesn't control me, and neither do you. What kind of alternative are you speaking about?"

"Time's up!" the security guard yelled over to the setting.

Sid held his hand up signifying one more minute.

"If you stay here thirty days to dry out and calm your temper, I'll get you to the best alcohol rehab facility in the region for the next sixty.

If all goes well, you'd then go to a transition facility, and after that, you may be forgivable to your wife, assuming that you never drink again."

Horace turned to the guard.

"Come get me!" he yelled.

He stood and looked back at Sid. "I'll see you in hell, old man."

CHAPTER THIRTY-FOUR

Viola Butters

HAL BUTTERS NEVER told anyone about Viola's difficult childhood. The Moses family of nine children grew up in a rickety wooden rental house with just one bathroom on Morris Street. She and her sisters learned to weave sweetgrass baskets. Her aunt sold them on weekends to the few tourists of the 1960s.

Her brothers crabbed during the summers to bring free meals home. Her mother took in sewing. Her father was imprisoned for multiple thefts and never responsible for their upbringing. Her maternal grandfather, Ed White, wore a chauffeur's hat and coat to drive wealthy white ladies to the hair parlors and luncheons. He waited in the car to take them home. His clientele included the high-society ladies of the East Battery area who had him wait while they attended meetings of the Daughters of the American Revolution and the United Daughters of the Confederacy.

Viola grew up in a household that harbored southern traditions of low-paid servitude in a classist and racist society. She had come to despise white society. She was angered by both history and reality.

The racial epithets had further aggrieved her that she often heard in her teenage years. She realized that she was one of the lucky ones who left the depressive neighborhood and found a responsible husband. It was if he had rescued her from abject poverty so that she could crawl into normal poverty.

Hal Butters was from Johns Island and left at the age of eighteen to join the United States Army. He received his GED high school equivalency certificate while in the service. He was honorably discharged in six years with a sense of patriotism, responsibility, and devotion. He learned a valuable trade from another combat soldier that placed him in demand. His brickwork was superb. But contractors routinely complained of the refuse, undercalculated mortar, or time down from weather events. He was paid late very often. Some contractors bankrupted and never paid him. Invariably, the people who took advantage of Hal Butters's good nature and poor business sense were also white.

It was not difficult to understand why the Butters family found all "whities" suspect. They had been abused and disappointed all too often.

When Viola found that she had pancreatic cancer, she asked for a black doctor and black nurses. She felt that only blacks could take care of blacks. When the clinic gave her Dr. Ramsey, she felt doomed to die. As the specialist was an upper-crust Caucasian, she felt that the doctor would have no compunction about another old black woman dying. She had convinced Hal that the end was near because there were no black oncologists to attend to her.

But Hal was God-fearing and an optimist. He prayed, and he looked to the heavens. He recruited others to pray. He brought fresh fruit and some cooked vegetables from home to feed to Viola. He told her that he had advances waiting from black subcontractors who would keep their cupboards full when she got back to the house. He was not ready to believe that Viola was going to leave him. Had it been Hal in the hospital and Viola at home, there never would have been a man as white as Sid Toile coming into their lives. Viola would not have paid any attention to the Boracle because he represented the untrusted skin color.

It was propitious that Hal had asked Sid for the use of his pen. Sid came quickly and worked diligently for no compensation or expected thanks. He studied pancreatic cancer in libraries across the world through the nuance of the World Wide Web. In twenty-four hours, he became the finest expert on the disease extant. But he was never going to convince Dr. Ramsey or even Hal Butters of his ability. He would need to use psychology. He arrived at Dr. Ramsey's office as scheduled for his ten-minute window of opportunity.

He waited well past the time of his appointment before a young intern led him into the office of Dr. Ramsey. He knew the crucial time it would take to render the course that could save Viola Butters. So he decided to use the ten minutes in a most awkward forum.

"Dr. Ramsey, thank you for giving me ten minutes. Unless you are going to stretch to eleven minutes, we will proceed without the pleasantries," Sid began, refusing to sit. "I'll talk for the first nine and leave time for your reply at the last.

"There is no reason to restate the Hippocratic Oath. I am aware of your learned professionalism and deep desire to save every life every time. So let me impart what we know about pancreatic cancer across the world. It's the worst. Owing to your stated legal caveat, I will cite this patient as a fictional person—a female, about fifty-eight, and a minority. Let's call her Vivian. OK?"

The doctor nodded.

"The fictional Vivian has gotten a break because her cancerous tumor leans up against her spleen. You wouldn't know it's there otherwise. That lucky circumstance means that the tumor discovery makes it early enough to operate."

Dr. Ramsey suspected that Sid Toile had stolen her chart from the hospital room or the nurse's station. He hadn't.

Sid continued.

"Her pain is at the lower left side, and the tumor is likely mid-pancreas. I suspect that it is an early tumor because the pancreas will not signal pain like the spleen. But I'm sure you already know that. Her oxygen levels are good. Her general health is good, though possibly a slight anemia persists. She also needs better hydration. Surgery will be her only solution to include the removal of the spleen. Her postsurgical protocol will require treatments to counteract the loss of her spleen."

The doctor was impressed by what this brilliant and confident layman knew.

"Are you aware that our fictional Vivian took six 10 mg Ambien sleeping pills the evening after she saw her oncologist for her prognosis? She has a predisposition not to trust Caucasians. She is convinced that only a black doctor can save her. She nearly went into a coma. Also lingering is her detachment from hope. She is certain that she is at the very end of her life.

"Part of the clinical standard is for the patient to trust the course taken by experts and to believe in the miracle that may or may not exist. Having me come to her through her husband's efforts is what she believes to be a path of hope. But I am the wrong color. It would help if you had a black doctor visit our Vivian. He could be an internist or a rheumatologist—doesn't matter. She's been stigmatized by white America over her entire life. A visit by a minority physician just before surgery would do her wonders. I'll take it from there."

Dr. Ramsey started to object to the idea of a minority doctor visiting by raising his hand slightly to speak.

"Hold on, doc. I know the rules and the ethics. But my being here is not precisely within the scope of either. We have to sell her on the surgery still. Let's just assume that our fictional patient's husband is already on board.

"The next part is critical. She needs this surgery in the next forty-eight hours. You are the best-qualified specialist for the job. The intricacies of pancreatic surgery are numerous. Only your skill can do this. Time is the enemy before the operation and the ally afterward. You will need the top OR assistants for this as well. Her recovery begins with the last stitch to her abdomen.

"After a few days, the same minority doctor whom you send to see her tomorrow needs to see her then. The body can recover much faster if the mindset is profoundly positive.

"To summarize, she needs hope and an intricate surgery within forty-eight hours, which should be performed by you as head of the surgical team with the best OR staff possible. Now I believe I have taken eight minutes and twenty seconds. The Hippocratic Oath compels your reaction. Do you have any objections to this course of treatment?" Sid asked.

He glanced down at his pocket watch to have the doctor assume he was keeping time.

The doctor was speechless. He asked Sid to sit. Sid took the sitting request as a gesture that the doctor was considering the layman's proposal.

"Mr. Toile," he started, "I fully intended to look at a surgical option for our fictional patient Vivian after more tests related to the tumor's growth and position. But you're telling me that you believe that the surgical timing is more critical than the assimilation of that particular information. Am I right?"

"Indubitably," Sid replied.

"I can entertain that thought," Dr. Ramsey conceded. "May I ask how did you know about her slight anemia or her oxygenation, sir?"

"Observation only. No information was requested or given by any hospital associate," Sid replied. "And the tumor placement came from her location signal interspersed upon my knowledge of anatomy."

The doctor tapped his pen on his desk, still contemplating the proposal.

"We are at ten minutes. I can stay as long as you need me," Sid added.

"What makes you audacious enough to think that I'll act on this information and schedule this surgery?" the doctor asked, no longer paying attention to the time.

"Because of two things I know, sir. One—you're the best surgeon-clinician in this discipline available. Two—our fictional Vivian will die from the disease if the surgery does not occur in the next forty-eight hours. These two facts are correlated by my first set of references and inured by the Hippocratic Oath. Waiting for other tests is a direct violation of the directive '*primum non nocere*,' or 'first, do no harm.'"

Dr. Ramsey stared at Sid for a few seconds. He then picked up the phone and spoke with the supervisor of the operating rooms. He scheduled the surgery in OR 6 for Viola Butters at 11:00 a.m. the next day. He also asked his friend Dr. Lloyd Freeman to visit Viola Butters. He told Dr. Freeman the preposterous reasoning, but Dr. Freeman understood. Lloyd Freeman was an African American specializing in geriatric medicine. He obliged Dr. Ramsey by stopping to see Viola Butters the next morning.

The surgery schedule went as planned. Hal Butters and Sid Toile were together in the waiting area along with other members of the large Butters family. After four and a half hours, Viola was sent to recovery. Dr. Ramsey came out to see her husband.

"Mr. Butters," he began, "it was a complicated procedure. We were successful in removing the tumor. I believe we got it all. We also had to remove the spleen, but that is not as critical. We can medicate for the spleen's absence."

"Doc, what I wanna know is will my sweet Viola make it? Dat's all I care 'bout," Hal expressed.

"Her prospects improve with time. We will have to keep her awhile and run other tests. But the good news is that the surgery was successful," he answered.

"Thank you, doc," Hal said while holding his old ball cap glancing down.

"She should make it, and you'll have plenty of people to thank other than me. One of them is that old man who was sitting there next to you." The doctor pointed.

The Boracle had already left the waiting area. He already knew the result. He did not want to be thanked.

"Musta had another i-mergency." Hal looked up.

"Dat man gets spread way too thin ta stay in one place," Hal acknowledged. "Speck he'll be checkin' layta."

CHAPTER THIRTY-FIVE

Established Residency

SID ARRIVED AT the San Jose Airport near Cabo San Lucas. He went through the customs area reclaiming his small duffel bag and proceeded to his predetermined rendezvous point.

The exit pavilion directed the travelers to the left or right into the warm Baja California sunshine. Young students surged to the taxi line on the left in high anticipation of a partying atmosphere that promised to become memorable. Other higher-income visitors were there to capitalize on time-share offerings or discounted "all-inclusive" hotel stays. Cabo San Lucas had even become a favored destination for the Hollywood elite. All of these travelers had a common item of apparel—sunglasses.

Sid watched as they came through from the international flights. One arrived from Rio de Janeiro. Another came from Panama City, Panama. The flights from Los Angeles and Vancouver arrived just before the Boeing 747 landed from Mexico City. Sid waited by sitting upon a twenty-four-inch concrete wall that divided the traffic from the exit. The taxi transports were depleted quickly to take passengers on the twenty-nine-mile trip to Cabo San Lucas. Shuttles ran constantly. Sid looked at his pocket watch frequently but was not looking at the time the facing recorded. He looked at Ida Toile often enough that one would think he was whispering to her small rounded photo.

Pablo Gutierrez arrived a half hour late but was glad to see the old man waiting on the sitting wall at the shaded area. Pablo carried his larger overhead storage suitcase on rollers, pulled with his good left hand. Sid was happy to see the young Mexican again.

"Pablo, *mi amigo,* your children miss you. Maria is making a special meal for your return tomorrow. We're meeting an old friend of mine at the Casa Dorada bar this evening at seven o'clock. Then we're flying back out at nine forty in the morning," Sid announced. "My rental car is waiting over at Alamo."

They walked to the shuttle area to retrieve the rental car.

"Pablo, it is very odd to me that the third-largest car rental company in Mexico is Alamo. Now, I know that it's a Spanish word for 'cottonwood tree,' but it is also representative of one of the worst U.S. land grabs ever perpetrated upon Mexico. *Remember the Alamo* became the battle cry for Texas independence. It would be similar to putting a large pizza chain in Israel and calling it Auschwitz Delivery," Sid explained.

Pablo did not fully understand.

The long drive to Casa Dorada gave Sid time to explain his entry plan to the United States. He knew that Pablo would be worried about crossing the border again.

"Pablo, my associate who will meet us tonight, has a delivery as well," he began. "But it's better than pizza."

Pablo inquired, "Mr. Sid, they say that if I try to cross the border again, they will put me in jail for ten years. Does your friend have a plan to stop that?"

"No, Pablo, he does not," Sid paused. "My plan does that."

"You will be given a new passport with the photo we obtained from Maria," Sid explained. "It's legal, and so are you."

"It took a senator I know and a six-week wait, but they can never deport you again. You have the option by accepting this passport to become an American with parents in Mexico and a family in North Charleston."

"But don't I have to pay a lawyer and wait seven years?" he asked. "What about my sister, Valeria?"

"We took care of the details. And Valeria can be issued a ninety-day visa at the asking. Does she want to come back or stay in Puerto Angel?" Sid asked.

"She wants to stay in Puerto Angel for now and maybe forever. She has a new boyfriend there," Pablo informed.

"You just have to obey the laws, pay your taxes, and build a productive life. You are entitled to all freedoms as long as you do not abuse those freedoms. You can even be called to serve on a jury," Sid developed. "You just have to do what you were doing before and make sure you are responsible to your family, your community, and your new country. You have already proven yourself before. So just do the same."

"When I get back, I will have no work, but I will find work and call up people who will hire me," Pablo committed in confidence. "I have been thinking about it, and I want to follow my dream to be a carpenter, like Jesus. No more tar mix."

"Yes, you can be a carpenter," Sid winked. "I'm sure of it."

They placed their bags into a small manual transmission Chevy Bolt. Sid knew that Pablo would have trouble shifting gears because of his missing right hand, so he assumed the role of driving him to the resort. There, they would finalize the journey to citizenship.

After their check-in to the resort, Sid went for a walk down to the marina. It was warm and humid and just five blocks away. Sid knew that the marina had many excellent shops lining the moorings of sizeable deep-water fishing craft. He wanted to find an appropriate gift for Maria and the children. The sombreros were tacky, and the shellacked and petrified armadillos were an animal rights activist's nightmare. He was interested in a mysterious and ornate Mayan mask. It was hand-painted on acacia wood. But when he turned the mask over to find the price, he saw that it was made in Indonesia.

As he began to ask the clerk for an authentic mask, a short and slightly built man tapped him on the shoulder. He was holding a manila envelope.

"Mr. Toile," he began, "you may not remember me. I am Carlos Enrique Rebolledo. We met in Cuzco in 1974. This is the Christchurch dossier. All the Edinburgh papers are there—certified and stamped. It is in order and as you instructed. The wooden box has the stone. I have verified its provenance. Thank you for what you have done for my father. Good day, sir."

Sid accepted the envelope and the small wooden box. He gave the small man a slight head bow and a Neuvos Soles coin as his verification. He said nothing but did recall the gentlemanly elder Rebolledo. He knew that the celebrated Peruvian agronomist had died in the last year. They were friends from another time. He watched Carlos Enrique leave as quickly as he appeared. The entire exchange took twenty seconds.

The dossier had everything he needed to extract himself from one life and emerge into the next. The box was for someone else. Only he knew when the timing would be right.

The good son Rebolledo disappeared back into the marina area. Sid placed the large envelope under his arm and proceeded to the jewelry counter. He bought a few silver and turquoise jewelry pieces for Maria and two Mexican-made wooden toy airplanes. He had them wrapped before proceeding in the thick Cabo heat back to the hotel.

As the sun went down casting a luminous hue upon the famed Lovers' Beach across the bay from Casa Dorada, Sid headed to the pool bar. There, Sid and Pablo met a floral-shirted stranger. He introduced himself as the U.S. diplomat to Mexico and handed Pablo his new legal passport. He then performed a quiet swearing-in ceremony at Sid's insistence. After the impromptu ceremony, Sid bought Corona beer for all three to toast to the newest U.S. citizen.

All of the attention temporarily humbled Pablo. He couldn't believe that he would never have to fear the INS officers again. He would be with Maria. The spontaneous ceremonial moment would change his life and inure his attitude of service to others. What Sid had arranged fortified Pablo's resolve to become successful in America and, in turn, help others in need.

The three of them proceeded to the beach setting down the walled stairs from the hotel. They enjoyed an authentic Mexican seafood dinner at the tented and informal Cabo restaurant the Office. The restaurant occupied the beach in front of the Casa Dorada. Pablo did not say much at dinner, still in awe of the U.S. diplomat. Even the diplomat took the opportunity to ask advice from the man that he even knew as the Boracle.

As the three of them finished dinner, Pablo spoke up nervously.

"*Senõr,* Mr. Sid, I am a poor Mexican who is now a rich American. But I have the same amount of money. Thank you for giving me a chance to be somebody for my family. I will not let you down," he offered. "Because I will not let myself down."

Both the diplomat and Sid were astonished by the bold and simple gesture.

Pablo and Sid flew out the next morning. It took three hours to get to Dallas and another three on a smaller commercial flight to land in Charleston. By Sid's instruction, Maria and their two boys met them at the Charleston airport. They had taken an Uber taxi. The reunited Gutierrez ran to hug the one-handed Pablo as he appeared at the baggage area. He showed Maria his passport, which was stamped by an immigration official in Dallas on his way home. The stern female officer that commanded the immigration booth in Dallas completed the process by saying, "Welcome home!" to Pablo upon handing his passport back to him. He showed the stamped imprint to Maria.

"Yea, Pablo. My passport Mr. Sid got for me was stamped in Texas too," Maria replied. "We never have to hide again."

They were both U.S. citizens. They went outside to wait for transportation with Sid, they assumed. But Sid was not to be seen.

Two vehicles pulled up as if they were signaled to do so. The driver of the new white Ford F150 extended cab pickup got out and rode away after jumping into the second car. He left the keys in the truck and left it idling with the transmission in park. Maria noticed the new script on the side that advertised Charleston Carpentry Specialist. Pablo's cell number was listed just below the artwork.

"Look, Pablo!" she shouted in surprise. "Sid must've done this."

Pablo was excited to approach the new truck. He saw a registration card over the visor showing his name. A fully paid insurance card was beneath it. He went to the back to lift the Tonneau cover. The opening revealed a portable table saw; metal saw horses, a circular saw, a rechargeable drill, and a compressor. A full array of other hand tools were stored in the locking toolbox drawers professionally installed under the cover in the rear. The truck had every tool the astonished Pablo needed to begin his new career.

He looked around to find Sid, although he knew that Sid had likely already left. He then helped Maria place the two young boys in the new truck. Three wrapped gifts from Mexico were on the front seat—the silver and turquoise jewelry and the two toy airplanes.

Pablo got into the driver's seat and adjusted the mirrors and the seat height. He was suddenly full of joyous emotion but held back from showing it. He blessed himself and said a silent prayer.

"My heavenly Father, thank You for delivering me to a path. May my travels always glorify Your Holy Name, and may You bless those like Mr. Sid who have helped to spread Your love of others. Amen."

Pablo blessed himself again. Maria blessed herself simultaneously.

She turned to Pablo and said, "My prayers have been fulfilled, and we have been blessed. We will always help others, Pablo. It is what we have to do to honor the blessings we've received."

Pablo nodded. He was with his family again. He was the newest American carpenter in Charleston.

He could not thank Sid because Sid left in the backseat of the dealer car that delivered the new truck. Maria knew why Sid was not available, even for the surprise. Sid was going to be back into his routine at booth 14 the very next day.

CHAPTER THIRTY-SIX

Keepsakes

THETA PULLED KEEPSAKES from a plastic box she had kept in her closet. She had her varsity letter from the cross-country team, her medal from the state championship volleyball team, her earned insignia for Phi Beta Kappa, old photographs of her grandparents, her confirmation crucifix from her godmother, and birthday and Christmas cards she treasured. She pulled the envelope with the one-page folded letter dated from late August of her sophomore year at Scott College. It was the cryptic poem from Billy Grayson.

On the outside of the envelope were the letters of the secret message that read, "To Theta: I love you. I need you." She opened the well-constructed verses written by her lover more than eight years earlier. She hadn't read it since she last saw it in the Atlanta hospital. She remembered crying in the revelation that Billy would live. She recalled placing the prose in a box for safekeeping. She prayed each day that

Billy would become functional and live a normal and healthy life, even if she was to be forgotten.

She was immediately inspired by the title. She hoped that both had sipped the enchanted wine. Poignantly, she read the hidden message once again. "To Theta. I love you. I need you."

Chance upon a Dusky Dream

To the glimmering glass of life's romances,
alizarin nectar, and circumstances;
Wondrous hopes—like rare aged wine, enhance
the journey—they intertwine.

No triumph of greatness can trace its cheers
To the barren groves of fruitless years.
Fervent blooms of bliss grow within a damnable depth of discipline,
Cannot joy and rapture guide your heart
'Til we mark synchronous lines on a chance-drawn chart?

Is this time of ceaseless want—a time to dare, or a time to daunt?

The wasteland extends from reality to sublime,
For it has no measurement for passing time.
Our cynical view of its void—fate, too often, has enjoyed. And
nothingness rolls onto its empty shore in whispered waves of yester-yore.

As in the sleepy dusk of past romances, by
moonlight cast on stilled advances.
No cloistered columns reach with stone to
hold what is dear or what is gone.
Melancholy the muse that once directs the
vigilant soul that virtue protects.

Fervently dwells in boundless space the love-filled joys of another place.

Holding dear the tender eyes—embracing what life glorifies!
The defeat of conscience nobly fought, thus betrayed by honor wrought.
The candles glimmer near the gate, and
shimmer in shadows of shifting fate.
As rain-washed dusk heeds the dawn, pure passion pulsates on.

Allow thy soul to cast thy youth to find the light of naked truth
And I, to last, shall toast to thine—with
mysterious, though enchanted wine,
Fragrant with a mellowed musk, vintaged near a shared and sleepy dusk.

Love, Billy

Somehow, the prose hinted to another meaning within Theta's view of the new Billy Grayson. He had the lyrical ability before the accident, and it exploded to a career after his rehabilitation. The sentiment was precious. This dreamy toast of literature—read differently than when she read it while crying years before—was prophetic. Theta saw the prose with new eyes. It was if he knew he was going away.

The revelation settled in her mind. She brought the prose to Sid the next day at booth 14. She wanted him to assess it and determine if there was any memory of her to be discussed with Billy.

"Have you ever brought this back to Billy?" he asked, knowing that she had not.

Theta shook her head to and fro. She knew what it said, but someone else wrote it to a person now forgotten by fate.

"May I copy it to study?" Sid asked. He did not plan to study the prose. He immediately conjured another reason.

She obliged the old man, handing the original to him. She knew he would return it. She trusted Sid as much as she trusted her late father, Simmons Barnwell.

"And you wrote a letter to him as well?" Sid asked.

"Yes, a love letter. Handwritten," Theta replied.

"Do you suspect that he has your letter?" Sid inquired, knowing that its existence would be beneficial.

"No. He has shown absolutely no attachment to the past and sees me as a complete stranger. Well, except for one subtle reference in one of his songs," Theta remembered.

"Go on," Sid followed.

"He has this verse, 'memories in the mists of mushroom fields,' that he wrote for a hit song called 'Soul Mate.' Sid, a mushroom field is an odd choice. So it's a stretch for a song. Billy and I woke up together with the window open and saw this field of mushrooms that had appeared overnight from the rains. It was misty. Is it possible that he found that little snippet deep in his lost memory?" Theta inquired.

"Brain injuries are difficult, child. His imagination has been enhanced by the trauma. The possibility of other recoveries still exists despite the expert opinions. I have read the journals and explored the brain pathologies."

Sid continued, "But then, why would he not remember you is the real question. Synapses. Neurons talk to neurons in the body. They might be electrical or chemical. Billy has lost his neuron to neuron attachments. The mushroom fields? Maybe that synapse fired off when he was writing the lyrics."

Sid gave the clinical explanation but felt that he had gone on a tangent and should return to the obvious.

"Will other synapses fire off later?" Theta cocked her head in puzzlement.

"Maybe." Sid offered. "But let's get back to the Billy Grayson we both know that is living, breathing, and now. You like him. You wish there were a way to reconnect when that may never be possible. So why not ditch plan A? Go with plan B. Reach out to him. I'd bet my little Monet that he needs a person exactly like you in his life."

"Monet? Really?" Theta had no idea that the Boracle collected art.

"Let me think about this information a bit, child. I'll see if I can solve for x," Sid concluded.

Both Theta and Billy had been nudged by the advice of the Boracle. He sensed that they could be very happy with each other. But neither had responded in any degree of haste. The Boracle knew that they belonged together despite the obvious responsibility objections both had harbored.

Theta knew that Billy was in actuality the post-traumatic and redirected Billy Grayson who knew little of her or the twins. She knew that he had no memory of their passionate love. She knew he had other responsibilities, a celebrity music career, a child by another, and a predisposition to remain independent.

Theta had even greater reservations. She dated no man since Billy. She was ultra-protective of her seven-year-old twins. She provided for them by a diligent and demanding schedule. She had no time for romance. She only wished the sequence of her life with the pre-accident Billy Grayson would have occurred within its natural course like the flow of the waterfall they enjoyed. Yet in the back of her mind, she kept thinking the Billy she knew could confound the medical journals and return to her. She brought the twins to the Saturday morning B & B events in the faded hope of that circumstance. Billy would return there only a fraction of the times that Theta arrived. His travels were becoming more and more difficult choices.

The Boracle had a plan. It had already manifested into the initial stage.

Theta was about to thank the Boracle upon leaving. But as soon as she stood and began to pronounce her appreciation, Sid raised his hand like a traffic cop at an intersection. She was surprised by the gesture.

"Theta, as silly as this sounds, I believe I have been channeled to a place and time to share myself humbly. I have no pretension that I am anyone or anything more than an old man cleaning up the far end of a life I have lived in the passion of servitude. My duty is my North Star. In its performance is its reward. And that is all that should ever be."

Theta smiled at the sincerity of his humility. She made a slight bow of her head and walked away.

CHAPTER THIRTY-SEVEN

Mithridates

ARLO CRUTCHFELD APPEARED to have outsmarted the savant. His rage had grown. Sid had an aversion to returning his calls or answering his letters. Sid avoided the twin brother of his deceased wife. He thought him to be a maniac. He was a wealthy maniac.

Arlo had followed the widower Boracle to Pennsylvania, Finland, Chile, and now Charleston. It was his life's ambition to destroy the man whom he felt had accelerated the death of his twin sister. Sid's devotion to her was inconsequential in Arlo's eyes.

Twice in the past, Arlo had planned accidents for Sid and even considered a faux-suicide event, complete with a typewritten note. But Sid was aware of the man's erratic and vehement behavior. He took precautions.

Maria Delgado had unwittingly brought in the strawberry yogurt with the death concoction. Arlo had made the switch and stayed in Charleston to read the obituary. He wanted to cut it out of the newspaper and take it back to Sparta as a trophy. He was confident that he had succeeded beyond suspicion.

Sid Toile was well read. Years before, Sid had become familiar with an ancient king—a mellifluous name cataloged among history's legends. Mithridates was a leader who defeated three Roman generals. He ruled a land surrounding the Black Sea in the century before Christ's birth. Many plots occurred over his life to dethrone him. He assumed that poison would become the most likely assassination tool. He made a habit of taking small doses of the known toxins so that he would build immunity. It was a known antidote. He took ever-increasing amounts of strychnine and arsenic with his food. His tolerance for the known poisons of the kingdom was considerable. Those that wanted to dethrone Mithridates were astonished as he defeated certain death and had the perpetrators brought to justice. Mithridates held his kingdom into old age. A thirty-five-ingredient mixture of antidotes had been widely dispensed for the same purpose throughout the Middle Ages. Mithridatum was named after the ancient ruler.

Sid Toile long believed that Arlo Crutchfield would find him as he had in other cities. His obsessive vengeance persisted. Sid had an early warning system that was natural and true. His dream cycle would cast the blue light when danger neared.

Sid read the blue signs. His senses were enhanced even more acutely. He knew when he was being watched or followed. He always escaped.

He always suspected that he was apt to be poisoned by Arlo Crutchfield. Arlo, Sid calculated, knew much about the various concoctions because of his significant farm maintenance responsibility and the various chemicals available to him.

Over twenty years, Sid took small samples of strychnine, nightshade, arsenic, and even the poison hemlock. He had ordered curare, used on poison darts in South America. He was also familiar with mithridatum. Sid was not afraid of the devious conspiracies that Arlo might employ and sensed that Arlo knew too much about various poisons not to plot a scenario that would appear as a natural death.

Arlo was incorrigible. Sid wrote early letters to Arlo, appealing to his reason. He wanted Arlo to know of his vehemence in trying to save the life of his beloved sister. He explained that he was desperate for unproven cures to pancreatic cancer—then unavailable in the United States. But the appeal to reason had no harbor in the mind of the vengeful. Arlo felt that his twin sister died much too soon. Her sad demise rerouted more than one life.

Sid became more aware that Arlo was and uncommitted psychopathic killer who was both evil and imbalanced. Arlo had the unfortunate resources of time and money.

As Arlo's earlier plans failed to eradicate his former brother-in-law at other discovered locales, Sid became ever aware of his malicious, conspiratorial energy. The cerulean dreams kept him ahead of the danger. In the time it took Sid to become immune to the poisons, Arlo's irrational intentions became a solvable problem to Sid.

The brilliant synesticist realized that he must die and that Arlo must own the conquest. He was nearly ready for the conclusion.

Sid had another cerulean dream. He knew that Tony the Blade Giancone would be sending a set of thugs to see him. "Torts" Tersini and Jocko Santo had been released after serving fourteen months. They drove a large black SUV to Charleston to get even with the old man in the coffee shop.

Sid had ingenious ruses stockpiled awaiting the predictable events others might employ. He owned the truth, the map, the science, and the sorcery.

His attention to the release of Horace Rhett was indicative of his calculated anticipation. Given Horace's final remarks ("See you in hell, old man!") from Sid's visit to the county jail, a whole strategic plan developed. As the judge released Horace on a $25,000 bail awaiting a trial for domestic violence and aggravated assault, he included a ninety-day renewable restraining order. The bailiff delivered a box of clothes from home, his incidentals, and a letter signed by his wife and daughter directing him to seek alcohol abuse counseling. He reclaimed his truck keys. The letter further stipulated that the door locks and alarm codes had been changed and that entering the home without permission was considered a home invasion. In South Carolina, a person can shoot first and ask questions later in the case of a home invasion. It's the law.

As Horace left the bench, he mumbled to the bailiff, "That old bastard's got it coming. Toile. I'll find that sumbitch."

Horace Rhett was angry enough to call Evelyn to threaten her. But her phone number and that of Anna's were also changed. Instead, Sid arranged that Evelyn's phone patched to a recording device at the sheriff's office. Horace raged when Evelyn's recorded voice of "hello" led him to assume he was speaking to her "live." The sheriff and a deputy picked Horace up and jailed him for thirty days because of the phone threat of physical harm. He was denied bail.

Once Sid received the threat news from the sheriff, he visited Evelyn. She met Sid at the front door while Anna was in school. Her swollen facial lacerations concerned Sid. She wore a sling on her arm.

"Evelyn, I'm afraid I have mixed news," Sid began. "Horace has been locked back up. He was foolish enough to threaten you on a recording that the sheriff has. He's in for thirty days. No bail."

"Sid, I'm so sorry to put you through this. These are my troubles," Evelyn stated. "This is going to be an ordeal."

"That's the other part. While we know where he is, you can serve him with anything that needs to be witnessed. It's your call. You only have thirty days to make it count because he'll evade you after that."

"Sid, do you mean the police charge of aggravated assault, or do you mean divorce papers?" Evelyn asked.

"The aggravated assault is already in place. You'll just need to sign that before the trial. You might want to talk over the divorce with an attorney and definitely with Anna," Sid advised.

"We've already talked. There is no other option. He's cruel, and he will not accept that he's an alcoholic. Even if he went to counseling, how will I ever trust that he will not revert?" she posed.

"Statistically, very few can quit and stay sober. It's just a fact. And he is violent. But if you love him and want what's best for him, you may be able to convince him to change," Sid considered. "It's something only you can decide."

"Sid, I'm embarrassed. I was living a façade of life. I don't love him. We lost that feeling years ago. I fear him. But the comfort of what he provided was too convenient. I settled. I rationalized that it would be best for me to tolerate the tirades for Anna's sake. I thought he might change, but deep inside, I knew that change was an unlikely possibility. I have to face it. He was bad for me and could be a threat to Anna as well. But he's her father. I feel like anything I do might be deemed self-serving or vengeful in a divorce. His assets are his contracts. He'll lose some of them over the next thirty days."

"What does Anna think?" Sid asked.

"She thinks we are oil and water. She fears him too. But, all of a sudden, I will need to provide her a college fund when I don't know if I can make a house payment beyond our meager savings. What will I do?" she asked.

"Trust your instincts. Get your real estate license recertified. Go back to work. Anna will understand. And she'll appreciate your sacrifices. No more bridge club. You won't miss it," Sid predicted.

While Evelyn was planning the rest of her life, Horace was planning the end of Sid's life. He knew that Sid Toile had planted the idea of independence into Evelyn's head. He would get even.

His cellmate, Rawl Richards, was a petty criminal but convinced Horace that he knew a "drive-by hit man" who lived in Kentucky. The petty criminal was being released at the end of the week. He gave Horace his number so that a post-incarceration hit could be arranged. He gave him the rules. It would be $5,000 cash down and the $20,000 cash upon completion. Unmarked bills. Horace agreed to the deal.

CHAPTER THIRTY-EIGHT

Flights

SID HAD A file he had given to Maria for safekeeping. She was to follow the instructions without deviation. He also delivered a packet to be held by his friend Thomas Leon. It was as if he were preparing for his own demise.

Sid was tidying his extensive list of solvable quandaries. One that he focused upon was that of the redheaded mother of twins.

Sid purchased a voucher from the Dream Site Travel Agency corporate offices in Memphis. It was for $2,000 in the name of Theta Barnwell. An "official" letter congratulating her on her sales record with their firm accompanied the voucher.

Sid also pursued the letter that Theta wrote to Billy. Theta told him what she remembered of its contents. He knew that it could be quite useful. He found Jackie Mann's contact information on the Internet and called him.

"Mr. Mann, I'm Sid Toile, a friend of Billy Grayson's," he began.

"Yes, sir. We have that in common," Jackie responded.

"I have been trying to piece together some of his pre-accident information to assist him in locating others here that may be of help. In doing so, I wanted to determine the location of his pre-accident personal effects, specifically a letter that may have arrived the day after his injury."

"Frieda and I got all of his books, clothes, everything—and took them to his parents when they were here. At their insistence, we kept his posters and his desk lamp. They have everything else," Jackie told him.

"I am trying to locate a letter only. Do you remember if you retrieved his mail from the post office?" Sid asked.

"I gave the post office key to his younger sister, Carla," Jackie volunteered. "His dad closed out the PO box, I believe."

"That makes sense, Jackie. You have been quite helpful. I'll contact his mom and Carla." After pleasantries, they hung up.

The number for Lucy Grayson was not likely listed. Since Billy had risen as a celebrity, the Graysons procured an unlisted number. Sid called Billy instead.

"Billy, my friend, I need your mom's cell number," he began. "I just called Jackie Mann to try and find a letter that I think will clear a lot of stuff up from before your accident."

"Really! That would be wonderful, Sid. Am I an orphan?" Billy asked in a humorous vein.

"No. No. Nothing like that. This is a letter from someone who might have known you better, but I do not want to get the details before I find the letter. Did you get a letter from someone after the accident that you did not understand?" Sid continued.

"Not that I remember, Sid. My folks kept all of my stuff. They paid my car payment and handled my departure from school. My parents were saints," Billy added. "Here's Mom's number. Call her and let me know of any other things I don't know."

Sid would use the call to prod Billy toward a direction he felt would be most beneficial.

"Thanks, Billy. Are you still procrastinating about a phone call? If that's the case, go back to what you weren't doing!"

"Timing's bad. Christmas is here. A tour with the band is in two weeks," Billy said. "But I did book my itinerary with Theta yesterday, Sid. It gives me a reason to call her back. But I don't think she's interested in me, or in anyone for that matter."

"Good, Billy," Sid confided. "Now you can grow old apart."

Billy laughed at the sarcasm. Sid liked to imbalance the odds with his sage wisdom and wit.

"What concert dates, and where are you playing?" Sid followed. "I might like to get out my old bell bottoms."

Billy told him of the dates and locations. Sid asked about young Ashton and his mother's joy in keeping him. He suspected he would see Billy's parents in short order.

Sid called Lucy Grayson and invited himself over. He knew that he did not want Lucy or Carla to find out about Theta and the twins by checking Billy's collection of the paraphernalia of the past. If Carla secured the mail, there was a small chance that the letter would still be in Billy's personal effects unopened. Lucy was most receptive to the Boracle's visit. She knew that Billy relied upon his advice.

He arrived at the Grayson home at four o'clock that afternoon by Lucy's arrangement. Billy's sister, Carla, was out. Lucy prepared a glass of iced tea, while Sid sat in the den.

Sid began, "Lucy, I have no magic wand to bring back Billy's past, but there are clues and hints that I feel I can pursue to get a better understanding and maybe assist Billy even further."

"Sid, how can we help?" Lucy inquired as she brought iced tea to him.

"Have you kept Billy's personal effects from college? I know it had to be a very difficult time. I wanted to look through them to see if there were any clues," Sid asked.

"There are two boxes in our FROG storage. Billy has the rest. It's all that we brought back and kept for him. We were not sure he was going to live. We even sold his bed and other things to help pay the medical bills. By then, we had hope," Lucy recalled.

"I can get them down," she followed.

"Thanks, Lucy. They may hold a clue but probably not," Sid suggested.

Lucy went to retrieve the boxes. Their television was on with the volume low. A rerun of the *Andy Griffith Show* was playing. Within a moment, she brought both boxes down and placed them on the coffee table next to the tea.

The tops were taped closed, but Lucy retrieved a steak knife from the kitchen to sever the wide packing tape.

Sid looked through the first box, extracting some of his college room décor, a Hooters wall calendar, class schedules, term papers, and miscellaneous loose items like his empty wallet, some handkerchiefs, old football programs, and his keychain. There were a few items from high school as well, including his senior yearbook. Sid looked through the items carefully, asking to retain the yearbook with the caveat he would return it in due course.

The second box was heavier than the first. It had his course books for the fall semester—courses he barely attended. There were loose notebooks and a few birthday cards he had saved. Sid looked through his books expecting to find the letter. He did. It dropped out of one of his notebooks. But he did not want Lucy to see it.

The unopened letter from Theta was placed on the inside front of his political science book, *Understanding Ideologies*. Sid placed the course book carefully under the yearbook. It's likely that Carla placed it there when she checked on his Tech campus mail for the last time. Sid spent no time looking at it. He simply closed the course book knowing the letter was inside.

"I'll bring these back tomorrow, just after lunch," he stated. "Not sure if they will signal any clues, but you never know."

Sid excused himself and took the books. He thanked Lucy for the refreshing tea. He got home and extracted the unopened letter to be used as part of his plan for Theta and Billy.

Sid Toile had the calculated mind of a world-class chess champion.

CHAPTER THIRTY-NINE

Dream Site

AS AN INCENTIVE for her attainment of a production goal, Theta Barnwell qualified for a free four-day stay at the Renaissance Resort in St. Croix. She could take the trip or the cash equivalent of $2,000. She had no idea that Sid had initiated the award. Being a single mother, she had decided upon the cash. On the day that she was to e-mail the voucher back to the Dream Site Travel Agency Headquarters in Memphis, Billy walked in.

"Billy, what a surprise!" Theta looked up.

She stood to hug him.

"Are you going somewhere I can help with?" she followed professionally.

"Yes, Theta. I have the concert trip I mentioned. It's short. If you're sure you don't mind helping me with the booking, I'd like to give you the details. It's two nights at Grand Turk, two at San Juan, and three at St. Croix. Can you get me there and back? January 4 to 11. The band is coming in on their own from Charlotte, but I have to fly from here," Billy asked.

"Billy, I'd love to do this for you." Theta shuffled papers on her desk. "I'll need a bit more information. Preferred flight times, seating preference, hotels, car rentals, and a credit card I can place on file."

"I like flying out early from here and other departures after one o'clock. I never fly first class but like aisle seats. The band will have ground transportation already. I'll have to call you back with the hotels. Can I take your business card?" Billy asked while selecting a business card from the corner of her desk.

"Of course. Billy, let me work on this for you. Can I call you back tomorrow? I still have your business card with nothing on it from months back. Is that number correct?" she asked.

"Yes. The number is right. I'm honored that you kept it. Call anytime," Billy replied.

"Are you taking Ashton or anyone else? Your tour occurs before the spring semester begins," Theta followed. "I can find youth fares."

"No thank you, Theta. It's just a short Caribbean tour. Ashton's gonna have to stay with my mom," Billy detailed. "I hate to leave the little guy for that long, but I have a contract.

Theta thought of the *taking-chances option* that Sid had recently suggested and decided to embolden her actions going forward. The serendipitous travel voucher could be a value used to get to know the new Billy Grayson. It was a gamble she decided to take.

Theta opened her Dream Site Travel program. She searched for solutions to Billy Grayson's travel with the intention to assist him in bringing young Ashton. She could do this if Billy allowed her and the twins to babysit Ashton while he was performing. She could validate the voucher she had been awarded by matching the dates Billy had given to her. She would not get in Billy's way but hoped to have an occasion to finally spend some time talking with the celebrity as they had both wanted. She carefully planned her bold intentions. Sid would be proud.

Within twenty-four hours, Theta called Billy.

"Billy, I have your information and the pricing for your trip," she began.

"Wow, Theta. That was fast," he responded.

"Billy, I want to ask you something first, but I want you to be honest with me as a friend," she followed.

"Honesty is the bedrock of life, Theta. Sid repeats that to me all the time," he stated. "I have no old lies to protect, so I might as well be completely honest."

Theta smiled at Billy's self-deprecation over his amnesia.

"Well, on the day that you walked in, I had just won a voucher that is an all-expense paid trip to St. Croix. It's an open-date voucher to be used within the year."

Neither Theta nor Billy knew that the Dream Site bonus voucher was arranged through the acute foresight of one Eliot Sidney Toile.

"When you walked into the agency to say you were going there, I was not planning on going and was going to opt to cash in the prize. But when you told me about the conflict of bringing Ashton, I checked the dates. I was thinking of taking the twins to St. Croix over the Christmas break. The bonus voucher makes it possible. They are still out of school until January 14. So I was thinking, that if you trusted me, I could offer to take Ashton too. We're staying on St. Croix. I can watch him while you do your concert."

There was a silence. It was long enough to have Theta thinking that she had put Billy on the spot.

"Be honest with me, Billy. Is this too forward of me or too imposing? Tell me so that I will not make a fool of myself. I won't get in the way of your groupies, I promise," Theta explained.

"Wow, Theta. Groupies aside—that does work. I'd love to take Ashton with me. He'd love it too. Since the band is staying at the Renaissance, he can stay in my room and spend time with your girls at the pool and beach of your hotel, if you don't mind," Billy accepted.

"Where are you staying, Theta?"

"Billy, with the voucher, I have already placed the same hotel, the Renaissance, on hold. It's available. I promise we won't get in your way," Theta followed.

"Oh, yes, that could be a problem. The groupies! Remember? They gather in the ballroom of the hotel and just swoon the entire time." Billy embellished the assumption.

Theta chuckled, relieved that Billy was kidding her.

Billy took a serious moment to explain further.

"Theta, I am not a 'player.' I do not subscribe to the media-expected travel life of a musician. I pretty much keep to myself. I once took on a girlfriend. In a flash, she was a fiancée. That person was, in fact, a groupie. I was foolish. The episode came from abysmal judgment at a time of my life when I was most vulnerable. Not smart! I made a terrible and senseless mistake, but I have a blessing—Ashton. But that engagement is a constant reminder of why I should keep to myself," he explained. "Don't get me wrong. I have a son whom I adore and treasure. He is my foremost priority."

Theta immediately thought of the parallels to her life. She internalized that Billy would never pursue a new romance because of his self-admitted mistake and his responsibility to Ashton. She wanted to dispel any other personal notion, though deep inside, she hoped to rediscover the former Billy Grayson.

"Billy, I am not trying to be anything but a friend. We're going there during the weeks of Christmas break, so the twins will not miss school. I thought I could help you with Ashton, and the girls would be delighted to help me babysit," Theta clarified. "Besides, it would not be an awful experience to hang out with you some. We could finally get that cup of coffee I've promised you for too long."

Billy feigned hesitation.

"Well, I don't know. I'm somebody that you may know better than I know myself! You take your chances," Billy enticed. "You might just be barely OK with me—given the high bar set by the groupies."

He added, "Can you fly Ashton to the first two stops with me, and we'll meet you at the Renaissance? He already knows the twins from the B & B, so that will work out fine. Maybe we could do lunch at the pool or something."

Billy smiled as Theta consented to be his friend and nanny for three days in St. Croix. She was elated as she hung up. Billy was also quite interested in the arrangement. He could finally take Ashton and then spend some exploration time with a refreshingly novel face—Theta Barnwell.

CHAPTER FORTY

St. Croix

BY CHRISTMAS THE following week, Billy had given Theta his credit card for the flights to all three Caribbean stops. She printed the itinerary of his flight arrival time at St. Croix and had personally rented a six-passenger Ford Explorer. She assured him that she would meet him at the airport to save confusion with the band and the equipment.

On the seventh of January, Theta took her one chance to see if the new Billy Grayson could become any semblance of the man she loved more than eight years earlier. She was quite cautious.

The daily JetBlue flight 2060 from San Juan landed on schedule near Christiansted, St. Croix, at 2:20 p.m. The flight only took forty minutes. Theta and the twins waited for Billy at the baggage claim. Theta took the airport opportunity to walk to Billy and give him the welcoming hug of an old friend. Billy had taken Ashton with him for the first two stops and then reintroduced Ashton to the twins.

"Theta, I didn't pay extra for the hotel shuttle. Thank you for doing this. You should be at the pool with the twins, though," Billy stated.

"Remember, we came yesterday. They are waterlogged," Theta responded. "Here's your room key and your welcome kit."

Billy was momentarily intrigued. It was as if she worked for the hotel.

"How did you pull that off?" he asked.

"I'm a professional travel agent. I had your credit card number and a face that is believable, I suppose. They think I'm your wife," she chided. "I didn't look anything like a groupie."

"Saves time. I'm for that," Billy added before asking, "Are you hungry, Theta? I hope so. I'm famished."

Theta looked at the girls. They had all eaten before coming to the airport. She didn't want to pass up an opportunity to revisit the sight and voice of this accomplished and handsome artist.

"We ate at the beach grill, but we have room for dessert. Any particular fare you'd like?" Theta asked.

"Let's get to the hotel, and it would be my pleasure to buy ice cream for three pretty groupies at the beach grill." Billy smiled.

Theta was at an end room on the first floor, furthest from the elevator. Billy's pre-booked room was a fourth-floor suite, complete with a stocked bar, valet service, and an indoor Jacuzzi. It had two bedrooms. Theta was tempted to change Billy's room to something closer to her but refrained.

They took the luggage to Billy's suite. Theta was amazed by the spaciousness and the ambiance of the more beautiful layout with a full view of the ocean.

"This is nice, Billy. Your travel agent needs to get a raise," Theta said, impressed by the openness and décor.

"Yeah, it's too big. I don't like the bigger rooms. I get swallowed up," Billy answered. "They assume all band members party all night."

"Let's go check out the grill, Ashton. I'll bet Mia and Leah can lead the way," Billy said as he placed his bags by the sofa.

The five of them went to the beach grill and ordered. Theta had a Diet Coke, while the twins ate ice cream. Billy and Ashton chose from the chicken and burger buffet.

"Theta, can we go by your room on the way back?" Billy asked.

"Whatever for, Billy? You'll be disappointed to know what you get with a prize voucher," she intimated.

"I just wanted to see it. But we don't have to," Billy replied.

"No. no. It's perfectly fine. We can then go back to yours to get Ashton into his bathing suit. The girls know all of the fun places to take him," Theta confirmed, hoping to spend available time with Billy.

Billy signed the room check and went with Ashton to see Theta's first-floor room. It had been cleaned and the beds made. All of the items the Barnwell girls brought were hanging up neatly or placed into the dresser drawers.

"Just as I thought," Billy started. "This room is near the emergency door; there are two queen beds, a big-screen TV for sports, and no hotel noise. You picked the perfect room," Billy disclosed. "I'll bet that path from the window leads right to the beach."

"Yes, it's a fine room. We like it," Theta reassured Billy.

"Theta, it's time for me to ask a favor of you. Be honest. Don't be pressured either," Billy started. "I would be doubly happy if we could switch rooms. Here's my key. The band will pick up my room bill, and yours is already free. Whaddaya say?"

Before Theta could answer, the twins began to voice their approval.

"Please, Mommy, please. We can have our own bedroom, and there's more play area. Please! Please!" They were in unison.

Theta cocked her head slightly while looking at Billy. "Are you sure?"

"I'll help you carry the stuff. My valet from the suite can come get it," Billy assured.

"While he's on the way, Ashton and I will go get our stuff and bring it down here," he directed.

Billy got the suite room key back from Theta.

"I'll bring your new suite key back in a flash," he promised.

Billy's spontaneous room change idea made the prospect of a great vacation better for both the Barnwells and the Graysons.

Billy asked Theta if she would mind Ashton and him hanging out at the pool with the girls. Billy invited them for dinner at Duggan's Point—provided they could use Theta's Ford Explorer. Theta did not hesitate to accept.

When Billy finished unpacking their luggage at the ground floor room, they headed to the pool to reserve space. The pool area was getting crowded. Snowbird vacationers had found St. Croix. But Theta was not there yet. Billy got into the shallow end to throw a Nerf ball and splash water on Ashton. He was looking every few minutes for Theta so that he could tell her where their towels were reserving chairs.

Theta came with her flat shoes, sunglasses, and a simple white cover-up. She had lotion for herself and the twins. She pulled her shimmering red-brown hair back into a beret. Billy pointed to the reserved chairs.

"Thanks, Billy," she mouthed with the slightest sound while dropping her sunglasses.

Theta began to apply lotion to Mia, who seemed in a hurry to jump into the pool. Leah was next, more patient—but still intent on getting wet. Then Theta adjusted her chair back up a notch. She removed her cover-up to reveal the lithe and model-like figure she had kept in fit condition over her hiatus from dating. She was still pasty white with splotches of freckles. Her light-blue two-piece bathing suit was still a size four with a busty floret top. She knew that she could not stay in the Caribbean sun very long.

Billy had placed arm swimmies on Ashton. The twins joined them. He threw the twins to a splash landing and then Ashton. They repeated the exercise with the sweet sound of children's laughter, while Theta watched. The three children began to play Marco Polo at the shallow end. Billy exited the pool to sit by Theta.

"Theta, you will be a deep shade of glorious red in an hour," he started. "It's no way to enjoy a vacation. I have sunblock."

"I have some 35 SPF on the table. I can't reach my back. Would you mind?" she asked, remembering her abrupt refusal from eight years prior that was the ironic initiate of their sexy waterfall experience.

She adjusted her chair and rolled over. Billy applied the lotion to her shoulders and upper back. He added more to her lower back.

"I can do your legs, too, if you'd like?" he inquired.

"I can reach my legs, but thanks," she replied. "Do you mind keeping an eye on the three of them?" She readjusted the poolside lounger flat and returned to a position on her stomach momentarily.

Theta thought about the setting and knew that the scorching sun was her enemy. Billy was there—sitting next to her watching the children. She realized that she was too insular. She decided to turn back over and to sit up—knowing that appearing cold, hesitant, and detached was not her way of reintroducing herself. She did not want to let Billy sit alone. She much preferred the companionship chatter because she dearly wanted to get to know him again.

She said nothing at first. She perused his physique from the subtle mystique of her sunglasses. He was twenty pounds or lighter from the hospitalized years of trauma and rehabilitation. But he had the same gray-green eyes; the same shaded beard, and the dark chest hair she admired many years ago. He wore his dark wavy hair longer to cover the brain intrusion scar. She remembered seeing him hanging on for life in the hospital room with his bandaged and swollen head. The thought made her tears well up behind her sunglasses. To know that he had emerged from near death to be at her side was touching, even though he had no perception of the sentiment she felt.

"They play so well together, Billy. That Ashton likes the attention," Theta began.

Theta chatted about the children's schoolwork and their gymnastics, realizing that Billy did not know that all three children in the pool were all his creations. She applied more lotion to her arms, upper chest, and legs as she talked.

"Listen to me," she interrupted herself. "I'm talking about the children and haven't let you get a word in. How's Ashton doing with your mom? How was Grand Turk?"

Billy updated Theta on Ashton's excitement about traveling "on the road" with Dad. After ten minutes, Billy brought an umbrella over to place near the table so that Theta would not get a surprise of redness.

"Billy, I knew you well enough when we were in high school to know that you were a gifted writer. I had no idea that that ability would underscore your career," Theta opined.

"I felt like I found the calling for lyrics when I was in rehab," Billy explained. "I had no idea that there was a market. I learned to sync guitar music to things I had written, and vice versa. I don't know how it comes to me, but it does."

Theta interjected. "You have nine songs now that made it to top-ten charts for other artists. That must be especially thrilling. They see you as a lyrical genius."

"I can't explain it. I just feel it, write it, score it, and play it. I'm blessed." Billy gave the insight. "It's like I received a prize for almost dying."

Theta was stunned by his personal revelation.

"But, Billy, you had this ability before, I know it. It just wasn't among your priority list of things to accomplish in life. You were set on becoming an architect. Instead, you have changed the music world. It must be a fate that was fulfilled."

"I think I have another fate, Theta. I just don't know what it is. I haven't found the compass direction to find it," Billy concluded. He looked at her in the shaded light of the umbrella. Her beauty was striking. Her distinctive green eyes were brilliant and warmed the mood.

Theta hoped that she could find her way back to him. But it would take a supersized dose of destiny.

"Theta, you probably have some idea of what musicians and other celebrities encounter daily, especially on the road. Though your perception would likely be pretty accurate, I did want to settle some questions you might have. I want to be honest with you because you deserve that. You have known me longer than I have known me. I have no idea of what or who I was. I can only be responsible for who I was over the last five or six years since I was released. Some information might repulse you, other parts will not," Billy stated.

"Billy, you owe me nothing. I am just a friend who cares. I do not need to know things you wish to keep confidential. I have no confidential information to trade either, so don't burden yourself, please."

Theta certainly did not want to divulge the vaulted information only she knew. She hoped he was not trying to pry into her past in return for his honest submittals. She presumed that Billy wanted to know what happened to the father of Mia and Leah.

"I am not looking to exchange information, Theta. I just want to come clean with you as someone I deeply admire. You did things for me without thanks or any other expectation. The fund-raising role you undertook was never acknowledged. And even now, you have not asked for anything, yet you have made it possible for Ashton to be with me by recommending your help. Again, you've asked for nothing in return," Billy noted.

"My father was my North Star, Billy. I do not do things to be thanked. I do things to help because it's the right thing," Theta said. "There should be no other motive, don't you agree?"

"Exactly," Billy answered. "That's why I feel I should be up front. Just hear me out. I messed up once because I got careless. There were a few other women, and you should know that. But I have gotten away from the trap. There are no women now because I won't let myself shun my responsibility to Ashton. Drugs? They are everywhere and given freely. My brain was already damaged, so I was wise in that regard. I stayed away. I was the same with booze. I have a wine or a beer occasionally but rarely have the second one. I certainly do not need alcohol to complicate my life any more than it is. I don't gamble, and I have never even smoked a cigarette—to my knowledge. I go to church occasionally and pride myself on my inner faith. So there you have it. The band members consider me to be very boring. I'm not what you think in many ways but probably worse than you think in others."

"Who am I to judge, Billy?" Theta replied. "What I knew of you before the accident matches your postaccident persona. The women?

Well, I'm sure they were everywhere. You probably didn't have a chance. So don't beat yourself up. If you were married, then that would be different. The faith part I understand. You're on the road a lot. That's a tough place to keep up with worship services. I'm traditional, and I like the Episcopal Church. It's not only very formal but also supportive. But, unlike you, I have a predictable schedule.

"If you're telling me this to clear up the unknown of the posttrauma Billy from the high school Billy, I get it. But it's none of my business, really. I like you, Billy. I always have. I am pretty well satisfied that I'm a good judge of character. You have no reason to be concerned with what I think of you because I'm not perfect. I see you as one of God's living miracles. If you can allow me the privilege of your friendship, then I promise always to be a good friend you can count on," Theta concluded.

"But suppose I wanted to see you more often for the potential of a relationship beyond friendship?" Billy asked.

"I'd consider it. It would take time. You might regret it, though," Theta indicated. "Billy, I would not be like the groupies. There would be no intimate privileges that come with the dating part. I've made that mistake already too.

"You have a world full of beautiful women without children or any baggage whatsoever. My priorities are my children. Dating—though it would nice—has taken a backseat. Be careful what you wish for!"

"Theta, I don't know what tomorrow may bring, and I'm aware of how you feel. You have an amazing sense of responsibility. You should know that I am infatuated with you at the very least. I know the rules. I admire that point as well. We will get along well. I'd bet on it. Our dinner tonight will be our first date—sorta. Let's see if we have common interests and go from there. No commitments. Just a trial effort to stay connected as friends and see if the relationship grows. You OK with that?" Billy posed.

"I have no objections. Whatever happens, I feel sure we will remain respectful friends for a very long time. So let's get to know each other and just see," Theta suggested.

They talked for another half hour, sharing wine coolers that Theta ordered. The children played. The sun slanted down the horizon. The breeze drifted to the northwest. Billy suggested that they gather the children to go out for dinner.

They departed at Billy's first-floor doorway to meet again in an hour for the ride out to the restaurant.

Billy had his concert "gig" the next night before flying back to Charleston on the third day. The dinner with Theta and the children would be his initial attempt to find out more about two people he vaguely knew—Theta and himself.

CHAPTER FORTY-ONE

Rest Stop

HORACE RECEIVED HIS formal charge of aggravated assault, the charge of threat to cause harm, and his divorce papers on the same day while in the detention center. He was to appear again before a magistrate upon release but had to submit to an electronic tracking device. He could not leave the state.

After his temporary release, Horace rented a room at an Extended Stay suite. On his second day out, he called Rawl Richards, the petty criminal with ties to an established hitman from Kentucky. Rawl gave him instructions. He was to bring $5,000 in unmarked and nonconsecutive one-hundred-dollar bills to a rest stop at mile marker 174 West. The date and time were exchanged.

He arrived earlier than scheduled so that he could perform his surveillance of the area. His contact was there early as well. He saw a dark green Dodge Ram pickup flash its lights. Horace got out and walked over. He noticed the Kentucky plates. The driver rolled the window down. He looked like a skinny Elvis Presley without sideburns.

"You Horace?" the strange man asked.

"Yeah, you Kenneth?" Horace shot back.

"Get in," Kenneth suggested.

Kenneth was wiry and rough-hewn. His hair was slick, and he wore a dark blue ball cap that had the initials "UK" scripted in white. The vehicle stunk with the thickness of cigarette smoke. He had a Wendy's cup in the holder between the seats and an empty half-pint of Jim Beam on the passenger floorboard. He took a sip of the concoction. Horace sat with his shoulders turned to the hitman.

"You got what I need?" Kenneth asked.

"Yeah, the photos. She's a creature of habit. You can catch her coming out of this bookstore on Wednesdays at about twelve fifteen. She does her grocery shopping at the Publix on Thursdays. I typed what I knew of her schedule on the second page. You can't hit her after three o'clock because my daughter's home then. I'd prefer that it's done away from the home.

"She's a classy-looking chick. Too bad. I'd rather she be ugly," Kenneth informed. "It's easier to kill ugly. Now, how and when I do this will be my choice. I have to scope it in. I'll plan it for away from her home. But what if she's with her mother or a friend?"

"Just take care of her. If you gotta whack a witness, I ain't paying extra. That's your choice. Just not my daughter. OK?"

"No problem, pal. Just asking in case. Consider it done," Kenneth declared. "When is best?"

"Oh, yeah. Yesterday wouldn't be soon enough," Horace said. "Make it look like a mistaken identity if you need."

"Are you sure? Whack this lady in broad daylight. OK. You got the bills, my man?" Kenneth asked.

Horace pulled a green envelope from his coat.

"Here's the five Gs." Horace handed it over.

Unexpectedly, Kenneth opened the envelope and counted the bills. Horace looked around, but no one was near the Dodge truck. He couldn't believe that the guy was counting it right in front of him.

"All there?" Horace asked.

"Yep. I always check. Now, this is important. You bring the other twenty at exactly four o'clock right here the day after the hit. Got it? And don't screw with me on the balance. Cash. Unmarked, nonconsecutive," Kenneth outlined. "No funny business."

"I need one more hit. Same deal?" Horace asked.

Kenneth shook his head in agreement.

Horace pulled out a white envelope. There was cash with two pages of information wrapped around it and secured with a rubber band. He was not going to give the other $5,000 cash unless they struck a deal.

Kenneth opened it and looked at the photo on the first page and the typewritten "habit" schedule on the second.

"This fella's got to be eighty. Why don't you just let nature do the job? He can't be too far away already," Kenneth suggested.

"That's the SOB who's gotten my wife to file charges and sue for everything I've earned. I want him dead yesterday too," Horace continued. "It may be easier to do an auto hit-and-run or maybe suffocate him with his own pillow. You decide."

"Got it. I oughta give a discount. This will be easy," Kenneth stated. He then pulled out the cash and began counting the second envelope's booty.

Horace was becoming impatient. He began thinking that he'd go hunting upstate for a bit with the ankle monitor. Knowing where he would be by the authorities would eliminate his direct involvement. Besides, they'd never trace down a hit man from Kentucky. He was spending his savings on the hits. He knew that the hits would cost less than the attorney's fees for the divorce. With the high alimony and child-support, a hit man could save him a multiple of his post-divorce expenses. Besides, the home mortgage was fully paid. He'd gain that value to start his new contracting business. It was a perfect plan with a tremendous upside.

"This old man here . . . what's his name?" Kenneth asked.

"It's in there. Sid Toile," Horace stated.

"Yeah, Sid. I can make it happen. But I don't want to make two trips. Can I whack both around the same time? Give me two weeks to plan and another to execute. OK?" Kenneth asked.

Horace shook his head yes.

Kenneth asked, "You got the moolah? I've got the time. Just watch the police reports for the details. I usually make the six o'clock news. From the day of the execution, you me back her as agreed two days later. You don't wanna know what happens if you and the forty thousand don't show up."

"Don't worry. I'll be here," Horace confirmed.

Kenneth took another swig from his Wendy's cup. Horace began to exit from the nicotine and Jim Beam odors that proliferated the green Dodge truck.

Both men drove away satisfied that a contract was properly transacted.

CHAPTER FORTY-TWO

The Frumpy Bellman

A FRUMPY BELLMAN DELIVERED a large nine-inch-by-twelve-inch Renaissance envelope to the fourth-floor room while Billy and Theta were away at his scheduled concert. Theta attended the concert at Billy's behest while a local middle-aged nanny supplied by the hotel watched all three children. She dressed conservatively, as always, not wanting to appear to be a groupie in pursuit of the famous singer-songwriter.

The curious envelope was placed under the door in the same fashion as if it were the final checkout billing. The nanny did not displace the envelope. It was addressed to Theta Barnwell, who was listed as the room occupant of the lavish two-bedroom luxury suite. It arrived promptly to the correct room despite their room change the day prior.

A similar large envelope was placed under Billy's door on the first floor. It was addressed to the famous lyricist and marked "open immediately." Theta's envelope was similarly marked.

The concert ended on time. The St. Croix noise ordinance curfew at midnight required the concert to close down as scheduled. Billy rode back to the Renaissance Resort with his new old friend Theta. Both were tired. They went to the fourth-floor suite so that Billy could pick up Ashton. The children were all sleeping—all three in the extra bedroom.

Theta picked up the envelope and placed it on the marble-top bar. She saw the words of immediacy but did not open the letter. She wanted to assist Billy in getting the sleepy Ashton into his arms. Once Billy lifted Ashton, Theta went over and kissed Billy and Ashton on their cheeks—a motherly peck. It warmed Billy's mood to briefly receive her goodnight tiding. He admired everything about Theta as someone fresh yet increasingly familiar.

Billy was about to leave to take Ashton down to their room. He shifted the tired three-year-old to the crux of his other arm and turned to whisper to Theta, "Breakfast? Nine-thirty? It would be just like a third date!"

Theta nodded. She was profoundly enamored that Billy proposed to meet at the hotel restaurant. The companionship hinted of becoming a mutually agreeable union. Billy closed the guestroom door behind him.

As the nanny was gathering her pocketbook and cell phone, Theta opened the envelope. She unfolded a one-page typewritten letter and recognized it immediately. It was the copy that Sid made of Billy's tribute poem to her. Billy had completed the beautiful tribute just days before his traumatic head injury. She was surprised to see it. But Theta immediately thought that it came from Billy, not Sid.

As the nanny was about to leave, she pleaded with her to stay a bit longer. She was immediately exhilarated and had to see her lover from eight years earlier. She presumed he had made a mental breakthrough. She couldn't wait to see him.

"Can you stay just a few minutes longer? I have a quick errand. I'll be back in a few minutes, maybe twenty at most," Theta implored. "I'll pay you extra."

The nanny consented. Jobs like hers paid well on an island without a viable industry beyond tourism.

Theta reread the heartfelt prose that the lost Billy Grayson wrote to her eight years earlier. It emboldened her to see him and embrace him as if the time had not elapsed. She was suddenly overtaken with sentiment. She was about to cry again. She had to see Billy immediately.

She went to her bathroom to reapply her lipstick and brush her hair. She also sprayed a hint of Dolce & Gabbana perfume to both sides of her neck under her ears. She was not angry about the reappearance and perfect timing of the prose letter but, rather, intrigued that Billy may have rediscovered her role in his former life. There was much she had to tell him that he did not likely know.

She had convinced herself that Billy had realized his full past suddenly and serendipitously. She was thinking of words to approach the issue once she got down to Billy's room, thinking that he could figure out that the sleeping twins were his girls and that she was the love of his life. She rationalized a complete explanation.

She did not realize that the letter in the Renaissance envelope was delivered by a mysterious figure and not by Billy. Billy had not regained his memory. Sid had interceded so that the two of them could regain their magic.

Theta was mentally and emotionally ready to rush down and see Billy at the odd hour. She had to know how much he had abruptly recalled from his past. Her heart was joyful. Her pulse was increasing by each step.

Billy, meanwhile, had placed Ashton in bed before returning presently to open the Renaissance envelope that was left for him. He assumed that the band manager had sent a change in their return schedule, as had happened in the past. He tore the top portion open carefully without damaging anything inside.

Billy was somewhat alarmed that the content was but a single unopened letter. It was postmarked more than eight years earlier. It only showed a return address as Scott College in Decatur, Georgia. He recognized the stamped date as three days prior to his life-changing accident. The envelope still showed a red lipstick kiss implanted next to his name. He had no idea who sent it long ago since there was no name on the return address line.

He unfolded the soft pastel handwritten stationery. He glanced at the name at the end to see who had written him this obvious love letter from years ago. He was momentarily confused as he discovered the author of the love note—Theta.

He thought to himself, 'Had she withheld this letter these many years? But it had to come from another source. It went to his college address, and the post office canceled the stamp.' He read the opening with heightened interest. Billy felt the intense anticipation of learning about a mysterious chapter trumpeting his unknown past.

My Dearest Billy,

You have me here by you. I am warmed in the glow. The fragrance of the midnight shower rides upon the furtive gusts of the nearby forest. It is a misty trace of tenderness we share. I shall never witness a nighttime rain again without conjuring your touch in my ardent dreams. I have given myself to you alone and completely. It is the surrender and trust of love.

You rest in the calm. My heart is swollen in the love of you. Could I ever be any happier? Could I ever find a greater peace or a more wholesome joy? The breeze brings my spirit into you and yours into me. There is a secure delight to be awake while you sleep. I can admire you without the awkwardness of your waking perusal. In this I am most contented.

We spoke of a never-ending conversation. Let us also cherish a knowing silence. Let us embrace a bond of gladness, a tie of kindness, and a pledge of adventure together. Let us remain as ourselves individually but as one together. There could never be a vision so vivid, a wish so vibrant, or a desire so wanting as the delectable trance of your companionship. I shun my doubts, my fear, and my vigilance in the face of the fully effervescent sunlight that will warm our future. It illuminates a new and glorious world. You have me here by you. I am warmed in your sunglow. I will love you forever.

Theta

Billy realized that he and Theta were lovers. Nobody ever told him of that fact. His parents didn't, but they probably would not have known. Jackie Mann seemed to say that they were casual friends only. His sister, Carla, never mentioned her. But the letter would explain her effort in fund-raising for him. She was in love with him at the time of the accident. But even Theta never said anything.

So why the letter? Why now? Billy thought. *Did Theta bring the letter with her? Impossible,* he surmised because of the canceled postage, and it because it had been delivered to his campus box. So who sent it to the hotel? Who other than Theta even knew he was in St. Croix?

He immediately suspected Sid. Only a mind like the Boracle could devise the time, place, and circumstance so brilliantly.

As Billy was deducing the answers that might fit the questions, there was a soft knock at the door. He looked through the door's peephole. It was Theta.

He was sure that she did not know about the letter he had just read and was still holding. He opened the door, not wanting to alert her that he had new information about their love relationship that was lost in his accident.

"Theta, you OK?" he asked. He looked at her as one would gaze upon a lover.

"The nanny is up with the girls still. But I got this letter that I figured was from you," she began in earnest. She cocked her head slightly to the side, expecting an explanation.

"Huh?" Billy shrugged, now aware that other forces were at work. It had to be the Boracle's doing. "Theta, I don't understand."

"This letter that you wrote to me before the accident." She lifted to show him while inquiring in a loud whisper. "You mean that you don't remember writing it? You didn't send it to my room?"

"Theta, please sit down over here. Ashton is dead to the world. We can whisper," Billy answered. "I received a hotel envelope too. It had an unopened handwritten letter. I just read it for the first time. It's from you. And it's dated three days before my accident."

Theta began to cry. She realized that Billy had not mentally connected to their mutual past. Billy immediately reached for her and held her close as she sobbed uncontrollably. They both had a lot of questions.

Billy perused the letter that Theta was holding. He saw his name affixed to the bottom.

"Theta, I do not recognize this poem. I suppose I wrote it before I had the accident," he explained. "I also suppose that you and I were deeply in love with each other in another life."

Theta was crying in both joy and revelation.

"Theta, we need to sort this out. Can you stay here while I take Ashton back up? Give me your key. I'm going to ask the nanny to stay a little longer," Billy proposed to her.

She realized that there was an immediate need to talk. She handed Billy her door key. Billy handed her the letter from where he had placed it on the counter before the knock on the door.

"While I am gone, see if you recognize this," Billy implored. "It's the first time I have ever seen it. That is, I think!"

Billy placed the sleeping Ashton back on his shoulder and took him up to the fourth floor. He placed the sleeping Ashton into Theta's bed opposite the girls' room in the suite. He handed the nanny $200 to stay until he or Theta returned. She was elated at the amount.

Theta reread the letter she had sent to Billy eight years earlier. It conjured an emotional sense of her love for Billy that she had revisited all too often.

Billy immediately went back to the elevator to sort out the mystery. On the way, he realized that Theta was in love with who he used to be. He was wary of the late evening and the chance of each misunderstanding the other in the upcoming conversation. He decided to speak of what he knew first before learning the past information from Theta. He thought it wise to exchange the information on a "neutral court." He had the choice of a quiet hotel lounge, the lobby, a pool, and a beach to consider.

He tapped on the door where Theta waited.

When Theta opened the door, her eyes were wet and reddened of the moments. She had the handwritten letter she mailed to Billy by her side. It recalled her surge of passion. Billy saw that she had just finished re-reading it.

Billy spoke first to try and console the thousand thoughts that invaded both of them simultaneously.

"Do you have some flats to put on?" Billy asked. "Can we go for a walk?"

Theta simply took off her low heels. She gathered herself, wondering what revelations would follow.

"I can walk barefooted. Pool or beach?" she asked.

"Beach. I'll bring a towel to sit on," Billy suggested.

"I'll bring a second," said Theta. She was bursting with questions but decided to calm down.

They proceeded by the short walk path through the pool area to the soft pulses of the tide rolling away from Carambola Beach. The beach was wide. The sand dunes were interspersed with large boulders, a geological rarity.

They sat near one of the boulders by the dunes, away from the receding tide.

"Theta, let me speak first so that you get the straight information. Are you OK with that?" Billy asked as he reached to hold her hand.

Theta was still crying quietly, trying to compose herself. She clasped his hand as assurance. She truly believed that he had miraculously recalled his past. Her mind was racing. She further calculated that he must know of the children's parentage. She thought that perhaps he was piecing other facts together and needed her help. For him to have the letter from eight years ago delivered meant that he knew the whole truth. She was searching her heart for the right reaction for the news that she anticipated.

Billy started with the simple. It changed the entire perception of what was known and not known for Theta.

"Theta, I do not recognize either letter. I have never seen them before. So I assume that I wrote one to you at the time that you wrote one to me," he began.

"Yes, that's right," Theta stated softly but emphatically. She was immediately deflated. She realized that the old Billy, her lover, was gone forever. The lover Billy was not magically reappearing. But she was riveted by the circumstance and the conclusions he may not have considered.

"There is no wonder that I was in love with you, Theta. I know I am a stranger to you now, but everything about you seems to suit me. You're sweet, bright, incredibly responsible, and so conversationally nice. I love sitting to talk with you. I hope you do not mind that I am being so forward, but it's evident that I did love you before, so I have an excuse." Billy smiled. "I'm proud of that, seeing you now."

"I did not read the printed poem, but if you leave it with me, I will," Billy added. "I'm sure that the Billy of the past wrote it for someone he loved. Maybe I can write something else to you."

"You already did," Theta stated. "Your song 'Soul Mate' has references that only you and I had experienced."

"Really?" Billy responded. "That's inexplicable. I wrote the first part of that in rehab."

Theta knew that Billy was piecing together a past by its facts, not its experience. She wished that he knew her from their experiences together. It was becoming clear that he did not.

"Why would you think I wrote that to you? I'm intrigued," Billy followed.

Theta realized that the mushroom field description was a quirk, an anomaly. "I suppose you didn't. It's because you described a fresh mushroom field in your lyrics. There was such a thing, and we saw it together."

"I'm sorry Theta that I do not remember a view. Using that lyric came from nowhere. I have never looked across fresh mushrooms," Bill qualified. "But it could be that my brain had a residue of a partial memory then."

Theta accepted the response reluctantly. She turned to follow the moonlit fiddler crabs scrambling frantically between the shallow breakers.

Billy paused to take in that the moonlit view of the lovely shoeless girl sitting on the beach next to him. They each awaited the next revelation.

Theta realized that nothing had changed except the knowledge that they were once lovers. But if she didn't speak up presently, that stagnant condition would persist. She thought of Sid's advice and decided to befriend chance over caution.

"Billy, what else can you conclude from the past that you just found out about?" she asked. She led him like a guide through a maze—solving the unknown by restating the known. She persisted to have him conclude their past by deduction.

"You didn't plant your letter, and I didn't plant mine. So this has got to be the work of Sid Toile," Billy stated. "What have I missed so far?"

"Yes. Sid," Theta agreed, nodding her head in approval of the first conclusion.

"Let's agree that we're sitting here by Sid's connivance," Theta said. "That's a good start. He wanted us here, and he wanted us to talk. He knew the missing pieces that we didn't so he planted the letters. The rest is up to us."

The half moon allowed muted lighting. The Caribbean breeze was salty and erratic. They adjusted their seating on the towels to face each other. Theta's angelic face was illuminated in the moon's glow. Billy still held her hand softly.

"Many questions remain. I give you that," Billy suggested.

Theta's alizarin hair seemed to tangle in the soft gusts.

"I'm a bit throaty after the concert," Billy explained to her as his voice struggled. "Tired, I guess. But the importance of this conversation may keep me up for weeks."

"You told me you graduated from the College of Charleston. But you lived in Atlanta. Was that because of me?" Billy asked.

"Mostly. Well, Billy, I should be completely truthful. That answer is a resounding yes. I liked Scott College. But let's go back before that. After we dated in high school, we broke up. It was amicable. It was because we were both going off to college and because I frustrated you. We truly liked each other. I fancied that our romance was not over. I knew that I could love you. So I followed you to Atlanta. Only you didn't know that I was there because I wanted to be near you. Truth! Nobody knew that we dated later—just the one time. It was the weekend before the accident that we fell in love. But when you had your accident, my whole world changed," Theta added, still in a misty tone.

"There's much more, isn't there?" Billy asked, knowing that Theta was reticent to tell the whole story.

Theta cocked her head to the side as she often did when considering a reply. She was trying to muster her courage to tell all of the truths but wanted to do so in a way that would not make Billy feel any guilt. She preferred that he drew the conclusions instead of her outright confession.

"Theta, dear . . . I think Sid placed us here for more reasons than we can know. It follows that I shouldn't know less than you know," Billy concluded. "Please let me know everything. I think I can handle it."

Theta looked at him, trying to get the words out. But she struggled.

"Do you trust me enough to tell me everything you feel I should know, even if that changes our friendship?" Billy followed. "I must be able to face my past and my future with the same tenacity. Only the truth can help me. Can you present all of the truths to me? I already like the first one. We were madly in love with each other. I had great taste!"

Billy added, "As indelicate as this is, your letter leads me to believe that we were lovers in every sense. I fear I may be stepping over the line, so help me out."

Theta preferred that Billy assume the result. She didn't want to say it. But it was now up for discussion. The moment that Sid had meticulously engineered was at hand.

Theta paused as she collected her thoughts and gained a better composure. She folded her bare feet underneath and inched closer to Billy, her green eyes glimmering in the moonlight. She took her hand from his and placed it on her chest below her clavicle.

"As I said, we dated in high school and then broke up. I wasn't ready for any physical commitment to anyone then. That's why you were so frustrated with me back then. I was a virgin. Better said, I was a determined virgin who was set to remain a virgin until my wedding night. You were going off to Georgia Tech on a soccer scholarship. You could have any girl you wanted because you were athletic, handsome, and personable. There was not an incentive to wait many years for me.

Yet I followed you because, deep down inside, I knew that you were someone special."

Theta bravely told the sequence without crying anew.

"We saw each other as friends several times after that but did not date. You dated others but had no interest in me other than as a friend. I understood the reason but did not retreat from my feelings. I did not want to crowd you. And as silly as it sounds, I envisioned you always while waiting for my wedding night. Truth. Make no mistake. I was waiting for you and you only."

"Was I a jerk?" Billy asked. "I must have been a real idiot jerk to you."

"No. Not at all. You were a perfect gentleman then as now," she replied. "I guess that is why my feelings for you were so strong. It was because you cared even when you knew that I would not give in. It made me love you even more."

"Thank God. I'm beginning to like me. My taste in women had to be exquisite." Billy smiled. "So what happened to you that I rerouted to other ventures and you drifted away?"

He still had no idea of what other information was to come.

Theta smiled accommodatingly before she went on to the more significant issue. She gulped in fear of the next full circumstance of her revelation.

"One weekend, you invited me to a cabin in North Alabama. You knew I was going as a friend only. I was still a virgin at twenty. You respected that I wanted to save myself for marriage, and you, Billy, were a perfect gentleman. I was completely safe. But after Jackie and his girlfriend Frieda left, we had the cabin to ourselves for the last day before driving back to Atlanta. It rained all weekend. The sun came out just after they left, and so did I."

Billy got the hint of the double entendre. Theta continued.

"We fell deeply and fully in love. I lost my virginity. You were, in every way, the exquisite and consummate character you are today. I initiated the consequence of our physical encounter, not you. It was the greatest first experience I could ever have imagined," Theta stated in a pleasant and factual tone. "Truth."

"Oh, Theta, I didn't know. I assumed we were just friends before my accident," Billy responded. "This must be awfully hard for you to tell."

"There's more," Theta added.

"Believe it or not, we never even had a picture taken together. With the rain that weekend, we never took a cell phone photo. Nobody could have suspected that we had fallen madly in love. Jackie couldn't have known. Your parents wouldn't know. The only indication was the two letters. I figured that the one that I sent to you was lost forever because your parents and Carla never mentioned it. Where could Sid have found it? I kept mine, the poem, in a box for eight years in my closet before giving it to Sid."

She continued to unravel the mystery to Billy. His eyes were still affixed to her brightened face as she stated facts to him. The breezes cooled the moment. Theta was somewhat relaxed getting past the story of her virginity. But what she had not told was weighing heavier.

"Well, nobody knew that this happened—the sex—except the two of us," Theta stated sheepishly. "You should never feel guilty about it. It wasn't your fault. I was definitely the aggressor. I had chosen you quite spontaneously at that place in time. I surprised us both."

Theta paused. She noted the look of concern in Billy's gray-green eyes.

"Actually, the whole episode was beautiful and lives on as my fondest memory to this day. So you know I was deeply in love with you. And I think you felt the same way about me. But we kept that part of our lives as secretive. You wanted to protect my virginal reputation, and I was so insular and private that I would never have shared it with anybody."

Billy was stunned into silence by the full revelation. He looked at Theta differently. He saw her as someone that his former self was in love with. He immediately realized that the amnesiac Billy Grayson could easily fall in love with the honest and attractive lady in front of him.

"There's even more, Billy," Theta added with a promise of surprise. She wanted to state the final fact quickly and succinctly without the drama.

Billy was temporarily taken by her soft candor in the report of their past.

"The last piece of the information I should tell you is the most critical part," Theta stated, forging forward to the conclusion.

"I have not made love to anyone else but you before or since that amazing weekend in Alabama," Theta reported.

She knew that she had just made the final and most impactful revelation.

Billy's eyes grew intense in the revelation. He realized that the last statement made him the father of the twins. He didn't know what to say. He calculated their age from nine months after his traumatic accident.

"Oh my god. Late August . . . Nine months . . . They were both born in May? Mia and Leah are ours together," he realized with enormous surprise. "I am stunned but overjoyed. Those girls are fabulous. And I'm their father!"

"Do they know about me?" he asked. "Have you told them who their father is?"

"No," Theta stated. "Leah looks just like you. She reminds me of you daily."

Billy immediately thought of Leah's darker skin tones and dark brown hair.

He replied upon the revelation, "And Mia favors you. The face, The hair. That was always obvious. This is happy news. I'm completely overwhelmed!" Billy exclaimed excitedly.

Theta saw that Billy's reaction to the fatherhood news was genuine and in the manner she had hoped. But she needed to temper the revelation.

"This is where it gets complicated," Theta explained. "No one but my father, God bless him, ever knew. My father died. Many others guessed that I was raped or slept around or was a surrogate mother who backed out. I never surrendered the truth to anyone else. Well, other than the Boracle. Sid figured it out."

"You never even told this to your mother?" Billy asked.

"No . . . Especially not to my mother. She wanted me to have an abortion. My pregnancy ruined her life. She never considered that I was living my life, not hers," Theta retold in slight disgust.

Billy could see that this had been a very emotional subject that Theta had borne for many years bravely and alone.

"My mother ruined our relationship over the mystery father that you just discovered. She was too immersed in her own life to understand that the only way I could find happiness from the love that you and I swore to each other was to have the baby. An abortion was completely against my principles. Later, I was overjoyed to find out that I would give birth to twins. I see so much of your personality and kindness in them every day. They are a special gift. They are my life. They became the *you* that I had lost."

Theta continued hesitating with the interruption of her emotions in the full revelation of the truth.

"I'll surely see them in a different way in the morning. But I suppose you don't want to change anything. I don't want to assume that I have earned any privilege of being identified to them as their father, Theta," Billy said.

Theta offered another view. *"The Boracle* brought this moment to us. I think he wanted us to talk it out and do what is best for the twins, Ashton, and each other."

Theta followed, "He knew because he figured it out. But he figures out a lot more complicated puzzles than this one. What would you suppose he'd say if he were sitting next to us?"

Theta spoke up to answer her own question.

"He really felt that you and I still had a very strong emotional connection to explore, but I wouldn't let anything get in the way of raising my twins. I have been crazy protective. He convinced me to take a step forward. My next step was merely to act on the timing of the voucher I had won from the travel agency and invite myself to help you with Ashton while going on a vacation out of the country for the first time. I did it for the twins as well. That was it. I was not expecting this conversation whatsoever. Sid must've known what he was doing getting those letters delivered to us.

"The letter I wrote to you must've been lost somehow. He found it. He sent it to you so that you would realize that we had a past. You said you had never seen it before?" Theta verified.

"Never, I swear," Billy stated. "And I didn't know about writing the prose either. But you told me I was a decent writer before the accident. This is how you knew?"

Theta nodded.

Billy was still stunned that his twin daughters were sleeping in the hotel and had never known him to be their father.

Theta's eyes were misty in the moonlight. She was bearing her soul.

"My parents never said anything either," Billy offered. "I'm sure they would have told me if they knew anything about you or the letter."

Theta interjected, "And Sid doubled down the bet, or we would not be sitting here. I gave him a copy of the cryptic prose you wrote to me back then. The secret message in it says, 'To Theta, I love you. I need you.' My heart leaped when I opened it in my room after we got back tonight. It has been in a box for eight long years. I couldn't read it without crying. So Sid decided to send it to my room with you in the hotel. He assumed that I would think that you had rediscovered your memory. My assumption would overpower me, and I would confront you about bringing the letter to St. Croix. He knew that I loved you so very much."

Billy was awestruck with the scheme his friend Sid had gone to great length to install. He realized that Sid wanted him to see Theta again through different eyes without divulging what he knew of the past.

"Theta, Sid is like a father to me. He did this for both of our benefits," Billy realized.

"I feel awful telling you this," Theta began. "But if they knew these details after your recovery, then you would have had other financial burdens, and the Billy Grayson that emerged from death to celebrity would have had two children he knew nothing about. That would have been really weird. My dad had incredible judgment. He even said that you truly should not be held responsible. That former Billy, the man I loved in every fiber of my heart and soul, never came back. I assume that Sid wanted me to rediscover this Billy in front of me. He has surreal powers when it comes to relationships."

Her wetted eyes told of the sorrow. Billy leaned forward to console her.

"You've carried these two girls as a single parent all this time knowing there was at least a financial solution just a blood test away?" he presented to her.

"I didn't want anything. I prayed to God every night that you would live, accepting that I would raise the twins on my own," Theta restated. "I knew then that the old Billy Grayson had, in effect, died from my life."

Billy was wholly astonished at Theta's selflessness.

"Look into my eyes, Billy," she said softly. "I promise this to you. You will never have to deal with what your former life and I had together. You are free to enjoy your life as you know it to be presently. We will fly out of St. Croix tomorrow and never ever burden you. I have what I want—two children that love me and remind me every day of the love I have carried in my heart for the lost Billy Grayson. I have been blessed. I have no bitterness and no motives. You are free to enjoy wherever your life transports you without me or the girls as responsibilities."

Billy stared into her dreamy green eyes that still held the edge of the moon within them. He was deeply impressed with her vigilance and the rarity of altruism.

His world was mostly devoid of truth. He knew that she recognized that he was not the former lover she had lost years before. That good man was her only lover. He knew that he could not likely become that person that Theta loved so deeply.

"Theta, Sid really made a mess of St. Croix for us to straighten out," Billy suggested. "He always knows what he is doing. But before we begin to unravel yesterday, today, and tomorrow, I think we need to establish two very important courses of action in front of us that could be helpful."

"What's that, Billy?" Theta asked, looking up to him in admiration of how he had handled the truckload of new details.

"First, I want you to know that the new Billy Grayson is melting by the minute. I've never met anyone like you. I am deeply impressed and fully enamored. Unless you want me completely out of your life, I would like to have the opportunity to apply for the job as father of my two daughters—even if it means you reject me. Please give me a chance to love them. I suspect that it will be an automatic impulse and that there will be a significant upside of having a father figure available to them. We can let them know on your time schedule, not mine," he proposed.

Theta contemplated the ramifications.

"I have to think about it, Billy. It's a lot to ponder. They have no idea that their father is alive. I didn't lie to them, but I've not told them the whole truth. I think that you are right and that I should not rob them of that benefit. I already know that you are a good man. Sid is an excellent judge of character. Can we work to that goal it carefully?" Theta asked.

"And what's the second course of action?" she pried.

Billy was awkward in the other request. "And, second . . . may I kiss you?"

Theta's heart pounded. She realized that she could love him. She had no idea that he could possibly fall in love with her. The old Billy Grayson was the last man she had ever kissed romantically.

They looked deeply into their mutual orbits of green. The oscillating wind freshened. The waves played as a liquid metronome in the foreground. The cloudless sky winked in the starlight.

Theta's eyes sparkled in their wetness. The tears gathered into droplets. Billy pulled her face to his by placing his right hand on her neck just beneath her left ear. He moved to her slowly, his eyes affixed upon hers before his lids closed in romantic anticipation. Their lips locked. It was a passionate first kiss that had no equal or precedence for Billy. It was a kiss of yesterday's wishes that brought the quaint promise of familiarity to Theta.

As their lips parted, Theta looked down to the sand. She did not want to ruin the mood but felt she had to change the assumptions that linger from a most passionate kiss.

"Billy, let's honor each other by approaching every step with certainty. If our love is to be, then time is our friend. Can we agree to go slow?" Theta asked.

"Theta, I think I have fallen in love with you for a second time. But I know nothing of the first. I'll promise you on Sid's gold watch that I will move at the pace you set. And I truly hope that I am worthy of you at each step along the way," Billy established. "I am sure that I am right about you. You need to take your time. I completely understand."

"Let's go relieve the babysitter," Theta said as she began to stand. "We have a lot to talk about. Just know that I have to make decisions that affect three people, so I'll need to go slow. It means that I am taken by you, as well. You're a prized catch for every single woman in America now. I don't want to compete for your affections. So let's set our own pace and hope that it goes the way we'd both feel confident about. But let's be sure about each other."

They walked slowly hand in hand back to the hotel, looking at each other by inspections of new interest. Though cautious, they each perceived the flickering ignition of a fresh and wholesome relationship.

Billy noticed the shimmer of her stone amulet from the moon's illumination and commented upon its beauty. Theta told him about its origin.

"It stayed in my father's safe for many years. It is probably very old, he told me. He gave it to me the day that I told him I was pregnant with your child. I had no idea I would have twins then. Dad told me that I would give it away one day. I would know to whom and when at a precise time. It is a mysterious stone. I wear it every day to remind me of my father," Theta explained.

"I have never seen another like it. I could tell that it was old and not a costume piece. Your father—or whoever gave it to him—had exquisite taste," Billy declared. "You rarely see that color."

They arrived at the suite. The elderly sitter was relieved, tipped again, and thanked.

Theta went to the kitchenette refrigerator and retrieved a chilled bottle of Rosa's Pinot Grigio. It is the only mood beverage she had ever considered since the weekend in the Guntersville cabin.

Billy opened it for her and poured two goblets high, hoping that she would sip hers slowly. She was exquisite, unlike any person he had known since his accident.

They sat up much of the night in the inquisitiveness of a promising blind date. There were serious moments of revelation and lighter moments for genuinely shared grins. They realized that they did not know each other at all but wanted to find out as much as they could before the sun came up.

Billy openly discussed Ellen and her drug-addicted passing. He said that he felt helpless in the witness of her demise. And then he felt alone again. It was the responsibility of Ashton that brought him forward. He had a deep aversion to the drug culture.

Theta told Billy about the various dates that others had arranged for her. They all seemed to seek an answer to her tight-lipped riddle. Ostensibly, the instant family prospect scared all suitors.

"And none ever measured up to my highest standards—someone like my father—or like the Billy Grayson lost to me on that dreadful day," Theta detailed. "I was destined to be a widow that was never married."

They were smiling with knowing warmth as they rediscovered each other again—whispering like teenagers in the quiet living area between the two bedrooms.

During a silent pause, Theta fell asleep on Billy's shoulder. He slowly laid her down on the sofa with the pillows propped under her neck. He breathed in the slight fragrance of her soft perfume and stared at her angelic face pensively for a moment. He lightly kissed her on the forehead and went to nap on the side lounge chair. Before the sun came up, Theta awoke to see Billy across the room. She got up to fix coffee for the both of them. She thought about the prior night's events and was enthused to see the sun rise upon the new day through the sheers at the balcony.

The sun ascended gloriously across the boulder-strewn beach. They watched it with their hot coffees from the balcony chairs. They had only three hours of sleep.

They had decided to get to know each other by traditional formalities. They would date. Fate and destiny would have to find their way in the darkness. But they had—at a minimum—kindled a small fire of guidance. They both held hope that a permanent and fulfilling romance could develop.

This new day yawned with promise.

All five of the suite occupants had a most delicious late breakfast the next morning. Billy was able to ask the twins about their school, piano lessons, and gymnastics. He had to temper his enthusiasm since they had not decided to inform the twins of the revelation. Theta already had an affinity for little Ashton from their interplay at the pool over the past forty-eight hours.

Billy stopped at the front desk coming back from breakfast out of curiosity to ask about the letter deliveries the evening prior. Though Billy deftly described Sid Toile, no one had seen a man of his exacting portrayal.

The frumpy bellman who had delivered the letters in the Renaissance envelopes never worked at the Renaissance. The desk clerk checked their hotel room delivery log and told Billy that the hotel had made no deliveries to either room he enumerated. Billy could not figure out how Sid procured the Renaissance envelopes. He would never know.

Sid Toile had brought the possibility of a resolution to more than two lives. Mia, Leah, and Ashton slept in the luxury suite the night before unaware of the impact that was to evolve. The twins' lives could be enhanced by the evening delivery of two envelopes if the pace of their biological parents' dating commitment proved providential. Ashton stood to gain two older sisters.

Those old delivered letters initiated a short sandy walk of lovers enamored by time and all of its defects.

CHAPTER FORTY-THREE

The Wish

THETA'S CELL PHONE rang. It played a refrain from the musical notes she'd downloaded. It was Colbie Caillat's "Brighter than the Sun." She read the name of the caller.

"Billy."

"Hey, Theta. I just had to call you," Billy replied. "I just received a record deal from Sony, and you wouldn't believe the zeroes that went to the right of the main number."

Billy's live St. Croix concert included two new songs. The musical genius was covered in *Rolling Stone* magazine as the "voice and lyricist that would define his age."

"That's great, Billy, and I know you're excited. We should celebrate at lunch on Wednesday," Theta suggested.

"No can do. I'll be in LA. Their studio is there, and I have to cut at least seven releases over the next four months. I'm going to be busy," Billy said in anticipation of Theta's exuberance.

"So you'll be out with the starlets and the bright lights for a while?" Theta posed.

"No, Theta, that's the real reason I'm calling. I thought maybe you might consider coming along. We can move there permanently. There will be another deal after this one. The girls will love California. And I can find a great place for Ashton's daycare," Billy reasoned. "Having you and the twins there with me will make all the difference. We can have time together to get to know each other like we promised in St. Croix."

The conversation transitioned to a moment of truth for their new and hopeful relationship.

"Billy, you know that I love you very much and I want you to be successful past your hopeful dreams. You deserve it. The girls love you too. But I just can't take them from here. They're so happy in school and at piano, gymnastics, and all. I don't want to change that. Besides, my career has been great here," Theta reasoned.

Billy paused, realizing that his megadeal with Sony might become a separation point from not only Theta but also his newly discovered twin daughters. Theta would need much more convincing to move to LA.

"Billy, you still there?" she asked.

She could tell that he was disappointed.

"Yes, I was just thinking about the girls. I hadn't considered that moving from Mount Pleasant was not an option. I really thought you might like the change of scenery," he reintroduced.

Billy added more explanation.

"Theta, there is nothing I want more than to be with the kids and you. I can find a very nice place there with this deal, and you won't have to work at all. You can enjoy the girls and Ashton even more. We can go on vacations. Maybe Hawaii."

He added, "Who knows—maybe we can get to know each other better and work toward a permanent commitment. We have both established that we would not force the issue out of convenience. But we'll have to start somewhere to build a lasting relationship. Finding the time to do things together is all we need. Even Sid told me that I have to take chances. Going to LA is not only a chance but also an opportunity. You might find me to be right for you. I truly hope so!"

Billy was trying to talk Theta into giving it all up to come with him, knowing that his large money contract could ease her financial pressure as well. But Theta had strong reservations.

"Billy, I want so much for things to be perfect for our children and also for you. But you have to understand. I dedicated my life to take care of them. They are my number-one priority. I cannot quit my career. And you probably already know that I will not move in with you. Getting an apartment without a job in a strange place scares me. A lot of bad things can happen," she posed.

She continued, "I am truly happy for you. But my life is here. My girls are here. Please, please understand."

Theta seemed to suddenly realize that Billy was highly incentivized to move far away. Theta's voice began to become unsteady. Billy could sense that she had already begun to cry.

"Theta, I promise you that I will never fall short of being a father to Mia and Leah again. They're more valuable to me than any amount of money. I should have thought this through. Don't worry, babe. Let me figure this thing out."

Billy stared at the contract in front of him. Artists like Adele, Madonna, U2, and Bruce Springsteen have topped $100 million for multiple albums with the big recording studios. Billy's unsigned contract was for $35 million, and it was just to add seven songs and publishing rights for seven singles already recorded for a new solo album. It was a spectacular deal. But he did not want Theta to know the sizeable financial consideration. He knew that it would make her feel guilty if he walked away from it.

He could still hear her sobbing softly away from the phone. He surmised that Theta saw the large contract as something ominous. It was not even a consideration for Billy to stay in Mount Pleasant and lose this magnificent deal.

Theta naively envisioned the contract at a much lesser amount but much more than she would make in a lifetime. She realized that he could not pass it up. She knew in her heart that this would end her attempt to reunite with the father of her twins—to discover the new version of the only man she had ever loved.

"Billy, I just can't do it. And I don't expect you to change your career for me either. That would be incredibly selfish of me. Maybe you could commute or something," Theta offered as she sobbed. "Do what you think is best. I'll survive. I always have."

"Theta, can you trust me on this? Please. Just keep your phone near. I'll call you back in a few hours," Billy promised. "There's got to be another way to make this work."

Theta continued to cry quietly.

"OK, Billy," she began with hesitation. "I'll be able to handle whatever happens. I'm strong from before. I just don't want to lose you a second time. The girls have found a loving father who cares. We just can't leave here. I'm sorry. Please call me back."

After solemn and polite good-byes, she hung up.

Billy's anticipation and excited phone call had taken his exuberance from the penthouse to the basement in record time. He decided that he should consult with Sid. He printed the e-mailed contract and headed for booth 14. He would need to extract the poignant relationship lessons of the expert. Sid could summon the insight of the ages.

CHAPTER FORTY-FOUR

A Record Deal

WITHIN TWENTY MINUTES of hanging up the phone with Theta, Billy was sitting in Sid's booth. The ageless savant was about to leave for a soup lunch Maria had prepared at his condominium.

"Billy, are you OK?" Sid began. "You're here at an odd time, and the look on your face tells me you have a dilemma."

"Sid, just point me away from failure. I am close to achieving everything I ever wanted, but the forces that I thought would converge are actually opposing each other. I asked Theta to move to LA because I have a new contract that is way more money than I expected," Billy began. "She declined, saying that her life is here with the girls—not with us all together in Los Angeles."

"Yes, son," Sid observed. "Too good to be true. Walk me through the deal."

Billy explained that he did not hire an agent. He had no lawyer. He showed Sid the unsigned $35 million contract.

Sid perused the deal.

Billy noted to Sid that as he began to sign it when he stopped to consider that he had arrived at the happy moment that would bring Theta and the girls into his life. He had decided to call her to share the moment without discussing the details.

"I explained that our future could be paved without worries. I did not divulge the amount of the Sony contract to Theta.

Sid, I was utterly confused and disappointed by Theta's response," Billy explained.

"I reconsidered signing the contract after Theta balked at the idea, Sid. What should I do? Sign it and let fate determine a course? Send a counter-offer? Dictate other workable terms? Quit the business? I was reeling." Billy detailed.

"You're frustrated by her response, Billy when she actually gave you a valuable insight into the best option," Sid pointed out.

His blue eyes stared at Billy over his glasses while Billy calculated what the insight was that Theta divulged. Billy didn't connect to the insight immediately and further, explained his viewpoint.

He explained, "I wanted so much just to return the signed megadeal to Sony, record the album, and deposit a healthy check into my account for Theta, the girls, and Ashton. This course would allow me to reestablish my focus to my personal life. But that course just didn't feel right after Theta hung up."

"Billy, listen to the voice," Sid tried to lead him to the solution.

"She was likely upset, maybe crying because she was sure she was going to lose you to your career. She began thinking that perhaps she was disposable or that the twins were disposable when she refused to go to Los Angeles. She's insecure. You're a superstar on the way up. That Sony contract validates your status. It's $35 million because you're worth that much. She thinks she's no better than a groupie at this point. She believes that you are meant for the world, and she will be left with nothing but the memories. Ask yourself, 'Is this what I really want?'"

Billy immediately understood.

"No price would buy me away from Theta, but I don't think she knows that. And the twins, I love them dearly. I think I just need to pass on the deal and focus on Theta," Billy realized. "Sid, I know that I love her."

"Reassure her at every opportunity. She needs to know that you are Billy and not Millionaire Billy. That doesn't matter to her. But you matter. What will you sacrifice to prove it to her?" Sid asked rhetorically.

"Billy, do you need to be in a certain place to write down notes or lyrics?" Sid asked.

"No, not really," Billy answered quizzically. "Why do you ask?"

"I can pull up articles from a London library and look at paintings in the Prado in the next five minutes," Sid noted. "The world is digital. Cannot the geniuses at Sony record where you are, my son?"

"Yes," Billy realized.

"There, you have your answer. The details you put into that answer have to include Theta and the twins foremost in your response. And now I get to go home and enjoy Maria's okra gumbo," Sid added. "And to imagine she couldn't butter toast four years ago."

The Boracle got up to leave. "Oh, can I study this contract, Billy? I'm pretty sure you won't need it."

"Yes, of course. We already know that one will not work," Billy said. "I'll put together a different one."

Billy stood to pay respect without thanking him. He then sat back down and took a blank music sheet from his notepad. He would need to craft a new proposal for Theta that would not require any benefit for Sony. But Sid had taught him to find the solution somewhere between the two. He began to scribble. But it was not notes or lyrics. It was a hodgepodge of ideas he wanted for his life. He began to list them across the bar graphs of the thin page.

"Mia. Leah. Ashton. Companionship. Fulfillment. A future to make me personally proud of my choices. To love and to be loved by someone. Happiness. Theta."

Oddly, he had not written down two words—success or wealth.

His friend and mentor, Sid, had always believed that living a good life was the essence of success. He knew that wealth was not a goal but a byproduct. More people, he figured, were ruined by wealth than had ever been corrupted by happiness. He knew that he was on the correct path to the Boracle-inspired solution.

He wrote down ideas. They came quickly. Within an hour, he had a plan. He would call Anthony Goble, Sony's powerful executive, and read off a bizarre list. Once he could achieve consent, if agreed by Sony, he would call Theta back. He knew that she was probably still crying over the last "good news call," so Billy had worked in earnest with urgency.

He dialed to Sony to speak with Anthony.

"Anthony, I wanted to thank you for this generous contract. It's just too good to pass up, so you'll have to trust me when I tell you I have to turn it down. I hope you'll understand."

"What? You want more?" Anthony began. His response was loud. "That's $5 million a song."

"Wait," Billy demanded.

"I'm going to give you a much better deal for much less," he replied.

"Huh? You want less?" Anthony asked.

"Yes, much less," Billy confirmed.

"But I have some stipulations. They could be sticky, but I think you'll see what I'm trying to accomplish. I'm not signing your contract. I want you to send another one to me that I will sign."

"Go on," Anthony suggested.

"First, the contract amount will be $9 million, not thirty-five," Billy started. "So you save $26 million."

"Next, I'll get you the seven songs and give you the rights to the other seven that have already charted," Billy added. "I'll only want the same moderate royalty that you would give to a new and unproven artist."

"You're doing this for only $9 million? OK. We get all rights to fourteen recordings. Got it. No complaints," Anthony said.

"There's more," Billy followed.

"I'll do these songs in one month, not four. And I will guarantee three top-fifteen charters or lose $3 million of the $9 million back to you," Billy added.

"This is even getting better," Anthony blurted. "Are you sick or drunk? Do you need to go to the Betty Ford Clinic?"

"No. I'm healthier now than I was before my soccer injury. My mind thinks better," Billy asserted. "The money will only make me different. I don't want to be different. I need it for three college savings accounts."

"If you say so," Anthony countered. "There must be a catch."

"No catch. Nine million. One month. At least three new top fifteens. So only the $6 million is guaranteed. Send half of that out with the contract. We begin sixty days after I sign the new contract. For the advance, I sign away the seven songs you already have."

"Billy," Anthony goaded, "you smokin' dope?"

"Listen, Anthony. All I want from Sony is to do it in my new studio here. That's it," Billy concluded.

"No problem there, bubba. I had no idea that you had a new studio, but that works. We'll just have to put the backup musicians up somewhere for a few weeks. But for $26 million savings, I think I can swing that part," Anthony conceded. "Just give me the studio address, Billy."

"Well, use my e-mail, and I'll send my account number for the deposit. I don't have the street address yet. I have to buy a building and contract the soundproofing, acoustics, and recording equipment in the next sixty days. That is why I need the $3 million now," Billy explained. "And this way you get first dibs on future albums made here."

"Billy, this contract will say what you outlined, so I don't care how you do it or if it's all recorded next to a train trestle. Hell, the seven songs you've already recorded are worth more than the $9 million. You know that, right?" Anthony offered.

"Yes. But the plan I'm putting together with you right now will be worth more than all of Sony's money can buy," Billy countered without revealing the reason.

"I hope so, kid. I hope so." Anthony hung up.

Billy then dialed back to Theta. He was personally humbled by not realizing the repercussions of the prior proposal. He thought about his foolish assumptions that drifted into a regrettable interchange from their last conversation.

"Hello, Billy," Theta answered without letting Billy speak first. "I am so sorry that I have ruined your plans for us."

Billy started to interrupt her, but Theta continued.

"Please forgive me. I'll be waiting here when you get back from LA. I promise you. You didn't deserve me acting like a child."

Billy seized the conversation. He had his mind made up.

"No, Theta, no need to forgive anything. I want to thank you for what you said about not upsetting the lives of the twins. You're right. You made me zoom over to booth 14, and Sid reprioritized my life. I had to think about what Sid told me. So I have a new plan that is all about you, me, the girls, and Ashton," Billy started.

Theta was immediately interested. "Will it keep my children's father here?"

"Yes. And more so, it will give us an opportunity to find out if we are to be as a couple. We have to find that out. It is essential. Actually, Theta, it is the most important point I'm making. I know that I love you. If it works and we are mutually in love, we'll make the twins much happier. If it doesn't, then we'll know that too. At least we will have tried."

"I'm interested, Billy. What did you come up with?" Theta asked.

"I just got off of the phone with Anthony Goble of Sony. They will allow me to put a sound studio in Charleston and do the album here. They'll send the ensemble talent. We've shortened the time and the demand. I will only have one intense month of work to record the songs. But I promise you will not even know that I am busy there. I'll do it while the kids are at school and you are at the agency. I will have them written and scored in the next sixty days, no problem. So the focus will be the performance and sound mixing. But, Theta, what I'm telling you is that my entire life is going to be focused on you. I hope that you will find me to be worthy of you," Billy suggested.

"That's it. You didn't have to give up anything?" Theta asked.

"It was a matter of what I would be giving up by going to California," Billy replied. "I have responsibilities here. Of course, that involves

Ashton, Mia, and Leah. They trump the old deal. You made me see that. I owe those girls seven years of fatherhood."

"And me?" Theta asked in relief.

"And you. No matter what I present to you, you have presented more to me than I can ever thank you for properly. I can't remember you from before, but I sure can give you 100 percent of my attention now. If I am not worthy of you, I will understand. But for now, I want to write those life lyrics and put the best possible score out there. And like the songs, I want to pursue you to a conclusion. And if that works as I hope it will, I will cherish you for the rest of my life."

Theta's green eyes became shiny with hinted tears. She was silent and hesitant.

"Theta, will this new contract give me a new chance?" Billy asked sheepishly.

"Billy, this is so hard for me. Please be patient. I've never told you this . . . But. . . I still have fantasies about you. Only they are not fantasies. It is an inspiring and romantic memory for me. It's just that you don't know me now. And, really, I don't know you. Every cell in my body loved that Billy from back then without hesitation. Trying to recapture that time is foolish. But seeing you and your love for the girls has moved me. Proceeding cautiously is my nature. It was before. I know that you are that same person, yet you're not. I'm trying to balance that with the memories.

"I think I really do love you. I'm just afraid of rushing in. Can't you see that I do want to be with you? But I still feel we have to pass the litmus test of sincere and devoted love instead of mutual convenience," Theta reminded him.

Theta posed the weighty issue.

"I want to be everything to you that you ever dreamed, but we have to work to make this right for not only us but also those three children whose lives will forever change if we make a mistake."

"I get that," Billy said. "I'm staying near you to explore my dreams. I'll give you space, but I also want to find time for us to be together when you want a companion. I'll wait for you. You already have my devotion and my heart. Just know that I am there. Give me the opportunity to be what I was before. If Mom watches the kids for us, would you consider celebrating my new contract this evening over dinner?"

Theta responded impulsively, "Shem Creek Seafood?"

"Seven fifteen. I'll pick you and the girls up at quarter till and drop them by Mom's."

"Deal. Can't be out later than nine thirty, OK?" Theta reminded him.

"Deal."

Billy was taking Theta out to celebrate giving up $26 million. It would be worth two hours of the never-ending conversation with the woman he loved.

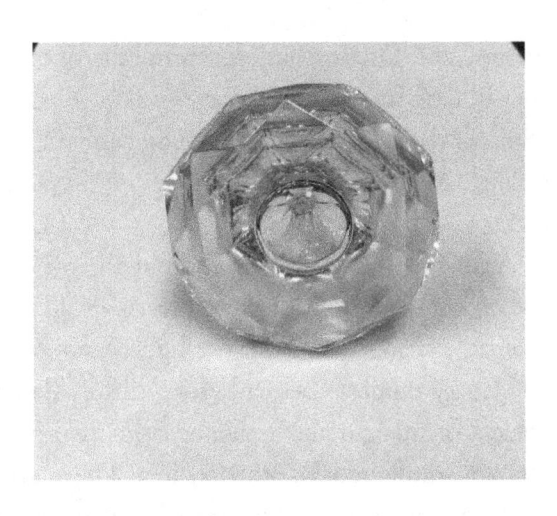

CHAPTER FORTY-FIVE

The Bracelet

JUST AS THETA was preparing to close the Dream Site Travel Agency, the phone rang. It was Sid.

"Well, hello, Theta. I hope you are well," Sid began. "I'm sorry to call late, but I need to arrange a complex itinerary for a friend. I'll just send his information to you. His name is Cailean, pronounced as 'Colin.' He's Scottish. His visit here was delightful, but he will have to leave by midafternoon on the third."

Theta took down the information.

"That's fine, Sid. Just give me a destination, and I can put together a few different itineraries in the morning. Do you have a facsimile machine or e-mail available?" Theta asked.

"Let me scribble it down, and I can fax it from my office at home right away," he replied. "And just call me when you have it, and I can place it on my credit card."

Theta read out the Dream Site fax number. She asked for the passport number in case international travel was involved.

"Thanks, Sid, for recommending Dream Site and me to your friend. I am happy to take care of this," Theta said before they simultaneously said good-byes.

She did not wait for the fax information at the office. She simply put a sticky note on her computer screen to prioritize Sid's request in the morning. She set the alarm, turned out the lights, and locked the entry door. She had to hurry home to be ready for a dinner date with Billy.

As Theta locked the door, a man emerged from a car parked in front. The suddenness and darkened lot startled her. The man approached without saying anything. He reached into his thin overcoat pocket and was about to pull out an unintelligible object. But just as he came forward looking directly at the vulnerable girl, another car drove up. It was Maria with Pablo. Their timing was a relief to Theta. She imagined that they had interrupted a kidnapping or a murder. The man immediately returned to his dark blue Buick Lacrosse. The approach and retreat were without words. There were no others near the travel agency.

"Maria, thank God. I thought that man that just left was going to accost me. I may have been mistaken, but I was scared. Why are you and Pablo here?" Theta asked.

"Sid said that you might need these copies. He just called us minutes ago. He left them for me to deliver this morning, but I had to pick up Pablo because his truck is getting serviced. I almost didn't make it in time," Maria said apologetically.

"Actually, you made it at just the right time. My heart is still pounding. It was probably nothing," Theta considered. "But that man looked scary."

Theta thanked them for the delivery. She put the papers in her purse and hurried into her car. She needed to get home, feed the twins, call Carla to babysit, and dress for a casual dinner with Billy. She only had an hour or so.

The man in the Buick had left quickly. Theta did not write down the license plate. Had she done so, she would have found that the car belonged to a person she had never met—Walter Bailloch.

Carla came early. She was excited that Theta was dating her brother. She admired Theta profoundly and found the twins to be excellent children. Carla helped to clean the table and began to assist the girls with their homework.

Theta showered quickly and dressed for seafood. She wore slacks and a floral print top to her neckline. She brought a light sweater in case they sat outside. Carla heard her hurried instructions and then intimated to Theta her light-hearted encouragement.

"It's just Billy. You could meet him in a burlap sack, and he'd compliment you. Relax. I've got this. You go and have a good time."

Theta gave Carla a knowing smile.

Billy was waiting in the lobby when Theta arrived. They greeted each other with a short hug and abbreviated kiss to the cheek. A hostess took them to an inside seat overlooking the sport-fishing fleet that had docked for the evening. A waiter poured their water glasses and asked for drink orders.

"Just a glass of your house Pinot Gris, please," Theta responded.

Billy put up two fingers. The waiter nodded and walked away.

"Thank you for coming, Theta. I have something for you," Billy began. "It's nothing big, but it reminded me of, shall we say, our mutual revelation on St. Croix."

Billy handed Theta a small, elongated wrapped wooden box. She looked up in surprise and placed her hand on her upper chest to gesture her demure humility.

"Why a gift? It's not my birthday or anything," Theta fluttered.

She reached to the box and opened it as if she were going to reuse the wrapping and the ribbon.

"When I left behind you and the girls, I had time to drift around the airport shops. Instead of waiting four hours for my delayed flight, I went to the outdoor market across the street.

"It was strange that a man approached me in the market. He was not from the island. He had a wooden box. He said it was old and that

I was supposed to buy it. I laughed in his face. But when he opened the wooden box, it revealed this single stone bracelet. I immediately knew that I had seen a similar stone before. It's much like the one you wore to the St. Croix concert and again out on the beach that fateful night." Billy explained.

"He told me that the stone once belonged to my great-grandfather who had been shipwrecked at Grand Turk Island a century before. How would he have known? My father's grandfather did shipwreck before settling in Beaufort in 1890. I knew the generalities of that family story, so I knew I had to buy the stone. But he didn't want money. He wanted my guitar. I made the trade. I turned to give my business card to him, thinking he might want concert tickets. But he left quickly. I put the empty wooden box in my checked bag, worried about customs. But I carried the bracelet in my coat pocket like it was costume jewelry. I went right through customs and immigration. After all, it was a good luck piece belonging to my great-grandfather. He did not drown in the shipwreck."

Theta was stunned. The wooden box contained cotton bedding displaying a thick silver chain and one bright tinted lavender stone. It dazzled. The box was similar to the one her dad kept in his office safe. She immediately thought of her dad and the story of the amulet she was wearing under her sweater. She took off her amulet necklace and placed it next to the stone bracelet. The bracelet stone was a near perfect match to her amulet. She believed that they once existed together at another time and were reunited—just like her and Billy.

"Billy, this is too weird. They match." She declared.

Billy responded, "Theta, as soon as I saw him reveal the bracelet I thought the stone was familiar. The strange middle-aged man said that the bracelet was very old and had special powers. But that wasn't the weird part. He said that I would know who to give it to. I had been thinking of you since the night before when we talked on the beach. I smiled and told him that I was sure to get it to the right person."

Theta put the Ethereal Stone necklace back around her collar and clasped it. She spun the stone back to adorn her upper chest.

Billy moved closer, rising to affix the mysterious bracelet to Theta's left wrist. It was a stunning gift.

Theta rose and moved in close to his chest and hugged his waist. She looked up slightly expecting a short kiss. Billy obliged her. The standing kiss over the soft music in the Creek House was exchanged as if no one else was in the room. Theta's spontaneity from eight years earlier had returned. Neither Billy nor Theta knew of the significance of the ethereal stones being together again. Their love would never die.

"When we shared those moments under the moon that night, my most meaningful discoveries since my accident were revealed to me. I just cannot get over the revelation. It is intriguing from every angle—you, the girls, the letters, the things you sacrificed, and all of the inner emotions that have thrilled me since," Billy intoned. "You are a reality that I had not considered. There had to be someone from my past that gave it meaning."

After the moment, she returned to her seat next to Billy. They shared the window view. They both gazed out in silence.

"Billy, I wanted to show you something, but first—I wanted to talk about a few things concerning us, Ashton, and the girls," she stated. "I hope we can continue to date, but we need caution, and we need patience."

"I get it, Theta. I screwed up today. I went to see Sid, and after we talked, I felt terrible. Please forgive my assumptions," Billy apologized.

The two glasses of Pinot Gris arrived. No appetizers were ordered. They both wanted dinner and time to talk. Billy requested the mahi-mahi with broccoli and brown rice. Theta decided upon the chef salad with broiled shrimp. The waiter left to place the orders.

"Billy, this might be one of those times that I ask you to hear me out. I have decided on much of what you need to know going forward. All of this is going to be a challenge for both of us. So I'm just going to put it out there and see where it takes us," Theta proposed.

"I get it. I'll shut up. You just slap me on the cheek when you want me to respond, OK?" Billy offered.

"Deal." Theta smiled. She couldn't imagine slapping Billy for any reason.

"OK, back to the St. Croix night. We both decided to keep our information secret. We know that Sid knows about us, but he'll never say a word. Your sister, Carla, knows that we see each other but nothing else.

"There will likely be a time and a place to reveal all, but I think the present timing is poor for Ashton and the girls. I could care less about nosey friends, and I know that we shouldn't hold the knowledge from Carla, your mom, or mine. But they'll understand why we kept it once the timing is right. So my first point is that Ashton and the girls are our priority. They should not know anything about us until we both feel the timing is right.

"Second, I appreciate that you are a national celebrity and that you may have other interests than me, either now, before, or in the future. You do not owe me anything. I realize that. I think about you all the time, but you are not my property, and you, Billy, are not to be held accountable for my situation or the girls' upbringing. They want you around. I want you around—but you should never feel trapped by a life you can never remember."

Billy looked as if he was impatient and needed to interject his feelings.

"I know this is taking a bit, but I have my mind set on the order of things. Billy, please be patient with me. There's just a little bit more, then you can comment, rebut, scream, or whatever," Theta continued.

"Last, I want to share my most personal feelings. I think I'm deeply in love with you. You have done nothing to make me hesitate. But this is happening too fast. I am scared. You have beautiful and smart women who will be waiting for you in every city. I don't even fear that because you have shown me over these few weeks that you have such a strong character. I cannot make a mistake. And neither can you. When you called me back today, it told me that you wanted to place me above what was probably a million dollars. You placed the girls there too. So you know that I cannot make a quick decision, pick up and leave, or even move in with you. It's the way that I am. And, Billy, I know that part of me will not change. You do need to know that."

Billy smiled at the insight, knowing he was devoted to the lovely dark redhead setting the rules. He knew that he should hear her out and not interrupt.

Theta continued, "Yes, I am in love with you. And, yes, we have to be sure. If you want to pursue what maybe we both feel, we'll have to have these ground rules I've laid out and just one more. I will not make love to you until and only if we are married. To get to my total commitment—heart, mind, soul, and body—we have to be sure of each other. This will take patience, effort, and devotion. Billy, I want you to know I'm in for the duration, but the rules will have to stand until we are both certain."

Theta looked down momentarily. She had said everything that was on her mind for the evening. She did have one more minor surprise, but she wanted to wait for Billy's response. So she slowly reached up with a devious smile and gently slapped him on his cheek.

Billy sipped his wine as if he needed it to wet his throat. He reached out over the table to clasp her hands. He placed both of his hands around hers. He took a full breath, expanding his chest slightly, before responding. He looked into her emerald eyes lovingly before uttering a heartfelt opening.

"I would marry you today, yesterday, or tomorrow—or in ten years. There is no other, and there will never be another but the angel in front of me tonight. I love you for who you are, what you mean to me, how you thrill me, and how you have inspired my career. You are my muse and my hope. Theta, I accept your terms and will place you above all other earthly enticements or contracts or opportunities that come my way. I am yours when you want me, and I am here for the duration too. I love you without restrictions, time clauses, or location rules. I will wait on you, and I will be the best father ever to our girls. One day, we will be together. I'm sure of it. We love each other. That will get us through any test of time. So once you're sure of me, just slap my cheek again, Theta, as hard as you like. Then give me just twenty-four hours to become worthy to kneel before you."

Theta had tears streaming when the meal arrived. The waiter and assistant server were aware that they had encroached a moment. They placed the food and asked if they needed anything else.

"All's fine, thank you. Can you bring us two more glasses of the house pinot?" Billy asked. Theta had taken only two sips from her first glass.

Theta composed herself. Her strongest compulsion was to answer Billy with approval and tap his cheek again. But she knew that she wanted to wait and think clearly through the romance to make sure her twins were fully considered.

"Billy, I do love you. Let's plan to dine more when we can, and I'd like to have you come around more to bring Ashton and do things with the twins," Theta suggested.

"I'd love that. Can you put my name in at their school to pick them up occasionally instead of your mother? I can bring Ashton and deliver them to your house until you get home. It's easy to call Carla to babysit if we go out for a few hours," Billy stated. "We can arrange our time to get to know each other with a plan that gives me better exposure to my daughters, you to Ashton, and us to each other."

"I'd like that," Theta replied. "Billy, I do have one other small item I wanted to share with you. It's silly. I hope you don't think me too forward. It's just an idea."

"No, no, Theta, nothing's silly. Let's share everything. No secrets, OK?" Billy decreed.

"OK. Deal. But don't think badly of me. I've been carrying this brochure around for a week. It came into the agency, and I immediately thought of us," Theta explained. "It's a silly dream. But it is so perfect, I had to show it to you."

She lifted the color brochure from her purse. It was folded in two to fit. She handed it to Billy sheepishly. He read it out loud.

"BVI Little Conch Island. Oh, this is exquisite, Theta. It couldn't be far from where we were in St. Croix," Billy started. "It looks like it's a private island."

"It is. I called the number, not for my clients but out of sheer curiosity. A family in London owns Little Conch. You get there by a short boat ride from Tortola. It's fifty-eight natural reserve acres to explore on foot or by a bike path. There are two houses, but the wealthy owner only comes twice a year. They rent the house on the other end, Seascape Cottage. It has it all. There are two secluded beaches on each side, a pool with a vanishing edge that becomes a grotto waterfall below before the water cycles back into another wading pool. It has a hot tub, a private walled garden, a grassy meadow, a dock, jet skis, a catamaran sailboat, an outdoor shower, four hammocks, and so much more. The master suite has a draped four-poster bed and a large modern bath. The place has Wi-Fi, TV, and a small theater with a movie library. It has numerous sitting areas and a wraparound veranda porch with ceiling fans. They stock whatever you order for the week prior to your arrival. The full-service staff is on call, and they are only a twenty-minute boat ride away. There is no one else on the island," Theta rattled off the details excitedly.

"You have done a lot of research, Theta. This sounds fantastic," Billy followed. "It sounds too romantic to be a vacation for the kids, but I don't want to ever assume anything again."

"No, it's not for them. For us," Theta stated. "You and me. One day, if we get married. This would be the perfect place for us to honeymoon. It was just something for me to dream about. I've carried the brochure because I thought about our revelation night in St. Croix. The dreams began. Billy, you need to know that you are in that dream. I have never been there, so I like looking at the photos in the brochure. But you keep appearing. If we ever get married, would you consider going there?"

"Are you kidding? You and I—alone on an island? Pinch me!" Billy replied.

"Now I'm being presumptuous. Forgive me, Billy. I just thought you should know that you are in my dreams, and they have drifted to this island brochure that arrived serendipitously through my agency channels. I might be able to get a discount too," Theta revealed.

Billy's imagination was reaching a steroidal stage.

"Theta, if you tap me on the cheek, we're going there, and I'd pay double, maybe triple. Just us two alone on a Caribbean island! That's really not fair. You shouldn't have told me. Now I'm going to be really angry with myself if I falter and blow this chance for lifelong happiness with you! I'll be thinking about that every moment of every day."

The waiter returned as they were finishing their meal. Billy passed him his credit card. The waiter returned with the completed transaction. Billy acknowledged to Theta that the waiter had been excellent and did not interrupt the enthralling conversation or the romantic moments. He was given a fifty-dollar tip.

As they rose to leave, Theta asked to keep the brochure. Billy suggested that he copy it first and give it back the next day. She agreed.

"It takes two to dream this dream," she chided. "Now let's both work to get to the Seascape Cottage. But be warned—it will take a lot of patience and understanding. You dissuade my skepticism every day, but my sense is that I not leap when I need to move slowly and be sure. Too much is at stake. We have to be sure for everyone's sake."

They walked with clasped hands to the lobby.

As Theta walked to her car, she turned to Billy to again thank him for the bracelet. They kissed again, her soft lips to his cheek. It was an invitation to fate. The ambient light glistened through the glassy tint of muted violet. The two stones reflected in a simultaneous strobe as if they had rendezvoused for the first time after centuries of separation. They had.

CHAPTER FORTY-SIX

Itineraries

SID HAD FAXED his request to Theta the night before, just as she left the office for her date with Billy. He had also sent the support document copies with Maria. There appeared to be a sense of expedition. When she opened the office the next morning, she pulled her sticky note from her computer. The two-page order from Sid was in the facsimile tray. Theta grabbed it and read the details on the cover page before beginning to plan the complicated trip.

Sid's friend, Mr. Cailean, had a Scottish passport. He would be flying from Charleston International by way of Denver to Los Angeles. He would be staying at the Los Angeles Airport Marriott until his flight to Papeete, Tahiti, the following evening. The nine-hour flight would allow a three-day stay at the Four Seasons in Papeete before a morning flight would take the client into Auckland, New Zealand. Three hours later, Cailean's flight would leave Auckland for Christchurch on the

South Island. She had the itinerary priced and taxed. She printed it and dialed back to the number Sid had given her.

As she dialed Sid's number, she saw that a back page to the fax had printing that did not have anything to do with the booking. It appeared to be the first page of a contract. Just as Sid answered, Theta noticed Billy's name on the top line. She nearly panicked before recovering.

"Ah, Sid. This is Theta," she began, now startled by the contract.

"Yes, dear. Do you have an itinerary planned for my friend Doug?" Sid began.

Theta hesitated before removing the contract copy from her view so that she could focus on Sid's client details. She assumed that the contract had come through by error.

"Sid, can I just fax it to you, since it is so complicated?" Theta asked. "Once you get it, you can call me back. If it's right, just give me authorization to book and charge, and I'll deliver everything to you at the Bib and Bibliothéque by noon today."

"Perfect," Sid replied. "Send it by e-mail, since I am away from the house, and I'll call you back in a few minutes."

Theta e-mailed the printed itinerary with hotel and flight confirmation numbers to Sid as agreed. She had scanned a credit card authorization agreement. After doing so, she pulled out the fax copy of the contract. It was the first offering from Sony to Billy from the day before. She noted that the fax came in from Sid's facsimile machine. She realized that Sid had sent it, and it was purposeful. She was startled to see that the contract amount was for $36 million. This was the contract that Billy had turned down to stay and be with Theta and the twins. It was well beyond the $1 million amount that Theta had assumed he had turned down. Billy would never have indicated the dollar amount to her. He was not materialistic, and she had not known him to brag about anything since their brief reintroduction to each other.

Theta thought that *Sid must have considered it important—or she would not be staring at the instant wealth that Billy dismissed as inconvenient to his higher pursuit.* She was completely awestruck by the knowledge. She could call Sid back, but he might act as if the contract copy was an accident. Billy had consulted Sid the night before his dinner with Theta at the Creek Restaurant.

As she sat in amazement of the character Billy possessed, her office phone rang at her desk. It was Sid.

"Hey, Theta, book it. It's exactly what my friend wants," he started. "Did you see the other item I sent?"

"Yes, Sid. I'm embarrassed. This should be private information," she professed.

"It is private," Sid reminded her. "Billy surrendered it to me yesterday. He said he had something much more valuable here and way too precious to lose. So he made an awful deal with Sony to do all of his work in Mount Pleasant. He would just die if he knew that I had sent a copy of his contract to you, so you can never tell him I sent it to you, OK?"

"But why did you, Sid?" she asked.

"Because, my dear," Sid explained, "I'd rather watch weeds grow in an anthill than to see two perfectly matched people delay their lives and their children's lives another minute. You love him. He loves you. He's the twins' father. He loves them. You love Ashton as if he were your own. I have seen people come to booth 14 for years but have never seen anyone so profoundly in love with another as Billy Grayson is with you. I can see it in his eyes every time. And you would be an awful poker player as well. I sent that fax to you out of respect for him. You may think that it was wrong to do so. My world is not as complicated as yours seems to be. It was quite timely and absolutely right, my dear girl. But he must never know."

Sid then moved the conversation to a new and penetrating direction.

"By now, you know the truth. I may go away in time. I'm an old man. I have, but one instruction left for you, Theta. End your loneliness and begin your happiness. You deserve it. Billy is your destiny. I know this in my old craggy bones. You must know it as well. You've heard of self-analysis paralysis? It's hard to escape. Those girls need their real father every day. Do not deny them. And you need your life back. Billy would wait for you forever. But why would you deny him for even another minute? That, my dear, is truth."

Sid paused while Theta took in the reasoning and made her own conclusion.

"Thanks for the itinerary. The authorization to charge was sent to you a few minutes ago from Mr. Cailean's card, not mine. It's getting close to your lunchtime. Invite someone you know to enjoy it with you. Make it count."

Sid hung the phone after a polite good-bye. He knew what would happen next.

"Hello, Billy," Theta started. "Can you pick me up in twenty? I want to go out for a quick lunch. Billy, I love you. I need you."

Billy would not recognize the anagram reference from the prose she held to her heart, but it meant much to Theta to say it out loud.

CHAPTER FORTY-SEVEN

And Do You?

BILLY STOPPED TO find his car keys. His Nissan Pathfinder needed to be washed, but he had procrastinated. He was presently busy on the notes and lyrics that Sony would expect from the $3 million advance that was deposited into his account at ten o'clock that morning. Theta's call changed every priority. He had just enjoyed dinner with her the night before and dreamed of Little Conch Island. He knew that he would need to focus on Theta more than on the Sony contract.

"Theta, I'm on the way. I didn't clean my car. I hope you don't mind," he explained.

"Billy, if the lunch is good, I'll wash your car in my driveway this evening," she promised.

Billy chuckled, not knowing how serious she had become from her last phone conversation with Sid.

"OK, look for me. I'll take the bypass and be there in a flash," Billy informed.

They hung up. Theta primped in the agency restroom. She brushed her dark wavy hair. The fluorescent lights showed the Irish red hue in its sheen. She sprayed Billy's favorite perfume from their encounter at St. Croix, Dolce & Gabbana. She looked at herself in the mirror and whispered, "OK, Sid, this is it. Billy's going to be shocked at the timing."

She told one of her coworkers, Rose Flanagan, that she planned to be back before one thirty. Then she went outside to sit on the bench under the awning, waiting on Billy. Just as she sat, she saw the Buick from the night before parked thirty yards away. There was no one sitting in it. She became immediately uncomfortable.

She was immediately relieved as she saw Billy's dirty silver SUV pull into the driveway. Billy drove to the curb and got out to open the passenger door. She met him there, her eyes studying his unsuspecting face. She began to get in but stopped and turned around facing Billy.

With a vigor she could not withhold, she slapped him hard on his cheek. Billy was startled. At first, he thought she was angry about something but knew this to be uncharacteristic. Theta smiled a broad and expecting grin. He realized the meaning of the forceful slap.

Billy immediately pulled her to him and kissed her inviting lips with an indescribable joy. He only paused between kisses to say two words.

"You sure?"

"Yes, I'm 100 percent certain. I love you, and I have loved you. I will love you again. I'm completely yours if you want me," she proposed.

"When?" Billy asked, adding, "I admire that you are so organized and careful yet unpredictable."

Theta directed, "I cannot wait the twenty-four hours. Let's eat lunch and then go get a marriage certificate at the courthouse. Rose is a notary if we need her. Am I moving too fast?"

Theta got into the dirty silver Pathfinder. Billy ran around to the other side. He sped off to an Olive Garden to get there before the lunch crowd began. They were led to a booth where they asked the hostess for an express lunch order. They wanted to plan the rest of their lives together.

"Tonight, tomorrow . . . Theta?" Billy began. "How?"

"No, not tonight. Tomorrow." She replied. "Trust me with the details. Let's enjoy lunch and go and get the marriage license first. I'll do the rest. You just pack and show up at nine thirty in the morning. Downtown courthouse. The kids will be in school. Can you get your mom and Carla there too?"

"Yes, I'll call them after lunch. You sure are spontaneous," Billy interjected. "I was sure I was in dating mode for at least a year or two."

"Yeah, I know. I am so emotional, but I am also so sure," Theta cried. "You are my life, Billy. I cannot be without you for another day."

Her iridescent green eyes were wet with joy.

Billy pulled out his handkerchief. He reached for her hand and looked into her wetted eyes. She took the handkerchief and patted the underside of her lower lashes.

"When you know, you just know," she explained. "Besides, the wait is difficult for me too. Maybe even more than it is for you."

"Shouldn't I get an engagement ring first?" Billy asked.

"Don't you dare! You haven't asked me to marry you anyway. What's keeping you?" Theta chided him.

"Oops, I assumed a good slap on the cheek one time was enough. I have no ring. Should I wait until I get the ring?" Billy asked.

"No, silly. Ask me right now. This moment. We don't need a ring. We just need a direction," Theta assured him.

Billy got down on one knee. Some in the restaurant took notice.

"Theta, you are the love of my life. I am totally devoted to you always. Will you make my life whole and marry me?" Billy formally asked.

"Yes, but only if you never embarrass me again in a restaurant," she answered. "Now, come sit next to me because I can't reach your lips across the booth."

Theta cried softly as Billy approached her. He sat next to her, embraced her with his strength, and kissed her as a rehearsal of the thousands of kisses that would follow—all as passionate as the first she knew eight and a half years earlier in the waterfalls.

He paused.

"I still don't understand. No engagement ring?" he followed. "Why not?"

"I want love, not trinkets. The marriage bands are symbolic. The engagement ring is for mothers, jewelers, and socialites. I just want you."

"Good, then I can save the money and wash the Pathfinder," Billy countered.

"No, Billy. I agreed to wash the Pathfinder for a free lunch," Theta stated. "A deal's a deal."

Theta couldn't help thinking about Billy passing up a fortune to stay in Charleston to be with her and the twins. Nobody else would have made such a commitment. They ate lunch hurriedly and went to apply for the marriage certificate.

Theta returned to her office and posted a notice, as the manager, that she would be on vacation beginning the next day. She diligently worked on the intricate travel and babysitting plans she would need. She called in her first assistant, Rosie, to finish a few of her pressing client requests. She told her that she would uncharacteristically be leaving early.

Billy went to a small King Street jeweler to buy two wedding rings. He had them inscribed. He declined the offer of presentation boxes or gift wrapping. He had hers engraved on the inside.

"To Theta, I love you. I need you."

His was inscribed, "Love is Truth."

He placed the loose rings in his jean pocket.

He called his mom, asking her to keep the impromptu wedding news secretive. He would have the same conversation with his sister, Carla. He instructed them to meet him the next morning at the downtown courthouse by nine thirty.

Theta called her mom to tell her the news. Owing to their past rift, Martha was very formal, cordial, and careful in her response. She had the initial impulse to ask her if she was pregnant but avoided the subject. When she asked about the wedding date, Theta was blunt. Theta stated the factual details.

"Mother, there will be no formal wedding. I'm marrying Billy, my prom date from senior year. Daddy liked him. You didn't. He's the musician that had the accident and lost his memory. We will tell everyone about our marriage only when we get back from our honeymoon. We're getting married tomorrow at the downtown courthouse at nine thirty. Billy's mom and sister will stand witness for us. You are welcome to come. There will be no reception. We will leave immediately afterward for our honeymoon. And no, Mother, I am not pregnant."

Martha was momentarily appalled at the information and final disclaimer. But she was, in fact, still thinking that Theta had gotten herself pregnant again. She wasn't sure to believe that Theta was not pregnant. But she did not want to reenter the dark tunnel of their prior years of discord.

"Theta, I wouldn't have suggested that at all, dear," she responded. "I was only thinking about who will be taking care of the twins."

"That's already arranged. Billy's mom is staying over, and his sister, Carla, is helping. You are welcome to see Mia and Leah if they fit your schedule. The little boy there—his name is Ashton—I will be adopting him when I get back."

"What? Why? Is his mother dead?" Martha asked.

"No, she's just a drug addict and cannot even take care of herself," Theta informed. "The little boy does not know that. Neither do the twins."

"Does your husband, the musician, approve of drugs?" Martha boldly asked.

"Yes, Mother. He loves drugs. He's going to go into the drug business when we get back," Theta replied sarcastically. "Do you really think I would be around drugs, Mother?"

"He had to be around them, then, right?" Martha pursued.

"Mother, you are impossible," Theta replied. "Billy is a recovering amnesiac. That's all. I love him. I want to have his children but only after we get married. Got it? And I promise you that I will have his children—guaranteed—as soon as we can. I know what I'm doing. You have to quit treating me as your mistake. I am not a mistake. I am your daughter."

Theta hung up and immediately dialed the booking number for Little Conch Island. It was a very expensive booking, even with the agency discount. She was able to reserve it with a guaranteed late arrival. Theta worked backward from a connecting flight to Tortola from Miami. The Charleston to Miami flight details had several options, but the Tortola flight only flew once daily. From the cross-island trip at Tortola, there would be a twenty-minute boat ride to Little Conch Island.

Theta arranged that the Little Conch staff was to fully stock the kitchen and bar with special requests. She gave them the name Mr. and Mrs. T. Barnwell and read off the agency's credit card for the confirmation guarantee. She gave the booking her name so that Billy's notoriety did not attract paparazzi. Her signature was also appropriate for the agency authorization. She met Billy at her house by five thirty to review the details. Billy helped her to wash his silver Pathfinder in her driveway.

Since the day had a chill, they washed the car without frolic. They used the time to discuss other issues.

"Theta, is your mother coming tomorrow?" Billy asked.

"I doubt it. I did ask her, but she seems suspicious of the timing. I'm sure that she thinks I'm pregnant again. After all, she lived through what was to her an embarrassment in front of her friends eight years ago," Theta replied. "She never got over it. And neither did I."

Billy hesitated to respond. He then set thoughts in motion.his

"Theta, you may never have a relationship with your mother again. Whatever direction you take will have my support. You have the moral high ground, but she probably has no idea just how special her daughter really is. She would brag about you to her friends if she knew the backstory from eight years ago. But she'll likely never know that information. Will she ever know that the girls are mine too? That's going to be your judgment alone," Billy offered.

"Eventually, she will know," Theta replied. "Not now, though."

Billy carefully selected his summation of the dilemma as if Sid was whispering in his ear.

"The two grandmothers should eventually know each other better. They are both widows and only have these grandchildren in common. My mother will be ecstatic to know about the twins. I can't wait to tell her, but I will wait until you feel it is time. She will also have to know your mother.

"Your mother has posed quite an obstacle to you over the years. My only advice would be that you ask yourself what can and cannot be forgiven. Knowing you as I have, you are a moral example for everyone. You have an amazing resolve and a set of ethics that inspire. Having the capacity to forgive what is forgivable is a lot to ask in your relationship with your mother. Only you know that answer."

Theta sprayed the tire rims and the rear bumper. She was mildly receptive to Billy's advice. There were deep scars.

"Billy, I can forgive her wayward assumptions and maybe even her placing her social status ahead of my convictions. Yes, I hold a deep injury from that whole episode—not only over the pregnancy months but also well into the early motherhood years. She was not there for me when I needed her most. Maybe I can find the strength to forgive these things. But what I feel I can never forgive is her insistence that I terminate the pregnancy for her convenience, not mine. It would have been destroying lives for fully selfish reasons. I could never do that."

"It's because of what you hold in your heart and what you believe. That's why I am so warmed to be a part of your life. But you have to also believe in Christian forgiveness, whether it's against your standards. Maybe you should think about whether you are ready for it, how to present it, and what it may mean to your children. That's it. We won't talk about it anymore until you're ready. When you are, I'd like to support you however you need me to do so. Right now, all I want to talk about is loving you forever," Billy concluded.

The car was left to air dry because of the brisk wind. Billy rolled up the hose while Theta gathered the washing utensils. He kissed her good-bye before driving away.

Billy left to complete his packing and prepare for the Caribbean. He and Theta spoke intermittently by phone over the next few hours to complete the details. Theta went to gather her clothes, toiletries, her lone one-piece bathing suit, and other essentials into her two small carry-ons. One was a roller-board for the overhead, the other a large beach bag. She told Billy to pack lightly as well because their flight connections would not allow a luggage check-in. Besides, they could always buy the things they need at Tortola.

The last call of the evening brought back the idea of forgiveness.

"Billy, you are right about me. I am so defiant sometimes that I don't leave room for my Christian soul to direct me. I wanted to tell you that I plan to offer forgiveness to my mother. Complete forgiveness. I'm not sure she will understand that she had done anything to be forgiven, but that's not what forgiveness is about. I will have this conversation with her when we return. I feel that I do not need to forgive her so much for her sake as for mine. Thank you for helping me to see it. I love you. I'll see you at eight thirty. Oh, and I need to buy a new bathing suit somewhere down there. Mine looks like one for the mother-of-the-bride, not the bride! For God's sake, don't forget the rings."

Neither Billy nor Theta slept well. They spoke by phone into the late evening, exchanging wishes and dreams that would be within their reach upon the coming day.

Billy picked up Theta at her house at eight thirty, after the girls were off to school. The girls were informed that she would be on a trip for a week. She had never left them before, so she depended on the joint effort of Lucy Mathews and her daughter, Carla—their grandmother and aunt—to ably assist and entertain the twins. Besides, Ashton would be staying with them too. The girls liked playing with little Ashton.

When Billy arrived at the courthouse, he was astonished. Though he told Sid about the sudden plans, he did not expect to see him there.

"Sid, are you lost?" Billy began.

"No, son, I will be going out of town myself soon and didn't want to miss this," he winked. "This is a special day. I hope you don't mind if I enjoy the ceremony too."

"This works out well, Sid. Would you do me the honor of serving as my best man?" Billy asked.

"Best *old* man, maybe," he replied. "Yes, of course."

Theta leaned over and kissed him on the cheek. She knew that he was the person most responsible for the day's ceremony and the joy that would follow for many years. He had changed her entire world.

Carla and Lucy arrived together. They were to follow the newlyweds to the airport and bring Billy's newly washed Pathfinder back home to Theta's driveway. Theta and Billy had decided to live where the twins would be least disrupted despite the lack of bedroom space.

Billy and Theta were surprised when Frieda and Jackie Mann showed up. They came in with the faces of excitement.

"Sid called me, old buddy," Jackie began. "I understand that Frieda and I are part of your reason for getting married. We drove over last night from Huntsville. We wouldn't miss this for the world."

A clerk came to retrieve the excited couple and led them to the chambers. The entire party entered the empty courtroom. The ceremony was performed in less than ten minutes, and the filing documents were signed and witnessed. Everything went speedily until Judge Finnegan concluded with "You may kiss the bride."

The long and meaningful kiss caused the judge to tap his pencil before it ended. He had others to marry waiting in the lobby. The kiss was more than eight years in the making.

The newly married couple thanked everyone and headed to the airport, just twenty minutes away. When they got into their car, the dark blue Buick that had been parked near the travel agency was parked across the street. Walter Bailloch was at the wheel. When the new Grayson couple left, he did not follow them. Instead, he followed the old man that moved deliberately down the courthouse steps. He had found his target.

Sid Toile had reckoned that Bailloch was near. He sensed that he was staring at him from across the street. Sid had come to the courthouse to divert the devil.

CHAPTER FORTY-EIGHT

Little Conch

THE FLIGHT TO Miami took less than ninety minutes. Theta reminded Billy that she had them placed near the front seats because the Tortola flight had a very tight connection. This was the transfer that would require carry-on baggage and swift feet. Tortola was just over two hours away on a smaller plane.

They made the flight with time to spare. Billy insisted that Theta enjoy the window seat since she was a travel agent that rarely traveled.

"I can't believe we pulled this off, Billy," she remarked as she took his hand into her lap. "The island staff will have a van waiting at the airport to take us to the west end dock. There, we'll be taken to the island. We could make it there by seven or so. Hungry?"

"No, these peanuts are very filling," Billy teased. "You wouldn't happen to have a pizza or a cheeseburger in that big bag of yours, would you?"

"They have the good stuff on this flight, hubby," she answered. "There's Snickers, potato chips, or Almond Joy."

"Let's splurge and share all three with that stale coffee they serve," Billy proposed.

"Great, I'll flag the maître de," Theta said. "Oh, they have apple juice too."

Theta turned to the window and stared, thinking about how her life would change. She looked down at her bright lavender bracelet. The stone sparkled from the sun's descending light intensified through the window. There was so much to discuss, but they would have a week to themselves to decide on everything. Would they seek a larger house because of Ashton? Would they remodel? How would they deal with Billy's concert travel? Who would keep the checkbook and pay the bills? Theta knew that there was plenty of time to discuss the essential details. Theta would not burden Billy with the issues unless he brought any of these things up on his own. She was amazed at the timing of his next question.

"Theta, there is something we forgot to discuss that we should take care of while we've got a serious moment," Billy started.

"Wait, Billy," Theta started. "Let's do this. Let's try to leave it at one item per day for each of us. We have a whole week. You get to ask me what's on your mind. Then I get to ask you. We should cover most of the important stuff before we get home. You go first."

"OK, my one thing for today," Billy began. "I have not been good at attending church. I go when home with Mom, but it's tough on the road. I don't remember anything about my spirituality from before—just what my mom told me. We were Methodists, then Presbyterians. After my accident, I learned much about Christ by reading the Bible. I became a self-taught Christian with every reason you can imagine to be a believer. I know that you take the girls to Sunday school and that you are Episcopalian. I think we should all attend church together as a family. I can go to yours or you to mine. Are you OK with that?"

"Let's do this. Let's go to yours a few weeks and then to mine," Theta answered. "We can decide from there. I will always attend church, and I hope Mia, Leah, and Ashton will see the example while in our home and continue as adults. Not to make it too simple, but being a good Christian is important to me. Which church? I prefer the one where I can talk to God."

"Perfect," Billy answered. "We've made our first lifestyle agreement. Now, what do you have for me?"

"Mine's a little more of an emergency decision," Theta offered. "We have three children as of a few hours ago. That's a big enough family for most. But I am not opposed to growing it. Are you?"

"Not in the least," Billy replied. "As long as we can give each one plenty of attention, I have no number in mind. I'll leave that up to you."

Theta answered swiftly.

"Good, because I never went on the birth control pill. I had no reason to do so. I have no protection over the coming week and had no idea what you expected. My menstrual cycle ended less than a week ago, but based on my only pregnancy and your past virility, I could easily get pregnant this week. Were you speaking in theory or in reality, because—chances are—this honeymoon could produce a result!"

"Theta, you have to remember, I don't know you as you know me. I have no knowledge of our last 'production' and have never seen you unclothed. I know that you are gorgeous in every way. So knowing that this could be very romantic and we will not be disturbed, I hope we have ample opportunities to grow our family. You can wipe the drool from my face with your peanut napkin!"

Theta smiled.

"I'm not what you have forgotten before anyway. I'm older and probably a couple of pounds heavier. I have a scar from the Caesarian section. You might be disappointed, Billy," Theta warned. "I'm far from gorgeous and even farther from perfect."

As the plane landed, Billy kissed Theta. "Welcome to your new life. Welcome to Tortola."

Theta looked down at her wedding band.

"Thank you for this," she whispered. "I am so happy. This is bound to be the happiest day of my life. I read what you put on the inside. It made me cry again."

As they departed down the stairs onto the warm and breezy island tarmac near the gate, Billy spotted a man holding a sign that said, "T. Barnwell."

"Wow, they know you're here," Billy stated.

"Don't ask. Just accept it," Theta hinted. "You see any paparazzi?"

"Brilliant," Billy added.

They were taken by a minivan across the island to the west-end dock. There, another staffer grabbed their luggage and handed each a frozen piña colada. They boarded a small motorboat and were deposited at the Seascape Cottage in minutes. The staffer brought their bags to their bedroom with the four-poster bed. He gave service instructions, showed them the kitchen and the provisions, and reminded them that they were twenty minutes away, twenty-four hours a day.

"Our maid service comes at noon every day to clean. She can bring our chef to prepare lunch if you like," the staffer began. "It is part of the package. You'll not be charged any more for any of our service or amenities. Any special orders?"

Theta suggested the next day's lunch. "I saw that you have a wide variety of sandwiches. Can she prepare two chicken salad pitas with two orders of the tiramisu? Is that OK with you, Mr. Barnwell?"

Billy chided, "Your order works for me. Will we be up by noon, Theta?"

"I'm an early riser, Billy. That's when I work out. But I can sleep in until maybe seven o'clock. We have an island to explore."

The staffer took notes on a pad. "Now, you have two massage tables at the far end of the east beach inside the cabana. Massages are on demand, anytime. You can have candlelight dinner at the water's edge or on the veranda. Just let us know. There is complimentary transportation back into Road Town. There are some very nice shops and restaurants there. The sailboat is a small catamaran, easy to sail with a few instructions, or we can send a captain. Meals are provided on the sailboat. The island is all yours. You have no one else here to disturb you, and we only come when you call us. The owner's house on the hill at the other end is closed. They left for London last Thursday.

Your Wi-Fi password is Conch1234. The staff phone is accessed by dialing 444. Will there be anything else, Mr. Barnwell?"

Billy smiled. He had already folded a cash tip into his right hand. He gave the staffer a one-hundred-dollar bill. The staffer accepted the tip without looking at the denomination and walked back down the dock to his motorboat. He waved back to the newlyweds and left.

Theta went into the large bedroom to distribute her luggage contents to the dresser drawers. She took her toiletries to the bathroom.

Billy called out to Theta from the den, "This place is awesome. We might never leave."

Theta walked from the bathroom and leaned demurely against the den door.

"I agree. It's everything that was in the brochure. They have sea turtles, a natural bird sanctuary, and we may even see iguanas. Can I put your things up?"

"If you don't mind. I'll set the music and fix us something you like to drink. We'll make our first toast together," Billy followed. "And you can place any of my stuff wherever there is room for Mr. Barnwell. I can help you after our first toast together."

"There should be some pinot grigio in the fridge. I want something light and chilled," Theta requested sweetly. "Would you mind?"

The house had a welcome basket of fresh fruits and crackers. A bottle of champagne was on ice by the bar top sink. He selected the silver goblets in lieu of the glassware. The wine corkscrew opener was in the top drawer.

Billy perused the stereo and decided to try and plug in or pair his iPhone list of soft music to the speakers. He liked listening to many classical artists of his parents' generation when he traveled by plane. The baby boomers owned the patent for the best romantic mood music. He paired the Bluetooth Sonos system to his phone and turned it to a medium volume. He did not want to distort the evening's conversation. Willie Nelson's "You Were Always on My Mind" followed Art Garfunkel's "Second Avenue." The chilled wine was opened and poured.

He saw the sun fading low through the window on the west view. The sunset highlighting small distant clouds was sure to be memorable. He called Theta out to the veranda to the brilliant show. He handed her a filled goblet. She had hurriedly finished her tasks, as she wanted to be with Billy for every following moment. She was excited about re-attaching yesterday's optimism through a long chasm to this day's new beginning.

Billy looked deeply into her brightened and anticipating green orbs. He filled his lungs with the resolution of his impassioned fulfillment of life. The pause made his words meaningful and dramatic.

"We have loved each other since before—and during—the confusion of our trying circumstances. We loved with purpose beyond every adversity. We loved in a way to gain love's promise of endurance. To the Lady Theta Grayson. I hope God will guide me to deserve you always and forever."

Theta smiled. She tapped her goblet with Billy's and sipped the chosen nectar. They kissed passionately, much as they had done in the courthouse earlier that day. They turned to face the sun as it dipped below the aqueous horizon. Theta leaned against Billy and took another sip from the goblet. She looked into his gray-green eyes. They embraced and kissed again. Her eyes were wet in the moment.

Billy then took her goblet away and placed it with his on the rail. He lifted Theta in the crux of his arms and carried her inside to the sitting area before depositing her on the four-poster bed just beyond.

"Billy, you have been so patient with me. You must be frustrated and ready to explode. Just give us ten more minutes. Let's do this right. It's a memory to be made," Theta suggested. "I've been waiting for you too."

They kissed again before Theta coyly suggested an exciting course to facilitate their tepid desires.

"I'll shower. You can come in to wash my back," she said as she sat up at the bedside. Billy smiled and nodded.

Theta got up and moved to the bathroom to turn on the shower. Billy followed. She tested the warmth of the water before turning to Billy. She unbuttoned his shirt, kissing his chest along the way.

She undressed slowly in front of her excited husband. Herb Alpert's old standard "This Guy's In Love with You" began playing from Billy's iPhone list.

Theta first removed her slacks and then Billy's jeans. She took off her blouse. She kissed him again. Then she removed her bra and panties. Her only remaining adornment was the silver necklace chain with the lavender amulet. She enjoyed that Billy was watching her wordlessly and while becoming aroused. She removed his boxer briefs slowly.

Billy turned Theta around to unfasten the necklace. He saw that Theta was taut and fit from her discipline of daily exercise. He placed the amulet necklace on the sink counter.

Her heart was pounding. Her curvaceous breasts were full, sensuous, and sprightly. Her skin was alabaster in the muted light. She initiated a romantic hug and another passionate kiss. She moved a step back so that Billy could peruse her fully nude figure.

"There, you're both the first and the second person to see me completely naked as an adult," Theta declared. "And you're still the only man I have ever seen."

Theta then pinned up her long wavy hair, while Billy watched in awe of her exquisite figure. She moved back to him and took his right hand to her left breast and kissed him again. She then pulled the hand away to lead Billy into the large high-ceilinged shower where they enjoyed discovering each other as if it were the very first time.

After titillating each other further in soap and shampoo, Theta turned the shower off and clutched one of the large luxurious towels. She dried Billy off carefully and slowly before drying herself. He watched as she moved deliberately. She hung the towel over the hook behind the bathroom door. She took his hand again and led him back to the bedroom. She pulled back the comforter to the bottom of the bed and entered the sheets, still damp and nude. He bent over to kiss her. He moved slowly into the bed next to her. They faced each other, his hands clutching hers. They gazed into each other's eyes still fascinated by the events that bonded them to the moment.

"Billy, you and this joy have been in my dreams for eight long years. Let's take our time to consummate our marriage and seal our future together," she whispered. Billy kissed her again.

The lamps were turned off. The ambient light from the new moon sufficed. Billy could see Theta's eyes shining with joyful tears. He embraced her and kissed her with renewed passion. He moved the large pillow under her head and repositioned his masculine torso above her, looking deeply into her emerald eyes. They kissed vigorously as she opened herself to receive him.

As if by coincidence, Norah Jones's *Come Away with Me* filled the room with the perfect ending to a beautiful setting. The breeze freshened from the window screen. Theta remembered the song from the Alabama cabin weekend. Theta's memory flickered back to the night of the rainstorm eight long years before. She was back within the life she craved over those many years. They enjoyed an active night of emotionally charged lovemaking before dozing off to a peaceful repose.

The following morning, Theta arose to write a thought into her notebook. She didn't keep a diary but had notes of the moments she relished—such as when the twins first walked; or when her father died. An inspiration struck her as the sun came up.

I am with the man I will love forever. Thank You, God, for giving me patience. Thank You for blessing me with health. Thank You for leading me in darkness to the right path. I will follow Your Word always.

When Billy awakened, he insisted on making breakfast. Theta made the coffee. It was a new day. They had not been married for twenty-four hours. As they enjoyed a scrambled egg and cheese breakfast with wheat toast and strawberry preserves, Theta wanted to get the next agreement settled. The coffee warmed the mood.

"Billy, I like my job. I want to work. It's not about the income. I like my clients, and I love setting itineraries to exciting places. Will you allow me to continue even if we have more children?" she asked.

"That's a no-brainer. You are welcome to work as much and as long as you like. But I'd like you to think about owning your own agency one day so that when we travel, you will not need to ask off," Billy replied.

"Good suggestion. I always wanted to do that, and maybe when we get back, I can look into buying the local franchise or setting up my own," Theta suggested. "The local Dream Site franchise has been for sale before."

Theta felt assured and at peace with her decision. She turned to Billy.

"Anything on your mind, hubby?"

"Besides making love to you, I only had one thing to settle," Billy responded. "It's really not a question as much as a commitment. I've been thinking about this. My career takes me to exotic and faraway places. You and the family should go with me whenever we can arrange it. You can make the travel bookings. So I am inviting you to join me anytime—or all of the time. The second part of my travel idea is this: when I leave in the morning—and whenever possible—I will always be back that same evening, no matter where I fly away. I want to be back by your side every night. If the trip is longer, I will either pass on it or take you with me. Deal?"

"Wow, Billy, that could stifle your career," Theta noted. "But I'd love to know you will be home most nights. Done deal!"

Billy took the soiled breakfast plates to the sink.

"Jet skis, bikes, hammocks, or the sailboat?" he asked.

Theta smiled. "Let's make love again and then walk the preserve. And if we feel the urge, make love again along the way. Then we can have lunch by the pool, make love, sail, make love on the sailboat, and then find a place that's stunning to make love again."

"You really are great with itineraries." Billy winked. "And you really understand vacations well."

Billy and Theta were enjoying a fantastic honeymoon. Sid had called Rosie at the Dream Site Travel Agency to pay their outstanding debt, admonishing Rosie to never divulge the source. When Billy called from Little Conch to transfer funds from his newly infused bank account of $3 million, he was told that the bill was already paid anonymously. Billy knew that Sid had paid it. He planned to reimburse him upon his return. He was aware of Sid's largesse, but no one knew the immensity of his estate.

Little Conch Island was shaped like a slightly crooked high-heel shoe. The high end was nearly 120 feet above sea level. The owner's estate was at the overlook. The luxurious Seascape Cottage was at the "toe" of the island and featured two small sandy beaches, native coconut trees, and the warm and crystal-clear Caribbean waters lapping its shores. It was over four thousand yards across the channel to the staffing dock at the western end of Tortola.

It was on the fourth day that Billy posed the question about Theta's first experience with him eight years earlier. They were relaxing on the porch swing facing Tortola with a snack of lemonade and Cheez-Its.

"Theta, I do have a burning curiosity. You do not have to talk about it unless you want. It's about me and you back then. The questions are more like why, when, how, and what?" Billy outlined. "Is that something you can tell me about, or should I wait to get to know you better?"

"Billy, you realize that I can tell you, but it would be much like telling you about an affair I had with another man," Theta stated. "It will not bother me to tell you since you are that man, but it could bother you."

"When you say it that way, I should withdraw the question. But since you used my body, I wanna hear about it," Billy pointed out.

Theta laughed at the twisted rhetoric.

"Well, you know we were completely alone at a private cabin encircled by a forest reserve. A tributary of the Tennessee River created an idyllic place with rushing waterfalls. There were birds and squirrels and frogs and even deer everywhere. We spent two days cooped up by the steady rain. On the third day, your friends Jackie and Theta had to leave. You and I had enjoyed them, and we had a wonderful time. But we had an understanding that prevented us from any physical activity. I had a creaky bed. You had a miserable sleeping bag on the floor for two nights in the same bedroom."

"You really were a prude," Billy interjected.

"Yes, I suppose so. I insisted on the arrangement. I was—and I still remain—very strong-willed. But—after Jackie and Frieda left—the scenery, the waterfalls, and your gentlemanly conduct enraptured me.

I was more than a little enticed by your playfulness. You gave me space and respect. Oddly, I became the aggressor." Theta was slightly blushing as she told the story.

"You just wouldn't know what was going on in my mind. I was twenty. I was sunbathing near a man I considered as the perfect suitor. But even you knew you would have to wait a couple of years. Yet you honored me with your understanding and patience. Yet, somehow, I knew deep in my soul that you were the one.

"When we played in the falls, we looked at each other lovingly, and you kissed me. It was the most natural inclination for both of us. I was waiting for that kiss more than you knew. I could have put up the stop sign, but I didn't. We kept kissing until, well, we got naked in the waterfall. I'll never forget what happened next. You took me and held me. You made sure that everything from then on was about me. You made it thrilling, natural, and took away my fear," Theta recalled.

Billy was enamored with the recollection.

"That sounds beautiful. No wonder you kept it to yourself. You wouldn't have been on the pill, and I probably wouldn't have even considered bringing protection. I suppose that's why we have twins today," Billy surmised.

"Billy, this is delicate. It might have been that time or the next time on the shore or the time we made love at midnight or the next morning. We didn't put our clothes back on for a full day. It was incredibly sexy. We dressed each other just minutes before we drove back to Atlanta," Theta retold. "I really thought we were safe by the timing of my cycle. So my miscalculation led to the pregnancy. In the end, that part was what I held dear all these years as an amazing blessing from that memory of you."

"And then you kinda reverted to your virginal commitment?" Billy asked.

"Really, I got great advice from my father. When I told him that I was fully and completely in love with a man who might die, he began mentoring me. It was my father who paid the balance of your medical bills from the Atlanta hospital. He did this because he believed in me. He knew that you were not to blame. Then when the twins were born, he was so happy. He reminded me that the girls were my priority. Everything else was secondary," Theta recited. "Then I finished college, took on a career I liked and focused on providing the best possible future for the girls you and I created together. That motivated me."

"No serious dates since then, really?" Billy asked.

"Oh, there were opportunities. There were a few sincere suitors that seemed interested, but once they saw that I had twins, most retreated. I had a few dates to things like Christmas parties and church functions but never anyone I saw as a serious contender. There were a few divorcees and even an assistant minister. Some I liked, but I had no real attraction. I kept thinking about what we had for those twenty-four hours. I thought of what built up to it and what destroyed it. One day, I quit feeling sorry for myself and realized I was the luckiest mother of twins on the planet. I had true love strike me. I assumed it might never cross my path again—that is until that same person became what I'll call my second perfect love."

"Theta, I am really jealous of your first lover," Billy said. "He was one very lucky guy!"

Theta leaned over and initiated a passionate kiss to her husband.

Billy and Theta would enjoy their honeymoon for three more incredibly relaxing days on Little Conch. They jogged the trails, sailed, biked, crabbed, and even found a zip line the island owner had recently added. Owing to Theta's fair skin, they used the early morning and late evening hours to frolic in the many water features. They had the hot tub, the pool, the grotto shower, and daily snorkeling adventures. Theta's early suggestion that the island water activities were to be clothing optional meant that their bathing suits never got wet. Billy was thoroughly enamored by her spontaneity. They spent much of their time enjoying each other's fascinating conversation. By the sixth day, they felt they had resolved most of the unknowns related to an abbreviated courtship and a quick marriage.

They called daily to check on Mia, Leah, and Ashton. They were excited to hear their voices together in one house.

With only one day left on Little Conch Island, they called Sid. The conversation was apocryphal.

"Sid, we're having a marvelous time. We both feel it is because of you," Billy began. "And we know what you did at Dream Site. You will not get away with it. Even my alternative Sony contract is pretty amazing, all things considered. We can pay our way."

"Ah, that you can," Sid replied. "But, my son, I was left with no option. You got married so quickly and left so soon. I hadn't the time to get a wedding gift. Besides, I may be out of town when you get back tomorrow. At seventy-seven, you do not have the luxury of making extended plans."

"Sid, you're the reason for my greatest leap in the recovery. You got my mind thinking of priorities over the clutter that gets in the way. It's a lesson I will never forget. And I've never paid you a cent because you would have been insulted. You've been like a father to me—one that always seemed to reset my value system. Now you're responsible for the best honeymoon ever because you made me realize that Theta was my destiny—well beyond my dreams. And then you paid the bill. It's just not right."

"But, Billy, it's right with me. Don't rob me of that inner peace. It doesn't have a price," Sid stated.

"OK, I understand, but I'm going to spend a lifetime making it up to you. Theta wants to say hello," Billy added.

He handed Theta the cell phone.

"Sid, Billy said it best," Theta began. "I wanted you to know that I took a chance eight years ago. Nobody but my father and me knew for certain that it was the right choice until I spoke with you. You opened my mind to my next important choice. And then you convinced me to take a chance again. Now, I have Billy. He's sitting here next to me, and we are so very happy. You saw it. You knew it first. I know that you will never accept thanks, but please accept that I am another small puzzle piece that you connected. This couple who you have joined will always be proud to be among your *frillionaire* group. We have made something positive of our lives, as you have suggested. Happily, we are doing it together."

"Your ordeal and resolution have warmed me, young lady. Witnessing that you were married was the culmination of a duty I relished more profoundly than you will ever know," Sid stated. "You have duties to meet as well. You will have to manage a new combined family, and all six of you will be blessed."

Theta did not correct him. She thought that he had miscounted.

Sid added a request.

"When you return, I need a small favor for a day only. Please let Thomas borrow your amulet and bracelet. He'll tell you when he needs them. It is for a secret reason that will mean much to me personally. He is picking you up at the Charleston airport tomorrow as a favor to me. He'll have the children and Mrs. Grayson with him. I know you miss them dearly."

Theta quietly said goodbye by saying, "Consider it done. Bless you, Sid. We will never forget what you have done for us."

She pressed the end button on the phone. After hanging up, she looked at Billy, and as if she were entranced by Sid's words.

"Sid said all six of us will be blessed," Theta reported quizzically.

She stopped to consider his revelation. Sid had clearly stated the number six. She paused and then turned to Billy and said, "I'm pregnant. I am with child."

Tears welled in her sparkling green eyes. Billy thought that she was emotional over Sid's words that he had not overheard. He hugged her.

"How would you already know that you are pregnant?" he wondered. "Theta, it doesn't work that way. It's not automatic," Billy told her. "Do you feel like you're pregnant after just a few days?"

"No, Billy," Theta explained. "I know for certain I'm pregnant. And it's not because of anything I feel. It's something that Sid said. He said that I 'need to manage a newly combined family of six.' Sid knows that the number is five. But he said six. He was letting me know. I'm going to see Dr. Inabinet when I get back."

Theta was so sure of Sid's prediction that she and Billy had a formal celebratory dinner in Road Town that evening. She had no wine with her meal.

Sid's long-distance synesticism was correct. Dr. Inabinet verified the unusual prediction within weeks. The obstetrician calculated the inception date as Billy and Theta's wedding night. The baby would be due in early November.

Sid had pieced together two people, a circumstance, and an outcome correctly.

Importantly, the ethereal stones were together with their rightful holder. They had been separated for seven centuries.

CHAPTER FORTY-NINE

Eternity Never Waits

THE BORACLE HAD a late breakfast and left his condo to drive to Professor Leon's eleven o'clock class. He had just spoken to Billy and Theta when they called from Little Conch Island. The evening before, he had experienced an intense blue-light dream deep into his REM cycle. He knew what it meant, and he spoke with Maria Delgado before calling Thomas. There were arrangements he needed to make. They would both be engaged to assist.

He was looking forward to interacting with the young student minds as the day's guest lecturer. Sid began another of his popular presentations in front of the lucky students who were chosen for the elective course, Theoretical Algorithms 402. Thomas was proud to have his best friend honor him again.

The topics were mind-boggling and the insights riveting. The Boracle's final summation subject was directed to cite an unfamiliar comet.

"The Tubbiolo Comet returns on August 15 of 2024," Sid told the gathering of students. "The perihelion distance is 4.4456. It has a trajectory, an inclination, and an eccentricity. Some would describe me in much the same way."

The class giggled at the parallel reference.

As in the past, Sid never read from notes. He followed a thought process that had never failed. His grasp of facts that related to life made him an exceptional guest speaker. He lectured with an ever-interesting set of scientific and societal postulations.

"On the day of its return, there will be observatories digitizing it to see where it will go, even though they already know. We know where it has been as well. Tubbiolo Comet is like the lives we live. The parabola is a constant. Your personal parabola is no different. We see part of it and guess the rest based on the speed, distance, and time. Tubbiolo Comet—it's a perihelion experience I will not see from this vantage point. I'm old and transient."

He struggled with a sudden flurry of coughs. He interjected, "Please pardon me," before continuing. His face was reddened as he temporarily lost his breath.

"You've heard me speak about PHCs—positive human consequence." He strained. "Can you take your parabola into a life that delivers your PHC? This is where I leave you—in the wonder of science—and the marvel of who you can be in its world."

The last words drifted off softly. The forty-five-minute lecture was complete. The class stood to applaud the fascinating Boracle of Wi-Fi but was stopped before they could begin their clapping by the professor. He knew that Sid would not like being thanked. Sid made the motion of a slight bow before turning back to his friend Professor Leon.

As the appreciative professor began to dismiss the class, Sid Toile collapsed. Cell phones were engaged as the cadets called for an emergency vehicle. The professor and two cadets rolled him over to his back. He did not appear to be breathing well. There were visible signs that the Boracle suffered a severe heart attack.

An emergency vehicle arrived within seven critical minutes. The crew tried to find obstructions, without success, before lifting the silent old man into the rear of the emergency vehicle. Medics continued to seek other means of life-saving techniques as they worked closely over him in the ambulance, out of the public view. They left with immediacy to the Emergency Trauma Facility at the Medical University's downtown complex. The trip would last only four critical minutes.

Thomas had jumped into the rear of the vehicle. He appeared deeply shaken.

On the way to the hospital, the medics applied oxygen. The frenzy of determining the sudden cause of his collapse and its remedy would be recorded in the journal that the assistant medic administered. The radio technician called in the problematic situation.

Eliot Sidney Toile was pronounced dead on arrival at the Downtown Emergency Trauma Center. He was just two weeks short of turning seventy-eight years of age. Other necessary functions followed, including the introduction of a human remains pouch, commonly known as a body bag.

Just as the pronouncement was made, the noon carillon bells at old St. Michael's Church rang across the city. The tintinnabulation heralded much as an introduction of a celebratory beginning. A mysterious wall of wind startled the lively tourists across the city. Table umbrellas blew over; flags fluttered loudly, and assorted debris raced across the thoroughfares. When the bells completed their serenade, all was suddenly quiet. Sid's ending seemed surreal.

The macabre sense of finality struck the onlookers as the ambulance unloaded the gurney at the Trauma Center. Sid's body was enveloped and zipped into a thick plastic bag. The human remains pouch—or HRP—was a morbid indication of his demise. The crew rolled the remains into a secured room to wait for the county coroner.

Thomas Leon knew that Sid had no living relatives. So he assumed control of the postmortem. As his best friend over the last few years, he knew Sid's instructions for the inevitable. Sid had given him a sealed copy for his safekeeping.

Several of Professor Leon's students came to the hospital out of respect. Maria appeared in the waiting room. She was like the others in her disbelief. They moved from the first sense to the second. They became distraught. Thomas tried his best to console her. Thomas took a folded index card from his wallet and called the numbers in the order that Sid had given. He told them not to come down to the hospital and that he would be in touch soon.

He sat by Maria in the lobby and dialed to Evelyn, Viola, and Charlie. Maria had already summoned Pablo. They had decided not to call Billy and Theta on their honeymoon. They were due back the next day. Thomas took notes down before leaving the waiting area. He had much to plan and prepare.

An odd man walked into the Emergency Room lobby. He looked around before inquiring at the desk. No one there had seen him before.

"Ma'am, I'm just checking on a relative. My name is Toile. I'm jus' seeing how my brother, Sid, is doin'."

"I'll check, Mr. Toile," she replied.

She pulled up the name in the computer and stopped suddenly. She wrote something down on a small sticky note. It was the time.11:59 a.m.

"Mr. Toile, I'm sorry to inform you that your brother, Eliot, died at a minute before noon. May I get the director here for you, sir? We're very sorry," she reiterated. "We have grief counseling at the hospital."

"No, ma'am. What did he die of?" he prodded.

"Well, it says a myocardial infarction. A heart attack. He was nearly seventy-eight," she stated in a low tone, not wanting to broadcast the information to others waiting in the area.

The stranger did not seem surprised.

"Do you want to leave a forwarding address and number for his personal items, sir?" she followed.

"No, ma'am. It ain't my stuff. I'll go to the car and get my cell phone to call all of the other family," he stated.

Sid had no other siblings and no living relatives. The slightly built and haggardly man left the Emergency Room to go to his car and never came back. The car had Tennessee license plates. Arlo Crutchfield was content that the poisonous concoction was part of Sid's breakfast. It appeared that, because of Sid's age and the appearance of a heart event, no forensic autopsy would be forthcoming. He had avenged his twin sister's passing.

Arlo stayed in the area for a few more days, reveling in the news that his mission was complete. He was convinced that Sid succumbed to the poison concoction in the yogurt. A party of one celebrated his devious revenge. By the following Sunday, he took the obituary section of the newspaper with him back to drive back to Sparta, Tennessee. As he surmised, there was no autopsy ordered. There was no police report because there was no reason to suspect a crime had been committed.

Time had begotten the malfeasance of the times.

Arlo stayed until the corpse was to be interred or cremated as the obituary cited. A private cremation was to be held. Arlo was relieved to read it.

Sid had drawn his will, planned a private and unscheduled scattering of his ashes, and even written his own obituary. The obituary was short and concise, causing quite a stir with all that knew of his immense abilities and personal generosity. Sid left a blank line for the date of his informal service. Thomas would already know these details.

His obituary appeared in the local and state newspapers just two days after the collapse in the classroom. Thomas also sent obituary notices out to more than a dozen other selected city papers as Sid directed. Among those on the list was the Sparta Expositor. His obituary was only six lines.

Eliot Sidney Toile, of Boston, widower of Ida Crutchfield Toile of Sparta, Tennessee, had enthusiastically pursued their awaited reunion since her death in 1985. For those of you that believe in true love, rejoice in his transition, Sid has long embraced his inevitable demise.

Sid's earthly history has always been unimportant except for what he hoped to inspire in others. He invites those that have acted upon their personal human consequence to attend a gathering that will be announced one year hence. Sid was appreciative of his life's calling because it allowed him the privilege of friends.

Sid Toile left several special people he had known a personal note. Each had a sealed manila envelope. Thomas had these notes cataloged for later delivery. As for his unknown estate, Sid had required Thomas to keep it sealed until nine months from the date of his death, coinciding with the release of his assets from the county probate judge. Much of his estate had been redirected prior to his passing. Thomas had access to funds by a power of attorney that would pay out any medical bills and other debt. Sid had made the task of his death quite easy to manage.

After the coroner's signature to the death certificate was affixed within twenty-four hours, Thomas arranged as instructed for a private cremation. The ashes were to be taken for a private ceremonial spreading at a future date by the professor-executor.

Thomas deliberated upon the precise instructions. He told the crematorium director the details that Sid expected. He would collect the ashes from the crematorium soon enough.

CHAPTER FIFTY

The Urn

A SMALL CREMATION CONTAINER was presented to Thomas Leon in the redbrick building next to the railroad. It held five pounds of ashes and a metal tag. There was no urn. The crematorium had been closed for an hour. A sweaty coat and tie adorned the assistant manager, who was there to welcome the mourners before they closed as a favor to the executor. He acted upon strict instructions. Only one mourner came.

Thomas arrived by late appointment only to collect the ashes. The date of the cremation was not advertised to anyone. The incombustible metal disc tag only listed a six-digit number logged by the Cremation Association of North America. The number could be submitted to CANA for cross-reference to a name and legal identification so that mistakes are avoided. This process became the universal standard to identify remains by cremation.

"These are the remains I was instructed to cremate from the coroner. Mr. Toile had prepaid the bill. Very kind man. I had suspected the deceased was headed to a potter's grave paid for by the county," the assistant manager noted.

His voice traveled lowly throughout the small chapel.

"Yes. Mr. Toile was my best friend. I'll miss him dearly," Thomas confided.

"It was odd that he did all of this planning but did not pre-purchase an urn. We have several nice ones from porcelain to smoked glass to brass to silver," the assistant manager began.

Thomas's interest was perked. He nearly laughed at the idea of smoked glass urns in a crematorium.

"I suppose smoked glass would be appropriate," Thomas answered while realizing the value of a subtle pun.

The pun did not register with the assistant manager.

"The blue, emerald, or the ashen?" the assistant followed.

"Definitely the ashen," Thomas responded furthering the pun that only he internalized as humor. Thomas wondered if the crematorium gave discounts to burn victims. He could ask the assistant manager, but he was sure that the apparent absurdity would escape him.

The assistant manager left and came back with a box holding an urn marked "Smoked Glass Ashen." He handed it to Thomas to see if it was what he'd like to purchase.

"The contents of that whole bag will fit nicely into that urn. Usually, I make the transfer for people, as they get a little queasy. Would you like me to perform the transfer, sir?"

"Yes," Thomas replied. "And please give me the identification disc for safekeeping. I will treasure having it."

"No problem, sir," the assistant consented as he took the new smoked ashen urn and the sack of the remains into a preparation room.

In a few moments, the man returned with the urn and matching urn cap professionally assembled and secured by a small strip of transparent tape. He placed it into a small canvas bag mindful of a grocery store wine carrier to present to Thomas. The tag tied to the ash remains carrier was written in pen as "Eliot S. Toile." The assistant manager handed Thomas the numbered identification disc too. Thomas placed the small stainless steel disc into his pants pocket.

"Thank you for your patience, sir," the assistant began. "That will be $43.12 with tax. Will you be using a credit card?"

"Do you accept cash?" Thomas asked.

"Certainly," he replied.

Thomas took a one-hundred-dollar bill out of his wallet.

"Just keep the difference and donate it to the next indigent's or pauper's cost—a cadaver's cremation maybe. Medical science doesn't always pay. Besides, Mr. Toile would like that some unknown someone else gets a freebie," Thomas stated.

"Why, of course," the assistant replied. "So kind of you. Mr. Toile did the exact same thing last month. Thank you, my friend. I wish there were more people out there like you and Mr. Toile."

Thomas left the crematorium with a giddy smile. He had the identification disc, the powdery remains, and the farce of a cheap glass urn in the small canvas carry bag. He knew that the smoked ashen model would have amused Sid as well.

There was a formal service to arrange and then a private scattering of the ashes. Thomas organized these events diligently and with dignity.

The formal service was held at the St. Andrews Church in Mount Pleasant. It was just three days after Billy and Theta returned from their honeymoon. Thomas had waited for their return to schedule the service, knowing that Sid cared much for the newlywed couple.

The news shook theta and Billy. Thomas knew Sid had found a special connection to this newlywed couple.

There was no casket. There was just a discolored eight-by-ten rendering of Sid at the age of forty-five in a teakwood frame set upon a small table in the middle aisle. After the minister performed the rites of Christian burial, Thomas slowly walked to the oak-carved lectern. He was deliberate in his actions and words.

"Sid Toile was not of this world in so many ways," Thomas intimated. "He never spoke of his parents except that they were Harvard graduates and they had bestowed him with a palindromic name. He missed his wife, Ida, every day for the last thirty years. He had no siblings and never spoke of cousins or nieces or nephews. He had no children. Yet, ironically, he seemed related to everyone. He had a housekeeper he treated as a daughter. A songwriter was, in many ways, his son. A brick mason was his brother. He cataloged his life in two terms nobody had ever heard, as a *synesticist* and a *frillionaire*. He solved people's problems and lifted hearts.

"He used special abilities to memorize facts and sew them together to predict outcomes. He helped others—too many to ever know—and never boasted of those tales of triumph to anyone.

"He would stock up a rented van to take water, diapers, canned food, and batteries to disaster victims. He was a volunteer at a dozen hurricanes from Andrew to Irma. He did the same for floods, earthquakes, and fires.

"He was old-world gentlemanly, profoundly humble, quietly generous, and innately selfless. He preached one gospel—the gospel of positive human consequence. I'm convinced that Sid didn't die. He just moved to another neighborhood. Some other beneficiaries are lined up. Some other age will find him at a place much like booth 14 at the Bib and Bibliothèque that so many of us visited.

"Sid was my friend. Saying 'friend' these days is not inspiring or noteworthy because of social media. They have stolen the essence of personal interaction from that word. They call it Facebook, Twitter, Instagram, and LinkedIn. Sid called them the Digital Four Horsemen of the Apocalypse. Now if you can't spell apocalypse, it's not the end of the world!"

Many giggled at the pun. Thomas paused.

"That's Sid's joke, not mine. But Sid would be glad that I remembered it. Right now, Sid is on his way somewhere else to perform what he calls a duty. To the rest of us, it would be called a life-changing kindness. May the Boracle of Wi-Fi piece together clues that will make God's heaven an even better place. Amen."

The church pews were full of Sid's many booth 14 visitors. People were crowded to the rear standing room area, and other mourners were assembled outside on the wide-marbled front stairs. There were very few dry eyes after Thomas's eulogy.

Once the benediction was given, Thomas returned home to begin work on the balance of Sid's instructions. Sid had allowed him a time of pause before completing the prescribed tasks.

Sid had requested that Thomas take the powdery remains to the marshy expanse behind Sid's condominium and spread them. This was to be done at a random time on a random day. The day chosen for the spreading of the ashes had a forecast of ominous weather in the late afternoon. Thunderstorms were likely.

Thomas performed the task diligently as directed, as he did not want to have the responsibility of harboring the ashes indefinitely. Thomas never procrastinated in any sector of his life—whether grading papers, paying bills, or maintaining his residence. Those that knew the professor Thomas admired this predisposition of responsibility.

Only Maria Delgado would need to know the place where the ashes would be dispersed. It was assumed that the unannounced ceremony might cause a sensation with the residents of Fiddler's Cove Condominiums. She knew when most of the residents were away.

In addition to Maria's attendance, Pablo Gutierrez, Hal and Viola Butters, and Evelyn Rhett appeared for the brief ceremony. They had been invited to view it from Sid's balcony. Maria had informed them of the place and timing.

Thomas lifted the smoked ashen container to show what was left of a life of an immense positive human consequence. He then looked down and repeated the verse from Genesis 3:19.

> In the sweat of thy face shalt thou eat bread,
> \until thou return unto the ground; for out of it was thou taken:
> for dust thou art,
> and unto dust shalt thou return.

Professor Leon's biblical words were not spoken loudly. He glanced up to Pablo, Maria, Evelyn, Hal, and Viola to tell them that they had met and befriended a wonderful man that belonged to other ages.

"He was many and much, available and near. He was a friend, a servant, and a calm answer in the eye of the most horrific of storms.

He did all things for others with the caveat that they were not to thank him. He saw his life as a duty to be performed with sensitivity, passion, and grace. Indeed, he was dependable and magical. He was in common as one of us yet not of common cloth. He asked to be returned to the salt marsh so that he could serve as sentry to the first light upon the continent. It is his duty," Thomas informed.

A simple life was honored. A simple death was acknowledged. There was no notice of the spreading of the ashes given to the newspaper, to the neighbors, or to the students at the college. Thomas performed the abbreviated task as Sid Toile had instructed, only adding his own words from his reflections and remembrances.

As he walked through the path crunching the dry and crusty surface of the marshland, he noted the rumbling of the distance. A storm was moving with the winds toward the ceremony. The ground was parched in anticipation of the next tidal return. Thomas stood reverently among the busy fiddler crabs, resting herons, and marsh coots. Thunder continued to warn the assembled mourners of nature's omnipotence. Clouds were hurtling the horizon to reach a zenith in the mid-sky.

Thomas spread the ashes slowly and evenly to both sides of the path. Maria placed her hand over her heart. Pablo Gutierrez removed his ball cap with his good left hand and stood in silent honor. Hal Butters consoled his wife, Viola. Thomas Leon performed the act prescribed as a matter of diligence. He never deviated or gave a sign of his profound personal loss of his best friend.

Singular heavy droplets fell sporadically from the sky. They multiplied rapidly as Thomas scurried back from the marsh to the parking area underneath the complex. As soon as he finished, a bolt of lightning struck the tower across the street. The noise was deafening.

A man in faded overalls watched from a white pickup truck just across the road was startled. He jumped in out of the rain. He drove away quickly. Another man stood in the shadows near the local television super tower. It was Walter Bailloch, who had pursued Sid over many years. Thomas was not sure whether he was within earshot but knew he would be there because Sid told him so.

A minivan parked at the side of the condominium complex nearest to Sid's unit and the marsh. It held five occupants. Billy and Theta looked into each other's green eyes in the minivan and hugged. Theta's eyes were wet. Billy was equally shaken by Sid's passing. The children remained quiet in the backseats until the lightning struck. They were immediately afraid.

A half block away across from the marsh, two men watched from a rented SUV. They were filming it from a cell phone camera until the rain started. It was an amateur documentary for a mob kingpin in Philadelphia. The recording captured the lightning bolt. But when they tried to forward it to a cell phone waiting elsewhere, it came through as a blackened screen without sound.

All were there to hear the eulogizing words see the final gesture of casting the ashes. For some, it completed a task. For others, it invited the warmth of truth.

The service was performed according to the wishes of a rare and humble man. He had changed their lives, and they had, in turn, changed others. All were in contemplative agreement of the ceremony's finality. The lightning had a purpose.

CHAPTER FIFTY-ONE

Retrospective Commitments

NEARLY A YEAR after the formal service and private spreading of the ashes, Thomas hosted the planned gathering at the Bib and Bibliothéque. He placed a small notice in the local newspaper. It was to be held on a Saturday. He did not expect but a handful of Sid's old friends to show up. As Callista opened the front glass doors at precisely 8:00 a.m., more than two dozen people were waiting. Thomas was earnest in heading straight to the booth, as Sid would have appreciated. He pulled out the same teakwood framed faded photo of Sid Toile that was utilized in the center aisle at the funeral. He displayed it at booth 14, along with a vase of multi-colored chrysanthemums. Sid's vacant office was open for its final business.

Thomas submitted his folded PHC into the empty shoebox he had placed at the center of the table. It read, "I have pursued life by realizing that education is malleable and by introducing new concepts to young minds that will enhance our world in untold avenues of significance many years hence."

Evelyn Rhett came over to booth 14 next. Her eyes were reddened as she placed a note in a small yellow stationary envelope. She opened it and handed it to Thomas to be read aloud. "I have gained a new life for myself because I found the channel that improves the lives of others." She kissed his photograph and left.

The visitors were lined up as if they had appointments to see the Boracle. Some stopped to get a cup of coffee or a latte as they waited in line.

A guy who owned a carwash left a note; Sid's next-door neighbor at his condominium did so as well. The line was serpentine and contained a succession of those who came to inform the missing Sid of their new lives: a guidance counselor from the high school, a grocery store clerk, a nurse from the oncology unit, a tour guide, a chef, a retired policeman, and others.

The line grew as the morning progressed. Sid had touched many more lives than anyone knew. Thomas sat in the booth collecting the PHCs in the shoebox. He knew that the one box would not be big enough.

Sid's plumber stopped by and then his barber. A popular local jeweler came next and dropped a gold tie tack into the box with his note. A bus driver, a laundry owner, and an army captain each followed. A magistrate, a gardener, and a member of the local orchestra had notes as well.

Thomas noted that an older couple holding hands gave over two notes.

The brick mason Hal Butters note read, "My consequence is that I build things with pride that last as you told me. I build trust and relationships."

Viola Butters followed. "My PHC is my realization that all of known humanity is in one place on one planet. We have to get along to move along. I preach that message in Sunday school to children of every color who will inherit our world."

In an hour, the shoebox had nearly one hundred and fifty notes extolling each remitter's change of course since meeting Sid Toile. More followed.

A minority minister came with a note letting Sid know the growth of his congregation. Sid knew the church on Bull Street. He had donated over $100,000 for its maintenance and repair needs years before. Sid even designed a meditation garden in the rear of the churchyard.

In quite a surprise, a short man dressed in an elegant suit and sunglasses moved forward. His note read, "My PHC is that I have a new self-worth and can deliver some small service to people I don't even know because of the transition Sid Toile required of me. I was a taker, but now I'm a giver. It's my new vigorish."

It was signed "Charlie Stanton."

A property manager, a housewife, an Episcopal minister, a lady's fashion designer, a lawyer, and a shrimp boat captain followed. There was a copy editor, a pizza delivery boy, a Vietnam veteran from the Marine Corps, and a chemical engineer. All had notes to place in the shoebox. They each described their positive human consequence and placed the words into the shoebox. It was overflowing.

A medic, an ambulance driver, an owner of a crematorium, a foreign diplomat, and a county coroner left notes. A customs official and a manager from vital records were also in the line. There were three senators, two federal judges, and four congressmen. There were two airline pilots, three mayors, and a national talk show host. Admirals and generals came as well. Sid had influenced people from all walks of life.

Billy and Theta Grayson arrived together. They were silently saddened and held hands as they approached. They showed respect as if they were in a church setting. Theta delivered the simplest PHC in the box. It was a family photograph taken at Christmas by the Grayson family's decorated Yuletide mantel. It showed Billy, Theta, Mia, Leah, Ashton, and the new baby that Theta held in her lap—Eliot Sidney Grayson, born on November 10.

Billy's note was heartfelt and in line with his talent as a songwriter.

"The life I have is all ahead of me. Seeing where it came from is foolish. Seeing where it can go is its only true importance."

Thomas procured plastic trash bags from Callista for the overflow of notes. After hundreds of people had visited booth 14, Thomas took all of the notes and mementos out to the trunk of his car. By one forty-five, Thomas had received the last PHC note and began to clean up the booth. It came from the adversarial coffee server, Callista. She wrote it on a formal greeting card from the B & B selection counter after she witnessed hours of people in line to pay their PHC respects. She felt compelled to submit her own. She took her time to write what was in her heart with tears in her eyes.

"It was my pleasure to serve you these past years. You skated on your tip, but I received it in a different form anyway. Watching as you helped total strangers made me realize that this world is not about me. I am the only real witness to the total of the miracles you did for others. I will honestly miss you. Callous."

Thomas sought to finalize Sid's estate after the Bib and Bibliothéque reception. No one but Thomas knew that it was to be dispersed on Sid's seventy-eighth birthday, February 3. Thomas delivered the probated proceeds precisely as Sid instructed before his sudden demise. The addendum page of distribution read much like a stock report. Sid owned hundreds of stocks. Some had paid dividends that matured over the past eleven months and further increased the impact of the gifts. Thomas made sure that all of Sid's debts were paid.

Among the list of stocks that were distributed by transfer of ownership were Google, Ford, Texaco, Apple, Coke, and Pfizer. Sid had procured the transfer documents and signed them, witnessed by Thomas, prior to the day of his collapse.

Some of the new owners received multiple stock transfer certificates.

Hal and Viola Butters were suddenly worth $3.2 million. Hal was gifted seventeen thousand shares of TexTron Brick Corporation. Viola received municipal bonds with extended maturity dates. Sid supposed she would outlive them all.

Charlie Stanton received three Canadian stocks that were worth $700,000. He also received Sid's 40 percent interest in the Jildare Corporation, a leading manufacturer of athletic socks. Charlie recognized the irony of owning a share of the white athletic socks manufacturer—a staple of his daily uniform as bookie Joey Preticos.

Evelyn Rhett received the media account, including several parenting and guidance periodicals. They amounted to $1.9 million if fully redeemed. But she declined to cash them in. Eventually, she was invited to join the board of directors of *Parents' Day* magazine.

Sid gave four endowed scholarships in the name of Thomas Leon to the Business School at the Citadel. They were meant to foster the concept of "theoretical algorithms" for cadets he would never know. He intended to enhance conceptual thinking beyond the boundaries of traditional learning. The value of the endowments amounted to $2 million and relieved Thomas of any tax burden. Thomas also received the balance in Sid's cash account from the probated estate, after taxes and distribution. The balance was nearly $932,000.

Thomas had indicated to Sid that he was happy with his state pension and his savings over his career. He did not want to risk any of his earnings in the marketplace. He was risk averse. So Sid also left Thomas fifty-five years of U.S. savings bonds in $200 and $500 denominations.

Sid had placed in trust a cash amount of $2.8 million to be given to Billy and Theta Grayson upon the birth of their first child. Sid witnessed their elopement marriage ceremony just days before his classroom collapse. The couple's agreed-upon dating period lasted only three weeks after their rediscovery of each other in St. Croix. Theta had the wedding night she dreamed, and Billy had a lifelong partner who was devoted to his future and that of their four children.

Thomas dutifully explained that Sid had actually intimated that the first child had already been born—the first of the twins, Leah. Thus, the trust was immediately available to them. Sid further endowed the Grayson family with an additional stock transfer of another $400,000 to benefit their children's education. It was $100,000 for each child. Sid had correctly surmised that a fourth child would be forthcoming.

He signed the title of his marsh view condominium to Maria Delgado. It was worth nearly $2 million. He also left her and her husband, Pablo Gutierrez, cash—and another $1.1 million in Cemex, a Mexican cement maker stock.

Even Will Henry, Sid's CPA, received a seven-figure gift. And since Will enjoyed golf, he left him 3,400 shares of Calloway Golf stocks. He knew that Will played with their equipment.

In all, nearly $181 million of Sid's unsuspected wealth portfolio became a windfall to dozens of others he had encountered. His postmortem largesse was a surprise to all but Thomas Leon and Will Henry. Will had arranged that most could be gifted as nontaxable events meant to enhance lives that were suited for positive consequences by prepaying any that were subject to IRS rules.

The sassy coffee clerk Callista had decided to return to her parents' home in Chevy Chase, Maryland, and attend a junior college there. She wanted to learn management skills and open a retail bakery. On the day that Callista had turned in her resignation, Thomas walked into the Bib and Bibliothéque just before her 4:00 p.m. shift was over.

Callista told Thomas that she wanted to attain what Sid called a PHC. She was inspired by all he had done for others to change careers. Over the past year, she had missed Sid and most of the crowd that waited to see him in booth 14.

"Callista, I'm sure that you will make a difference in your transition to a new career. The Boracle would be proud," Thomas began. "In fact, he wanted me to leave something with you that he said he owed to you."

Callista's brown eyes grew large. She instinctively knew that Sid had left the tip he had frequently promised. Thomas handed her a large manila envelope with her name on it written in Sid's handwriting.

"Oh my god! He was telling the truth all along. That's my tip!" she blurted. "He didn't forget."

Callista opened the envelope in front of the professor excitedly. Once extracted, she looked at the paper contents quizzically, followed by confusion and disappointment.

"This is a joke. I thought he was leaving me something like some money," Callista shrugged. "These are just fancy papers with old printing to frame on a wall. I know he meant well, but he's still messing with me even after he's dead."

"Let me see them, please?" Thomas asked. Thomas knew that Sid would not be pranking the young girl.

Callista handed them over to the professor.

"This is better than cash, Callista. These are bearer bonds," Thomas cited. "They do not have your name on them, and they do not have to—they are better than cash. These are U.S. Treasury Bonds written in 1982. Sid's last will and the transfer certificate he signed listing the bond issue numbers mean that they are yours—free and clear."

Callista became energetically excited again, although she didn't know anything about bearer bonds.

"So what could they be worth today?" she asked nervously.

Thomas looked through the thin stack. "You have more than a dozen here. They are in allotments of $50,000 each. With growth to the present, they are likely worth at least four times the face value . . . Maybe five. It's a helluva tip."

Callista was calculating in her mind as Thomas gave the envelope back to her.

"You mean that Sid may have left me a $3 million tip? No way!" she speculated.

"I'd bet it's closer to four. Put these in a safe place. And have a good day!" Thomas concluded.

Thomas smiled at the irony of the tip's presentation, knowing that Callista had been most difficult in her attitude concerning Sid. But she did give him his nickname.

Thomas had fulfilled all of Sid's requests. He was honored by the duty. Callista's bearer bonds were his last delivery.

"Wait, Mr. Leon. Let me get you a free coffee. It's on me. And it's the last cup I'll ever serve in this place," she stated. "I'm going to own a bakery in Chevy Chase!"

CHAPTER FIFTY-TWO

Pocket Watch

THINGS ARE NEVER as they seem.

When the ambulance arrived at the Trauma Center days earlier, the role-playing had to begin immediately. There was no paramedic in the ambulance. All were imposters.

Thomas's brother from the Medical University Gross Anatomy Department applied the blood pressure cuffs. He brought a cadaver, as instructed, zipped up in a body bag already inside the ambulance. Hal Butters, also in an EMS jumpsuit, helped lift the wheeled gurney and then transferred Sid to the rear of the vehicle. He looked as if he were stooped over the laying of bricks when the ambulance drove off. Thomas's sister, a CIA agent, felt the pulse in Sid's neck and also helped lift him to the gurney, along with Pablo Gutierrez, who wore white gloves to disguise his missing right hand.

Once they were all in the ambulance, Thomas's sister provided a new Scottish passport and other needed identification for a new person named Cailean. All documents were placed in Sid's briefcase.

Pablo Gutierrez drove the ambulance at a controlled speed from the Citadel to the hospital. His wife, Maria Delgado, had already shipped Sid's most cherished belongings to the new secret address. They included Ida's wedding portrait.

Sid slipped on a paramedic jumper suit over his old clothes and hugged everyone and while delivering each his heartfelt thanks. He remained seated in the front until the cadaver was taken away. He then grabbed his briefcase and pre-packed roller bag and slipped into the waiting vehicle. The stunned onlookers focused upon Hal Butters' act of zipping up the body bag of a cadaver. Thomas's brother drove Sid to the airport where a private jet took him to Memphis. There, he connected through LAX to Papeete and then Auckland to Christchurch. In thirty hours, he was in another hemisphere nearly eleven thousand miles from Charleston.

Thomas Leon had the last conversation on his last day in Charleston with Sid. It was in the ambulance on the way to the MUSC emergency room.

"Sid, the trust account for Mr. Cailean is through this account at Kiwibank NZ. They have your new home title in the lockbox. It's all in the notes with the envelope. Taxes are paid to December. Here's the lockbox key. I'm going to miss you, my friend," Thomas said. "I'll do everything you set out for me at the right place and time. I'll be looking for a postcard or two from you. Mind if I start calling you Mr. Cailean?"

"Thomas, I may never find another true friend such as you!" Sid exclaimed. "And now you can save money on the twenty-dollar coffee cards."

"Sid, I knew that you knew and would not deny me that small gesture." Thomas smiled. "The cadets will miss you. But the bottom of the globe will get better every day! Any last instructions?"

"Yes, if you need to reach me for an emergency, just send our usual coded message through Bailie's Pub, Christchurch. I'll check there regularly," Sid promised as his Santa blue eyes looked over his glasses. "And take good care, my friend."

Their message was simple. Thomas would call the establishment and describe Sid in detail by the name "Thomas Leon" to answer an emergency phone call. Once the message was delivered, Sid would show his name to be someone else; not the Thomas Leon they were seeking. He would then call Thomas back within the hour. If the name was reversed as "Leon Thomas," it meant that Sid should call as soon as possible.

Sid began his next purposeful journey.

The world's only synesticist still enjoyed the free run of humanity. He had found a new calling within his next set of puzzle pieces. He would resume building his frillionaire legacy. He would embark upon anticipated duties that compelled him to discover odd trivialities that would connect the universe.

The details of Sid Toile's demise were most difficult for the Bib and Bibliothéque visitors. Sid's affinity for connecting small puzzle pieces had served the coffee shop patrons well. They came to depend upon him. The service, the cremation, the scattering of ashes, and the distribution of assets were done as Sid had meticulously planned. The foreboding intersection of evil had been calculated. It was as if their resolutions were predicted, prescribed, or predestined.

Sid had a few lingering resolutions.

Critical criminal evidence arrived in an anonymous package to the FBI Special Investigative Unit in Washington, DC. It came just two days after his friend, the county coroner, signed Sid's death certificate. The new evidence would eventually convict Tony "the Blade" Muzon and his thugs, Myles Tersini and Jocko Santo. It reopened several cold cases that gave irrefutable insight into multiple murders in South Philadelphia over a fourteen-year period. Within the year, a federal trial convened. They were each found guilty. All three thugs received sentences of life plus ninety-nine years.

Arlo Crutchfield met his end just days beyond his personal celebration of what was a revenge-fueled by psychosis. He drove his white pickup truck back to middle Tennessee by skirting Atlanta north to Chattanooga. The weather began to worsen as he headed up Interstate 24. The old farm truck had poor traction on icy roads. The February storm that moved from middle Tennessee down across the Cumberland Plateau froze the incline. The treacherous ascent up Monteagle Mountain near Suwanee could not be negotiated, and Arlo lost control of his truck. It slid sideways into another lane and was struck by a tractor-trailer rig. Arlo's pickup truck flipped over twice, killing him instantly. He had no heirs.

Sid was unaware of this circumstance. Revenge is a caustic motive. The Boracle would never decimate his character by the corruption of morality.

Justice is the proper antidote to all wrongdoing.

Horace Rhett's contract for two homicides appeared to give both Evelyn Rhett and Sid Toile the latitude to associate proper justice. Once Horace arrived back into Charleston from his *rest area agreement*, he remained smug and patient for the inevitable outcome. He planned to go hunting in the upstate, as hitman Kenneth would dispatch the planned signal of completing the contract. When that signal arrived,

Horace took the balance owed by way of a cash-filled duffel bag. He was instructed to deliver the final payment at the Ladson rest stop on his way upstate. As he was packing his truck outside the Extended Stay suite, an unmarked police car pulled next to him.

Two officers got out. Simultaneously, the county sheriff pulled up behind his pickup with another armed officer. Horace was placed against his truck and handcuffed.

"Mr. Rhett, you are being charged with two counts of conspiracy to commit murder. You have a right to remain silent . . ."

He was booked back into his former cell. Rawl Richard had given him what he thought was a solid contact. However, hitman Kenneth was an undercover detective from Kentucky. It was Sid Toile's intuition that Horace not only was temperamental but also had a much darker side. He knew this from his meeting with Horace at the detention center after the domestic violence charge.

The evidence was overwhelming. Hitman Kenneth's cigarette-reeking Dodge truck included a hidden videotape system that operated from his rear-view mirror. It showed the verbalized intention, the names of the victims, the details of the intended murder, and the money paid—both in stacks of one hundred dollars being counted out meticulously.

It took a world-class synesticist to predict the likelihood of such an arrangement. Ominous ends befell onerous men.

Satan's stand-in, the dark-eyed Bailloch, was a detestable person who had escaped death as if it were a game. He could not be held in any cell. He could not be defeated by military action. Sid surmised that he could only be enticed to an unsuspected point of imminent doom. The ethereal stones would bait the trap. Sid knew the place, the conditions, and the circumstance. He cataloged the optimum setting at his condominium over the past two years. He realized that he might possess the knowledge of the only antidote to the constant malady.

Indeed, Walter Bailloch was accorded ironic justice by the hand of God. It was when Thomas was spreading his ashes in the marsh a few days after the ambulance ride and coroner's death certificate signaled Sid's ending. Bailloch's seven-century malevolent task was to find benefit in the extraction of others from his nefarious pursuits. He either arranged, caused, or witnessed death. The talisman stones would become unprotected by way of Sid's demise. Bailloch would seek a hidden and solitary viewing to witness Sid's ceremony in hopes that the prizes would be evident to him at the event.

Sid had seen storms pass through the marsh view often. He measured the conditions meticulously with instruments from his fourth-floor porch. Lightning occasionally hit the grounded television tower north of his view just two blocks away. By Sid's meticulous calculations, Thomas's marsh-side ceremony would experience dangerous atmospheric conditions.

It was the ethereal stones that would protect and deflect all that was harmful. Sid had removed the tower's grounding mechanism. He reminded Thomas to continue scattering until the rain began—knowing a thunderbolt was imminent. The stones were laid below the tower to triangulate the impact. The 1.5-million-kilowatt bolt found its mark. Yet Bailloch did not perish. He was blasted away from the tower shaken—his face burnt and deformed. It was a warning from the savant.

Bailloch immediately knew that he had been outwitted again and that the wizard was still at large. He would need a year to heal the wounds, and his centuries-long chase was arrested forcefully.

The staged exit gave Sid the head start he needed to begin anew. Bailloch and others would not impede him. The time was nigh.

Thomas recovered the ethereal stones and gave them back to Theta. She and Billy would be forever protected. Not even Bailloch could extract the power of the talisman from true love.

The Boracle truly believed he would never die. He had lived many years past his expiration date. His later years were saddened without his perfect mate, Ida. He had often described each completed mission to his confidant and friend Thomas as one of duty. It was a calling that was presented to him as a sign from the ages when he was only nine and a half years of age. There was no deviation from his task—only benevolence extended as his deeds multiplied through time. His frillionaire friends helped him at every interval. The magical cache of all information of all times conspired at a confluence to sanction him as unique and timeless.

Thomas recalled his friend's insightful words when they first met. "It is likely all of us know when and where we were born. It's the uncommon person who knows why."

In time, a frumpy old man was seen on the New Zealand's South Island by a former student of Thomas Leon's futuristic class. The sequence was as anticipated. He was spotted as he was passing through the maze of frozen displays at the International Antarctic Centre. He looked so much like Sid Toile that the traveler suspected that he was the identical twin of the late savant. Or maybe he was the reincarnated savant.

The former student approached him with a confident zeal.

"Excuse me, sir, are you Mr. Toile?" the young traveler asked.

The exchange was brief. The thin man in the wrinkled suit appeared momentarily confused. He gave the former student a slow peer of unfamiliarity and responded.

"Ah am a bairn ay scootlund fa has lived haur oan mah wee pension. Ah am Coh-lin," the man replied. His heavy-brogue response puzzled the student.

The old man pronounced his name in a Gaelic intonation, a strong inflection remnant of his Scottish citizenship. The young traveler tried to translate the brogue to understand that the old man was a Scottish retiree living on a modest pension.

"I beg your pardon, sir. I must be mistaken. You looked quite familiar. I thought you were someone else—perhaps the twin of someone I knew," the former student replied in a lower tone.

"Ta, laddie. Wid ye ken whaur ah kin fin' a coffee shop?" he asked.

"There's a coffee shop across the square from the cathedral," the young traveler directed.

He pointed up to the skyline over a grove of trees.

"Follow to that steeple, and it's on the left. It's called *Bailie's*. I was there this morning," the young man stated. "You'll pass a pond with a hundred ducks, it seems. Bailies will have a menu with scones and sandwiches as well as Wi-Fi."

"Ta," the old man said. He tipped his tweed cap.

The elderly gentleman sauntered away down to the adjoining park to walk through the botanical gardens to the Christchurch Cathedral.

At the end of the gravel walkway, he stopped to assess the time as the still-puzzled student looked on. He reached into his trousers to pull out a gold watch. He opened it carefully, pausing to glance pensively at the photo within. He knew the former student was still watching him. He did so because he realized that the student would report the sighting to Thomas Leon. He then looked up at the sky to see where the sun was positioned. It was his habitual way of telling the approximate time. He had read the sun's position for many years because the sun would never lie.

The student-traveler reported all of the information to his mentor, Professor Leon. He said that the man gave his name as Colin, a very common Scottish moniker.

Thomas explained to the former student, "I knew of a man by a similar name. It was a name that crossed centuries in lore. I sense that the man was actually saying 'Cailean,' a man cited as the wizard who had transported Duhbghall mac Suibne, Lord Knapdale, away from imminent doom. The legend of the ethereal stones grew from the experience of leaping into a thunderbolt."

The former student looked puzzled.

"It wasn't the Boracle, son, and Mr. Toile had no kin," the professor declared.

"But Cailean—the wizard of lore. Now that's a tale for the ages. In time, Cailean conjoined the rightful Lord with his lost love, the maiden Màire. She was the bride with the alizarin hair."

Of this, he was certain.

EPILOGUE

The medieval poet Blind Robert Barrow penned the final stanza of the legend. The apocryphal words danced into the centuries beyond.

> Bailloch followed each path
> Each upon each converged
> The wizard planned each ending
> Lovers united in bliss
> Ethereal stones glimmered anew
> The bloodline flourished for all time

Castle Sween exists. It is considered the oldest remnant castle of Scotland. It overlooks a sea route to Ireland. It is believed that the MacSween clan reunited in Ireland where they emerged to become consequential to the history of the Emerald Isle. The MacSweens built Doe Castle and Ronan Castle in Ireland. They were allies of the Earl of Tyrconnell. They were most notable for their hospitality, carving a stone marker on a highway that extended through their lands. The marker invited all travelers as welcome for warm meals and shelter upon their journey.

ABOUT THE AUTHOR

W. Thomas McQueeney is a native Charlestonian and graduate of The Citadel. He has written seven books in genres to include historical, contemporary, and biographical subjects in addition to literary humor. His *Pilgrimages*, *Passages*, and *Voyages* columns have given rise to his reputation as a Lowcountry humorist. He is self-described as the "Poet of the Pluff Mud."

McQueeney's lifetime of service to others includes board membership to the Medical University of South Carolina Children's Hospital Development Board, the American Cancer Society, the American Heart Association, Our Lady of Mercy Community Outreach, Coastal Council of Explorer Scouts, Patriot's Point Museum Maritime Foundation, Bon Secours St. Francis Hospital, The Hibernian Foundation, The Citadel Brigadier Memorial Fund, The Citadel Foundation, the Charleston Metro Sports Council, and the South Carolina Athletic Hall of Fame.

He has been elected by the South Carolina Legislature to serve on The Citadel Board of Visitors. He served as Chairman of the Medal of Honor Bowl (NCAA Football), and the Southern Conference Basketball Championships. He also chaired the Johnson Hagood Stadium Revitalization Project, a $44.5 million fundraising effort. He is chairman and founder of Santa's Kind Intentions, Inc. He also served as Grand Knight of Knights of Columbus Council 704 and as

Chairman of the K of C Turkey Day Run, the largest 5-k race in the state of South Carolina.

McQueeney served as President of the South Carolina Athletic Hall of Fame, is an Honorary Member of The Citadel Athletic Hall of Fame, a recipient of the Southern Conference Distinguished Service Award, and the T. Ashton Phillips Community Service Award. He is married and has four children and four grandchildren. He is a recipient of the Order of the Palmetto, the highest award conferred upon a citizen of the State of South Carolina.

CPSIA information can be obtained
at www.ICGtesting.com
Printed in the USA
LVHW05s1754300918
591921LV00010B/375/P